Threat
Case

Also by J. C. Pollock

THE DENNECKER CODE
MISSION M.I.A.
CENTRIFUGE
CROSSFIRE
PAYBACK

J.C. POLLOCK

Threat
Case

Delacorte
Press

Published by
Delacorte Press
Bantam Doubleday Dell Publishing Group, Inc.
666 Fifth Avenue
New York, New York 10103

Library of Congress Cataloging in Publication Data

Pollock, J. C.
    Threat case / by J. C. Pollock.
        p.   cm.
    ISBN 0-385-29959-1 (hc)
    I. Title.
PS3566.O5348T47 1991   90-19121
813'.54—dc20   CIP

Manufactured in the United States of America

Published simultaneously in Canada

June 1991

10 9 8 7 6 5 4 3 2 1

BVG

For Lieutenant General Samuel V. Wilson USA (Ret.)
Friend, advisor, confidant, and a commanding
officer in every sense of the term.

Threat
Case

-1-

ST. BARTS—FRENCH WEST INDIES—OCTOBER 2

Maria was certain she had seen him before. She lowered her camera and studied the tall, lanky man more closely. He appeared to be in his early forties. Sandy blond hair curled over his ears and at the base of his neck, framing a strong, angular face and cold, deep-set eyes. It was not the type of face you forgot. He was trim and fit and wore jeans and running shoes and a long-sleeve white T-shirt rolled up to the elbows. A golden Caribbean tan suggested he was no stranger to the islands.

She didn't recognize him as a crew member off any of the few luxury yachts now in port, and she couldn't place him among the countless professional boat people she knew—a loosely knit community of crews who frequented the same bars and hangouts in yacht harbors around the world and knew each other by sight and boat affiliation, if not by name. But still he seemed vaguely familiar. He could have been one of the day-trippers who came across on the catamarans from St. Martin each morning, but she doubted it; nothing about him said "tourist." Maybe he was just one of those people who remind you of someone else, she thought; but failed to shake the overpowering feeling it was more than that.

Le Select Café, where Maria sat on the outdoor terrace taking pictures, was on a street one block from and parallel to St. Barts' Gustavia harbor. The small, ratty restaurant and bar was better known as "Cheeseburger in Paradise" (or greaseburgers, as Maria thought of them) after the song written about it by a once-popular rock star. The place drew its share of tourists and island locals, ranging from shop owners to trust-fund dependent beachcombers to those who just stepped off their yachts. But it was off-season, October, and the tourists were not out in full force and the beautiful people who wintered on the fashionable island had not yet arrived. Only a few of the café's rickety outdoor tables were occupied, and the foot traffic along the quay and on the harbor town's narrow, boutique-jammed streets was at a minimum.

Maria snapped a quick picture of a slack-jawed, unkempt young man in cutoff jeans and a grimy T-shirt. He had languid, lizard eyes, distant and unfocused, and he sat against the wall near the bar, the back of his chair propped at a precarious angle as he stared off into space. Whatever substance he had abused to alter his consciousness was having its desired effect. She took a second photo of him, capturing the interesting play of shadows and light on his fleshy, indolent face. Her attention then shifted back to the table in the far corner of the café where the man whose features kept nudging her memory sat in the dappled shade beneath the branch of an overhanging tree.

Unaware of Maria's scrutiny, Jerry Sincavage slouched in his chair, declaratively alone, his legs stretched out beneath the table as he drank from a long-necked bottle of beer. He was relaxed, interested in everything but part of nothing as his eyes swept idly back and forth across the café. He had the look of a man waiting for something to happen, unconcerned about what it might be, but ready for it, regardless.

Maria raised her camera and slowly turned the lens until the Leica telephoto zoom brought the tough, no-nonsense face into sharp focus. The rapid clicking of the shutter and the whir of the camera's motor drive instantly jarred Sincavage from his reverie. Hard eyes that held a hint of danger flicked toward Maria and locked on her. She smiled only to have it returned with a cold, unwavering stare as she got up and approached his table.

"Mind if I join you?" She stood before him, her shoulder-length chestnut brown hair backlit by what remained of the late-afternoon sun.

Sincavage, having assessed the situation as no immediate threat, shrugged and took a pull on his beer as she sat opposite him. It was not the usual reception Maria got. Her stunning figure and classic Castilian beauty were seldom, if ever, greeted with indifference by members of the opposite sex.

"Maria Padron," Maria said, extending her hand.

Sincavage leaned forward and shook the proffered hand without introduction. He gestured toward the camera resting on her lap. "You make a habit out of taking pictures of strangers?"

"Photography's my hobby, and you have a great face, very photogenic," Maria said, then added in further explanation, "I have this feeling we've met before. I don't know where, but you look very familiar."

"Isn't that supposed to be my line?" Sincavage said. There was nothing friendly or flirtatious in his tone.

Maria's expression changed, the moment of recognition shown in her eyes.

"The album," she said with a look of minor triumph. "That's where I saw you. You were a friend of Jim's in Vietnam. You were part of that Special Operations Group he served with."

"Jim who?"

"Jim Boos. He was a Navy SEAL in Vietnam. From 1968 until 1972, I believe."

Maria thought she saw a brief glimmer in Sincavage's pale blue eyes, but his stolid face remained unchanged.

"There's a picture of you in Jim's photo album, with him and his SEAL team. It was taken after some sort of special mission you ran. He used to talk about you every now and then, when he was in the mood to reminisce about his Vietnam days. Your name's Terry . . . or Jerry something?"

"You've got me confused with someone else, honey."

Maria frowned and shook her head. The eight-by-ten photograph she now saw in her mind's eye was almost twenty years old, which was the reason she at first had difficulty remembering where she had seen the man sitting before her—but she was sure it was him. The character lines were more deeply etched in the forehead and along the prominent cheekbones and the crinkled corners of the eyes, but it was the same face, the kind that doesn't change much with age, not when the owner bothered to stay in shape.

"You didn't know Jim Boos?"

"Sorry. Never heard of him." Sincavage again glanced at Maria's camera. "Never had the misfortune of being sent to 'Nam. You a tourist?"

"No," Maria said. "I'm captain of the *Cheetah.*"

"Captain?" The incredulity was heavy in his voice.

"Yes." Maria said evenly, accustomed to the chauvinistic reaction. A woman captain was an uncommon occurrence in the male-dominated profession, but Maria, even though only in her late twenties, was a first-class sailor and had more than earned the position.

"What's the *Cheetah*?" Sincavage asked.

"She's a sixty-five-foot sloop," Maria said with pride, then added on a more solemn note, "Jim Boos was the captain until he was killed two years ago." Again there was a flicker of something other than disinterest, but it vanished as quickly as it had appeared.

Sincavage nodded and scanned the café. "You staying here long?"

"Another week," Maria said. "I've got some downtime until the new mate gets here. Then when the owner arrives we're going on an extended cruise."

"You a charter boat?"

"No. The *Cheetah*'s never chartered."

Sincavage studied Maria carefully, taking in the smooth, flawless olive-tone skin and the expressive dark-brown eyes that held steady with self-confidence. "Maybe we can have dinner some night. I'll be here for a few days. Since you're here alone."

"Maybe," Maria said tentatively. She detected a subtle change in Sincavage's tone and demeanor. It was a change that told her she might have made a mistake in admitting she was alone on the

Cheetah. It was nothing tangible, but a subconscious alert put her on edge.

As Sincavage raised his beer to take another drink, Maria noticed a prominent scar on the back of his hand; it covered most of the area from his knuckles to just below his wrist. The skin was parchmentlike and lacked pigmentation, and the outer edge of the area was ringed in dark brown. Maria had seen burn scars of a similar nature before, usually caused by white phosphorus grenades or incendiaries.

Sincavage caught the focus of her attention, and turned his hand to look at the scar as though it was something long forgotten.

"Training accident," he said with detachment. "Some damn fool laid a mortar round in too close."

"White phosphorus," Maria said.

Sincavage cocked an eyebrow. "That's an interesting observation for a sailor . . . and a woman, at that."

"I'm full of surprises."

"I'll just bet you are."

As Sincavage slouched deeper into his seat he paused, then shifted uncomfortably, gingerly settling his frame at an angle against the back of the chair.

Maria caught a quick glimpse of the reason for his momentary discomfort: the outline of the flat grip of a small automatic pistol under his T-shirt. She guessed it was a .380, probably a Walther PPK or a Beretta. The weapon was tucked inside the waistband of his jeans at the small of his back, all but unnoticeable to anyone who hadn't spent time around men who carried concealed weapons.

Born into Miami's Cuban expatriate community, Maria knew such men well. She was only two months old when her father, a leader of the anti-Castro movement, died at Giron Beach while commanding Assault Brigade 2506 during the Bay of Pigs invasion; her mother died a year later in an automobile accident. She was raised by an uncle and aunt who were employed by the CIA and deeply involved in the Cuban liberation movement. Her childhood was spent in the Bahamas, the Florida Everglades, and various secret locations for anti-Castro guerrilla training camps throughout the Caribbean. Along with her tutored formal education, she had received an extensive indoctrination in weapons and guerrilla tactics, and there were few, if any, small arms she couldn't handle with remarkable proficiency. She had lived with danger and intrigue all her life, and now instincts she had learned to recognize and act upon were warding her off, making her feel uneasy about the man sitting across from her.

"Got to go," she said, getting up from the table. "Sorry for the intrusion."

Sincavage nodded and tilted the neck of his beer bottle toward her. "See ya around."

"You know, you've got a double somewhere in this world," she said as she turned to leave.

"They say everyone does."

Maria flashed another friendly smile and waved. Sincavage continued watching her until she left the café and disappeared in the direction of the harbor.

•

St. Barthélemy, better known as St. Barts to most visitors, is a winter hideaway for the likes of the Rockefellers, Rothschilds, and Philadelphia Biddles, along with chic, wealthy Europeans (mostly French) and Americans. A beautiful, pastoral island of white sand beaches in the heart of the French West Indies, there is little to suggest its turbulent sixteenth- and seventeenth-century days as a port and provisions center for pirates and corsairs who preyed on the Spanish treasure fleets, lurking among the cays and islets waiting for the hapless galleons to sail past, laden with gold.

Narrow, winding roads have replaced centuries-old footpaths only in the last thirty years, and timeless villages perched on hillsides overlooking sparkling bays and inlets help give the island the ambiance of the Côte d'Azur in its heyday. There is an unmistakable French influence, derived from descendants of the original Breton and Norman settlers, and older women still wear long black dresses and *quichenootes,* the starched white bonnets of Brittany.

Unlike much of the Caribbean, poverty is virtually nonexistent among the industrious local population, and brightly colored, well-maintained houses and luxurious villas dot the island's beaches and mountainous slopes. Gustavia, the tiny island capital and only town, with its pastel-colored buildings and Mediterranean feel, is clustered around a harbor crowded during the high season with tall-masted luxury yachts, and is home to an array of exclusive boutiques that line the quay and narrow, cobbled streets. Hermès, Gucci, and other trendy, outrageously expensive shops, along with gourmet restaurants as fine as any in Paris, set the tone for life on the island for the wealthy winter residents and credit-card-bearing tourists fresh off the cruise ships.

It was Maria Padron's hands-down favorite port in the Caribbean. Relaxed, sophisticated, seductive, and remarkably un-crowded and unspoiled, it was the place she most looked forward to visiting each year. If she ever gave up sailing and settled any-where, she had decided, it would be on St. Barts. The encounter at the café had brought back bittersweet memories of Jim Boos, and she had spent what remained of the afternoon on Petite Anse de Galet, a small beach awash with a variety of sea shells, near the edge of town. With a handful of lacy murexes, mottled brown cowries, and smooth olive-colored shells for which she didn't know the name, she had returned to the *Cheetah* in time to sit on deck while the day gave way to what the French call *l'heure bleu* —the blue hour—when the last rays of sun disappear beyond the horizon. In the failing light, pelicans glided over the harbor, swooping high into the sky and then plummeting into the water to catch their last meal of the day. It had been a particularly beautiful sunset; the sky glowing with pinks and scarlets and ever-deepening reds as the sea darkened from luminescent turquoise to deep blue to onyx as dusk gave way to night.

It was late evening when the winds from a brief rain squall blew through the narrow harbor and over the island, bowing the trees and churning the waters to foam. In a matter of minutes the wind subsided, leaving behind blue-black tropical skies swept clean of clouds and twinkling with the pin lights of countless stars.

The *Cheetah* was docked stern-to between a large motor-sailer and another sloop that had just arrived from day-sailing around the nearby islands. With her nine-story mast usually towering over all others in the harbor, the *Cheetah* drew attention wherever she went. A sixty-five-foot aluminum-hulled maxiracer, her owner, Zack Shafer, had spent millions converting her into one of the most luxurious sailing yachts in the world. Maria was belowdecks, sitting hunched over the chart table at the navigation and control station. She directed an overhead light onto the pages of an old, somewhat mildewed album and held a magnifying glass close to an eight-by-ten photograph secured inside one of the protective plastic sleeves. She brought the magnifying glass in closer, then back out again until she had the subject enlarged and focused.

She was concentrating on the man kneeling beside Jim Boos in the picture of a group of twelve disheveled young warriors just returned from a dangerous top-secret mission into North Vietnam. Their jungle fatigues were frayed and filthy and stained with perspiration, their hair was matted above bandannas tied around their foreheads and they all sported three- to four-day growths of beard. Some knelt with their weapons propped on the ground in support of weary bodies. Two men standing in the second row held up opposite ends of a captured North Vietnamese flag, their unoccupied hands flashing the *V* for victory sign. The "adrenaline high" of a successful combat mission was fading. Lopsided grins on faces streaked with camouflage paint spoke of relief; flat, penetrating stares told of exhaustion and stress. Maria recalled Boos telling her that the picture had been taken after a highly successful joint Special Operations Group mission, and that six of the twelve men in the special team were Army Green Berets, the rest were members of his Navy SEAL team. Another forgotten fact came back into memory: Boos had told her that all but three of the men in the picture were now dead, killed in action on subsequent missions.

Maria continued to study the photograph. "It's him," she said aloud, remembering that Boos had told her that the man whose face stared back at her across the years was one of the Green Berets. She changed the point of focus for the magnifying glass, but was unable to find the burn scar on the back of the man's right hand—it was hidden behind the receiver of his weapon. But there was no mistaking the chiseled features and hard, deep-set eyes. It was definitely the same man she had talked with at the café.

On the occasions when she had met friends of Jim Boos who had served with him in Vietnam, there had been a few who would not discuss the war, acting as though it had never happened, begging off Boos's attempts at drawing them into reminiscing with him about their exploits. They hadn't been much for war stories, or for that matter even remembering. Maybe that was the case with this Terry . . . or Jerry. Or he could be doing contract work for the CIA as Boos had done for a while, and recognition was the last thing he needed. Whatever, he certainly had the right to leave it all behind if he chose.

Maria thought of her friend, Jack Gannon, and smiled. He had served with Boos in the Special Operations Group, and she planned to visit him on her yearly trip to the States at the end of the upcoming cruise. She removed the photograph from the album, slipped it into a manila envelope and scribbled *Ask Gannon about him* across the front.

She turned her attention to the small diary she kept of her photographs. She was meticulous in recording the content of each roll of film, neatly logging the aperture and shutter-speed settings from the scribbled notes she had made when taking the shots, further noting the date, time of day, and type of available light, and any comments about her subjects.

That completed, she poured herself a glass of wine and went topside. Stretching out on the padded bench seat in the entertainment cockpit, she propped an oversized pillow beneath her head and listened to the reggae music playing softly over the built-in stereo system. Her attention was drawn to the large motor-sailer docked beside the *Cheetah*. The interior lights revealed an attractive middle-aged couple preparing for what Maria guessed was a formal affair on shore. The man in his tuxedo, and the woman in a designer evening dress sparkling with sequins, came out onto the aft deck, where they paused and looked in Maria's direction. Maria raised her glass to them and they nodded back as they stepped onto the gangway and went ashore.

Breathing deeply of the sweet-scented salt air carried across the harbor on the night breeze, Maria closed her eyes and relaxed to the music and the gentle rocking motion of the *Cheetah*. Her thoughts were again of Jim Boos, and how she missed him and what a good friend and teacher he had been. The effects of a day in the sun, the glass of wine, and the caress of the ocean breeze made her drowsy and she soon drifted into a dreamy half-sleep.

–2–

WASHINGTON, D.C.

Steven Whitney Bradford III looked and dressed the part of the young Washington politico on the fast track to success. He believed, correctly, that his greatest asset was that people underestimated him; he did not appear to be what he was, a facade he used with great success on those who succumbed to his easy charm and amiable manner. With practiced social skills and hard work, he had made his way up the beginning rungs of the political ladder, first as a Republican party student organizer on campus, then as a tireless volunteer campaign worker in the last election. The reward for his efforts was the position he now held with the President's Staff Advance Office, a prestigious post for someone his age, and one he hoped to parlay into a long and profitable career.

On the surface, Bradford had it all: a patrician lineage, keen intelligence, aristocratic good looks, degrees from the right schools, and the proper social connections. What he did not have, and valued above all else, was money. The fortune his great-grand-father and grandfather had made was squandered by a recently deceased father who was described by even his most charitable friends as a financially irresponsible reprobate and a drunk without the excuse of alcoholism. The small trust fund left to Bradford by his paternal grandmother was enough to pay his way through Princeton undergraduate school, but not enough to see him through Yale Law, a situation that brought forth his amoral, expe-dient side.

His proper Bostonian accent and Ivy League manners hid a conceit and arrogance that denied the immorality and incongruity of selling drugs to fellow students to pay his way through law school. He had, after all, been unfairly deprived of his rightful inheritance. He was owed. His initial small-time foray into the world of easy money—selling a few ounces of grass or grams of cocaine to his college buddies for a slight markup over his costs—had only whetted his appetite for more of the same, a great deal more. During the summer following his first year of law school, he had journeyed to Miami, and through contacts provided by a friend, made a connection with a trafficker that allowed him to circumvent his former supplier. As his confidence and customer list grew, so did the amount of cocaine at his disposal. He exploited the volatile "pass-along" market to the fullest, acquiring an exper-tise in "cutting" his supply with lactose to add weight and volume, amphetamines to give a cheaper high, and procaine to simulate cocaine's numbing effect. The product he finally passed on to his unsophisticated customers was no more than 12 percent pure co-caine. The process allowed him to stretch a four-ounce purchase to as much as one half kilo, increasing his profits proportionately.

By the time he graduated from law school, he not only had paid off his student loans but managed to cache in excess of one hun-dred seventy-five thousand dollars in various off-shore bank ac-counts. His subsequent year with the President's campaign staff provided him with a new clientele, as did the acquaintances he made since joining the President's Staff Advance Office. His new, upscale clients now included Senate and House aides and fellow White House staffers—Washington's young, achievement-ori-ented, pill-for-every-ill hard-chargers drawn to the nation's capital by dreams of fame, power, and money. The opportunity was there to expand his market to as much as a kilo a month, if he chose, translating into a potential tax-free income of approximately two thousand dollars a day. But although greedy, Bradford was not impatient or reckless. Expanding his market meant increasing his risks, a trade-off he was not willing to make.

Careful not to draw attention to himself, he did nothing that was noticeably out of line with his current position and salary. There were no flashy sports cars, no impeccably tailored custom-made suits and no ostentatious displays of cash, just a small town house with a large mortgage in Reston, Virginia, thirty-five minutes from his office in the Old Executive Office Building. And he was not a user, and never had been. He didn't need cocaine to feel masterful and invulnerable; his ego provided that. Neither did he need the euphoria or the chemically induced drive, sparkle, and energy; the challenge and thrill of beating the system and the money he earned provided that.

It was all going well for him. Better than he ever imagined it would. That was until two weeks ago, when the man from Miami contacted him, using the name of his supplier by way of introduction. The man had frightened him, badly. He had made no overt threats, but this was a dangerous man, who knew that if the information about his drug dealings were leaked to the proper authorities, Steven Whitney Bradford III would spend the next twenty years in prison. The man's proposal was not without its up side— five kilos of the purest cocaine for every pertinent piece of information passed along at an opportune time. There was no conscious decision to be made; no choice but to give the man what he wanted. For the first time since childhood he felt threatened, his self-assurance shaken. The substantial amount of money to be made from the promised cocaine payments assuaged his fears somewhat, but a small knot of discomfort formed in the pit of his stomach whenever he thought about the unpleasant turn of events—the loss of control and being under someone else's thumb. The specific information the man wanted left little doubt in Bradford's mind what purpose it was to serve, but as had been the case throughout all his twenty-nine years, Bradford's needs came first and everyone else be damned.

The cool autumn air threatened rain as Bradford walked along Pennsylvania Avenue, past the Treasury building and across Fifteenth Street NW to the Old Ebbitt Grill. He entered the Washington landmark, the oldest restaurant and bar in the capital, and walked past the crowded booths in the dining area, nodding to an occasional familiar face as he made his way to the warm, wood-paneled ambiance of the more private bar at the rear. The bartender smiled and nodded knowingly, drawing a draft Bass ale, which he promptly placed in front of Bradford with a friendly, "How's it going, Steve?" He was one of Bradford's customers—an occasional user, two or three grams a month.

Bradford mumbled a reply, glanced at his watch, then at the phone booth in an alcove at the far end of the bar. It was almost time. Another nervous glance at his watch, a quick drink, and he slid off his stool and crossed to the telephone.

●

The BMW seven series sedan with blacked-out windows cruised smoothly along the Dolphin Expressway, heading west, leaving Miami's darkening skyline behind. Jorge Madrigal was following the same route he always took from his office to his upper-middle-class home in the suburbs of southwest Dade County. A real-estate broker with a wife and two daughters, and involved in community affairs, Madrigal was the image of respectability.

His real estate business provided him with a legitimate income in excess of one hundred thousand dollars a year. As a second tier drug-cartel manager operating under cover, the cocaine shipments —four hundred kilos at a time—he orchestrated and coordinated from the Bahamas to a warehouse in Miami earned him six to seven times that amount. Madrigal planned and scheduled the smuggling operations, while his wife spent hours on pay phones and the mobile phone in her Mercedes, arranging the final transfers of the cocaine shipments to traffickers and the deliveries of suitcases full of cash to the top-level managers of the Medellín cartel. It was a family affair, with the exception of their two bright and attractive teenage daughters, who knew nothing of their parents' double life.

As Madrigal slowed the BMW to turn south at the Palmetto Expressway, the chirp of his cellular car phone broke the cocoon-like silence of the luxurious leather and burled-walnut interior. He removed the receiver from its cradle, secure in the knowledge that his conversation could not be monitored.

It was a false sense of security. The widespread belief that cellular telephones are a secure means of communication had long since been invalidated by the electronics wizards of the intelligence community. A sophisticated ultrahigh-speed scanner, equipped with an inband signaling decode device, and programmed to automatically scan only the cellular channels for a given area, can within seconds of a mobile telephone being put into use, locate and intercept the radio frequency signals of the targeted transmission.

Unknown to Jorge Madrigal, a silver van, painted with the logo and graphics of a carpet-cleaning service and traveling one-half mile behind his BMW, was doing just that. The van, the latest in mobile surveillance posts, was designed to be used as close as fifty feet from a target without arousing suspicion. A solid partition divided the driver's compartment from the back, where the electronic surveillance console and the equipment's operators were located. Visual surveillance, including night-vision capabilities, was accomplished by a hidden periscope able to rotate 360 degrees; the images it captured were viewed on a monitor on the console and automatically recorded on a video recorder with a feed to an instant printer that could produce a hard copy of any scene, on the spot, in fifteen seconds. The van's audio surveillance system consisted of synthesized high-performance receivers for monitoring covert transmitting devices (bugs), and a state-of-the-art scanner. Four ultrasensitive microphones hidden under the vehicle gathered sound within a fifty-foot radius when the van was parked at a static observation post.

Consequently, the communications intercept on Madrigal's mobile telephone was not the only surveillance measure used by the men in the back of the van. Hidden under the hood of the BMW, disguised as part of the electrical system, was a tiny black cube, no bigger than a thumbnail: a transmitter powered off the car battery, whether or not the engine was running. Such was the sophistication of the transmitter's technology that it was capable of broadcasting a signal to a directional indicator anywhere within a thirty-square-mile area of the car, enabling a surveillance team to locate the BMW and follow it at a safe distance without fear of being spotted or losing track of it. The transmitter had the added feature of being turned on and off by remote control—allowing the Drug Enforcement Agency people to deactivate it when it wasn't being monitored or when the car was being checked for bugs by Madrigal's people.

Expertly concealed inside the BMW's roof liner, another bug, even more intricately engineered, captured the conversations of any passengers in the car. Using a technique known as "snuggling," the bug was designed to transmit at a frequency just barely different from that of a Miami television station, allowing it to go undetected, or if noticed, mistaken as a bleed from the TV station's signals by the "sweepers" who went over Madrigal's house and car every week to check for electronic surveillance. It was this bug that picked up the chirping noise of the mobile phone and transmitted it to the DEA van, alerting the two technicians seated at the built-in electronic console to the incoming call, prompting them to turn on the scanner.

A mountain range of blue peaks danced on the screen as the scanner found and locked on to the channel carrying Madrigal's call. Reel-to-reel voice-activated recorders linked to the scanner clicked on and began recording the unsuspecting subject's every word. The caller did not identify himself and the conversation was succinct and to the point, almost cryptic. It was later misunderstood, and its significance lost on the men who listened to the recording at Miami's DEA field office. It was interpreted as confirmation of a drug deal or money transfer in New York City, of little concern to their office.

The teletype sent to the DEA's New York headquarters the following morning read:

Communication Intercept—Miami—2 Oct 90—18:40 Hours
Subject: Jorge Madrigal
Caller: Unknown Subject

Madrigal: Hello.

UnSub: I have some preliminary information on the subject you requested.

Madrigal: Go ahead.

UnSub: October thirteenth and fourteenth. New York City. United Nations and Waldorf-Astoria. The dates are firm, but the detailed itinerary is not complete.

Madrigal: When will you have complete details?

UnSub: Three or four days. Final arrangements are in the process of being made now.

Madrigal: Call me as soon as you have them. I will provide a New York contact for you for the dates you gave me.

UnSub: Ah . . . [Pause] A New York contact?

Madrigal: If there are any last-minute changes once you are in the city, you will pass them on to another contact. Understood?

UnSub: Yes.

Madrigal: I'll expect to hear from you within the next few days.

Disconnect

That night, Steven Whitney Bradford III got little sleep. The call he had made to Miami was an irretrievable first step into a dangerous and deadly world in which he knew he was ill-suited to survive. He lay awake most of the night, trying to conceive of a plan of action in the event his world began to fall apart, and trying to convince himself that the situation was not as grim as it appeared.

•

Jorge Madrigal had a restful night after making love to his beautiful wife. He slept soundly, knowing that the cartel bosses would be pleased with his success in compromising and recruiting a man so close to the information they wanted—a man actually involved in the planning. He had done well, and if he knew his bosses, he would be richly rewarded.

Three months later he would also be arrested, along with his wife, much to the horror of their daughters and the shock of their neighbors and friends. They would plead guilty, to receive reductions in sentences, to charges of narcotics trafficking and money laundering and spend the next seven years of their lives in prison. But this would all happen too late to have any effect on what Jorge Madrigal and Steven Whitney Bradford III had set in motion that October evening, with a telephone call that had lasted less than thirty seconds.

—3—

Created in 1865 as a law-enforcement bureau of the U.S. Treasury, the United States Secret Service is the nation's oldest general investigative agency. Its sole mission until 1901 was to preserve the economic structure of the country by preventing the counterfeiting of currency and the forgery of government checks and bonds. No Protective Operations Division existed until Teddy Roosevelt took office following the assassination of President McKinley, and until the 1950s, when the Vice President was included, only the President and the First Lady were afforded personal protection.

The Secret Service remained a small agency of only 284 agents until the assassination of John F. Kennedy in 1963, and the subsequent assassination of Robert F. Kennedy in 1968, after which the service grew rapidly. Congress, responding to public outrage over the assassinations, ordered the service to shift its focus and primary allocation of manpower and funds to Protective Operations as opposed to Investigations (counterfeiting, forgery, and fraud), resulting in a situation that still causes internecine battles between the two departments for budgetary resources. The much-expanded Protective Operations Division was now tasked with what had become the service's principal responsibility—a responsibility that continued to grow after 1968 to include not only the personal protection of the President, First Lady, and Vice President but all presidential candidates during election years, visiting dignitaries and foreign heads of state, and all living former presidents.

Adhering to a code of silence that rivals that of the Mafia, the Secret Service has managed to keep the details and extent of its methods and operations from the press, and consequently the general public. The most secret of all the service's departments is the Intelligence Division. The ID is, among other things, concerned with threat cases—or "nut cases," as they are often referred to by the agents who work them. In a warren of office cubicles on the eighth floor of 1800 G Street, two blocks from the White House, a force of twenty agents and forty intelligence analysts keep track of hundreds of known threat cases in an extensive, computerized data bank.

Letter writers and telephone callers are categorized according to the nature of the threat made. In the case of an anonymous letter threatening the President's life, research analysts check the data bank for intersects on handwriting, and known sayings or phrases in common with previous threat cases. If none exist, the letter is tracked to its place of origin, a threat case is opened, and the investigation is assigned to the Secret Service field office in the city nearest the letter's place of origin. Once the letter writer is found, he is interviewed and assessed by agents, and a permanent file is opened on him, resulting in a check being made on his whereabouts every sixty days. In the event of a presidential visit to a locale in which a known threat case resides, the local Secret Service field office assigns round-the-clock surveillance, or in extreme cases the person may be taken into custody until the President has left the area.

Telephone threats to the White House switchboard are immediately shunted to the Intelligence Division's operations center, where an agent attempts to keep the caller, who still believes he is talking to the White House, on the line while the call is being traced. The duty operation at ID is manned twenty-four hours a day, seven days a week, gathering intelligence and responding to requests for information or data-bank searches from the eighty field offices around the country. Along with its terrorist section, foreign section, and regional sections of the U.S., ID has agents assigned as liaisons with the rest of the intelligence community, including the Central Intelligence Agency, Defense Intelligence Agency, National Security Agency, and the FBI.

The worst nightmare of Secret Service Protective Operations is the unknown threat case. The potential assassin who works alone, intent on killing the President, but giving nothing away in emotional and abusive outbursts in letters or telephone calls. What every agent has to admit, despite his expertise and devotion to duty, is that an assassin willing to sacrifice his own life in the process has a better-than-even chance of success, regardless of Secret Service precautions. The Hinckley attempt on President Reagan graphically illustrated that bitter fact. Every agent securing the inner perimeter around the President on that day had done his job precisely as he had been trained to do it, and reacted instantly and properly to the assassination attempt. Yet it was due to mere chance (the small caliber of the weapon used) that the President was only wounded and not killed.

It was a nightmare every agent assigned to the Presidential Protective Division lived with, and it was on a rainy October evening in the nation's capital, in the office of the Intelligence Division's liaison agent to the Special Agent in Charge of the Presidential Protective Division, that the first signs of the nightmare that was to follow began to surface.

SECRET SERVICE HEADQUARTERS— WASHINGTON, D.C.

Susan Olsen was at her desk in the Intelligence Division, working late as usual, having early on in her career accepted the irregular hours that went with the job. If asked, she would have admitted that her current assignment was a marked improvement over the constant stress, travel, and shift work she had endured while part

of the First Lady's protection detail—a two-year tour that had put
an end to an already shaky marriage.

The teletype she scanned had just been handed to her by the
ID's CIA liaison, who was on his way out the door, mumbling
something about his wife throwing his clothes out on the lawn if he
missed another of his daughter's recitals. Susan gave him a sympathetic smile as he turned and dashed into the hallway in response
to the chime of an arriving elevator.

The intelligence report he had given her had been routed to ID
by CIA's newly formed Counter Narcotics Center in response to a
request made ten months ago by Mike Maguire, the Special Agent
in Charge of the Presidential Protective Division—he was to be
kept apprised of all intelligence information received on the
whereabouts and movements of the hierarchy of the Colombian
drug cartels.

Persistent rumors of assassination and kidnap plots aimed at
the President and his family in retaliation for U.S. drug policies
had brought the cocaine barons under close scrutiny by the Intelligence Division and the CIA's Counter Narcotics Center. There
had been no hard intelligence information to date that indicated
the plots were anything but rumors or breast beating on the part of
the drug barons. But as with all potential threats to the President
and his family, regardless of how obscure or farfetched, they were
never taken lightly by the Secret Service. They were rated in order
of probability of materializing into an overt action—from Class I
through Class III, with Class I being the highest rating—and responded to accordingly. The drug barons, with the enormous
amounts of money behind them and their stated intentions, were
in Mike Maguire's eyes rated Class I.

•

The report Susan Olsen held in her hand had been received two
hours earlier at the operations center at CIA's Langley headquarters. It had originated on the Caribbean island of St. Barts, where a
CIA Counter Narcotics Center (CNC) surveillance team had
tracked one of the drug barons, only to stumble inadvertently onto
a gathering of the heads of the Medellín, Cali, Bogotá, and North
Coast cocaine cartels. Four men, wanted by the Colombian govern-

ment and the United States Department of Justice, had arrived in private aircraft at intervals during the day. The hunted and harried men each brought a coterie of bodyguards to the tiny out-of-the-way island, and had sequestered themselves inside the grounds of a luxurious hillside villa overlooking St. Jean Bay. A fifth man, identity unknown to CNC, joined them shortly after their arrival.

The Counter Narcotics Center surveillance team immediately set up an observation post to keep them under twenty-four-hour surveillance, and were now requesting Delta Force support to organize a snatch operation to capture the wanted men and bring them to the United States, to stand trial before they were again scattered to the four winds. The request was one that CIA Deputy Director for Operations Richard Houser had not bothered to take to the Director, knowing full well the futility of trying to get the required cooperation from the French government to carry out an armed clandestine operation on an island that was their sovereign territory. Fat chance, Houser had grumbled, with more than a little bitterness. Not from the same high-and-mighty bastards who had refused our aircraft permission to overfly their territory for the raid on Libya.

Despite the President's authority to approve such extraterritorial operations under special circumstances, with or without a foreign government's knowledge and approval, the DDO knew this one would never get off the ground. At best, they faced being involved in a protracted gun battle with the drug barons' bodyguards, who according to the report numbered twenty-eight and were armed with submachine guns smuggled in aboard the private planes. And the surveillance team's description of the location where the drug barons had holed up made it clear that any attempt to assault the hillside villa would amount to a minor armed conflict in the heart of a peaceful tourist mecca frequented by the wealthy and influential, with a high degree of probability of innocent bystanders being killed. With no guarantee of taking the drug barons alive short of a well-planned Delta Force commando-style operation that would take at least a few days to plan and deploy, and no way to accomplish any improvised operation quickly and cleanly with the personnel now in place on St. Barts, it had been the DDO's decision to let the opportunity pass. The surveillance team was ordered to keep tabs on their quarry, but to take no independant action.

As the Secret Service Intelligence Division's liaison to the Presidential Protective Division, Susan Olsen carefully reread the two-page report and the DDO's comments where he had signed off on it. She decided, correctly, that it did not require immediate attention and slipped it into a folder with the other data to be included the following morning in her daily briefing of PPD chief Mike Maguire. She locked the folder in her desk safe, crammed a thick batch of summaries to be read that night into her briefcase, then pulled on her raincoat and left the building. Turning up her collar against the rain as she skipped between the traffic-snarled cars on G Street, she made a mental note to stop off at her favorite deli in Tyson's Corner. Another prepared dinner she would eat at home, alone, in front of the television.

-4-

ST. BARTS

The seedy bar and restaurant on a narrow side street just off
Gustavia harbor reminded Jerry Sincavage of one of those tropical
places that time forgot. A broad-bladed ceiling fan turned lazily
overhead, sending bluish clouds of stale cigarette smoke drifting
out windows open to the night air. A few of the tables were filled
with bronzed, colorfully dressed tourists laughing easily at ani-
mated stories of their day's island adventures. At the far end of the
room, leaning against a shadowy corner of the bar, were three men
Sincavage eyed carefully. They were out of place among the rest of
the clientele. To an observer with a fanciful mind, it would be easy
to imagine that the tough, hard-looking trio were plotting the
overthrow of some government. In fact, one of the men, the one
with the tight, curly black hair and heavily pockmarked face, had
been involved in just such an operation three years earlier. Sincavage tagged them correctly as muscle. All three, he guessed, were

probably in the employ of the man with whom he had an appointment within the hour.

Picking at the mystery-meat meal he had ordered simply to pass the time, Sincavage thought about the girl who had approached him at the café. He had followed her at a distance after she left, and watched her collecting shells on the beach, continuing his surveillance until she returned to the *Cheetah*. In the back of his mind he had known it was always possible that someday he would be recognized by someone out of his past, but this had been only the second incident in nearly twenty years. The first had been in Saigon, a few days before the city fell to the NVA, in a back street café in the Cholon section. He had waited for the man outside, snapped his neck, and left him dead in an alley.

Presently using an expertly forged Canadian passport that identified him as Roger Carlson of Montreal, Sincavage always carried four passports and four separate and distinct sets of identity papers, including pilot's licenses, in a hidden compartment in the lining of his carry-on luggage. Two of the passports, British and Australian, contained photographs of him with his appearance altered—glasses, dyed hair, and a beard had sufficed to make him unrecognizable—and it was these he had used on the half-dozen trips he made to the United States since returning from Vietnam.

Sincavage doubted there were more than a handful of people in the world who were ever associated with him long enough to remember his features, let alone his real name or any of his background. There were no boyhood friends; he was an orphan, a difficult child, passed around from foster home to foster home until he was old enough to enlist in the army. All of the friends he had made had been in Special Forces during the war, and most of them were killed in action, leaving him, as was the case with most men who spent extended periods of time in combat, with more dead friends than live ones. With the passing of the years, he had relaxed his guard, becoming less cautious in his efforts to disguise himself in remote locations such as St. Barts, and now it had caught up with him.

The incident that afternoon brought back a rush of memories of Vietnam, the Special Operations Group and Jim Boos. So the "Coon Ass" was dead. His boyish grin flashed across Sincavage's mind. The hard, wiry New Orleans Cajun had been one of the best pure warriors he had served with during his six tours in Vietnam. The girl had said he was killed. Not that he had died. Well, if someone had killed the Coon Ass, he must have been damn good. Professional curiosity had almost made him ask how it had happened, but any such inquiry from a supposed stranger would have confirmed the girl's suspicions immediately.

After signaling the waitress and paying his bill, Sincavage left the restaurant and climbed into the Mini-Moke he had rented that morning. The Australian-made jeeplike vehicle was the most common form of transportation on the island, and with good reason. Small and nimble enough to negotiate the narrow, winding roads, it also had a sturdy transmission ideally suited to the hilly terrain. From Gustavia, Sincavage followed the main road north out of town, climbing into the hills, where a breathtaking moonlit vista opened up as he crested the road above the tiny white-knuckle airport that was the bane of every tourist. Hairpin turns led down a steep mountain route barely wide enough for the pint-sized car, and he shifted into a lower gear to gain more control until reaching a flat stretch of coastal road that skirted a bay and led to the village of St. Jean. The tiny village, a hub of daytime tourist activity, was quiet. Shops, galleries, and water-sports concessions, which elbowed each other for prime space, were closed, but a few of the chic restaurants that overlooked the bay and crescent beach were still open. Glimpses of couples enjoying romantic candlelight dinners on flower-decked stone terraces flashed by as Sincavage continued on, into the countryside.

A mile or so outside the village, the scenic road cut closer to the ocean and paralleled the rocky, windswept shoreline. Inland, occasional clusters of quaint houses, painted in the vibrant colors of the Caribbean palette, appeared perched on steep hillsides. Another mile and the scenery became even more rural as the road climbed then dropped into broad valleys sprinkled with small native houses, eventually becoming no more than a thin black ribbon winding its way between the rocky shoreline and stone walls that edged arid meadows where goats grazed. Here and there, through brief openings in the lush vegetation of well-landscaped grounds, he saw the glitter of lights from some of the island's luxurious villas, tucked low-slung and sprawling into the rugged hills above the ocean, aspiring not to be seen.

Sincavage stayed on the main road along the coast, enjoying the twists, turns, steep ups and fast downs of the roller-coaster terrain. He carefully retraced the route followed that morning when he had scouted the area where he was to meet the man who had sought him out and summoned him to the island. Decreasing his speed, he drove one mile past a long, curving entrance drive that led up to a villa on the crest of a bluff overlooking the ocean, then back again to cover part of the route he had just driven from the village. He was checking the small secondary tracks that branched off the coastal road and coursed through the hills, to see if any surveillance vehicles were posted in the vicinity.

The area was virtually deserted, with the exception of the one-hundred-twenty-foot motor yacht *Southern Cross,* anchored for the night in the secluded cove below the villa. The luxury yacht hadn't been there that morning when he made his reconnaissance. Two couples sat at an outdoor dining area on the aft deck, having drinks in the peaceful setting. Sincavage cut his headlights and parked the car on a rough, unmarked lane a hundred yards from the villa's driveway. He sat on the hood, and through high-powered binoculars taken from his nylon carry-all in the backseat, he saw two more men moving about the yacht, inside the main salon. Above the aft deck, the boat deck was dark and quiet, too dark to make out anything other than indistinct shapes, but from behind one of the tenders, a silhouetted shape stood out—a portion of what appeared to be a video camera, fixed on the villa, and definitely not a standard piece of gear on a pleasure cruiser. After determining the line of sight and angle of view from the yacht, Sincavage plotted a course that would leave him unobserved.

Leaving the Mini-Moke out of sight of the main road, he pulled on a black silk windbreaker against the cool night air, and from beneath his T-shirt removed a Walther PPK kept tucked in the waistband at the small of his back. Jacking a round into the chamber, he released the safety and slipped the small automatic into a Velcro wrap holster, which he strapped on the inside of his lower left leg, just above the ankle. He walked a few steps, paused to adjust the ride and snugness of the holster, and then set out on foot.

The expansive one-story villa of white stucco and glass sat high on a rock promontory, commanding a panoramic view of the secluded cove, its deserted alabaster beach, and the Caribbean beyond. It was in a world of its own. Jagged cliffs rose up from the cove, flanking it on either side. Directly below, where moonlight sparkled on white powdery sand and reflected off black waters, the ocean rose in gentle swells, breaking listlessly on shore in tiny wavelets that slapped the beach with a soothing, rhythmic sound enhanced by the soft rustle of palms and the echo of the surf on a distant reef. Oblivious to its primal beauty, Sincavage heard it only as a useful tool—background noise carried on the night wind that would mask any careful movement in the immediate area.

The terrain leading from the road to the rear of the villa was steep and rocky, with enough tropical vegetation and underbrush to conceal an approach to the low stone wall enclosing the estate. Upon reaching the wall, Sincavage moved slowly along its perimeter, pausing and watching until he located all of the security guards posted about the property. There were twelve of them, all armed with submachine guns—Uzis, Sincavage noted. Whatever else they may have been good at, they were obviously poorly trained for the task of securing a perimeter. Rather than dividing the property into sectors and patrolling the area, they had taken up static positions that left blind spots in large sections of the grounds. Sincavage chose a spot deep in shadows and slipped over the wall. He stayed low, and carefully made his way from cover to cover, using the trees and shrubs leading up to the edge of the stone terrace that wrapped around the house. Eight more guards with automatic weapons were posted randomly around the terrace, again leaving gaps in their fields of vision.

Inside, five men sat sipping drinks in plush leather easy chairs and sofas grouped about the villa's massive living room, its glass doors on two sides open to the ocean breeze. The angry tones of a rapid-fire conversation in Spanish stopped abruptly as four of the men reacted with a start to Sincavage's unannounced entrance from the terrace. The fifth man sat unruffled, a bemused look on his face. He didn't know the intruder by sight, but instinctively knew who and what he was. He raised his hand to calm the man across from him, who was reaching for a weapon in a shoulder holster beneath his jacket.

"A very dramatic entrance," he said to Sincavage. "I'm impressed."

"Don't be," Sincavage said. "It's amateur night outside."

The calm man stood and extended his hand. Sincavage shook it. "I am Raphael Calderon," he said, in perfect, unaccented English.

"And I'm the man you sent for," Sincavage said. "I know the others by reputation," he added, gesturing to the remaining four men, who hadn't bothered to stand or make any pretense of social graces. "You, I don't know."

Calderon considered himself an excellent judge of character, and what he saw in the expressionless deep-set eyes of the man before him was what he had expected—a commanding presence that emanated cold, calculating efficiency. The others in the room eyed him suspiciously, sizing him up by their own standards.

Calderon smiled pleasantly and sat down, gesturing for Sincavage to do the same. Few men knew Calderon as anything but a wealthy Bolivian landowner, scion of a socially and politically prominent family. His life as an international narcotics trafficker on a massive scale was a secret he'd managed to keep from everyone outside the business, with the exception of the high-level government officials on his payroll. He was the brains behind the cartel's expansion into the lucrative Japanese, Scandinavian, and European markets, and the architect of a brilliantly conceived computerized nerve center for their intricate multibillion-dollar financial operations, which included sixty-five shell companies designed to hide the illicit drug profits. His organizational genius was responsible for the bloody, ruthless drug wars that had virtually eliminated the Cubans from the cocaine trade in Miami, and for the cartel's diversified investment strategies in real estate, small businesses, and financial institutions, including currency-exchange houses, which increased their ability to launder their huge profits. The villa chosen for the meeting was his, though that was a fact nearly impossible to prove, the title being held by a holding company in the Netherland Antilles that was itself held by three firms in the Bahamas, the stock of which had no identified owners—it was this type of elaborate precaution that kept him out of the files of law-enforcement agencies.

Sincavage had noticed immediately that Calderon was a cut above the other men in the room, in his mannerisms, his cultured voice, and the way the others deferred to him. His custom-tailored suit fit perfectly, and rather than being adorned with gold chains beneath an open-necked shirt, as Sincavage expected of the others, he wore a silk shirt with an expensive tie neatly knotted in place. He was relaxed, in control, his eyes calm and fixed on Sincavage, studying the man whose international reputation for professionalism and thoroughness intrigued him.

When Calderon began his discreet inquiries for a man with special talents, Sincavage's name (one of his aliases) was the first whispered in the elite, secret circles that dealt in the shadowy world of political assassinations and international intrigue conducted outside the sanctions of national governments. A few knew of specific contracts he had carried out, and rumors of others attributed to him; but most knew him only by reputation, and not by name. A man with no equal, Calderon had been told. A killer's killer. A specter to be called forth when the need arose. A mail drop in Vienna had been the only point of contact given, and it was in this manner that Calderon had set things in motion, stating only the time, date, and place of the meeting desired. It was all that was necessary. The fact that Calderon had used the mail drop told Sincavage that the people who referred him would also vouch for him. There was no doubt what the subject matter of the meeting would be, only who was the target.

As Calderon was about to speak, one of the security guards appeared in a doorway open to the terrace. There was a confused look on the man's face as he realized the equation inside had changed. He hesitated, unsure of what action to take, if any, then sheepishly stepped back into the shadows when Calderon dismissed him with a disdainful wave of the hand.

"Our ever-vigilant guardians," Calderon said, handing Sincavage a glass of brandy.

Sincavage's eyes flicked slowly about the room, lingering momentarily on each of the other four men. They looked like what they were—uneducated, cold-eyed hustlers, peasants from violent slum neighborhoods, who by the age of eight were carrying knives or guns or anything else that gave them an advantage in the day-to-day struggle to stay alive. Yet despite appearances that suggested otherwise, they were deceptively cunning men, close-mouthed, creative, and utterly single-minded in pursuit of their goals. They had all started their criminal lives humbly enough: a kidnapper/mugger, a pickpocket, a car thief, and a psychopathic street urchin who fancied himself an assassin. Tested constantly, they had survived rival traffickers, police, even governments, to reach the top rung of their profession.

They were the kings of cocaine. *Narcotraficantes.* The most successful, the richest, and the deadliest criminals on earth. They had come to dominate the cocaine business, as well as the economies and governments of several countries, through guile, guts, and a willingness to do whatever it took to get what they wanted. Their realm extended from the coca fields of Peru, Bolivia, and Ecuador to the jungle refineries of Colombia and Brazil. Their outposts were remote airstrips and piers in Mexico and the Caribbean, their ports of entry spanned the American South and Southwest. With combined profits in excess of six billion dollars a year, they vied with Third World governments in wealth and power.

Their organizations were kept separate, but they frequently made common policy and cooperated on major deals, sharing both risk and profit and enforcing discipline with a savage violence. Together they controlled over 80 percent of the cocaine coming into the United States—as much as seventy-five metric tons a year. They had thousands of employees: campesino peasants to grow and process the coca, pilots and mules to smuggle it, an elaborate clandestine distribution network to market it, lawyers to handle legal problems, bagmen to offer bribes and launder the billions of tax-free dollars earned, and hired killers to eliminate their enemies. Theirs was a world where murder was an accepted part of doing business. Those they couldn't compromise, they terrorized. Greed and fear were the keys to their success—*plomo o plata* (lead or silver), take the money or the bullet. Those who stood up to them died untimely, violent deaths.

The man sitting directly opposite Sincavage was Eduardo Vargas, head of the Cali cartel. Next to him sat Virgilio Martinez, his counterpart in the Bogotá cartel. Luis Morales, chief of the Medellín cartel, sat off to the side, his gaze alternating from Sincavage to the doors opening onto the terrace, not thoroughly convinced that the stranger was who he represented himself to be, or that he had come alone. One man sat off by himself, watching the others and Sincavage through eyes that suggested a full-blown case of paranoia. He was Claudio Valencia, chief of the North Coast cartel and the most dangerous man in the room. His head was on a swivel, eyes wild and suspicious. Valencia's father and brother had only recently been tracked down and killed by the Colombian police, while trying to escape from their once-secret hideaway in the Colombian jungle.

Despite their control over billions of dollars and large personal armies, these were frightened men, unsure of once-solid alliances, finding doors slammed shut in what were once safe havens—Panama, the Bahamas, and even Nicaragua were no longer willing to risk involvement.

They found themselves fending off a series of probing assaults from the Sicilian Mafia (not satisfied with their dominance of the heroin trade), aimed at taking over the cartels' processing and distribution networks, looking to expand inroads already made into Brazil and Venezuela. And from within their own cartels, they had fought internecine battles with younger members, who smelled blood and were jockeying for position. There were even rumors of CIA covert paramilitary operations in the planning stages, aimed at assassinating them. And in the eyes of these four men, their darkest nightmare, one that had already befallen more than a few of their associates: the targeting of key players by the Americans, for capture and extradition to the United States, where trials and long prison sentences awaited them, which would take them away from their money and influence.

This untenable situation had led them to turn to Calderon, who had listened to their anger and cries for vengeance. They knew who was to blame, where the real threat lay. There was no doubt in any of their minds that without the instigation, support, and collaboration of the United States, the hated yanquis, none of this would have happened. And they were now reacting to that threat as they reacted to all threats, with mindless violence. In the past eight years their assassins had bombed or gunned down two presidential candidates, 178 judges, eleven of the twenty-four members of the Colombian Supreme Court, two successive Justice Ministers, an attorney general, the Medellín police chief, and the editors of two newspapers. Now it was time to show the *norteamericanos* that they could not declare war on them with impunity.

It was Valencia who spoke first, his voice tight and angry, his English thickly accented. "You know why we send for you?"

"Let me take a wild guess," Sincavage said. "You want someone eliminated." He instinctively disliked the man; he looked as if he were about to jump out of his skin.

Valencia bristled at the sarcasm directed toward him.

"Yes, someone," Calderon interrupted before Valencia's volatile temper could flare. "Someone very special."

"Am I supposed to guess," Sincavage said, "or are you going to tell me?"

"The President of the United States," Calderon said flatly.

There was no surface reaction from Sincavage. He had sorted through the probable reasons for the meeting upon entering the villa and seeing who was in attendance. He knew that the target had to be someone who was hurting the cartels, but the President had not come immediately to mind, though it did not completely surprise him.

Calderon put down his drink and leaned forward in his chair, taking Sincavage's lack of response as a cue to continue. "Furthermore, we want him assassinated on a particular day, in a specific place."

Again there was no response from Sincavage, only a steady gaze fixed on Calderon.

"We have gone to great lengths to gain access to information on his movements, inside information," Calderon emphasized, "to aid you in your planning."

"When and where?" Sincavage asked.

"Eleven days from today, in New York City. He will be addressing the United Nations General Assembly . . . a speech on international cooperation for his war on drugs. That same evening he is scheduled to be the guest speaker at a ten-thousand-dollar-a-plate fund-raising dinner at the Waldorf-Astoria Hotel. But we want you to assassinate him before that, as he is entering the United Nations."

A small smile spread slowly across Sincavage's face. "An object lesson for all to see."

"Precisely," Calderon replied. "I'm sure you can appreciate the beauty of it."

"What I can appreciate," Sincavage said, the smile gone now, "is the stupidity of it."

Calderon stiffened, but retained his composure. "Bold, yes. But not stupid. Not with proper planning and in the hands of a professional such as yourself."

"Are you people at all familiar with the concept of cause and effect?" Sincavage asked.

"The time for logical response is past," Calderon said evenly. "My colleagues want a message sent to those who would destroy us. We do not seek your approval of our decision, only your specialized talents in carrying it out. For that we are willing to pay you far more than you have ever been paid before . . . ten million dollars."

If Calderon and the other men in the room expected to see an immediate reaction, they were disappointed. Sincavage sat quietly, his eyes fixed somewhere in the middle distance. The amount of money offered had indeed made an impression, but not to the extent that it affected his judgment. He was dealing with desperate men. Men who were striking out in blind rage, without thought to the consequences of their actions, but who seemed willing to accept whatever repercussions there might be. Violence had served them well all their lives; it was all they knew, all they believed in. Although at home with violence, Sincavage had never been a fanatic motivated by hate or blood lust as these men were, throwing caution and common sense to the winds. Rather, he approached each contract with a calm rationality, attacking obstacles with logic and precision. The target presented near-insurmountable odds, but that was part of what appealed to him—to his sense of challenge and competition. He had pressed his luck in the past few years, and he knew it. Maybe it was time to get out of the business. Time to disappear. After one final contract. One that if carried out successfully would be the crowning achievement to an already renowned career.

"Will you accept the contract?" Calderon asked.

Sincavage nodded. "Maybe. If you agree to a few stipulations."

"Of course," Calderon said expansively. "Name them."

"First of all," Sincavage said, "the current President of the United States is the most visible leader in the world, and consequently the most heavily protected; a strong deterrent in itself. His assassination will set off an international manhunt the likes of which the world has never seen. Whoever assassinates him can never work again. So the price is twenty million dollars. Pocket change to you, but financial security that allows me to disappear, pay off the necessary officials, and with a little luck and proper planning, possibly live out my life in luxury."

Sincavage paused to note any objections. There were none and he continued.

"Secondly, you're giving me extremely short notice. And by dictating time and place, you've increased my risks tenfold. The time factor can be overcome, but it will require me to work from inside your organization, specifically from your terrorist training camp in Peru. And I'll need arrangements made allowing me to select some men with special qualifications to train as an assault team, and provisions for all the weapons and equipment required to do the job. I'm not unaware that working from within your network means giving up some of my anonymity and exposing myself to whatever informants may have penetrated your ranks; that's another reason for doubling the price."

Calderon nodded, surprised that Sincavage knew about the top-secret training camp in Peru. "I will put you in contact with a man who will help you select the best possible men for the task, and instruct the man in charge of the camp to give you his full cooperation, no questions asked."

"He nor anyone else is to know anything about my mission."

"Of course," Calderon said in response.

"And I'll need a point of contact in New York City," Sincavage continued. "Someone who's in touch with your inside informant, to keep me advised of any changes in the President's schedule."

"Agreed," Calderon said.

"And I will decide where the target is hit," Sincavage added emphatically. "If it's possible to do it when he arrives at the United Nations, then I'll do it there. But the only guarantee I'll give you, in deference to the amount of money you're paying, is that he will die before he leaves New York; either way, your object lesson will be just as emphatic."

Calderon glanced at each of the men in the room, gaining a consensus as each nodded in agreement. "Agreed," Calderon said, raising his glass to Sincavage, who responded in kind without taking a drink.

"Who else knows about this?" Sincavage asked.

"No one outside this room," Calderon replied.

"Keep it that way, gentlemen," Sincavage said. "The President of the United States is the most difficult target in the world for an assassin who wants to stay alive after carrying out the contract. And I intend to be alive when it's over."

"We will pay you ten million dollars now," Calderon said, "and the remaining ten million when you have fulfilled the contract."

With a nod of his head, Calderon sent Vargas and Martinez into an adjoining room to return with three large, overstuffed suitcases, which they placed on the ottoman before Sincavage and zipped open. Inside each were neatly stacked bundles of one hundred dollar bills crammed into every available space.

"Ten million dollars," Calderon said. "Your first installment."

Valencia turned toward Sincavage, a contemptuous grin on his face. "Your politicians want your people to 'just say no' to drugs," he said, "but nobody says no to money, eh?"

Sincavage shook his head and smiled. He had, of course, heard about the huge sums of cash at their disposal, but had never witnessed such an ostentatious display of it. He also recalled that before their dominance of the cocaine trade, the Colombians had been the world's best and most prolific counterfeiters of American currency—a fact that caused him to make another decision.

"Keep the cash," he said, and removed a pen and notepad from his jacket pocket. He scribbled the code for a numbered account in a Liechtenstein bank on a slip of paper and handed it to Calderon. "I want the entire twenty million deposited in this account within forty-eight hours. When I receive confirmation of the deposit, you can consider our contract valid."

Calderon again looked to the others for approval, and got it, albeit reluctantly from Valencia, who was glaring at Sincavage in an openly hostile way.

"You lie, you die!" Valencia spat the words out.

Sincavage didn't rise to the bait. He didn't even look at the man. Instead he handed Calderon the notepad and pen. "I'll need telephone numbers for the contacts we discussed."

Calderon complied. "The first number is in Cartagena; I will tell him to expect your call. The second is in New York City; he, too, will be instructed to do whatever you wish."

"Once the deal is set, there will be no calling it off. Understood?"

"Understood," Calderon replied.

"If any of you are captured once the operation is under way, it's my call as to whether or not I continue. In the event that I do not, half of your money will be returned. The other half is mine to keep. Compensation for the absolute certainty that my identity and the matters discussed at this meeting will be revealed."

Calderon ignored the insult implicit in the last remark. "Everyone in this room will be at my estate in Bolivia until the job is finished," he told Sincavage. "I can assure you, no one will be in any danger of capture."

"And what about our money if you fail?" Martinez asked, pointedly.

"If I fail," Sincavage said, "I'll have died trying. Consequently, I won't give a damn about your money."

With that, Sincavage stepped out onto the terrace and disappeared into the shadows as quickly as he had appeared.

●

Eighty feet below the villa, and one hundred yards out in the middle of the secluded cove, a camera shutter clicked in rapid succession from the darkened recesses of the boat deck on board the *Southern Cross.*

"Shit!" The man behind the tripod hissed to himself, and quickly swung the 1000mm lens in the direction he had seen the man disappear. But his severe angle of view encompassed only the front edge of the terrace that overlooked the cove, preventing him from photographing anyone farther back or inside the villa. The elusive figure, which he had seen too late to photograph when he had appeared out of nowhere and entered the villa, was gone again. The cameraman's only hope was that the infrared film had captured the unknown subject in the few seconds it had taken him to cross the terrace and disappear into the night.

The second man on the boat deck, seated in the dark at a small portable console set up behind one of the tenders, removed his headset and shut off a recorder attached to an elaborate array of equipment. "They've left the room. Nothing coming in but intermittent clutter."

"What did we get?" the first man asked.

"Not sure. The take was pretty spotty . . . broken up. I think we'd better let the boys down below have a listen; I've got a sneaking suspicion it's not what they thought it was going to be."

—5—

The two vacationing couples aboard the *Southern Cross* had retired for the night. It had been the most exciting day of their trip, and one of the few nights they had gone to sleep without first drinking themselves into a stupor. The men, highly successful law partners from Chicago, had spent fifty thousand dollars to charter the luxury yacht, complete with crew, for two weeks. It was to be their wives' dream vacation, and it had started well enough—a new experience, relaxing and enjoyable, being pampered by the crew and enchanted by the magic of the Caribbean islands.

But by the end of the third day the novelty began to wear off and daily activities were deteriorating into boring repetition, especially for the men, who were accustomed to a more highly charged existence. It was the most concentrated amount of time the two couples had ever spent together and they had gone a long way toward proving the old axiom that the best way to get to know someone is to spend an extended period of time with them on a boat. By the end of the fifth day they had said everything they had

to say to one another—and a few things they wished they hadn't—
and the confined space, though beautiful and luxurious, was taking
a terrible toll.

On the morning of the eighth day, dreading what promised to
be six more interminable days, but not about to forfeit the paid-in-
full nonrefundable money, they had jumped at an opportunity
presented to them by the captain. Would they be willing to allow
four men, intelligence officers, to come on board to conduct a
surveillance on a matter of national security? There wasn't a dis-
senting voice to be heard, certainly not among the crew. The
secretive men boarded in Marigot harbor on the island of St.
Martin, and later that day the *Southern Cross* made the short trip to
St. Barts and dropped anchor in the secluded cove below Raphael
Calderon's villa.

The two men who had boarded first were CIA case officers, a
surveillance team from the Agency's Counter Narcotics Center—a
newly minted unit involved in building biographies of the drug
lords, tracking their communications, identifying their delivery
routes, and infiltrating agents into their organizations. They were
the same two men who had followed Claudio Valencia to St. Barts
and stumbled upon the secret meeting. Realizing the significance
of their find, and that they would need a surveillance platform to
eavesdrop on the villa, preferably a boat, they contacted a CIA
support agent in residence on St. Martin. He had suggested the
Southern Cross—the captain was a friend and former naval intelligence officer who would cooperate without prying. The other two
men, who boarded later in the day, were technical support personnel flown down from CIA's Langley headquarters in response to
the surveillance team's request. The intelligence officers were cor-
dial but close-mouthed around the crew and the lawyers and their
wives, and the desperate couples were more than content to play
the role of tourists enjoying their vacation (a not undemanding
performance considering the events of the past eight days) and
fantasizing about what an important contribution they were making to their country's national security.

With the meeting in the villa over, the crew on watch or in their
quarters, and the lawyers and their wives sound asleep, the CNC
surveillance team gathered in the main salon for a conference with

the technical support people from Langley. It was 1:00 A.M. when they finished listening to the recording. The take was indeed spotty, but playing and replaying of the tape began to reveal key phrases that suggested the purpose of the meeting was far more ominous than a discussion of how the drug barons could circumvent the latest interdiction measures taken against them by Colombian police and American DEA agents—the subject matter the CNC surveillance team initially thought was the purpose of the high-level meeting.

The large gaps in the recorded conversation were sections rendered unintelligible by interference from both interior and exterior noise. And the portions that had been lost or "walked on" by the peripheral noise had occurred at crucial moments, obliterating information that could have given the CNC team a better sense of the meeting and perhaps revealed the unknown subject's identity, or a clearer idea of the reason for his presence.

Unlike conventional electronic surveillance devices, which there had been neither time nor opportunity to install in the villa, the laser communications device that the technical support team had brought aboard was innovative and state-of-the-art, but not without its drawbacks. Like most highly sophisticated, ultrasensitive electronic equipment, it was dependent on perfect operating conditions, which seldom existed outside the testing laboratory.

Operating under the less-than-perfect conditions aboard the *Southern Cross,* and hoping for the best, the technical support team had set up their esoteric equipment on the boat deck, mounting the laser transmitter—approximately the size of a video camera—and its receiver on a tripod platform out of sight among the yacht's tenders. After a half hour of trial and error, they managed to sight it in on one of the glass doors of the villa living room, only minutes before the unannounced stranger arrived. An invisible laser beam was bounced off the door (which acted as a diaphragm), picking up the slight vibrations from the sound pressure generated by the voices inside. The vibrations caused a shift in the wavelength of the beam, modulating what was reflected back to the yacht to enter the receiver, whose focusing lens concentrated the modulated beam's infrared signal onto a photomultiplier, which transformed it into a series of electrical impulses. The impulses were then fed into an amplifier and a computerized demodulator, which separated audio from light, recovered the original voice signals, and allowed the output to be recorded or listened to.

All of the lost conversation could have been captured had they been able to gain access to the villa ahead of time and plant tiny flexible reflectors, allowing them to bounce the beam off objects within the room, thereby eliminating all extraneous window vibrations. But circumstance had precluded that, and along with the gentle intermittent pitching and rolling of the yacht, which necessitated occasional realignment of the laser beam, there had been a series of errant noises: the clinking of ice in glasses, the scrape of a shoe, the squeak of the leather chairs when someone shifted position, the security men walking by outside on the terrace, the night wind in the trees and the sound of the surf, had all conspired against them, adding their own sound waves that vibrated off the glass and disrupted the take. But the technical support team had done the best they could under hurried and difficult circumstances. Others would now be called upon to build on their foundation.

The decision was made to immediately transport the tape to CIA's Office of Technical Services audio laboratory, where an attempt could be made to clean it up and perhaps recover some of what was hidden among the clutter. At 2:15 A.M. the captain put the two CNC case officers ashore to continue their surveillance of the men in the villa. The *Southern Cross* then weighed anchor and headed for St. Martin, where the technical support team would board the CIA aircraft that had brought them to the island. Three and one-half hours later, the tape of the conversation and the infrared film from the camera would be hand-delivered to OTS scientists at Langley.

—6—

At three o'clock in the morning, Gustavia harbor was silent and deserted, save for a couple locked in embrace, leaning against the seawall a hundred yards from where Sincavage stood in a darkened doorway. Nothing stirred on board the yachts moored along the quay, and he waited patiently until the enraptured couple moved on, arm in arm, pausing for one last passionate kiss before they turned down a side street that led away from the harbor.

Maria Padron slept peacefully, stretched out on the padded bench seat in the *Cheetah*'s entertainment cockpit, where she had dozed off earlier that night. The gentle rocking motion of the boat as Sincavage moved catlike across the gangway was not enough to disturb her beyond a muffled groan.

Sincavage went unseen as he stepped down into the steering cockpit and dropped to one knee to lower his profile. He again scanned the quay and the boats docked alongside, as he removed the Walther PPK from his ankle holster and screwed a silencer onto the threaded tip of the barrel. Moving in a low crouch, he crept silently toward the main companionway and the entertainment cockpit, where he stood motionless over Maria Padron, the barrel of the Walther only inches from her head as he watched her chest rise and fall with the slow, even breaths of a deep sleep.

"What a waste," Sincavage whispered to himself. The remark was devoid of emotion; an assassin's observation.

He paused a few seconds to again admire her beauty, then fired two silenced shots in rapid succession that tore into the base of her skull and killed her instantly. The only sounds were the hiss and spit of the deadly hollow-point projectiles as they left the tip of the silencer, and a sharp clicking from the weapon's receiver as the bolt was blown back to pick up another round. A light blanket lay across the lower half of Maria's body, and Sincavage pulled it up, covering her completely. With the exception of a possible split-second flash of pain, Maria Padron had felt nothing; whatever she had been dreaming were the last thoughts of her young life.

Sincavage retrieved the empty shell casings and tucked the weapon into his waistband before he moved to the companionway. He swung nimbly down into the main salon, where dim night lights cast a soft golden glow over the interior. A quick sweep of the master stateroom, the guest stateroom, and the crew's quarters confirmed his earlier conclusion; there was no one else on board the sixty-five-foot sailing vessel. Returning to the main salon, he immediately spotted what he was looking for. The Leica camera sat on the bar counter at the end of the galley closest to him. Three film canisters sat next to it. He popped open the back of the camera and pulled out a half-exposed roll of film that lay against the sprockets, stuffing it, along with the three exposed canisters, into his jacket pocket.

He crossed to the starboard side, and stopped at the navigation and control station aft of the main salon, where he studied the array of instruments and systems monitors mounted on the bulk-head. Behind the communications console, he felt for the wiring harnesses. This would do fine, he thought, as he took a small circular device made of stainless steel from his pocket. One-half inch thick and three inches in circumference, the deadly incendiary resembled a miniature hockey puck in configuration. The inside of the stainless steel container was packed with Pyrenol, a substance the consistency of sealing wax and designed to ignite for only a few seconds at an extremely high temperature, just below detonation speed but intense enough to burn through one-half inch of steel in two seconds.

Sincavage placed the device behind the communications panel, the hole in its face plate against the back side of the outer bulkhead amid a tangle of wires. He inserted an igniter into the container's receptacle and connected the wires that extended from the igniter to a digital timer the size of a watch face and powered by a camera battery. When the timer reached the preset time, the circuit would close and current from the battery would fire the igniter for the instant it took to start the flash burn of the Pyrenol. The ensuing electrical fire would spread quickly, gutting the interior of the sailboat and burning with enough intensity to melt and fuse the stainless steel container and the timer to the point of being un-recognizable to anyone but an arson expert.

Sincavage set the timer to go off in ten minutes and went topside. The fire would destroy anything he had missed, and de-pending on how badly the girl's body was charred when the fire reached the entertainment cockpit, possibly lead the less than competent local police to suspect that what had taken place was something other than a professional hit. With one final glance at the sloop and the motor-sailer moored on either side of the *Chee-tah,* Sincavage crossed the gangway and disappeared into the dark-ness on the far side of the quay. He walked casually down a cobbled alleyway to where he had parked the Mini-Moke, and paused to pull on the leaders protruding from the canisters, stripping the film from them and tossing the lot into an open garbage bin behind a restaurant. Five minutes later, as he drove slowly away from the center of town, a small circle of brilliant orange-white light flashed for an instant behind the *Cheetah*'s communications panel. Thirty seconds later, an acrid cloud of gray smoke began to accumulate in the main salon and drift slowly up through the companionway.

•

The young couple aboard the sixty-foot sloop *Masquerade,* docked alongside the *Cheetah,* had met only three days ago on the island of Anguilla. He had invited her to join him on his boat and she had accepted; neither regretted their decisions as they lay in each other's arms, bathed in perspiration after a long night of lovemaking.

The woman sighed contentedly, disentangled herself, and got out of bed. She pulled on a pair of shorts and a T-shirt, then took the half-empty bottle of champagne from the ice bucket on the nightstand and went topside.

"I need some air," she called back to her lover, who slipped on his swim trunks and joined her.

On deck they embraced, enjoying the cool night air that sent a tingling sensation through their overheated bodies. The woman raised her head from the man's shoulder and looked in the direction of the *Cheetah,* her eyes settling on the entertainment cockpit and the main companionway. A frown creased her sunburned brow as she realized what she was looking at.

"There's smoke coming from that boat," she told the man.

A quick glance was all he needed before grabbing a fire extinguisher from the locker behind him and dashing onto the quay and boarding the *Cheetah.* The girl followed close behind, waiting on deck as the man went below, choking back the fumes as he managed to put out the fire before it had spread much beyond the bulkhead around the communications console.

A shrill scream, immediately followed by another, brought him scampering up the companionway, to where the woman stood staring in horror at the bloodied, lifeless figure she had just tried to awaken.

–7–

Immediate access to CIA's Office of Technical Services section is strictly limited to senior OTS staff. Only they have the seven-digit combination for the cipher lock key pad that secures the main door. All other personnel are required to ring a buzzer, drop their laminated identity card in the tray that flaps open, and wait for a metallic voice to tell them to enter.

Tony Covington, chief of the Agency's Counter Narcotics Center, had done just that, entering the inner sanctum as the lock clicked open. A uniformed security officer inside the door returned his ID card and directed him down a long corridor flanked by doors painted in cheerful pastel colors to offset the drab institutional feeling of the area. Behind the doors were the offices and laboratories of the myriad specialists responsible for developing the Agency's most sophisticated weapons, drugs, and the arcane equipment of espionage tradecraft.

As Covington passed the Explosives section, he recalled a recent trip with two of their technicians to CIA's top-secret isolation compound at Harvey Point, North Carolina, where he was given a counterterrorist demonstration featuring the most recent advances in applications for plastique—the malleable explosive substance capable of being molded into any conceivable shape and disguised to resemble things as innocuous as a vase or a soap dish.

Through a glass wall halfway down the corridor Covington peered into the Toxic Agents lab—a double-door vacuum-sealed goldfish-bowl environment where the agency researched and developed deadly poisons, toxins, and bacteriological and chemical agents. Farther on was the Weapons and Ballistics section, where every conceivable type of exotic weapon and ammunition was created to suit any need.

Other esoteric sections followed: Flaps and Seals, specializing in the surreptitious opening of mail, or reading it unopened by applying various chemicals to the exterior; Disguises, where makeup artists created complete physical make-overs, everything from contact lenses that changed brown eyes to blue, to artificial moles and scars to draw attention away from distinctive, and therefore memorable, facial features. Next was Photography and Imagery, which not only experimented with innovative film techniques, but designed cameras disguised as everything from tie clips and rings to automobile headlights and dental bridgework. Identification section was the lair of master forgers and engravers, who could reproduce documents issued anywhere in the world. Nothing was beyond their purview—a Danish passport, a Czech visa, birth and death certificates from any country, a Moroccan driver's license, and credit cards from any bank were just a few of their expert reproductions. Thorough to a fault, whatever identities they created they backstopped—constructing an elaborate personal history and the complex web of ancillary documentation that was part of a computerized society. Even minor details, such as pocket litter, were not overlooked; pictures of a nonexistent wife and children, club membership cards, and department store charge cards, all were included to complete the new identity.

Behind the blue door at the end of the corridor was the Electronic Services section and the audio laboratory where Dan Gardner awaited Covington's arrival. Here resided the best wiremen in the world. To them there was no such thing as a private conversation, and no one was safe from the ingenious, insidious devices they created.

"Were you able to work your magic?" Covington asked the scientist, who looked the stereotype with his tousled hair, rumbled white lab coat, and steel-rimmed glasses perched on the tip of his nose.

"Magic we do every day; miracles, less frequently," Gardner said. "This stuff needed a miracle, it was walked on pretty heavily."

Gardner motioned for Covington to follow as he moved to a cluttered countertop below a console of reel-to-reel recorders that filled one wall of an office cubicle crammed with computers, spectrum analyzers, and various electronics modules.

"Unfortunately the laser communications device our boys used hamstrung us. With conventional bugs scattered around a room, our computers can compare the sound tracks from different angles, discriminate among them, pick out the voice vibrations and edit out any covering or background noise; faucets splashing, radios blasting, none of those old tricks work anymore. Even if they manage to completely obscure the voices, our computer-enhancement specialists can still focus in on the conversation and reproduce it. But the laser bug works on a different principle, and unless you've got plenty of lead time to set it up right, the take's going to be limited."

Gardner moved a stack of files aside, picked up a computer printout, and handed it to Covington. "This is the hard copy of the take. There's more if you want to see it, but I condensed it to those parts of the conversation that reveal the nature and intent of the meeting. The ellipses indicate where words are missing, the length of the ellipses are in relation to the number of words we couldn't recover. Look it over, then I'll tell you what conclusions we drew, but I think you'll find it self-evident."

Covington rested one hip on a stool beside the counter and slowly read the text of the conversation captured by the laser device aboard the *Southern Cross*.

Identified Speakers: (1) Well-educated man; possibly Bolivian
(2) American; Pennsylvania coal regions accent.

Bolivian:
"I am . . . . . Calderon."

American:
"And I'm . . . . sent for. I know . . . .
. . . reputation. . . . . . . don't know."

Bolivian:
"The President . . . . States . . . .
. . . . on a particular day, in a specific place . . . .
. . . . . great lengths to . . . .
. . . . . . movements. . . . . aid . . . ."

American:
"When and . . . . . . ?"

Bolivian:
"Eleven . . . . today, in . . . . City . . . . .
. . address . . . . Assembly . . .
speech . . . . cooperation . . . .
. . . . drugs . . . .
. . . Waldorf . . . ."

(Following twenty-six seconds lost and unrecoverable)

Bolivian:
". . . . . logical . . . . past"
(Fifteen seconds lost) . . . . . "million dollars . . . .
accept?"

(Six seconds lost)

American:
". . . . . current President . . . .
States . . . . visible . . . . world . .
. . . . deterrent . . . .
assassination will . . . . manhunt the . . . .
. . . .
work again. Twenty . . . . dollars. Pocket . . . . . .
. . . . . financial security that . . . . to
disappear . . . . officials and with a little . . .
. . . . possibly . . . . life . . . .
. . . . extremely short notice. And . . . . . .
dictating . . . . you've increased . . . .
tenfold. The time . . . . overcome, but . . . .
. . . . . . require . . . to work . . . . your . . . . .
. . . . organization . . . . from . . . .
training . . . . . arrangements . . . men . . . .
qualifications . . . . assault . . . .
provisions . . . . weapons and equipment . . . .
. . . job. . . . not . . . ."

(Eight seconds lost)

Bolivian:
". . . . . contact with . . . . will
help you select the . . . . . . possible . . . . task,
. . . . . instruct . . . . charge of the . . . .
give you his full cooperation, no questions . . . . ."

American:
". . . . . . need . . . . . point . . . . York City.
. . . . . . touch . . . . informant . . .
keep . . . . changes in the President's
schedule."

Bolivian:
"Agreed."

American:
". . . . . decide . . . . is hit . . . .
. . possible to . . . . arrives . . . .
Nations, then . . . . there. *(Seven seconds lost)* . . . . .
. . . lesson . . . . as emphatic."

(Twenty seconds lost)

Bolivian:
". . . . . will . . . . ten million now . . . .
. . . ten . . . . have . . . . contract . . . . .
. . . . installment."

American:
". . . . . cash . . . . the entire . . .
. . . million . . . . account . . . .
. . . . . hours . . . . confirmation of . . . . . .
consider . . . . valid . . . .
I'll . . . . numbers . . . . contacts . . .
discussed."

Bolivian:
". . . . . number is . . . . . . Cartagena; I will . . . .
. . . . to expect your call. The . . . . New York
City . . . . will be . . . . . to do . . . .
wish."

(Remaining twenty-eight seconds lost)

"Are you sure about one of them being American?" Covington
asked.

"Our linguistics experts are positive," Gardner said. "The other guy is a probable; could be from Peru. He was speaking excellent English, but his trace accent was either Bolivian or Peruvian."

"The bastards have brought in a top pro to assassinate the President of the United States. Our President," Covington said, taking the affront personally.

"And he must be damn good," Gardner said, "to demand and get twenty million dollars."

Covington reread a section of the take. "They want him hit when he enters the UN. To make one of their sick statements, no doubt."

"That's our conclusion," Gardner said. "But what's really interesting is that the announcement of the President's plans to address the UN on the drug problem wasn't made until about a half hour ago. Whoever leaked it to them has access to inside information."

"From what I make of this," Covington said, "they've given the shooter a contact in Cartagena to arrange for weapons and an assault team, and someone in New York City to keep him abreast of any changes in the President's schedule." Covington paused and looked at Gardner. "How many people have timely access to information regarding changes in the President's schedule?"

Gardner shrugged. "Secret Service Presidential Protective Division, the President's staff advance people, the host committee in the city he's visiting . . . quite a few."

"Twenty million for the hit," Covington said. "There can't be more than two or three pros in the world who could command that kind of money, even from drug barons."

"Should narrow your search," Gardner said. "You want me to send a copy of this to Secret Service Intelligence Division?"

"I'll take care of it."

With that, Covington thanked Gardner for a job well done and left. Farther down the corridor, he stopped in the photo lab. The infrared film had been developed, but his luck had not held. Five frames contained images of the unidentified American. All were taken at bad angles and were partially out of focus. In one shot only the back of his head was visible, in another no more than a portion of the left side of his head in profile, from the ear back. The only identifying features revealed were that the man was approximately six feet tall and had sandy or dark blond hair worn long at the neck.

Deep in thought, Covington left the Office of Technical Services section, crossed the hallway and entered the elevator. As he pressed the button for the sixth floor, he decided to first do a computer run on known assassins. And for that he would need the help of a friend in Operations.

-8-

It was 7:45 A.M. on October third when Mike Maguire inched his government issue midnight blue Mercury Marquis through the maze of concrete crash barriers in front of the southwest gate to the White House complex. At the guard house, he exchanged pleasantries with one of the Secret Service Uniform Division officers on duty as another opened his trunk and looked inside the car. It was standard procedure that all vehicles entering or leaving the White House complex, regardless of the rank or political status of the driver, be checked for explosives—a precaution taken against terrorists concealing a powerful explosive charge, wired for remote detonation, beneath an unsuspecting subject's car. After this cursory check, an orange tag placed on the windshield tells the Uniform Division guards patrolling the inner perimeter that the check at the gate has been done. A short time after a vehicle is parked inside the complex, a UD officer teamed with a dog trained to detect explosives conducts a more thorough check, removing the orange tag upon completion.

With the initial inspection finished, Maguire threw a choppy salute to the guards and continued on through the gate. Partway down West Executive Avenue, he turned left and drove through the tunnel entrance into the south court of the Old Executive Office Building, where he parked in the space reserved for him as Special Agent in Charge of the Presidential Protective Division. He entered the administration section of his office on the ground floor of the OEB and poured himself a cup of coffee from the fresh pot brewed by his secretary, Molly Arnold, who for the two years Maguire had been SAIC/PPD, had always arrived at work before he did—at least an hour earlier than was required.

"Anything I need to know?" Maguire asked her.

"Nothing earthshaking," Molly answered. "The kid got lost in the halls last night, but they found him before he panicked."

Maguire chuckled at the remark. The "kid" Molly was referring to was the Vice President, whose office suite was one floor above them. She had given the young VP the nickname and it had stuck, and was now used by most of the Secret Service agents when out of earshot of the Vice President.

A small, perky woman—Maguire described her as being wired for 880—with bright, inquisitive eyes and a quick wit, Molly Arnold was a dedicated and hard-working government employee. She had seen seven SAIC/PPDs come and go, and Maguire was her favorite. She had once told him, at an office party where she had exceeded her self-imposed two-martini limit, that if she were twenty years younger she would climb on top of him and wouldn't get off until the Board of Health pulled her off.

"The purchase orders and memorandums on your desk require your signature," she said, and handed him a small stack of telephone messages.

Maguire flipped through the phone messages, and as he walked down the corridor to his office, shuffled them into the order in which he would return them. He paused in the office doorway and glanced at the large display board against the corridor wall that contained wallet-sized color photographs of all the agents assigned to the Presidential Protective Division. The photos were pinned to the board in groups, arranged according to their shift assignments, and he noted that two of the agents now on leave were due back today.

It was too early to return any of his messages, and signing off on the purchase orders and memorandums, he returned them to Molly. As he was about to leave for his morning rounds of the White House west wing, Susan Olsen, his liaison with Secret Service Intelligence Division, appeared in the doorway.

Maguire glanced at his watch. Her daily briefing was scheduled, as it always was, for ten o'clock. "You're early."

"Our CIA liaison just got some information I thought you ought to see immediately."

Her usual cheerful smile was missing. Maguire motioned with his head toward his office, and followed her down the corridor.

"Four of your all-time favorites on the druggie hit parade just surfaced," Susan said, and handed him the ID intelligence summary she had compiled that morning, and a copy of the teletype from CIA's Counter Narcotics Center containing the transcript of their "take" from St. Barts. "Unfortunately, CIA didn't have enough lead time to send someone in to grab the bastards." Susan's hatred of drug traffickers was on a personal level. Her older brother, a former DEA agent, had been severely wounded during a drug bust gone bad and was now confined to a wheelchair for the rest of his life.

"Calderon?" Maguire asked of the only name with which he wasn't familiar.

"We're not sure who he is, but if CIA is right about him being Bolivian, he might be the mystery man we've heard about."

Maguire sat at his desk and propped his feet up as he read; his body tensed as the purpose of the meeting on St. Barts became clear to him. His eyes moved over the transcript of the take, then abruptly stopped as one of the words leapt off the page at him. He looked up, stared briefly out the window at the E Street traffic, and continued reading.

"I don't agree with CIA about a high-level inside informant," Susan said. "Maybe someone who knows someone who talks too much. We've got a city full of jackasses with inflated egos who can't keep their mouths shut. The fact that the President was going to address the UN on the drug problem sometime in October has been known for a couple of months. Not the exact date, but they could have gotten a close guess from someone in the news media."

"Did you read this?" Maguire asked, referring to the printed copy of the CNC take.

"Yes."

Maguire pointed to the word "Waldorf." "The UN security people were advised of the date for the President's speech to the General Assembly before we announced it; that could account for that piece of information getting out, but the fact that the President will be staying at the Waldorf-Astoria and the fund-raiser will be held there hasn't been released to the host committee or anyone else. Hell, the decision wasn't even made until two days ago."

"The Republican National Committee didn't know the location for the dinner?"

"A few weeks ago they were told they could hold it in New York City, and they were given the date and three possible locations with available facilities, so they could start lining up all the big spenders —another possible source for the leak about the date of the UN speech," Maguire said. "But they won't receive confirmation of the Waldorf as the site until later this morning."

"Who was in on the decision-making process?" Susan asked.

"Us and the President's Staff Advance Office. That's it."

"Someone's talking out of school."

"Let's hope it isn't intentional," Maguire said.

"You think this one could be serious?"

"Twenty million dollars' worth of serious," Maguire said. "And if they follow through with it, we've got a major problem . . . DEA, FBI, CIA, and DIA files, and our own intelligence information on known narco/terrorists, are virtually worthless if they've brought in an outsider."

"Brian agrees with you," Susan said, referring to Assistant Director Brian Davidson, the head of Secret Service Protective Operations. "He said it would be a little premature to start pressing buttons, but he's instructed all liaison personnel to keep track of any developments through their opposites in the rest of the intelligence community."

"I want everything you get as soon as you get it," Maguire told

Susan. "Work your sources outside our liaison community; make sure nobody's holding back on us."

"I'm on good terms with the second in command at CIA's Counter Narcotics Center," Susan replied with a wink. "He asks me out every time I go over there for one of our joint intelligence seminars."

"Accept in the line of duty," Maguire said, and again scanned the CIA teletype looking for something that had caught his attention earlier. He found it on the last page. It was a brief annotation dated and time stamped early that morning and concerned a murder aboard a yacht moored in St. Barts. "How does the murdered woman tie in to the meeting at the villa?"

"I don't believe she does," Susan said. "I followed up on it with our CIA liaison before I came over. It came in with the latest intel report Langley got from their CNC surveillance team on St. Barts. Looks like an unrelated incident. The local cops are treating it as a crime of passion. They have a suspect."

Maguire nodded and removed a large file folder from his desk. He placed the ID intelligence summary and the transcript of the take inside, then as an afterthought, scribbled a note to himself that read: *Disposition by locals of Maria Padron murder?*, and put that in with them. The mention in the teletype that a silenced weapon had probably been used had piqued his curiosity.

•

One floor above Mike Maguire's office, on what is considered the first floor of the OEB, is the suite of rooms occupied by the President's Staff Advance Office. Coordination and cooperation between the President's staff advance teams and Maguire's Secret Service Presidential Protective Division advance teams are crucial to the President's security outside the White House. The Staff Advance Office determines the President's itinerary and the locations of the functions he will attend, choreographing down to the last detail all photo opportunities for the press and all public exposure during the trip. Nothing is overlooked: who will be at the bottom of *Air Force One*'s steps to greet the President upon arrival, who will ride in the limousine with him, who will accompany him in the elevator at the hotel. No one is ever in immediate proximity to the President of the United States unless it is planned that way, and that planning is the domain of the President's Staff Advance Office.

Though the Secret Service PPD advance teams work closely with the staff advance teams, their goals are completely opposite. Responsible for the President's security at every location he visits, and along all motorcade routes, the PPD advance teams want minimum public exposure for the President, and even then only under closely controlled conditions. Consequently they are, by the very nature of their objectives, at odds with the presidential staff and their desire for maximum public exposure for political purposes. The relationship between the two, though professionally correct on the surface, is more often than not cool and adversarial.

Maguire's relations with Tom Gibson, the newly appointed head of the Staff Advance Office, were strained at best. Unlike his predecessor, who when he erred, preferred to err on the side of security considerations for the President, Gibson was a self-important, social-climbing political hack, with little regard for the security precautions that dominated all of Maguire's waking hours, and some of his nightmares. To Gibson, anything that got in the way of a photo opportunity or a film clip for the evening news was intrusive and there only to be gotten around.

"You're still seeing bogeymen lurking in every doorway," he told Maguire, who had just finished briefing him on the meeting on St. Barts and the conclusions drawn from it—telling him nothing of the details of the take or how it was obtained, or by whom, only that he was working a threat case based on information about a possible assassination plot organized by drug barons.

"This isn't something to be dismissed lightly," Maguire said, doing his best to keep the edge from his voice. "I'd appreciate your looking into the source of the leak."

"Do you expect me to believe that one of my staff is actually passing on information to drug dealers?"

"I didn't say that," Maguire said evenly. "But it's possible one of your people is discussing sensitive information with someone who is passing it on. It's not as though it hasn't happened before."

"Did it ever occur to you that there may be a simple explanation for this?" He was using his most patronizing tone. "The last two times the President visited New York City, he stayed at the

Waldorf Towers. That's common knowledge, Mike. No big secret.''

"And the two times before that he stayed at the Plaza, and the
time before that, the Pierre," Maguire said. "I'd like you to put
someone on this and get back to me. At least make your people
aware that a problem exists and remind them of security considerations."

Gibson nodded an impatient accord. "I'll look into it. But
please don't start dictating ridiculous security measures for this
trip based on another nebulous assassination plot. We get one
every week, for Christ's sake. If you've got something concrete,
fine, but I'm not arranging the President's movements around
some baseless rumors."

"You'll be kept informed of all developments," Maguire said.

"By the way, the Chief of Staff wants to add another stop to the
President's Ohio swing next month . . . Cincinnati." He handed
Maguire the revised itinerary for the trip.

"I'll have Operations section arrange for another advance
team," Maguire said, and turned to leave.

"Lighten up, Mike," Gibson called after him. "If we took every
threat seriously, the President would spend his entire term huddled in a corner of the Situation Room with the lights out."

Maguire didn't respond as he headed back down the steps to
his office. Now wasn't the time to press the issue, but he had a gut-
level feeling that it would soon come. It had been ten years since
the afternoon of March 30th, 1981. An afternoon that had left him
feeling powerless and inadequate for the first time in his life. There
had been no warning. Just the six shots in rapid succession, and
then chaos. The President's press secretary lay on the ground,
gravely wounded; a Secret Service agent was down, shot in the
stomach; and a D.C. policeman was shot in the neck. Unknown to
Maguire at the time, a .22-caliber round had penetrated President
Reagan's chest cavity under his left arm, collapsing a lung. Maguire
literally threw him into the back of the limousine and dove on top
of him to shield him. He had been the shift leader for the working
shift that day; it had happened on his watch and the vivid memory
still haunted him. The ride to the hospital had been the longest
journey of his life, and when the doctors finally announced that the

President was out of danger, Maguire had vowed that he would do everything in his power to ensure that it would never happen again.

●

Steven Whitney Bradford III's initial reaction to Gibson's lecture to the staff on being more circumspect in their discussions of sensitive information was sheer panic, which he managed, with great difficulty, to keep from manifesting itself externally. By the time Gibson had finished, Bradford realized that it had been a reprimand for everyone, nonspecific and nonaccusatory, as his boss went on to more pressing business. Bradford's pulse rate, however, did not return to normal until the meeting was over and he had left the conference room. Taking refuge in a rest room stall, where he promptly threw up the undigested portion of his lunch, Bradford mentally assessed the personal damages and decided that at this point they were negligible. A few minutes of deep breathing and applying logic to the situation, and he began to feel in control again.

The Secret Service suspected the drug barons were plotting to assassinate the President. That was all. Nothing they hadn't suspected for the past year and a half. There was no need to panic. They were chalking the leak up to an inadvertent slip of the tongue to the wrong person by someone who should have known better. But how the hell had they learned even that much? Maybe Gibson hadn't told them everything he knew; maybe he was laying a trap for him. No, he dismissed the thought immediately. The man wasn't smart enough by half to plan anything that convoluted. He would arrange to have an afterwork drink with him in the next few days and find out just how much he did know. It wouldn't be hard. Gibson enjoyed listening to him talk about the exploits of his great-grandfather and grandfather, mentally taking notes of interesting stories he could repeat, hoping others would infer that he was intimately acquainted with the Bradford and Whitney families. He was easily manipulated if one understood, as Bradford did, that man's foremost instinct was not self-preservation, but preservation of the image he wanted to present to others. Know the way a man wants others to see him, and you can manipulate him at will. It was one of the few worthwhile things Bradford had learned from his father. And Gibson's weaknesses and feelings of inadequacy were more readily apparent than most. The ridiculous way he combed what little hair he had on the sides of his head over the bald dome on top. And his accent. Born, raised, and educated in Kansas (a state so boring, Bradford felt, that it produced no discernible accent), Gibson had affected a quasi-Ivy League/Eastern Establishment patois that fooled no one except other people from Kansas. It was time to cultivate Gibson on another level, one that might warn him of any further inquiries by the Secret Service.

Glancing at his watch as he left the rest room, Bradford noted that four hours remained before he could call his contact in Miami. He'd tell him what had happened. Maybe they'd call it off and let him off the hook. Sweet Jesus! How could he have let himself get in this deep?

–9–

Maxim's Hotel and Casino in Las Vegas, Nevada, bustled with the sounds of fools and dreamers clinging to the peculiar American myth that you can be a rest-room attendant at noon and a millionaire by dusk. They would all, however, soon reach a more sensible accommodation with reality. The truth of the dream is sad, and graphically attested to in pawnshops just off the famed, gaudy neon Strip where false teeth, prosthetic devices, even a glass eye can be seen among window displays crammed with guitars, jewelry, once-treasured birthday and anniversary gifts, and every imaginable personal item of any value—the pathetic, hard-earned possessions of people who had lost it all and needed just another hundred or two to guts it out at the tables and get back on top.

The get-rich-quick fever of Vegas is as pervasive and deadly as the desert heat. Gambling-crazed parents leave children in locked cars in asphalt parking lots where temperatures often reach one hundred ten degrees, and forget about them. Sometimes the children die. The suicide rate is three times the national average. It is a city of more than four thousand gaming tables and over sixty thousand slot machines, with no clocks or windows in casinos, which exist in a timeless, air-conditioned present where the house always wins, beating the players out of some five billion dollars each year. But still they keep coming; the Las Vegas airport handles more than one million incoming passengers a month.

The notion of gambling away money was anathema to Zack Shafer. He had amassed a fortune in excess of one hundred million dollars in the business world, through exhaustive preparation and hard, relentless work, never once trusting to luck. What was going on all around him was something so far beyond his comprehension that he averted his eyes as he crossed the casino floor and weaved his way past intense, desperate people on emotional roller coasters, hunched over green felt gaming tables and rows of video-poker games and churning slot machines.

Shafer took the staircase to the mezzanine level of Maxim's Hotel, overlooking the casino, and stopped at the sign-in desk at the entrance to one of the hospitality suites with an adjoining banquet room. A large, colorful poster on an easel just outside the doorway displayed the gruesome image of a human skull adorned with a green beret, and the announcement that the annual reunion of the Special Operations Association was being held inside. The Association was a fraternal organization for those who had served in combat in Southeast Asia with the Special Operations Group (euphemistically named Studies and Observation Group to keep the press from learning its true mission). The majority of its members were former Army Special Forces, Green Berets, but the Navy SEAL and Marine Corps Force Reconnaissance units that had played a vital role in SOG operations were also represented, as were the helicopter pilots who had flown them in and pulled them out, and fighter jocks who flew support missions for their operations.

At first glance, the gathering could easily be mistaken for something as normal as a Rotary Club meeting, but not for long. These men had seen too much ever to be quite normal again. Approximately twenty-four hundred people out of the millions who served in Vietnam qualified for membership in the association. And 75 percent of them were dead—killed in action. Of those present, many were now retired military, all had served multiple combat tours, and most were highly decorated. They wore conservative sport coats and suits, and their civilian occupations varied; there were entrepreneurs who took the same all-or-nothing risks in the business world that they had taken in the jungles of Southeast Asia, there were some still connected with the darker side of government service as CIA contract employees and case officers, and assorted consultants and specialists operating throughout the intelligence community. None of them had ever lingered around war memorials waiting for the cameras to turn on so they could hug each other and cry because they didn't get a parade when they came home. They had never been on drugs, never murdered or raped civilians, never hated the army or LBJ or their country. And they didn't feel that America owed them a free ride because they had defended her.

These were men with a special place in history; men who had participated in a little-known side of the war—a side still fully known only to those who fought it. They had been part of America's shadowy top-secret war in Vietnam, running missions into denied areas: Laos, Cambodia, North Vietnam, and China. Theirs had been an unconventional war of interdicting troops and supplies along the Ho Chi Minh Trail, conducting prisoner-snatch operations to capture high-ranking North Vietnamese army officers for interrogation, assassination missions aimed at NVA and VC political cadre, and a wide assortment of CIA controlled "black" operations for which no records were ever kept, or those that were were destroyed soon after the mission. They ran some of the hairiest operations of the war, bordering on suicidal; the killed-in-action rate of their units at times exceeded eighty percent.

These men had been gamblers, too, but unlike those bathed in the soft timeless light of the casino, who were wagering their paychecks on games of chance against house odds, they had wagered their lives in a lethal game of skill and courage against a cunning and resourceful enemy. And not in the hope of material gain. It was the first day of their three-day reunion, and they were still arriving from every corner of the world. They drifted in, alone in most cases, without fanfare, quietly, as they so often did throughout the jungles of Southeast Asia. They were initially greeted with tentative nods, in vague acknowledgment from those already there, then with hearty handshakes and heartfelt embraces at the moment of recognition by old comrades, some not seen in many years, or last seen in Vietnam under far less comfortable and secure conditions than a luxury resort hotel. There were the inevitable war stories, elaborated and embellished, but not to enhance the status or courage of the teller—these men had been weighed on the scales and not found wanting, they had nothing to prove— but rather to add humor to frightening experiences that were funny only in retrospect, not when the sheer terror of the missions was still fresh in their minds.

Choruses of laughter rang out and drinks were refilled as the men settled in once again to enjoy the camaraderie found among those who shared common experiences and backgrounds—the strength of their bond could be found in the association's motto: *You have never lived until you have almost died.* Occasionally there was something different about the laughter brought on by the stories being told. A subtle nuance, a distant look or a change in timbre of the voice, a momentary pause—as a story brought unwelcome memories of another mission, one that had not ended well; one that reminded those present of friends that had been killed, or of entire recon teams that had vanished without a trace. The pain and the sorrow went unspoken, but they were there, just behind the eyes, rising from the dark chambers of the subconscious, where things best not thought about too often are stored. The stories continued, but for a brief moment each man had felt the presence of friends he had lost and would never see again.

Zack Shafer stood in the doorway and looked inside at the group of sixty or seventy men, most in their mid-forties, who sat in small clusters at tables scattered about the room—a few held up the bar at the opposite end, flirting with the two attractive hostesses mixing drinks.

"Can I help you?" the man at the sign-in desk asked.

"I'm looking for Jack Gannon," Shafer said.

"He's inside," the man answered. "Just got here an hour ago." He studied Shafer's face for a long moment, then asked, "You a member?"

"No. Just a friend."

"Go on in. Any friend of Jack's is welcome."

Shafer entered, his eyes moving slowly over the room until he spotted Gannon seated with three other men in a far corner. As he moved closer, he noticed the unusual pin on Gannon's sport coat —a small blue rosette with white stars on it—then realized what it was: the lapel pin worn by those who had been awarded the Medal of Honor. He had spent only a few hours around the man two years ago, but he was someone you remembered once you met him. His size wasn't imposing—slender, just a shade under six feet tall with a tapered, athletic build that suggested upper-body strength—but he had presence, and an aura of raw power and ability emanated from him that was out of all proportion to his size.

Gannon saw Shafer approaching, recognized him after a moment, and stood to greet him—a quizzical look on his face as he remembered that this was not a man to pay a casual social call in an out of the way place, especially when he had had to go to some trouble to find him. "Zack, good to see you. It's been a while."

"Two years," Shafer said. "Is there somewhere we can talk privately?"

"Sure." Gannon saw something in the man's eyes that precluded any further small talk. He excused himself from his friends; men accustomed not to ask questions of people who declined to introduce themselves.

Gannon motioned to the adjoining banquet area. One of the doors was open, revealing a huge room crowded with dining tables already set up for the evening's scheduled activities. Shafer followed him inside, closing the door behind them. As they sat across from each other at a table near the dais, Shafer opened his briefcase and removed a manila envelope and a partly charred diary.

"Maria's dead," Shafer said. The words were delivered bluntly, without emotion, but his eyes misted over and he looked away after he said them.

Gannon said nothing at first. Maria's beautiful face flashed before him. "What happened?"

"Someone killed her."

"When . . . why?" Gannon's mind was flooded with vignettes of Maria and Jim Boos and the brief time they had spent together on the *Cheetah* two years ago, when they had helped him track down his wife's killer.

"Sometime between midnight and three this morning," Shafer said. "The local cops are calling it a crime of passion. They think it was a *Cheetah* crew member I fired last week . . . Jeff Newcastle. I know it damn well wasn't. Newcastle went back to England two days after he left the boat. He's been there ever since. I checked."

"What are they doing about it?" Gannon asked.

"Nothing that's going to lead them anywhere except where they've already decided to go. I spent most of the day in Gustavia at the gendarmerie trying to make some sense of it, but all they want to do is sweep it under the rug. If they resolve it as a crime of passion, committed by one foreigner against another, they eliminate any black mark against the locals and the tourist business isn't affected. They don't care who did it as long as they can exonerate their own people. Typically French," he added with disdain.

"How was she killed?"

"Two shots in the back of the head with a .380-caliber weapon . . . execution style," Shafer said. "They found her on deck, curled up on the bench seat in the entertainment cockpit with a blanket over her as though she had been sleeping. And there were people on board the boats moored alongside the *Cheetah*. No one heard anything."

"A silencer."

Shafer nodded. "Not the usual scenario for a crime of passion, I would think. And whoever it was also set fire to the boat. Fortunately, someone put it out before it spread."

Gannon's mind moved ahead of the conversation, his eyes coming to rest on the charred diary lying on top of the manila envelope on the table. He pushed the diary to one side to see the partially hidden writing on the outside of the envelope, and read: *Ask Gannon About Him.*

"What's this?" Gannon said, picking up the envelope.

"I was hoping you could tell me. I found it on board the *Cheetah,* along with the diary Maria used to keep track of the photographs she took."

Gannon opened the envelope and removed the eight-by-ten photograph inside. "That's Boos," he said, immediately, and pointed to him. "And Scotty Lyon; he's here at the reunion. Looks like a joint SEAL–Special Forces team, judging from the mix of weapons and jungle fatigues. Probably a black operation laid on by the Agency; it was usually their deal when we ran combined forces ops."

He continued studying the photograph, letting his memory drift back twenty years. "I knew two of the other guys," he told Shafer. "They're dead. Killed in action." One of the men he had recognized in the photograph and knew to be dead, one of the few people he had ever truly hated, had brought back a memory that he quickly forced from his mind.

Shafer handed the diary to him. "Read the entry Maria made on the second of October, the afternoon before she was killed."

Gannon paged halfway through the book and began to read.

October 2nd—St. Barts

Bright sunny day. Subjects at Le Select Café. First man leaning chair against wall—looks like he's in a nod. Interesting play of shadows. Second man at corner table under tree—spooky. Carrying concealed weapon under shirt in small of back. Probably a Walther .380. See if it shows up in any of the shots. Also check for white phosphorus burn on back of right hand. Strange conversation. He lied about knowing Jim. Wasn't pleased about being recognized.

There was more information, listing the aperture settings and shutter speeds used, but nothing pertinent to their conversation. Gannon handed the diary back.

"Where's the film?"

"Missing," Shafer said. "I found the camera on the bar counter in the main salon with the back open. Maria would never leave it that way. She was meticulous about her equipment."

"What about places on the island that develop film?"

"There are only two. I checked them both," Shafer said. "She hadn't dropped anything off since she made port."

"Was anything stolen from the boat?"

"Nothing. It wasn't a robbery," Shafer said emphatically. "One of my security people was with me when I examined the *Cheetah*. He said that whoever tried to burn it used a very sophisticated incendiary device. Not something readily available on the open market. None of what happened suggests a crime of passion, a robbery, or any other simple explanation."

Gannon was silent for a long moment, another rush of poignant memories came as the fact of Maria's death began to sink in. "Maria was special," he finally said. "I really liked her."

"She was my friend as well as my employee," Shafer said, his voice revealing another rise of emotions. "And I want whoever did this caught and punished."

"What can I do to help?"

"I've given it a lot of thought, and I think the man mentioned in her diary is in that photograph," Shafer said. "And my instincts tell me it's the same man who killed her."

"On the surface, I'd have to agree with you," Gannon told him. "We're in the right place to start asking questions. There are quite a few former Special Forces personnel and SEALs out there." He gestured toward the hospitality suite. "They'll probably be able to identify the others in the photo."

They returned to the hospitality suite, where a dozen or so new arrivals were milling about the room. Over the next hour Gannon showed the photograph to every man attending the reunion. Scott Lyon, one of the men in the picture, was a highly decorated former Navy commander and a SEAL who had served with Boos. He could account for the other four SEALs—all dead, never having made it home from Vietnam—but he knew only two of the six Green Berets who had been on the mission. He went on to explain that it was a night operation, and the SEALs had deployed the Special Forces segment of the team from a submarine off the coast of North Vietnam. Using inflatable rubber boats equipped with silent-running motors, they had inserted them south of Haiphong on a beach, which they then secured while the Green Berets went inland and carried out their phase of the operation. Four hours later, with the NVA close on their heels, they returned to the beach with their kidnapped prisoner—a North Vietnamese general. After a brief firefight with the pursuing NVA, the SEALs had transported the Special Forces troops and the general back to the rendezvous with the submarine.

"The only contact I had with them was at the premission briefing and then at the brief-back before insertion. I doubt that I said more than a few words to any of them," Lyon told Gannon. "It was a green beanie mission, our primary function was as a security element. I don't think I ever knew their names. Except for the two who ran a couple of other operations with us, I never saw any of them again."

"When was the picture taken?" Gannon asked.

"Late March . . . early April of seventy-one," Lyon said.

Walt Shumate, a retired sergeant major with twenty-five years in Special Forces and seven combat tours in Vietnam, and now connected to the CIA in some unspoken way, identified one of the Green Berets on the team that Gannon had not known; again, the man had been killed in action late in the war.

After having shown the picture to everyone present, Gannon made a notation on the back of the photo of the three unidentified men. All Green Berets.

"We have positive IDs on all but three of the people in the photograph," he told Shafer, "and confirmation that those identified died over fifteen years ago, with the exception of Jim Boos, and that man over there," he pointed to Scott Lyon. "And I can personally guarantee you he's not the man we're looking for. But at least we've narrowed it down."

"Are you still with Delta Force?" Shafer asked, noticing the pager clipped to Gannon's belt—a device Delta Force personnel often referred to as the electronic leash for the dogs of war.

Gannon didn't respond, but it was a nonresponse that Shafer understood. No one with Delta Force ever revealed their affiliation with the top-secret counterterrorist unit, but Shafer already knew and Gannon saw no point in using his cover story. He had been with Delta from its inception in 1977, and after retiring from active duty as a lieutenant colonel at the age of forty, three years ago, he had gone back to work for them as a civilian operations and intelligence specialist.

"Are there any military records you can check that would help identify the others?"

"We have a few former SOG types back at 'the Ranch,' " Gannon said, using the Delta Force euphemism for their highly classified headquarters and training compound at Fort Bragg, North Carolina. "I'll run the photo by them, and take it from there."

"I appreciate your help," Shafer said.

"Maria was my friend, too, and I owe you." Gannon was not one to forget that without Shafer's cooperation, the man who had murdered his wife might have gotten away.

"When are you returning to Fort Bragg?"

"I had planned on spending the next two days here at the reunion, but I'm not much in the mood for that now. I'll try to get a flight out tonight. I'll be in touch as soon as I have anything, and you keep me apprised of anything on your end."

"That goes without saying," Shafer said. "I have my plane at the airport, and I'm headed back east. It's no problem to drop you off in North Carolina."

Gannon accepted the offer and excused himself while he made the rounds in the hospitality suite and said his premature good-byes. No one asked why.

As he and Shafer left the casino and climbed into the waiting limousine, Gannon asked, "How did you know where to find me?" He had told only the Delta Force operations officer about attending the reunion, in the event of an emergency.

"I have friends in high places," Shafer said with a smile.

Gannon recalled his impression of Shafer when they had first met: not a man he would want to face across a bargaining table. And he remembered something Shafer had said two years ago that gave insight into his character, and his eastern Tennessee roots: "Life's just like business; you've got to take a firm position. There's nothing in the middle of the road except yellow stripes and dead opossums."

•

Forty thousand feet above the desert floor, heading east into a darkening sky at 450 knots, Gannon settled back in the plush leather seat aboard the Gulfstream G-IV business jet. Shafer had managed to close his eyes for only four hours in the last two days, and was sound asleep in a recliner designed for that purpose at the opposite end of the spacious cabin. For Gannon, closing his eyes did nothing to stop the onslaught of images flashing across his mind's eye. He was again reminded of what he had come to accept years ago: the war would always be with him, affecting the path of his life in one form or another, constantly changing him. He had stopped trying to cut himself loose from it. There were times when he felt that the war had been the only reality, and the rest of his life had been a dream. Nothing ever ends, he thought. Every damn thing you've ever done or was done to you is still around in some form or another, working away.

Was he the same young staff sergeant who had served five combat tours in Vietnam with the Special Operations Group? No. He wouldn't even recognize that person today. Was he the same man after Kate was killed on the whim of a psychopath, taking away the one loving constant in his life and leaving him without a family, and at times, he felt, without an anchor? No, he was not the same and never would be. He saw Jim Boos's face before him, as he lay dying from a bullet that had been meant for him. And now Maria Padron. Someone on the periphery of his life, but nonetheless connected to it. Someone who had unselfishly helped him and asked nothing in return. And now she had died a brutal death. There seemed to be no escaping the vortex of violence that sought him out and caught hold of him at will—the price he paid, he reasoned, for the kind of life he had chosen to lead. *Ask Gannon about him!* And it had found him again.

The trick, he ventured, would be to live in the eternal moment, no beginning, no end, just the immediate present. He laughed to himself at that errant thought; philosophy was not his strong suit. Something Kate had once read to him came to mind; she had said it was probably the origin of the SOG motto: Heidegger had written that for authentic living what was necessary was the resolute confrontation of death. Well, if that was true, he had certainly lived authentically.

He reached into the carry-on bag at his feet and removed the photograph from its envelope. He stared at it, concentrating on the faces of the three men yet to be identified. Had one of them killed Maria? And if so, what forces were at work that had laid it at his doorstep? It was a rhetorical question. He knew it was, again, the war.

●

Twenty-three hundred miles away, in a telephone booth outside a 7-Eleven store in Arlington, Virginia, Steven Whitney Bradford III listened to the voice on the other end of the line in Miami. Nothing was over until he said it was over, the voice screamed. Did he understand? He was to continue to provide any and all information just as they had discussed. Bradford held the receiver to his ear long after the line went dead, still not fully recovered from the shock of the meeting at work and now shaken by the other's refusal to call things off in light of his recent revelations.

Maybe the man in Miami was right. So they have reason to believe there was an assassination plot in the works. So what? There was nothing to tie him to it, or to the information leaked from the office. To cut and run now would be premature, casting suspicion on him where there might never have been any. And these were dangerous and vindictive men; if he did not carry out his end of the deal, they would probably hunt him down and kill him. Finding some consolation in the logic of his own argument, Bradford went into the 7-Eleven and bought a quart of chocolate milk and a box of powdered doughnuts, which he drank and ate in the car as he drove—brushing crumbs from his lap all the way to Reston.

●

The two men in the back of the DEA surveillance van tailing Jorge Madrigal's BMW as he pulled out of the Dadeland shopping center exchanged questioning glances.

"What the hell was that all about?"

"Sounds like a hit. Some druggie's got a contract out on his competition. Same old shit."

"Must be somebody pretty high up."

"We'll know when we find his body in the trunk of a car."

The van broke off surveillance ten minutes later as Madrigal pulled into his driveway. The agents in the static observation post one block away would take over for the next eight hours. The men in the van returned to DEA's Miami office to turn in the recorded telephone conversation, which would be transcribed the following morning, then filed and forgotten.

It has been said, by people in a position to know, that all the information that will ever be needed by America's intelligence-gathering agencies comes into their possession on a daily basis. Collected by competing, autocratic, turf-conscious bureaucracies, who do not share with rival agencies, it is buried somewhere among the tons of raw data that are intercepted, partially processed, and filed away each day, rather than being disseminated to the agency that might recognize its value and put it to use. Clues to the identity of every mole and deep-cover agent, revelations of coups and assassinations in the planning stages, new weapons under development, troop deployments, and governments on the verge of toppling—it is all there. They just don't know that they have it.

—10—

Shortly after leaving the Office of Technical Services audio and photographic laboratories that morning, Tony Covington, head of CIA's Counter Narcotics Center, received a report from his surveillance team on St. Barts: the five men at the villa were preparing to leave the island in their private planes—filing false flight plans that would enable them to disappear without a trace, or so they believed. With the drug barons' departures imminent, Covington put through an emergency request to the Defense Intelligence Agency, and a Navy E-2C Hawkeye surveillance plane on station off the coast of Cuba was "loaned" to the CIA.

The Hawkeye, equipped with the sophisticated APG-63 radar, was capable of detecting both airborne and surface moving targets as well as providing vectoring information to other surveillance or intercept craft. Its systems locked on to the five separate planes within minutes after they left the runway at St. Barts airport. Upon reaching the limit of its operating range, the Hawkeye was replaced with another of its type out of Panama—vectored from a routine surveillance mission along Nicaragua's Caribbean coast. In concert with a network of American military radar tracking facilities throughout the Caribbean basin and Central America, it continued plotting and tracking the courses of all five planes as they headed for the South American continent and their final destination in Bolivia.

•

It was 8:00 P.M. when Covington got his first break in the search for the mystery man who the previous night had accepted the contract to assassinate the President of the United States. Immediately after learning of the drug barons' departures, he had assigned six of his brightest and most dogged CNC research analysts at headquarters to do what they did best, and they had demonstrated their worth sooner than anyone had a right to expect.

Tapping into airline reservation computers, they obtained the manifests for every commercial flight that had arrived on the island of St. Barts, and the neighboring island of St. Martin—which served that part of the Caribbean as the main hub for connecting flights to the smaller islands. They went back three days prior to the drug barons' meeting, and also included the manifests for the morning and afternoon commercial flights departing that day.

At Covington's request, CIA's resident agent on St. Martin instructed his support agents to check with car rental agencies and the managers of the hotels, motels, and inns on the island, compiling a list of guests who had checked in within the past three days. The CNC surveillance team that had been watching the drug barons did the same on St. Barts.

It was the off-season in the Caribbean, so their tasks were far less time consuming than if it had been mid-winter, and by three o'clock that day the majority of the information was faxed to Langley headquarters, where the computer whiz kids, as Covington called them, went to work on it, availing themselves of every authorized computer data bank—and more than a few for which they had no authorization, including those of four foreign governments. A total of eleven hundred and sixty-seven names had to be processed. The information from credit cards and driver's licenses and passports, used at hotels and car rental agencies as a means of identification, were checked against the federal and municipal records in the country to which the person claimed citizenship. Five hours later, the CNC analysts believed they had found their man, or at least the man he was pretending to be.

A Roger Edward Carlson, using as identification a Canadian passport and a driver's license that gave an address in Montreal, had rented a car on St. Barts on the morning of October second. The list of hotel guests from St. Barts further revealed that Carlson had checked into a small beachfront resort on St. Jean Bay the evening of October first and left early in the morning on October third. A cross-check of the airline manifests showed that he had arrived in St. Martin on the Eastern Metro Express from San Juan, Puerto Rico, the evening of October first and departed October third shortly before noon from St. Martin on a flight back to San Juan. He was ticketed for a connecting flight that same day on Iberia airlines from San Juan to Bogotá, Colombia, continuing on to Cartagena and arriving at seven-fifteen that evening.

It was the Cartagena destination that set off the alarms and focused the analysts on Carlson. Covington recalled the Colombian coastal city was mentioned as a contact point in the take from the conversation between the Bolivian and the assassin. A call to CIA's liaison at the Royal Canadian Mounted Police Security Service—Canada's CIA—revealed that no passport had been issued to a Roger E. Carlson of Montreal. A further check of city records verified that the address on Carlson's driver's license was a proper address located in the Main, Montreal's immigrant district. One hour later, RCMP Security Service reported that no Roger Carlson lived at that address—the three apartments above the Korean grocery were occupied by Palestinian émigrés, and had been for the past seven years.

As Covington suspected he would be, the man they were looking for was using an alias backstopped with expertly forged documents. But an alias was a beginning, a thread to start the unraveling by making discreet inquiries to friendly foreign intelligence services for information on known aliases of suspected professional assassins. The description of Carlson that one of Covington's men on St. Barts had gotten from the young woman at the car rental agency was vague: tall, perhaps six feet, maybe forty years old, dark blond or brown hair—she was wearing her sun-glasses and couldn't be sure—and handsome, she thought, in an exotic way.

Covington glanced at the clock on the wall. The assassin had landed in Cartagena approximately one hour ago. He had missed the chance to arrange for a surveillance team at the airport, but a call to CIA's station chief at the U.S. embassy in Bogotá might avail him of whatever assets and agents they had operating in Carta-gena.

•

The Colombian resort city of Cartagena de Indias—its proper name—is a shadowy, lived-in museum of baroque facades, derelict forts, and ancient ramparts, where crooked, cobbled streets, so narrow that balconies almost touch, echo with the sounds of history. Like all aging beauties, Cartagena best recaptures her allure and mystique in the dim light of streetlamps and candles during the "hours of mysterious flourishings," as a poet has called them—the hours just after the sun has slipped abruptly into the Caribbean Sea, and strong steady breezes that once filled the sails of Spanish galleons whip up whitecaps and blow across the city, delivering it from the oppressive heat of the day.

It is in the cool of the evening, in the soft glow of lamplight in the Old City, that lovers look for quiet corners, and artists and intellectuals gather over tall iced drinks at favored sidewalk cafés. On the waterfront, barges and coastal sailboats moored for the night and laden with cargoes of bananas and hardwoods rise and fall in the gentle swells as sailors come ashore and prowl the bars on Halfmoon Street, bargaining with tawny, acid-tongued ladies of the evening. Shoeshine boys near the old clock gate fold up their kits as elderly people stroll the ancient streets and rest on benches in quiet parks and squares, where disparate crowds watch im-promptu dancers step to Afro-Colombian folk tunes and spicy salsas while nearby vendors sell shaved ice with syrup, and sea-shell jewelry.

Once a strategic stronghold and center of trade in Spain's New World empire, the wealth of a continent—gold, platinum, timber, and coffee—flowed into the fortress city for shipment to Spain.

Still a major port and commerce center, another more sinister and lucrative trade now flourishes. The city has become a major transshipment and distribution center for the tons of cocaine processed in jungle laboratories and destined for Mexico and the smugglers who will take it across the border into the United States in ever more insidiously inventive ways.

The handsome man who sat sipping a drink at the sidewalk café on a corner of the Plaza de Bolívar profited greatly from the illicit drug trade. He was José Fedor Ospina, second in command of the infamous *Movimiento 19 de Abril,* a leftist insurgent movement and terrorist organization known as M-19 that has plagued the Colombian government for the past fifteen years with bombings, extortion, and kidnappings, the latter two being their primary source of financing their activities before trading in their principles for a piece of the drug trade. International in character and scope, M-19's support comes from leftist student and intellectual groups attracted by its radical revolutionary chic, accounting for its tentacles reaching to other Central and South American countries as well as European capitals and to the United States, where they publish an English-language newspaper in New York City.

Ospina had been with the group since its inception and had survived their nearly being wiped out in 1980 by the military and police. After training in Libya and Cuba, he had come home to put his newfound skills to use by organizing and participating in the carefully staged media events of seizing foreign embassies in Bogotá, and the 1985 bloody seizure and burning of the Palace of Justice. The recent signing of a peace pact with the government, giving some M-19 leaders amnesty for past crimes, had weakened the organization, but Ospina had cast his lot with the faction that had broken away from the main body to join in the lucrative drug trade.

A phone call Ospina had received that morning from Raphael Calderon was the reason for his presence at the café. It was through Calderon that Ospina had carved out a piece of the cocaine business for his organization. It was a natural alliance. With logistic trails for his guerrilla movement already established across Colombia's frontiers with Panama, Peru, Ecuador, Venezuela, and Brazil, M-19 was in a position to disrupt, and in effect, control the movement of drugs from the far-flung coca fields and processing labs into Colombia's metropolitan distribution centers. Ospina had promised secure routes to the traffickers, guaranteeing their safety and the uninterrupted flow of cocaine; and to provide the cartels with additional well trained and heavily armed muscle against their competition and the government. In return Ospina demanded, and got, a piece of the action, including control of the highly profitable distribution end of the cocaine business in the Brooklyn and Queens sections of New York City.

The request from Calderon earlier that day had been an inconvenience, necessitating a hurried trip from Barranquilla, a modern industrial city on the Caribbean coast one hundred fifty miles north of Cartagena. In no position to refuse the wealthy and powerful Bolivian, he had reluctantly complied and agreed to give his full cooperation to the man named Carlson. He had asked for no explanation of the purpose of the meeting, and Calderon had offered none. Ospina had gone directly to the apartment of an M-19 colleague in Cartagena and waited for the phone call Calderon had told him to expect, instructing the man who called to meet him at the sidewalk café.

From his vantage point in the park across the street, Sincavage watched the man with the faded red bandanna around his neck, worn as Ospina had told him it would be, as a means of identification. Sincavage didn't trust or respect revolutionary zealots, considering them unstable and loyal only to their own paranoid delusions. He had spent the last thirty minutes observing Ospina and studying the rhythm of the crowd, the casual ebb and flow of his surroundings, looking for anything out of sync.

Not far from where he stood, in the deep shadows beneath a tree, a group of students gathered on a corner of the plaza. One had a guitar, played none too expertly, and their songs dissolved into gales of laughter. An old couple, reverential and bent with age, shuffled toward the Church of San Pedro Claver while other couples, young and impious, strolled along city walls lit with amber floodlights, looking for darkened niches to stop and embrace.

A couple sitting on a bench near the edge of the park, ostensibly lovers enjoying the evening air and the antics of the student balladeers, had drawn Sincavage's attention. As he scrutinized them with a cold professional eye, he saw no whispered conversation where lips brushed in the telling, no holding of hands or any of the countless intimate displays of affection that lovers do without thinking. Instead, their attention shifted metronomically from the students to the café table where Ospina sat impatiently nursing his drink.

The man's name was Ricardo Villegas, a CIA support agent. His companion was Ileana Posada, recruited as a local asset two years ago. They knew nothing of Sincavage, and would not until the following morning when Villegas made his scheduled contact with the CIA case officer in Bogotá who controlled him. Ospina was the target of his surveillance effort, and had been for the past three days after spotting him in Barranquilla. Earlier that day, he had been caught off guard when Ospina made a hurried trip to the airport and boarded a flight to Cartagena. Not wanting to chance his exposure, Villegas booked a later flight and telephoned ahead, instructing Ileana to pick up the surveillance upon Ospina's arrival.

Sincavage allowed himself a small, humorless smile at his discovery of the surveillance team, and stepping out of the shadows onto the pathway, passed directly in front of the hapless couple as he crossed the square to the café.

With instincts that had kept him alive and out of government prisons for years, Ospina recognized Sincavage for what he was the moment he entered his field of vision. He had never seen the man before, he was certain of that, but he had known men like him. The predator's look about him set Ospina on edge.

Without a word of introduction, Sincavage took the chair across from him at the rickety café table. He got the waiter's attention and pointed to Ospina's drink, indicating that he would have the same.

"A mutual acquaintance said you would be able to help me," he said to Ospina.

"Perhaps. What is it you need?"

"Six of your people; two of them women."

"And the purpose they would serve?"

"That's none of your business," Sincavage said without rancor. "They must be fluent in English, must have spent some time in the

United States and be qualified with assault rifles and light antitank weapons."

"How soon do you need them?"

The two men fell silent when the waiter arrived. Sincavage managed an unobtrusive glance in the direction of the park as he took a long, slow drink. The lovers' eyes were hard on him.

"Two days from now. I want them transported here"—he removed a slip of paper from his shirt pocket and handed it to Ospina—"ready for a week of intensive training."

"I will do what I can," Ospina said. "The best people may not be available on such short notice."

"Get them, wherever they are," Sincavage said. "I won't tolerate incompetents. They get people killed. And I'll need a plane, twin-engine, that can operate out of unimproved strips. Can you manage that?"

Ospina nodded. "There is one available; it is a Mitsubishi . . . MU-2, I believe. A smuggler's plane equipped with special radar," he added. "It is at a small private airstrip approximately twenty kilometers outside the city. I will take you there. Is there anything else?"

"No. Just don't play games with me. If you send me unqualified people, you'll never see them again, but you will see me."

The renowned Latin machismo surfaced. Unaccustomed to being insulted and bullied, Ospina's face flushed at the thinly veiled threat. A muscle along his jaw line twitched as his body stiffened, then relaxed just as quickly as he stared into Sincavage's quiet eyes and again saw the feral atavism that his instincts had caught the moment he saw him crossing the square. This was a man ruled by discipline, not emotion, allowing him to kill without conscience or remorse. Not a man to be foolishly challenged over pride.

Sincavage had remained silent, his face a stone mask, for the long unspoken moment of Ospina's decision to live and fight another day. He rose from the table, again stealing a glimpse of the couple in the park.

"You said you could take me to the airstrip?"

Ospina nodded. "Come with me. My car is nearby." Reaching into his pocket, he handed Sincavage a neatly folded and creased piece of paper. "I was instructed to give you this. It is a second telephone number for your contact in New York City."

Villegas and Ileana waited in place until the two men disappeared down an alleyway. At the sound of a car engine starting, they rushed to the opposite side of the square, where they had parked.

Sincavage sat at an angle in the front passenger seat of Ospina's rented car, his back against the door, watching the street behind them. The flash of headlights that appeared from around a corner exiting the square brought another humorless smile.

"Something is funny?" Ospina asked.

Sincavage decided the game had gone on long enough to serve his purpose. "You've got a tail," he told the terrorist.

"How would you like to handle it?" Ospina said after a quick confirming glance in the rearview mirror.

"You mean do we lead them into an ambush and kill them?" Sincavage said. "No. Want me to drive?"

A cheshire cat grin spread slowly across Ospina's face. "That won't be necessary. I would, however, advise that you fasten your seat belt."

Sincavage did, just in time, as the tiny Fiat rattled and screeched at being thrown into a near-impossible series of turns down slick, cobbled streets barely wide enough to accommodate it. By the time they reached the outskirts of the city, the surveillance vehicle was no longer in sight and Sincavage released his death grip on the dash and the armrest.

—11—

The home of the top-secret Delta Force, the U.S. Army's elite counterterrorist unit, is a heavily secured 550-acre compound in an isolated corner of the sprawling U.S. Army base at Fort Bragg, North Carolina. The huge, low-slung modern building that dominates the facility houses the headquarters detachment, operations center, and squadron bays, while scattered around the compound are various training sites, including demolition areas, rifle and pistol ranges, and a shooting house complete with a full-size mockup of the interior of an aircraft and numerous rooms with movable walls for changing assault scenarios. It is the state-of-the-art in training facilities for highly specialized units.

The men of the Delta Force number just over two hundred, with one hundred fifty of them being "shooters"—members of the three operational squadrons. They are some of the deadliest soldiers in the world; an eclectic group, chosen not only for superior intelligence, physical dexterity, and stamina but for patience, the ability to remain cool under pressure, and the diverse special

qualifications required to fill the esoteric needs of a counterterrorist unit. Some, as "service brats," spent the formative years of
their lives in foreign lands, and possess language skills and in-
depth knowledge of people and locales in trouble spots around the
world. Others have attracted the attention of Delta recruiters by
excelling at their previous military assignments. All are capable of
working in small teams or independently, operating on their own
in unfriendly locations for extended periods of time under adverse
conditions without feeling the debilitating psychological effects of
loss or dependency.

They are as much clandestine operatives as they are soldiers,
with the ability to infiltrate a foreign civilian population and blend
in to conduct intelligence-gathering missions prior to a Delta
Force assault. All are cross-trained in operational skills that range
from small-unit assault tactics, explosive-entry techniques, HALO
and HAHO (High Altitude, Low Opening and High Altitude, High
Opening) parachuting of pinpoint accuracy, to scuba insertions,
hand-to-hand combat, sniper training, aircraft refueling, heavy
equipment operation, and high-speed driving. Theirs is a life of
constant, rigorous training in preparation for missions that can
occur at any time: a hijacking in Rome or the sighting of a long-
sought-after terrorist leader could send them into action with only
minutes to prepare a response. They are finely honed, highly
trained men who fit the stereotype of the Hollywood secret agent.
But they are not actors, they are the real thing, living on the cutting
edge where they can be under fire on any given day.

Jack Gannon had given the last fourteen years of his life to the
Delta Force, serving as deputy commander for his final two years
on active duty, and had never regretted a moment of it. His pride
in the unit and his respect for the men who were part of it were
what brought him back to work as a civilian operations and intelligence specialist—a position that was created especially for him.

He had arrived at the Ranch at six o'clock, as he did every
morning, and had just finished showering after running the obstacle course and completing his daily workout on the Nautilus equipment in the physical fitness center on the lower level of the main
building. Climbing the open stairway to the mess hall, he poured

himself a cup of coffee and stood at the entrance, scanning the rows of tables.

The troops were arriving, drifting into the mess hall after stopping in the squadron bays to change from their civilian clothes—their uniforms outside of the compound—into the olive-drab one-piece jumpsuits worn for their daily training. The young men—mostly in their mid- to late twenties—could easily be mistaken for college students, construction workers, surfers, or any other segment of society they chose to emulate—their civilian-style haircuts and casual dress code were due not to lax regulations, but were part of a deliberate image that allowed them to go anywhere in the world on a moment's notice without being recognized for what they were.

Gannon saw Lou Burruss, an analyst in Delta's intelligence section, sitting off by himself, his face buried in a French language newspaper from Fort-de-France, Martinique. The young staff sergeant's area of responsibility was LANTCOM (Atlantic Command), which included the Caribbean basin and parts of Latin America. His efforts were channeled into collecting all intelligence information originating from that area and sifting through it to find anything that related to Delta's wide-ranging interests, including the activities of the drug cartels, whose members were now classified as narcoterrorists.

Burruss looked up from his paper to see Gannon take the chair opposite him. "Morning, boss," he said, using the familiar Delta greeting accorded to superiors.

"I need a favor, Lou," Gannon said. "It's unofficial, not Delta business."

"Sure. Name it."

"Anything out of the ordinary crop up in your section lately?"

"You looking for something in particular, or just general updated stuff?"

"Specifically anything from St. Barts?"

"Pretty quiet little place," Burruss said. "Haven't had a meaningful piece of intel out of there in . . . since I don't know when."

"This would be recent. Within the last three days."

"I'll check the overnight take."

"And you might want to touch base with your liaisons at CIA and DIA."

Burruss cracked a knowing smile, understanding that Gannon wanted him to pump his sources throughout the intelligence community. "I'll give 'em a holler. See what they got."

"I'd appreciate it."

"Any names or other pertinent info you can give me," Burruss said, "a starting point to interrogate the computer?"

"See if the name Maria Padron sets off any bells and whistles."

"No problem, boss," Burruss said, and went back to his paper as Gannon got up from the table and left the mess hall.

The safety officer's office was on the same level as the mess hall and only a short distance down the catwalk that ran the length of the huge two-story open area in the center of the building. The door to the small, narrow office was cracked open, and Gannon knocked once and entered to find Dan Pitzer at his desk, elbow-deep in paperwork.

Pitzer was a legend in the special operations community. A retired command sergeant major with thirty years in Special Forces, twelve of them in the Delta Force, he had served seven tours in Vietnam, and had been a part of every major Delta operation since its inception. Like Gannon, he had come back to work as a civilian, and his assignment as safety officer was seen as the ultimate in putting the right man in the right job. None of the young troopers dared give him a fanciful excuse for an incursion of the rules and safety procedures. "No way they're going to pull anything over on Pitzer," the Delta commander was fond of saying. "That jeep-stealing, Rolex-watch-wearing master scrounger of a hillbilly's broken every damn rule there is himself . . . and gotten away with it."

Pitzer's trademark grin creased his tough, craggy face as he looked up from his paperwork and saw Gannon standing before him. Their friendship went back twenty years, to when they had both served in the Special Operations Group in Vietnam and had run "over the fence" reconnaissance missions together.

"Hey, pardner, take a seat," he said in his West Virginia hillbilly twang, and put his paperwork aside. "What can I do you for?"

Gannon sat in the chair opposite the standard government-issue metal desk and removed the eight-by-ten photograph from the envelope he had brought with him.

"You can put that epic memory of yours to work," he said, and handed him the photograph.

"A combined op, SEALs and SF," Pitzer said at a glance. "I know some of the SF guys. Most of them bought the farm."

"I'm interested in these three," Gannon said, pointing out the three men who were still to be identified.

Pitzer studied the faces for a few moments. "Yeah, sure," he said, and pointed to each one as he spoke. "That's 'Squirrel' Watson. Used to put his team up in trees when the NVA was on his ass. Bought it in a chopper crash at the Phu Bai launch site in seventy-two or three. And that's Pete Michaels, poor bastard. One week before he was due to go home shrapnel from a mortar round tore his spinal cord all to hell; put him in a wheelchair for the rest of his life. After five tours too. He's around somewhere, either here in Fayetteville or the Raleigh-Durham area, I forget. I see him every now and then at the old timers' breakfasts at the NCO club."

A smile came to Pitzer's face as he stared at the third man. "And this is my old sidekick. Salami-eatin' Johnny Jocabetti. Used to get a stick of that stuff every week from home. Called him J.J. Damn good recon man. We ran a bunch of missions together out of Kontum, Command and Control Central."

Gannon's attention focused on Jocabetti. Nine of the men in the photograph were now known to be dead, and of the three identified as still being alive, Jocabetti was the only one whom Maria could possibly have seen on St. Barts. "Do you know where I can find Jocabetti?"

"Probably in a padded room somewhere."

"What do you mean?"

"He's been in and out of the VA psycho wards for the past fifteen years. We kept in touch for a while," Pitzer added, "but he really went off the deep end about ten years ago, and except for a Christmas card every year or so, I don't hear from him anymore."

"What happened to him?"

Pitzer shrugged. "Who knows? Saw too much, did too much. Remember the navy hospital on Treasure Island off San Francisco?

They had a detuning center for SOG personnel who did multiple combat tours?"

Gannon indicated that he did. "We were sent there for a physical after being in-country for an extended period . . . a checkup for malaria, or any rare viruses we might have picked up."

Pitzer chuckled. "That's what they wanted us to think. Remember how the soda and cigarette machines didn't work, just ate your money? And the surly nurses and doctors, and the cold meals?"

"Yeah."

"Well, that's the way they planned it. Anyone who threw a fit and trashed the machines, or pitched their food around in protest, or gave the doctors and nurses any static ended up staying longer than those who just let it slide. It was their way of finding out who needed a little help before they were let loose on society. Anyway, Jocabetti really snapped. Pushed over vending machines, threw a doctor through a window, and like that. He spent about six months there before they let him out. Gave him a medical discharge . . . a Section Eight."

"When's the last time you heard from him?"

"Christmas card last year."

"Any return address?"

"No. Postmark was somewhere in Pennsylvania," Pitzer said. "But I can almost guarantee you the VA's got him in the system."

"You wouldn't happen to have any VA contacts, would you?" Gannon knew the answer before he asked the question. Pitzer was known for his networking; he was wired into every nook and cranny of the government bureaucracies through old service buddies now in the civilian sector.

"Yeah. Tom Jeffries, former SF. Went through training group with him. He's got a cushy job with them in D.C. Tell him I said to call."

"Thanks, Dan," Gannon said, and put the photograph back in the envelope as he got up to leave.

"Mind telling me what you're on to?"

"I'm not sure," Gannon said, "but I'll let you know when I find out."

●

Much of the lower level of the main building at the Ranch is taken up by an area within an area: the Operations and Intelligence section located inside the Sensitive Compartmented Intelligence Facility (SCIF). Totally enclosed and hardened to ensure that no audio, visual, or electronic penetration of the facility is possible—not even the faintest of electronic emissions can escape it—the SCIF is the joint domain of the intelligence officer and the operations officer and their staffs. It is where Delta's crown jewels are kept—its sensitive files, intelligence data, and contingency plans—and where its operations are planned, and monitored and controlled by means of a satellite communications network that is remoted into the Tactical Operations Center, keeping the Delta commander in touch with his troops anywhere in the world.

Entrance to the SCIF is gained by running a magnetic security card through the slot on the cipher lock and punching in the required code numbers. A central computer then reads the individual's card, determines whether he has access to that particular door, and records it on a printout, providing a record of who has entered and exited what doors and at what time he did so.

Inside the SCIF, corridors branch off in several directions. Along the corridors are offices for the operations and intelligence officers and their assistants, and larger common rooms in which operations sergeants and intelligence sergeants, clerks and "worker bees" schedule training exercises, aircraft needed for training jumps, and handle the mundane chores of processing security clearances and other routine paperwork.

Lou Burruss's office was halfway down a narrow corridor lined with the offices of the intelligence analysts whose responsibilities spanned the globe: Eurcom covered the U.S. European Command; Southcom, the U.S. Southern Command responsible for Central and South America; Centcom, the Central Command covering the Mideast and Southwest Asia; Pacom, the Pacific Command encompassing East Asia and the Pacific Islands; and Forscom, Forces Command, which is responsible for U.S. forces inside the United States. The stacks of computer printouts and foreign newspapers and periodicals that could be found cluttering every available space in the offices attested to the reams of material that was perused on a daily basis.

Burruss was hunched over his computer in the Lantcom office, welcoming the break from his daily routine of collating, analyzing, and filing the intelligence information gathered the previous day. He stared intently at his video monitor as he scrolled through a seven-page document looking for any occurrence of St. Barts or Maria Padron in the text of the Defense Intelligence Agency's weekly intelligence summary for the Caribbean Basin.

All around him, Lantcom regional maps, with acetate overlays depicting hot spots, covered the walls of the office, along with satellite photos of military installations, civilian airports, and other strategic locales that would demand Delta's attention in the event of an operation into that specific area. Tacked to a cork board above his desk were a selection of Hagar the Horrible and Kingdom of Id cartoons, along with mementos from his contributions to past operations brought back by members of the assault forces in gratitude for his excellent work. His favorites were a bikini top from a fondly remembered Danish tourist encountered by an amorous trooper during a clandestine reconnaissance mission to Grenada prior to the invasion, and a rules and regulations poster in Spanish, taken from the warden's office in the Panama jail that Delta had stormed to free a CIA agent just before that invasion kicked off.

Burruss had spent the past three hours tapping into the data banks to which Delta had access at CIA, FBI, National Security Agency, Drug Enforcement Agency, Department of State, Joint Chiefs of Staff, U.S. Southern Command, and finally DIA. All had given him a "dump" on what they had, but he had come up empty. Glancing at the telephone numbers on a card taped to the desk beside his secure phone, he decided on a more direct approach and dialed the number for his contact at CIA's Caribbean desk.

In a profession where knowledge is power, and is therefore jealously guarded, intelligence-gathering agencies are prone to hoarding, rather than sharing their hard-earned information. But Burruss, like all Delta analysts, took competitive pride in knowing all there was to know about his region, and went to great lengths to ensure that nothing slipped past him. Cultivating analysts in other agencies was of the utmost importance in accomplishing this, and it was in this area that Delta had a distinct advantage over their counterparts in the rest of the intelligence community.

Delta's relationships with other analysts were developed not only through periodic interagency seminars but, unlike most other agencies, during crisis situations, when the person being asked to help could fully realize that his or her information could have a direct bearing on national security or be put to immediate use in an effort to save lives, thereby providing a transcending motivation that made the contributing analyst feel his or her hard work was actually accomplishing something tangible and rewarding. Consequently, Delta's requests were treated as the exception to the unwritten rule of "give them as little as possible."

An invitation to the Ranch is extended to those who have been most helpful; it is a rare and highly coveted privilege afforded to very few outside of Congressional oversight committees and high-ranking military with a need to know about Delta's capabilities and methods of operation. The special visitors, as the outside analysts are called, are treated to an elaborate dog and pony show selected from Delta's bag of magic tricks. As a grand finale, they are allowed to sit in the mock-up aircraft as it is assaulted and real bullets tear into the targets affixed to the seats alongside the unsuspecting visitors—a never-to-be-forgotten experience that would be their main topic of conversation at work and at home for weeks to come. Upon returning to their respective agencies, the visitors become fans for life, eagerly complying with all future Delta requests with an alacrity and candor previously unknown in their profession.

Burruss's contact at CIA's Caribbean desk gave him what she had, apologizing for not having more and promising to get back to him if anything else turned up. She had been invited to the Ranch last month, and the memory was still fresh in her mind as she once again toiled away at a usually tedious and repetitive job.

A second call to CIA yielded nothing, and just as Burruss ended the conversation, Gannon knocked once and entered the office.

"Anything turn up?"

"Sure did, boss," Burruss said. "A police report from St. Barts shows a Maria Padron found dead on a yacht . . . murdered.

Predawn, October third. No arrest. Suspect is a former crew member."

"That's a dead end," Gannon said. "Nothing else?"

"One more item," Burruss said, "which is quite a lot, considering nothing ever happens on that laid-back island paradise. Five or so cocaine kings had some kind of high-level secret meeting there on the night of October second. Came in one day, left the next."

"Any details?"

"My source at CIA's Caribbean desk says there's a take from a laser device, but she doesn't have access to it. Their Counter Narcotics Center compartmented the investigation and slapped a top-secret classification on the intel."

"Do you know anyone at CNC?"

"I already tried him. He's too new at the job, does everything by the numbers. He got nervous and clammed up when I pressed him," Burruss said. "You want me to stay with it, follow up on the locals' murder investigation and the druggies' meeting?"

"Yes, if you will."

"You think the two are connected?"

"I don't know. But whenever I've chalked something up to coincidence in the past, it's turned out not to be one," Gannon said. "I'd like you to add another name to your search: John Jocabetti. Try your DEA and FBI contacts. See what they have on him, specifically any connections to the drug business, no matter how remote."

"Who was Maria Padron, boss?"

"A friend . . . she was a very special friend."

"Sorry," Burruss said. "I'll keep at it; whatever I turn up I'll get to you ASAP."

"Appreciate your help, Lou," Gannon said, giving him a pat on the shoulder as he left.

Back in his own office, Gannon placed a call to the Veterans Administration headquarters in Washington. Pitzer's friend was helpful, locating Jocabetti in less than an hour and calling back with the information: as of ten-fifteen that morning, John Francis Jocabetti was a neuropsychiatric patient on a locked ward at the VA hospital in Coatesville, Pennsylvania. He had just been readmitted the previous night after disappearing from the hospital grounds two months earlier.

A friend in Delta's operations section located a military flight scheduled to leave nearby Pope Air Force Base early the following morning for Dover Air Force Base in Delaware, less than an hour's drive from the VA hospital. He arranged for Gannon to be on it.

-12-

The rivets in the twin engine turbo-prop's metal skin groaned and creaked as winds buffeted and rocked it throughout its descent from fifteen thousand feet. In less than a mile the topography had plunged to one quarter of its former elevation and updrafts pulled against down drafts as Sincavage finessed the controls, holding the small plane on course as he crossed the last of the foothills that ran along the base of the Andes mountains in the north central corner of Peru.

After following the coastline south from Cartagena, he had stopped in Quito, Ecuador, to refuel before crossing the spine of the magnificent mountain range. It had been a demanding flight, requiring constant attention as he flew through gaps between peaks towering to twenty-three thousand feet, and skirted steep, rocky crags that poked through ballooning puffs of cumulus clouds harboring unstable air masses that rose thousands of feet higher.

His eyes now searched for a landing strip that appeared on no aeronautical charts. Below, as far as the eye could see, nature dominated a prohibitive landscape of tropical forest, broken only by mountain streams cascading over waterfalls into broad, fast-flowing tributaries that snaked through the uninhabited wilderness for hundreds of miles, eventually to swell the waters of the mighty Amazon on its four-thousand-mile journey across Peru and Brazil to the Atlantic Ocean.

In the distance, off to the south, a dark wall of rain approached, a threatening element Sincavage realized he would soon have to contend with unless he found the strip quickly. Then he saw it, appearing magically out of nowhere, a crude, narrow clearing hacked from the floor of a jungle-choked mountain valley. A tattered orange windsock stood forlornly at one end.

With one eye on the approaching storm, he banked the aircraft steeply from what the fluttering windsock told him was a down-wind course, to his base leg and then on to a final approach. The grassy runway sloped ten degrees downward to the north, and Sincavage estimated its length at no more than thirty-five hundred feet. Limestone cliffs guarded the approach while a steep drop off into a wild river gorge fell rapidly away at the far end, both harsh reminders that the region's rugged terrain was an invitation to tragedy for careless pilots.

As Sincavage looked out the window, the ridges and ravines directly below were convincing, the shadows dark and deep. He was flying on "dead man's curve," with absolutely no margin for error. In seconds, he was beyond the point of no return, committed to the landing. The ground rushed up, and feeling the force of the crosswind, he dipped a wing and managed to hold it there in compensation for the powerful intermittent gusts as he aligned aircraft with airstrip. Wrestling the plane to the ground, he fought the wind that meant to keep it aloft, and managed to come to a full stop only a few feet from the green abyss at the runway's end.

Dense jungle closed in on either side, and the cockpit quickly became stuffy and humid; the air was so thick it verged on becoming rain. It was not until Sincavage exited the plane that he saw the heavily armed men appear from the tree line—young men, some still in their teens, with dark, solemn faces and suspicious eyes. They carried an assortment of weapons, ranging from Soviet AK-47s to Belgian FAL automatic rifles and American M-16s, and looked as though they knew how to use them. They were guerrillas, peasants from the mountain valleys for the most part. Some bare-chested, others in T-shirts, all wore frayed and faded jungle fatigue pants and hats in an assortment of camouflage patterns.

Sincavage's gaze fell on a squat, powerfully built man with fair skin and hair, obviously not a Latino. With a wave of his hand, he commanded the guerrilla force to lower their weapons as he walked toward the plane.

"You're either the man Raphael Calderon told me to expect, or you're a dead man." The words were delivered with a pronounced Australian accent and a crooked smile that was more practiced than genuine.

"Carlson," Sincavage said.

"What's in a name?" the man replied. "Actually, the identification numbers on the plane told me all I needed to know. I'm Anderson," he added without the pretense of a handshake.

Sincavage took his nylon carry-all from the rear compartment and went about securing the aircraft. "You know why I'm here."

Anderson shook his head. "Been told to help in any way I can."

"I'm expecting six people to arrive tomorrow," Sincavage said.

"So I've been given to understand. Can I ask the purpose of your stay in our little hideaway?"

"You can ask" was all that Sincavage said.

Another crooked, humorless smile and Anderson made a sweeping gesture with his hand toward a barely visible break in the tree line off to the side of the airstrip. "If you will follow me, Mr. Carlson."

The break in the wall of green was no more than a crude, hand-cut jungle trail. Two machete-wielding young guerrillas led the way, swinging occasionally at thick trailing vines and encroaching underbrush that threatened to reclaim the hard-won path at any moment. In a matter of minutes, Sincavage's denim shirt was soaked with perspiration. Taking a bandanna from his jeans, he twirled it tight and tied it around his forehead, feeling more at home in the harsh environment with each passing minute, the atmosphere reminiscent of his years in Vietnam.

The rain squall that had threatened to envelop him during his approach to the airstrip now passed overhead, unleashing a thunderous downpour that despite its intensity scarcely penetrated the thick triple canopy. Broad-leaf plants and vines dripped heavily from the second-level growth, and water trickled from ferns and orchids down the necks and backs of the sweating men. The rain ended as suddenly as it had begun, and a cool mist soon hung over the trail like a damp shroud. A squadron of vibrant green parrots squawked at being disturbed, and zigzagged through the lush foliage, followed by the distant, chilling roar of a troop of howler monkeys crashing unseen through the upper branches. As the men trekked deeper into the jungle, countless other sounds, accompanied by brief flashes of movement, betrayed a host of indistinct creatures in the deepening shadows of the creeping bamboo and tangled, impenetrable vegetation.

They had gone a little over a mile when the forest opened up to a sprawling jungle camp expertly concealed beneath the overhead canopy. Sincavage immediately understood why none of it was visible from the air. Only the first growth, the understory up to ten feet, had been cleared to accommodate the structures scattered throughout, and as they reached the center of the camp, the place took on a pale-green unearthly glow from the diffused shafts of sunlight that penetrated the upper reaches. Sincavage saw two thatched roof open-sided dormitories containing enough bunks and hammocks to accommodate a hundred men, and a dining and kitchen area complete with a dishwasher, microwave oven, and refrigerator, all powered by the camp's generators—and judging by the meal being prepared in the open-air kitchen, a fresh supply of meat was available on demand. After pointing out that there were enclosed bathrooms with showers and flush toilets, Anderson then pulled open the door of a tin-roof shack, revealing a large common room with an extensive library of pornographic magazines and a large-screen television with a video recorder. No imagination was needed to guess the subject matter of the stacks of videotapes on the shelves beside it.

"All the comforts of home," Sincavage said, impressed with what were luxurious accommodations by jungle camp standards.

"A little bit of heaven where you least expect to find it," Anderson said, dismissing the guerrillas with another unspoken command. They faded from sight as quickly as they had appeared.

Sincavage followed the Australian across the main part of the camp down a short trail to where a second area spread out beneath towering trees. It was larger than the first and contained more structures, some thatched roof open shelters, others fully enclosed tin-roof shacks, approximately twenty in all. A quick glance around revealed their purpose. Hundreds of containers of chemicals and plastic mixing barrels were stacked on raised pallets beneath tarps strung from tree limbs. The interior of a long building with a tin roof was brightly lit by heat lamps suspended from the ceiling, the intense heat they generated directed at a snowy blanket of filtered cocaine—in excess of three hundred kilos—in the process of being dried before packaging.

The floor of another, even larger structure—again, a drying shack—was covered with a thick layer of coca leaves being slowly raked back and forth by a worker in the initial process of drying the leaves before they were processed into paste. Nearby, another man slogged through a large vat of coca leaves immersed in a mild solution of sulfuric acid—a process repeated several times a day for four to five days to extract the cocaine from the leaves, creating a liquid then mixed with lime, gasoline, ammonia, and other chemicals to make the cocaine base.

A weary campesino led a mule and six tethered burros into the camp on a trail that entered from another direction. The animals were burdened with twenty-five-pound sacks of coca leaves. After unloading and resting for the night, the man would repeat the grueling trip of four eighteen-hour days across three mountain ranges, returning to his coca fields until they yielded another crop and he would make the journey again.

Sincavage was impressed by the extent and ingenuity of the operation, capable of producing three tons of cocaine a week, according to Anderson. Its remote location was due to jungle laboratories in the Upper Huallaga Valley being discovered and destroyed by American DEA agents and the Peruvian military. Here, deep in the wilderness on the eastern side of the Andes, they were farther from the government's staging bases, secure in the mountain strongholds of the left-wing terrorist group known as the *Sendero Luminoso* (Shining Path)—areas where DEA agents and Peruvian soldiers hesitated to venture for fear of being outgunned and outmanned by the guerrillas and subjected to hit-and-run attacks and ambushes that historically have proven resistant to conventional military tactics.

The Shining Path's virulent and brutal revolutionary guerrillas were nothing more than anarchists who had never bothered to explain what they were fighting for. They were best known for their policy of selective annihilation—assassinating local politicians, reluctant peasants, and foreign aid workers, or starving entire villages for not joining their ranks—a policy that had left one quarter of Peru's towns and villages with no one in charge. After their alliance of convenience with the cocaine barons, their unstated political manifesto became a moot point; their leaders concluded that when running drugs makes you rich, ideology is relegated to nothing more than an academic matter.

Sincavage estimated there were fifty of them in the camp; the rest of the inhabitants, numbering approximately sixty, were peasants involved in producing the cocaine. Half of the guerrillas were young trainees, there for a ten-week course under the tutelage of Anderson and his two-man training staff, the others were a permanent cadre of experienced jungle fighters serving as a security element for the camp.

"However," Anderson quickly pointed out, "they sample a little too much of the nose candy to secure much of anything. Chewing the bloody leaves used to satisfy them, but not once they got a jolt of the finished product. I've threatened to shoot the ones I catch; that gives them pause . . . for a while."

Leading the way down a footpath that branched off from the cocaine-processing part of the camp, Anderson chatted away about the merits of his training program and the quality of the trainees. "Not very good, mostly scared, homesick lads forced into volunteering, but a reasonable facsimile of a fighting man when I've finished with them."

Out of sight of the rest of the camp, they stopped at a cluster of eight small bamboo and thatch huts. Behind the huts was an obstacle course, and in the distance a natural, boulder-strewn clearing Sincavage estimated to be the size of a football field.

"Thought you might appreciate the privacy," Anderson said,

indicating the huts. "They'll accommodate you and those you're expecting. I was told you'd be needing some special weapons."

"Fragmentation grenades, LAWs," Sincavage said, using the acronym for bazooka-like light antitank weapons, "and mini-Uzi submachine guns."

"No problem, except for the Uzis," Anderson said. "I have MAC-10s, just as concealable, if that's your purpose."

"Fine," Sincavage said. "And I'll need some improvised targets set up in an open area."

"What are the targets to represent?"

"A limousine, two vans, and three cars in a motorcade."

"And the plot thickens," Anderson said with a wink and another humorless smile. He then jerked a thumb in the direction of the clearing beyond the obstacle course. "I use it as a weapons and demolitions range; it's yours for the duration. Anything else?"

"The best sniper rifle you've got."

"That would be a Remington 40XB; a bolt action seven-millimeter Magnum with a twenty-four-inch barrel. It's got a two-piece Kevlar stock, breaks down just behind the receiver. And the barrel's been customized to accommodate some rather special ammunition I think you might find interesting."

"And the scope?" Sincavage said.

"Leupold, three point five by ten power. Has a two-inch adjustable objective to adapt for varying light conditions."

"Perfect," Sincavage said.

Anderson glanced at his watch and turned to leave. "After you get squared away I'll patch you through to Calderon. He was anxious to have a chat with you on your arrival. You'll find the commo shack behind our little porno theater."

After stowing his gear in the hut at the edge of the trail, and making a quick tour of the immediate area, Sincavage found the communications shack, where Anderson waited for him.

Sitting incongruously on a rough-hewn wooden table in the middle of the bamboo and thatch shack was a satellite radio, complete with a digital voice protection system.

"State of the art," Anderson boasted.

The modern secure-voice radio came as no surprise to Sincavage. On his brief walk around the area near the huts, he had noticed a satellite dish, three feet in diameter, concealed at the edge of the clearing near the obstacle course.

The connection took only seconds, and Calderon's voice came through crystal clear, bounced off a commercial communications satellite from his ranch in Bolivia to the remote jungle camp.

"Our inside source has informed us that the Secret Service knows of our arrangement," he told Sincavage.

"What do they know?"

"That we have contracted a professional assassin."

"Do they know you by name?"

"I must assume that they do," Calderon said. "They must have had the villa on St. Barts under electronic surveillance."

Sincavage smiled to himself. *That was a given, you idiot,* he almost said, but didn't. "What difference does it make? Besides, that was the point, wasn't it, to let everyone know who was responsible?"

"Yes, only after the fact," Calderon said. "But more to the point, if they know about us, they in all probability know about you, and the location and time frame of your attempt."

"Those are my problems," Sincavage said.

"I thought you would want to be informed," Calderon said. "Your chances of success would appear to be seriously diminished now that they know of your plans."

"My intent, not my plans," Sincavage said.

"As you say. I will keep you informed of any further developments through the contacts I gave you. Good luck," Calderon added, none too convincingly, and then Sincavage heard the disconnect over the small handset.

Anderson had heard only Sincavage's side of the conversation, but it was enough to intrigue him even more. It had been a year since he had left the training base and cocaine-processing camp he had set up for Calderon in Colombia, slipping across the border into Peru one step ahead of the government troops that raided and destroyed the compound hours later. And it had been a long time since he had had a conversation with a fellow traveler, someone, he imagined, with a background similar to his own.

"Care to join me for a drink?" he asked as they exited the radio shack into the cool evening air.

Sincavage declined the offer. "It's been a long day. Maybe tomorrow."

"Tomorrow, then," Anderson said. "I'll have your weapons ready first thing."

Walking back to his hut at the far end of the camp, Sincavage's thoughts were on Calderon's message. He had expected the drug lords to be under heavy surveillance and their ranks infiltrated by any number of agents and informants, riddled with them from top to bottom, especially since the creation of CIA's Counter Narcotics Center. With the Company's experience and expertise in penetrating organizations, the equation had changed drastically, and he had suffered no illusions about his mission going uncompromised. Quite the opposite; he had counted on just that going in, planning on using it to his advantage. And so far things were going as he had expected—they knew only what he had intended for them to know.

—13—

The updated report that Tony Covington at CIA's Counter Narcotics Center had forwarded to the Secret Service Intelligence
Division was waiting on Mike Maguire's desk when he arrived at
work that morning. He now had a name, Roger Carlson, who was
traveling under forged documents and had been on St. Barts at the
time of the drug barons' meeting. Adding to the significance of
time and place, the CNC report informed Maguire that they had
tracked Carlson to Cartagena, where two days ago a man matching
his description had met with a known terrorist, though both were
lost after spotting the surveillance team that CIA's Bogotá station
had assigned to the terrorist. But the name was a starting point,
and Maguire immediately called Susan Olsen, instructing her to
pass the information on to Interpol on the off chance that the alias
he was using might be in their files.

Adhering to his usual morning routine, Maguire left the Old
Executive Office Building at eight-fifteen and crossed West Executive Avenue, entering the White House through the west wing

basement. Exchanging greetings with the Uniform Division officers at their post just inside the door, he continued along the hallway, past the Situation Room and the Navy Mess to W-16, the Secret Service's main command post in the White House. Inside W-16 was the nerve center for the extensive measures taken to protect the President and First Lady when they were in residence. The working shift supervisor monitored and oversaw the agents on duty, making certain, among other things, that every thirty minutes an agent came out of W-16 and "pushed" the agents posted around the White House to the next post—a rotation system that combated boredom and inattentiveness. Filling one wall of the command post was a bank of video monitors capable of displaying every inch of the White House grounds through cameras strategically placed around the complex. There were wall-mounted panels lit with readouts for all locks, alarms, telephones, and radios, and a small cubicle for the Radionics system—a recent addition that Maguire considered not only worthless and moronic in concept, but dangerous to the extent that it provided a false sense of security for the President's children.

The Radionics system was, in effect, a computerized central monitoring station for the conventional alarm systems in the homes of the children, who were scattered about the country. Any incursion into their residences that tripped the alarms sent a signal over telephone lines to W-16, where the floor plan of the affected house could be called up on a monitor, displaying the precise entry point of the break in. The duty technician at the console in W-16 then dialed the number of the residence to make certain it was not a false alarm, and if it was, requested a code number to verify that it was indeed one of the President's family to whom he was speaking. If no one answered, or no verification code was given, the alarm was considered valid and the duty technician then called the local Secret Service field office, who in turn called the local police and reported the break in.

Maguire had fought against the installation of the system from the start, but existing manpower in the Presidential Protective Division was already stretched thin—a minimum of one hundred agents would have been needed to provide around-the-clock protection for the President's five children and twelve grandchildren

—and morale would have been a problem, with no one eager to be stuck standing in a backyard in Denver at two o'clock in the morning in the dead of winter. Consequently the Radionics system had won out, despite Maguire's argument that it would have been far more practical to have the individual alarms wired directly into local security companies, who could provide the same service, with much quicker response time, with the Secret Service out of the loop—a solution that was anathema to the upper echelon of the Service.

Maguire noticed an entry on the previous night's log—the alarm in the home of the President's son in Denver had been tripped; it had taken twenty-five minutes to establish that it was a false alarm. Maguire shook his head in disgust. Twenty-five minutes was enough time to kidnap or assassinate not only the President's son and his family but all of his immediate neighbors as well. The Radionics technician on duty avoided his gaze, well aware of Maguire's feeling about the system.

Putting the entry log back on the table, Maguire checked the electronic status board that constantly displayed the location of the President and the First Lady. The board read POTUS (for President Of The United States)—RESIDENCE, and FIRST LADY—EAST WING OFFICE. A brief conversation with the shift supervisor brought him up-to-date on what had happened since last night: the Washington field office had locked up a man found with an automatic weapon in Lafayette Park, and the New York field office had succeeded in tracking down a particularly vitriolic letter writer. Maguire checked the time, and left the command post, taking the stairs to the upper level, where he stopped off at a small office between the Oval Office and the Cabinet Room and checked in with the President's appointments secretary for any changes in the President's itinerary for that day. There were none.

At eight forty-five, after a quick tour of the posted agents, he went over to the main part of the White House, where he waited in the hallway for the elevator to come down from the President's private quarters. The highly coveted ritual of escorting the Chief Executive from the elevator to the Oval Office provided the one time during the day when the agents of the Presidential Protective Division were assured of direct contact with the President, provid-

ing an opportunity to discuss any concerns regarding his safety—
an adjustment in his body armor or a gentle reminder that he wear
it more religiously—or listen to any unfiltered comments and criti-
cisms he might have of their performance.

The President was alerted only to significant, imminent threats
to his or the First Lady's safety, with the reports of the countless
"nut cases" never reaching him or his Chief of Staff. Maguire knew
that mentioning the drug barons' hiring of an assassin was premature at this point, and out of line, since the initial report of any
noteworthy threat case was always first discussed with the deputy
chief of staff. But Maguire also knew the value of working the
system, priming the pump for an immediate response if and when
it came time to take action. His presence alone, as head of the
Presidential Protective Division, as opposed to the usual custom of
the working shift supervisor waiting at the elevator, would alert the
President to a heightened concern and that something out of the
ordinary had prompted his being there.

At eight-fifty the elevator door opened and the President
stepped out. His attention immediately fell on Maguire, whom he
had not seen in weeks.

"Morning, Mike. How ya doin'?" The trace of a brief inquisitive look told Maguire his presence had had the desired effect.

"Fine, Mr. President," Maguire said, and fell in step as they
walked down the hallway to the glass-enclosed Palm Room and on
outside to the colonnade bordering the South Lawn.

The President smiled politely, looking up from a draft of a
speech he had been working on in his study in the second floor
residence since early morning. He commented on the beauty of the
crisp fall day, then as they reached the door to the Oval Office, he
fixed Maguire with a sharp, penetrating stare. "Anything I should
know about?"

"Not yet, Mr. President."

The President nodded thoughtfully. "Nice to see you, Mike,"
he said, and entered the Oval Office, where his Chief of Staff could
be seen waiting on one of the sofas, casting a proprietary look of
disapproval upon seeing Maguire alone with the President.

•

Forty miles west of Philadelphia, the Coatesville Veterans Administration Hospital sits on a hillside overlooking the rolling countryside of Chester County, Pennsylvania. It is built around two quadrangles in a park-like setting of autumn-colored woods and manicured lawns. The attractive complex of red brick buildings could easily be mistaken for an Ivy League campus, rather than a twelve-hundred bed neuropsychiatric hospital housing the most hopeless cases in the VA medical-care system. The majority of its patients were those who failed to respond to treatment, or proved too unmanageable for other VA institutions; it was the last stop in a long road of misery and despair for hundreds of mentally disturbed veterans of the Vietnam War.

The psychiatrist who met Gannon at the reception area and led him through a maze of corridors and along a below-ground walkway to the second quadrangle, where the locked psychiatric wards were located, was a woman of forty-two, a Vietnamese refugee who had come to the United States two years after the end of the war. She had been Jocabetti's doctor for the past eighteen months, or the portion of that time when he had been in the hospital.

"He stays four or five months," she told Gannon, "then checks himself out against my orders."

"He can do that?"

"There's nothing we can do to keep him here," she said. "No one can be kept against his will. But he always comes back, he's what we call a census patient, or a revolving-door patient. Sometimes, when he's earned privileges and is allowed off the ward during the day, he simply walks off the grounds without telling anyone. But he's seldom gone for more than a week or ten days."

"Where does he go?"

"According to the local police he has a shack somewhere in the woods outside of town. They occasionally see him walking the streets in the early morning hours. When he's ready to come back, he usually commits some minor crime; throws a brick through a window or gets into a fight in a bar. The police take him into custody and call us."

"I was told he was gone for two months this time."

"Yes. That's unusual, for him." The doctor stopped walking

and turned toward Gannon. "Does that have anything to do with your visit?"

"I don't know."

"You're not family."

"No."

"A friend?"

"No," Gannon said. "I've never met him. We have friends in common, though. We served in the same unit in Vietnam."

"May I ask the reason for this visit?"

Gannon considered lying, but didn't. "There's a possibility he was involved in a murder."

"I can't say that would surprise me," the doctor said. "He's prone to violence . . . his clinical diagnosis is Intermittent Explosive Behavior Disorder, among other things. He can be a very disruptive patient."

"Is he dangerous?"

"At times," the doctor said as they continued walking. "Jocabetti's not one of our success stories. He's never opened up, resists therapy. Most of our patients we've been able to medicate and stabilize, get them back to near normal and out into the real world before they lose their skills or become institutionalized. If they stay on their medication and come back for out-patient treatment we've got a pretty good chance of helping them lead a decent life. But I'm afraid Jocabetti doesn't fit into that category. No one's been able to get through to him, and more than a few have tried. He simply withdraws, somewhere deep inside himself, and won't let anyone else in."

"Does he remember the things he does when he's violent?"

"There's nothing wrong with his memory. The fact that he remembers the past so well is probably the root cause of his problems."

"I guess we're all prisoners of the pictures in our minds."

"An interesting observation, Mr. Gannon."

"I've seen some of the same pictures," Gannon said. "I'm just one of the lucky ones. Is he all right now? I mean, is he feeling all right to talk?"

"He had to be put in four-point restraints and heavily sedated last night, but the charge nurse on the ward told me he was feeling a lot better this morning. Are you certain he's going to want to talk to you?"

"I don't know. Does he mind getting visitors?"

"I checked his file when they called and told me you were here. In the eight years he's been under our care you're the first visitor he's had."

"He has no family?"

"None of record."

As they reached the end of the underground passageway, the doctor led him up two flights of stairs and unlocked a door that opened onto what Gannon immediately thought of as a corridor of lost souls. A half dozen or so men wearing brown print pajamas and robes shuffled back and forth in floppy slippers; some gazed suspiciously at him, others ignored him, their blank eyes cast downward. The walls and woodwork of the area were painted an institutional beige, and a tile floor in the same color was waxed to a mirror finish. At each end of the corridor was a ward containing the patients' rooms and a common day room for games and television. The door to the ward on the left was locked, and a gaunt, tortured face filled the small glass and wire mesh window, the eyes intent on Gannon. A patient with a harmonica in his mouth approached the doctor, playing a constant discordant note, increasing the volume as he drew nearer. Upon reaching her, the man paused, inhaled and exhaled loudly through the harmonica, then moved on, lowering the volume of his cacophonous song as he disappeared in the direction of the day room.

"Wait here," the doctor told Gannon. "I'll see if Jocabetti's feeling up to a visit."

Gannon had to make a conscious effort to keep from staring at a man, or rather what was left of him, who approached from the opposite end of the corridor. The man's face was literally destroyed. He had no hair or eyebrows and his ears were rimless holes. The pasty pink flesh of his scalp and face, streaked with blotches of purple, was stretched drum-tight over his head, leaving a perfectly round hole the size of a dime in the front of his one patchless eye. He had no nose, only two tiny openings beneath a molded lump of surgically reconstructed flesh. The orifice marking his mouth was as perfectly round as the one eye, but slightly larger, its saliva-coated circumference remaining unchanged as air was sucked in and out, sounding like the hissing of a scuba tank regulator. His left arm ended at the elbow, and he moved along the hallway haltingly, hampered by a thick black shoe clamped between the tongs of a metal brace on his left leg. As he passed by, Gannon noticed that black cloth wings, the insignia of an army aviator, were sewn onto his bathrobe.

The doctor reappeared from the doorway to Gannon's right, accompanied by a tall, heavily built man who immediately pegged Gannon as a stranger and glared at him with open hostility. He stood back, and off to the side, as the doctor reached Gannon.

"John, this is Jack Gannon, he's here to visit with you."

Gannon moved forward and extended his hand, but there was no response from Jocabetti, his brow knit into a perpetual frown of disapproval and suspicion.

"I'd like to talk with you for a few minutes," Gannon said.

Jocabetti continued to stare openly and made no reply.

"The day room's a little crowded right now," the doctor said. "I suggest the room across the hall." She gestured to a small room with a few folding tables and chairs off the central corridor, where patients were allowed to have a more private lunch with their visitors. "I'll be at the nurses' station if you need me," she told Gannon.

Jocabetti hesitated, then out of curiosity followed Gannon into the small lunchroom, noisily scraping a chair across the floor and spinning it around to straddle it as he sat down. His eyes never left Gannon, who took a chair at a table opposite.

"I know you?" Jocabetti asked, gruffly.

"No."

"Then what do you want? And make it quick. I got a TV show I want to watch."

"I'm a friend of Dan Pitzer."

Jocabetti's expression changed slightly, his gaze less accusing. "Where were you?"

Gannon knew what he meant and said, "Da Nang. Command and Control North."

"How many tours?"

"Five."

"Gannon, huh?" Jocabetti locked eyes with him, then slowly nodded his head. "Yeah, I heard of you . . . Medal of Honor, right?"

Gannon nodded a response.

Jocabetti's demeanor softened further, now more comfortable with someone he considered one of his own. "How's Pitzer doin'?"

"He's fine," Gannon said. "Retired a few years ago, but he's back working for the army as a civilian."

"A double-dipper, huh?" Jocabetti's gaze shifted to the barred window looking down on the inner quadrangle. He was quiet for a long time, lost in a memory he didn't choose to share. "I taught that hillbilly how to speak New York, ya know."

"He told me."

"How about my shrink, huh?" Jocabetti said, rolling his eyes. "Vietnamese. Believe that shit? And she wonders why I won't open up to her. Probably was a goddamn VC; for all I know I killed half her family. . . . What are you doing here, Gannon?"

"I need to know where you were on October second."

"What day is it?"

"October fifth."

"Three days ago . . . shit, I don't know. Probably sleeping off a drunk in my hooch. Why?"

"Where's your hooch?"

"In the woods." He gestured with his hands toward the window. "Not far. Why do you want to know?"

Gannon's eyes were watching Jocabetti's hands; they were both jammed deep in the pockets of his robe and had been except for when he pulled out the chair.

"What the hell are you lookin' at?"

"Are you sure that's where you were three days ago?"

"Isn't that what I just told you?" Jocabetti said, his voice taking on an intimidating edge. "And stop talking to me like a goddamn shrink, answering a question with a question. I hate that shit. It's like nobody hears you or nobody's listening, like all that matters is what they want to know. I asked you, what are you looking at?"

"I was trying to see the back of your hands."

Jocabetti pulled his hands from his pockets and stared at them. "What the hell for?"

Gannon stared too. There was no evidence of any scarring. "Have you ever been to St. Barts?"

"I don't go to church . . . and there you go again with that question with a question shit. Once more and this conversation's over. Understand? What about my hands?"

"I wanted to see if you had a scar on the back of one of them."

"I got scars any number of places, but not there. You a cop now, Gannon?"

"No. Retired military, back working for the army."

Gannon opened the manila envelope he had brought with him and removed the eight-by-ten photograph of the combined SEAL/ Special Forces team. He handed it to Jocabetti. "Everyone except you and two others in this picture are dead."

Jocabetti looked at the photo and grinned. "Yeah, I can believe that. I remember this mission. Like it was yesterday, ya know? Sometimes I just close my eyes and watch the war all over again on the back of my lids. Flash cards of the mind. I don't remember any of the SEALs, but I know all of the SF guys. Who's still living?"

"Scott Lyon, one of the SEALs, and Pete Michaels. And you."

"Yeah, I know Michaels," he said, placing the photograph on the table. "So what's this got to do with anything?"

Gannon saw nothing to be gained by any further questions. His instincts and Jocabetti's ingenuous answer to his question about St. Barts had told him he was talking to the wrong man. There wasn't the slightest indication that Jocabetti was concealing anything. He didn't even know that St. Barts was an island, let alone where it was.

"Someone killed a friend of mine. There's a good chance that person's in this picture. Lyon and Michaels were ruled out as possibilities. That left you."

"Who am I supposed to have killed?"

Gannon shook his head. "I'm sorry to have bothered you with this; I really am."

"Why'd you ask about a scar on my hand?"

"The person I'm looking for had a white phosphorus burn scar on the back of his right hand."

"Well, you got the right picture, but the wrong guy. You're looking for Mad Dog, not me."

The name from the past had an immediate effect on Gannon. It was the nickname for the one man in the photograph for whom he felt no remorse when two years after returning from his final tour in Vietnam he had learned that the man was dead. "Jerry Sincavage?" He could feel the old hatred begin to rise again even as he spoke his name.

Jocabetti picked the photograph up from the table and pointed to a man kneeling in the first row. "Yeah, him. Jerry Sincavage. Mad Dog. He had a real bad burn scar like you said."

"I don't remember him having a scar on the back of his hand," Gannon said.

"Well, he did," Jocabetti said with conviction. "When's the last time you saw him?"

Gannon thought for a moment. "May of sixty-nine."

"It happened after that," Jocabetti said. "I remember when he came back from a mission with it all bandaged up."

"But he's dead. I was told he was killed in action in seventy-one."

"Missing in action, body not recoverable," Jocabetti corrected. "In Laos. Probably rotted to worm food by now, in a shallow grave about eighty klicks from the launch site for his last mission."

"Are you sure about that?"

"Hey, Gannon, I'm crazy, not stupid," Jocabetti said, impatiently. "A heavy team was sent in to find him and the rest of his recon team. I went in on that one, came up empty. Walked right into the middle of an NVA staging area. We damn near didn't get back out . . . lost half the heavy team."

"Did anyone see Sincavage get hit?"

Jocabetti shook his head. "None of us. They radioed a Prairie Fire emergency, said they were surrounded, everybody was wounded. By the time we got there the place was like a Wild West show; you couldn't hear yourself think for the weapons goin' off. We didn't have time to look for bodies. There were enough of them around, but we started taking our own casualties and had to get the hell out of there. I never busted bush so fast in my life gettin' back to the choppers that pulled us out. I think they sent another team in about a few days later when things quieted down, but they got shot off the LZ before they had time to look around. I don't think any of the bodies were ever found."

"What kind of operation was he running?"

"He had a special four-man team, Thai-Vietnamese, one of those indigenous mercenary tribes out of the North that the CIA hired to run operations with SOG. Jerry wasn't running normal missions; most of the ops he ran after sixty-nine came out of headquarters, probably CIA, even his commanding officer didn't know what the hell he was doin' half the time. A special Blackbird flight would take him and his team to Saigon, then a week or two later he'd be back. Never talked about what he did."

"Did you run any operations with him, besides this one?" Gannon asked, indicating the photograph on the table.

"Couple. Right after he transferred to SOG from the Phoenix Program," Jocabetti said. "But I didn't like running with Jerry; nobody did. He had a self-destructive side that got people killed. He once told me that real power is not caring if you live or die—he believed that shit . . . and they think *I'm* crazy."

Jocabetti began laughing softly to himself. "He really hated officers, especially those that weren't airborne, hell he hated any kind of authority figure." After another brief private laugh, he continued. "We were in Saigon together once, being debriefed at SOG headquarters for a mission we just ran, and he saw this great-looking French broad sitting on the terrace of the Continental Hotel with some rear-echelon-major type. Jerry, half in the bag, got pissed off for some reason, walked right up to their table, sat down, and proceeded to whip out his dick and stir his drink with it, all the time smiling politely at this major, who was too scared to do anything about it. . . . Jerry had that look about him, ya know, you didn't want to mess with him when he got that look. He was a real piece of work."

"I know," Gannon said, and cut the conversation short as he picked up the photograph and put it back in the envelope. The murder of Maria, which had made no sense, now took on a different light. If Jocabetti was right, and his recollection was all Gannon had to go on at the moment, a "dead" man who wanted to stay dead would certainly feel threatened by someone who had recognized him, and had taken his picture. Gannon fought back the powerful emotions that were beginning to surface at the thought of Sincavage still being alive, and once again being responsible for the death of someone close to him. There had to be another explanation, someone else with a burn scar, maybe not someone in the photograph at all. A series of coincidences that could be rationally explained with further investigation. But the more he tried to force his thoughts in another direction, the stronger his instincts pulled him back to what he did not want to accept—the fact that Jerry Sincavage was still alive and had killed Maria Padron.

"You've been a big help," Gannon said, getting up from the table. "Thanks." He extended his hand; this time Jocabetti shook it. "You take care of yourself; and I hope you get better soon."

Jocabetti forced a small smile. "You got to be careful in casting out the devil; lest you cast out the best that's in you. I read that somewhere. Makes sense to me."

Back in the hallway, Gannon found the doctor at the nurses' station, and as he waited while she unlocked the door for him to leave, he looked back to see Jocabetti leaning against the doorway of the visiting room. Slowly straightening to a semimilitary posture, he threw Gannon a salute. Gannon smiled and returned it as he stepped into the stairwell and the door slammed shut and locked behind him.

–14–

A bright orange fireball rose from the remote jungle clearing as a powerful explosion rocked the nearby trees and shattered the silence, rumbling outward and resonating off the surrounding hills. The target, a collection of empty chemical drums and plywood, constructed vaguely to resemble a van, disintegrated into a smoking heap of rubble. At the opposite end of the clearing, lying at the edge of the jungle, a young woman dressed in camouflage fatigues with a rocket launcher on her shoulder turned and smiled at Sincavage, who gave her a thumbs-up for her effort.

At Sincavage's command, a young man took her place. Dropping to the ground into a prone position, he shouldered another of the German-made Armbrusts—a man-portable rocket launcher with an effective range of three hundred yards against an armored vehicle. The compact, deadly weapon, four inches in diameter and thirty-four inches in length when folded into the carrying position, could be slung over the shoulder and suspended beneath the arm by an average sized person, making it readily concealable beneath a topcoat.

The guerrilla took aim and fired at the second target in the line of four remaining improvised vehicles. The rocket projectile roared from the weapon, trailing a plume of smoke across the clearing to where it impacted into a rock outcropping at the base of a hill just inside the tree line, missing its target by a wide margin and sending a storm of granite shards, leaves, and small tree limbs soaring into the air.

"Try it again," Sincavage said. "Take your time and align the sights properly."

The young guerrilla reloaded the weapon and did as he was instructed, this time hitting and destroying his target.

"Good," Sincavage said, pleased with the expertise four of the guerrillas had shown with their weapons. The girl's ability with the rocket launcher was especially gratifying. Attractive women drew far less scrutiny from security details. "Bring the launchers and the rest of the rockets with you," he told the group. "We've got some classroom work to do."

The six young guerrillas followed Sincavage along a narrow jungle footpath to a small open area in front of their huts, where he had set up a chalkboard. They watched with rapt attention as Sincavage diagrammed a line of vehicles and began explaining their respective positions and areas of responsibility in a presidential motorcade.

Twenty yards away, hidden by the dense undergrowth off the jungle trail, Juan Osorio stood silently watching the man who spoke like an American, and whom he had heard the Australian call Carlson. He had been shadowing him and the team of guerrillas, who had arrived just after dawn, since early that morning. His job as one of the camp's chemists provided the cover for his activities as an agent for the CIA. Recruited just after graduating from Seton Hall University, he had undergone extensive training at the Farm —CIA's secret training base in Virginia—before returning to his native Peru and as his first assignment infiltrating the major drug cartel operating out of Lima. He had been in the remote jungle camp since it was built, reporting on the activities of Anderson and his guerrilla trainees, identifying them and passing the intelligence information on to his control, a case officer with CIA's Counterterrorist Group section at the American embassy in Lima.

The blond American's presence, and the subsequent arrival of the six young guerrillas he judged to be Shining Path recruits from the conversations he had overheard, intrigued him. Though they weren't part of Anderson's guerrilla-training program, their activities were interesting enough to bear watching and reporting to his control.

He checked the time, and silently withdrew deeper into the jungle, moving cautiously toward the opposite end of the obstacle course. He stopped and knelt in the undergrowth, and waited a full five minutes, watching and listening for any sign that he had been followed. Once certain that he was not being observed, he crawled into a dense stand of bamboo and pulled aside what appeared to be a clump of dead plants and vines rotting on the jungle floor. From the shallow hole that served as his cache, he removed a small moisture-proof bundle wrapped in several layers of plastic and stored in a small knapsack.

Inside the bundle was a sophisticated dictionary-sized satellite radio with burst transmission capabilities, a small collapsible dish antenna eighteen inches in diameter, and spare batteries. Unfolding the antenna and orienting it in the proper direction and at the proper angle, he connected it to the radio. A tiny green light glowed when he turned the unit on and began whispering into the handset. It took thirty-five seconds to record his message, which was automatically encoded as he spoke. Pressing another button on the front panel caused the thirty-five-second message to be compressed to a burst of less than a second of transmission time as its signal was bounced off a satellite orbiting high above the earth's atmosphere.

•

The Communications Programs Unit (CPU) in the American embassy in Lima is on the top floor in the northwest corner of the building. It is constructed as a room within a room within a room, a tightly secured galvanized steel chamber behind a vault door, where the secrets of CIA, NSA, and the State Department are shielded from outsiders. The measures taken to make the CPU as secure as humanly possible are extensive. The thousands of screws used to erect the metal walls were designed to create their own threads, effectively forming a seal against microscopic tolerances that would allow electronic or radio-wave penetration. The steel vault door, flanged to give it a knifelike edge, is coated with beryllium to ensure a smooth, snug fit when closed. The air vents are fitted with honeycombed filters, and all power lines pass through special electronic filters and circuits. To prevent leakage in the communications lines, data is converted to light beams and carried over optical fibers, making physically tapping into the lines—a virtual impossibility without being detected—the only way to intercept any of the transmitted data.

The CIA's code room, a separate inner sanctum within the CPU, gleams with metallic-gray cipher machines and ultrasophisticated radios for transmitting and receiving messages beamed off satellites from around the world. Through this equipment flows the top-secret details of CIA's operations throughout South and Central America, its messages enciphered by an intricate system of substituting random digits for each letter of the alphabet, with the digits constantly changing according to a complex preprogrammed mathematical formula, then double encoded by being passed through two cipher machines.

A CIA code clerk watched as a red light blinked on one of the electronic panels, then dimmed and went out as the incoming message was received, decoded, and recorded.

"It's from 'Aztec,' " the code clerk said to the CIA case officer standing over him. "He's on schedule and his identifiers indicate his cover is secure."

The code clerk did not know that Aztec was Juan Osorio, or where he was transmitting from, but he did know that had his identifiers not been correct, it would have been a prearranged signal alerting his control that he had been compromised and was being forced to transmit under duress.

The CIA case officer took a seat at the console, put on a headset, and flipped a switch, playing back the message.

> An American arrived at the camp yesterday. (Break) Tall and blond. Using the name Carlson. (Break) Joined by six probable Shining Path recruits who arrived early this A.M. (Break) The American is conducting special training in assaulting a motorcade. (Break) They

*are separate and apart from Anderson's guerrilla-training program.
(Break) I will follow up on their activities and further advise.
(Break) End transmission.*

The case officer removed the tape containing the recorded message from the console and placed it in his pocket. Within the hour he would send a flash cable to CIA headquarters, relaying Aztec's information to the head of the Agency's Counter Narcotics Center in response to a request received the previous day for any information on a man using the name Carlson, last seen in the company of a known terrorist in Cartagena two days before.

15

It was six-thirty in the evening at CIA's Langley headquarters, and Tony Covington's talented and dedicated staff of research analysts in the Counter Narcotics Center were again working overtime. The flash cable from the Lima station had given them an added impetus: they now knew where Carlson was and what he was doing, but still not who he was.

A thorough check of Intellofax—the CIA database in which the general files normally appear and for which thousands of Agency officers are cleared—had so far revealed nothing. At Covington's request, and in light of the serious nature of the investigation, the Deputy Director for Operations granted the CNC analysts limited access to his records division, specifically allowing them to run a name trace on Carlson through the huge computer database the clandestine services kept on all individuals suspected of having radical anti-American associations in this country and abroad. Again, the results were negative.

Granted further permission to expand their search to the next level, the analysts were now running a name-specific trace on Carlson through the Operations Directorate's tightly controlled and highly classified "soft" files, which officially did not exist—a measure taken to protect them from requests under the Freedom of Information Act or subpoena by Congress. In addition to details of covert operations these files contained personal information—friends, associates, lovers, habits, vices and outside interests—on case officers involved in those operations, and noted their principal agents, who were identified only by code names.

The exhaustive process was long and involved, as the analysts looked for any occurrence of the name Carlson in the numerous covert operations and investigations run by the Agency in the past twenty years, or for intersects under the broader headings of assassins, terrorists, drug traffickers, or rogue foreign agents.

Brian Kinsolving, a recent honors graduate from Stanford University, and the newest addition to the CNC staff, absorbed salient facts at an incredible rate as he scrolled through the file now on his computer screen. Using his own esoteric method of ferreting out information, he had decided to note any code name that appeared in more than one of the categories being searched. The recurring code name would then be used in his subsequent searches based on the supposition that an assassin—especially one who could command a fortune in payment for his services from the drug barons—would be no stranger to the intelligence community, and might even, at one time, have done contract work for them, and over the years had probably used a code name as well as an alias.

Kinsolving called up another file and continued to scan at a rapid pace. His eyes locked on a word halfway down the screen. There it was again: code name—*Viper.* According to his notes, the name had appeared in twelve previous synopses of operations for which he did not have the necessary clearance to access the entire file. Unlike the countless other files he had perused, the sanitized synopses for these twelve revealed none of the details of the operations, stating only where they were conducted, the dates they were activated and terminated, their security classifications and a coded index that was useless without the key and specific code word access for further information. All the operations had taken place in Southeast Asia between 1971 and 1975, and all had the highest security classification.

Going back over the notations he had made, Kinsolving noticed that the case officer in charge of the twelve operations was the same person, and his name was not given; in each case, under the heading of "control," he was identified only by a hyphenated eight-digit code number with the first four digits always remaining the same. Suspecting that the first four digits served to denote the case officer, and the second four to categorize the type of operation, Kinsolving entered the first four and made a global search, requesting information on any operations in which the man was involved. To his surprise, a three column single-spaced index came up on the screen, listing over seventy separate operations by their code names, all conducted in Southeast Asia beginning in 1961 and ending in 1977. Printed in bold letters opposite each entry in the index was: SPECIFIC CODE WORD ACCESS REQUIRED.

Kinsolving continued on, now interrogating the computer for any singular occurrences of Viper not linked to the code-designated case officer, but there were none. Viper did not appear in the files until 1971. He took part in twelve operations over the next five years, all in Southeast Asia and all for the same case officer, then vanished from the files without any further reference after 1975. On a gut instinct, Kinsolving tried entering the name Carlson along with Viper, asking for intersects, but found none. The time frame for all of Viper's operations was the same as that of the Vietnam war, and it occurred to Kinsolving that the war might be the reason for Viper's disappearance from the files; perhaps killed in the performance of his duties, or if he was an area-specific agent indigenous to Vietnam, his services may have been terminated when Saigon fell.

As he scribbled a series of notes on the information he had just retrieved, Kinsolving realized that the last four digits in the hyphenated code varied for all the mysterious case officer's operations, with the exception of those in which Viper was involved. Perhaps he was a specialist, conducting the same type of operation each time—and, of course, an assassin was a specialist. Whatever he was, Kinsolving decided, Viper was an anomaly, involved in more black operations than any single person he had run across in the files so far. And his control, an old Southeast Asia hand, had spent his entire career, it appeared, on the darker side of the Agency's operations. It also occurred to Kinsolving that he was the only case officer he had come across whose identity was protected by a code number—an unusual precaution considering that the files he was accessing were already highly classified, with access severely restricted.

Kinsolving didn't like anomalies, always considering them suspect in an otherwise orderly system. But as he found his mind going off on unsubstantiated tangents, and with nothing even remotely to tie the agent known as Viper to the man known as Carlson, he forced himself back on the original investigative track, making a mental note to throw Viper into the equation as he continued his search.

•

Interpol, the 146-member-nation International Criminal Police Organization, does not, as is commonly believed, maintain a force of international police officers. Instead it is an international information and intelligence service that gathers, processes, and disseminates data in support of a worldwide telecommunications network, addressing criminal activities that include international terrorism, illicit drugs, economic and financial fraud, the capture of international fugitives, and the tracing and recovery of stolen works of art. Each member country maintains its own sovereignty. Each has a Nation Central Bureau, working within the parameters of its own laws and policies, which serves as that country's point of contact with the international law enforcement community.

At 8:15 A.M., on a gray, drizzly fall morning at Interpol headquarters in the Parisian suburb of St. Cloud, Henri Ducret's research assistant brought him the cable that had just come in from the Vienna office in response to his inquiry of the previous day. It was the third reply he had received; the first, from Brussels, and the second, from Hong Kong, had come in as overnight cables. The initial request for assistance from the United States Secret Service Intelligence Division had received Ducret's immediate attention on seeing that the inquiry concerned known or suspected assassins.

The name of Roger Carlson and the limited physical description the Secret Service had provided were sent out to all member nations over Interpol's encrypted global satellite communications network, which connects the General Secretariat in St. Cloud with National Central Bureaus the world over. In response to the replies received, Ducret next interrogated Interpol's Files Accountability and Control System database. Available to agents and analysts twenty-four hours a day, the IFACS monitors and controls the inventory of cases and has the capability of tracking the movement of all files within the organization, providing their exact location and status (active or inactive) at any given moment.

The cables from Vienna, Brussels, and Hong Kong referred Ducret to three specific case files submitted to headquarters by their respective offices over the past thirteen years, cases that involved a man using the name Roger Carlson. Their common denominator dovetailed with the Secret Service's suspicions; each was a murder case, believed to be a contract assassination, and to have been committed by a lone gunman. All were unsolved. The information in the files was sketchy, but Ducret did a printout of the available facts and flagged it for immediate transmittal to the Secret Service Intelligence Division in Washington, D.C.—Attention: Susan Olsen, Presidential Protective Division Liaison.

16

Susan Olsen was having her morning coffee with Molly Arnold when Maguire entered the office to hear them laughing over a remark Molly had just made. His secretary held up something in her hand and said, "Tomorrow's the kid's birthday. Think he'll like it?"

"All right, I'll bite," Maguire said. "What is it?"

"A secret decoder ring," Molly said with a sly smile. "The top pops open and there's a hidden compartment. He can use it as a sort of archive to store copies of his most memorable speeches . . . or he could keep all of his military decorations in it."

"That's cold," Maguire said, knowing full well his secretary had no intention of giving the toy ring to the Vice President.

"It's the thought that counts," Molly replied.

"One of these days he might just walk past the office and hear you taking his name in vain."

"Yes, but the question is, will he understand what he heard?"

Maguire laughed. There was no winning with Molly, a lifelong ardent Democrat who made any and all Republicans a target for her jokes—with the exception of a handsome newcomer to the Senate from California. "I give him the benefit of the doubt," she had told Maguire, "because I'd like to jump his bones."

Maguire saw the impatient look on Susan Olsen's face, and the thick leather portfolio she held in her hand. With a nod of his head, he motioned her toward his office.

"We've got some more feedback on Carlson," she said, taking the chair opposite his desk. "CIA's located him in Peru. A druggies' jungle camp. He's apparently training six guerrillas in the fine art of assaulting a motorcade."

"Any details?" Maguire asked.

"Just that it's his third day there, and the recruits are probably Shining Path fanatics," Susan said. "My Agency liaison's promised to keep me informed with any updates as soon as they get them."

"Do you think they're holding back on us?"

"No. That wouldn't be in their best interest. And they can always be counted on to do what's in their best interest."

She extracted a page from a file in her portfolio and handed it to Maguire. "This came in overnight; it's what Interpol's got on Carlson."

The sheet of paper was similar to a standard flyer for a wanted criminal, but lacking information in almost every pertinent category. The small square in the upper lefthand corner where the criminal's photograph normally appeared was blank. The double row of five squares where the fingerprints were placed was also blank. ROGER CARLSON was entered in the space after NAME, but was followed with (BELIEVED TO BE AN ALIAS SUPPORTED WITH FALSE DOCUMENTATION). Under DESCRIPTION was simply: Approx. Height —6'0". Approx. Weight—165. Hair Color—Blond. Eyes—Blue or Gray. A SUMMARY OF KNOWN FACTS listed the reference numbers for three separate cases from Brussels, Vienna, and Hong Kong, adding that the suspect was wanted for questioning in all three cases, and that extradition was requested by any country having an extradition treaty with the three countries where the cases originated.

Susan began reading from the annotated memorandum she had prepared from the case files. "The Brussels case involved the murder of a British colonel in August of 1978. He was attached to

NATO, and at the time was under investigation by British Intelligence for leaking secrets to the East Germans. The Brits were just about to confront him with it when he was killed. Interpol believes the contract may have been put out by the Stasi, the East German secret police, to cover their flanks when they learned that the colonel was going to be exposed."

"How was he killed?"

"Two shots in the back of the head with a silencer-equipped .380-caliber handgun," Susan said. "Approximate time of the murder was one-thirty in the morning . . . on a side street off the Grand Place Square. A couple of Italian college students on vacation caught a glimpse of the killer getting in a car and driving away."

"What tied Carlson to it?"

"The witnesses got a partial plate on the vehicle and the Brussels police traced it to a rental agency who had rented it to a man using an international driver's license under the name of Roger Carlson.

"Hong Kong in September of 1982 looks like another contract hit," she continued. "The murdered man was a Tokyo investment banker on the run from Japanese authorities. He was wanted on embezzlement charges, but he was apparently only a small fry; his real value to them was his ability to bring down some real heavy hitters involved in a lot of shady dealings with millions in government money. They found his body in the harbor. The only witness was an old woman, a sampan dweller, who gave a partial description of a man she saw talking with the victim on the waterfront; basically the same description the Italians gave."

"Same M.O. for the murder?"

"Exactly," Susan said. "And Interpol made a ballistics match with the bullets from the Brussels killing four years earlier, which tied Carlson to it."

Maguire frowned and stared across the room, then opened a desk drawer and removed a file. Paging through it, he found what he was looking for stapled to the initial report on the drug barons' meeting on St. Barts.

"Contact the St. Barts police and ask for a ballistics report on the bullets that killed the woman on the sailboat . . . Maria Padron."

"You think they might match the ones from Brussels and Hong Kong?"

"It wouldn't surprise me."

"I doubt the St. Barts cops have a ballistics lab."

"Then ask Interpol to intercede on the premise that it's tied in to their cases," Maguire said, putting the file away. "What about the Vienna case?"

"Variation on a theme," Susan said. "Proves our man isn't limited to the 'up close and personal' approach. This time the target was a West German cabinet minister visiting Vienna for a conference in April of 1988. The weapon was a sniper rifle . . . seven millimeter Magnum. Killed as he came out of his hotel with his mistress. Night illumination shot from a distance in excess of nine hundred yards. Not bad," she said, raising an eyebrow at Maguire. "I'd say our man Carlson had some expert training somewhere."

"Since he's believed to be an American," Maguire said, "it might be worthwhile asking our DIA liaison for some help in checking out the military sniper schools—once we can give him some solid parameters to narrow down the search."

"Here's something you might find interesting," Susan said, after scribbling a note regarding the DIA liaison. "Carlson's not a completely inhuman mechanic, at least not so completely that he doesn't succumb to weaknesses of the flesh. The manager of the apartment building where the shot came from never saw him in the daylight, so consequently he didn't get a good look at him. And the apartment Carlson used was rented for him by someone else a week earlier, but the manager did see a lady of the evening leaving the place the night before the shooting. The police tracked her down and she gave them the name of Carlson, along with a description and the unsolicited comments that he was a gentle lover, nothing kinky, and a big tipper."

"Any reason given for why the West German was a target?"

"They suspect the Red Army Faction terrorist organization was behind the contract, but they have no idea why."

"Any other cases?"

"No. Three assassinations in the last thirteen years, that's it."

"Three that Interpol knows of," Maguire said, pointedly. "And you can bet Carlson isn't the only alias he uses. I'm going to brief the deputy chief of staff on what we've got. I think it's time he knows we have a potentially serious problem on our hands."

"I'll leave my notes and the Interpol files for you," Susan said. Rising to leave, she asked, "Are you going to increase security for the President?"

"Not yet," Maguire said, "but everything that's been relaxed at the Chief of Staff's request is going to be brought back up to regulation procedures."

Pausing as she stepped out into the hallway, Susan said, "If you need me for background when you brief the DCS, just give me a shout."

Maguire waved a farewell as she turned and continued down the hallway toward the outer office. The mention of the West German terrorist organization, Red Army Faction, had given him an idea, and in his personal address book, he found the telephone number for Jack Gannon's office at Delta Force headquarters.

The relationship between Maguire and Gannon went back fourteen years, to the founding of Delta Force. Initially underfunded and undermanned, the fledgling counterterrorist force sought help wherever they could get it, and the Secret Service was both a willing and able source. At the time, Maguire was head of the Uniform Forces and Firearms branch of the service's training division, located at their training camp in Beltsville, Maryland. Gannon and the Delta Force commanding officer had asked for help in training their shooters, and Maguire had provided use of the facility at Beltsville, and instructors with the required expertise from the service's world-renowned countersniper program. They had trained the Delta troopers in sniper tactics and long-range shooting, and had put them through their "Attack on the Principal" course—highly specialized training in responding quickly and forcefully to an attack on a protected subject. During the intervening years the arrangement between the two elite units had come full circle, the student becoming the teacher: Secret Service Counter Assault Teams were now trained at the Ranch by Delta personnel.

Since becoming Special Agent in Charge of the Presidential Protective Division, Maguire had worked with Gannon on numerous occasions when the President's travel took him outside the country. With Delta's primary mission responsibility being overseas, where Secret Service had a limited capability and its least effective support, Delta was often called in to stand by, ready to deploy, in the event of a terrorist threat to the President. With their respective professions demanding most of their waking hours, the two men seldom had the time to get together socially, but their personal friendship had managed to endure and grow over the years.

Maguire inserted a small plastic key into the side of what appeared at first glance to be a standard office phone, picked up the handset of the STU-3 secure telephone system, and dialed the number at the Ranch.

•

Gannon was in the Operations and Intelligence Section, sitting in Lou Burruss's Lantcom office. The young analyst had just gotten off the phone with his contact at CIA's Caribbean desk.

"Not much, boss," he told Gannon. "Over breakfast in the cafeteria, she managed to pry a few words out of a friend who works in the Counter Narcotics Center. Seems they've been tracking some guy . . . something to do with the drug honchos' meeting on St. Barts, that's all she could get. But if you factor in a request I got from a CNC analyst just after I got in this morning, things get pretty interesting."

"What did they want?"

"They asked me to dump them all we've got on that combination drug processing and terrorist-training camp we've been keeping an eye on in Peru . . . up in the northwest corner." Burruss flashed a silly grin. "Think it could be a coincidence, boss? Somehow I doubt it."

As Burruss finished speaking, Gannon's beeper sounded. Unclasping the device from his belt, he glanced at the readout, not recognizing the number of the caller. "Mind if I use your phone?"

"It's all yours. Need some privacy?"

Gannon shook his head as he dialed the number on the secure

telephone. At the sound of Maguire's voice, he smiled for the first time in days.

"What are you up to, Mike?"

"About six two," Maguire said, "but I don't think I'm going to get any taller."

"Your jokes are getting as old as you are," Gannon said. "What can I do for you?"

"I'm working a threat case, and something just turned up that made me think you might have this guy in your files."

"Run it by me."

"Are you on secure voice?" Maguire asked.

Gannon reached down and turned the small plastic key at the side of the telephone and depressed the SECURE button on the front panel. The readout window above the button immediately flashed SECRET, then displayed the number from which Maguire was calling. "I am now," Gannon told him.

"The name is Roger Carlson." Maguire then spelled the last name. "It's an alias backed with phony Canadian documents. Can you run a name check and see if he turns up in your files? He might have a tie-in to the Red Army Faction."

"Wait one," Gannon told him. Turning to Burruss, he said, "Run a check on a Roger Carlson, possible Red Army Faction connection." Burruss typed in the access code for the proper database, then entered the name into his computer and waited as it began to search the files.

"Anything else you can give me on him?"

"Sketchy stuff. Six foot, one sixty-five, blond hair, blue or gray eyes."

"You're right, it's sketchy."

"Got another wrinkle your Caribbean area specialist might be able to help with."

"I'm in the Lantcom office now; he's the man running the name search."

"Has he picked up anything on a high-level drug cartel meeting in St. Barts four days ago . . . and the murder of a woman on board a sailboat?"

There was a long silence on Gannon's end.

"Jack, you there?"

"Yeah. I'm here. What's the nature of the threat case?"

"From what we've got so far, Carlson's been hired by the drug barons to assassinate the President. He's been tracked to a jungle camp in Peru, where he's training a team to take out a motorcade. This guy's for real, Jack, Interpol came back with information that tags him as a top pro operating on an international scale. They have ballistics on two of his previous hits. The same type weapon was used on the girl on the boat; our intelligence division's in the process of finding out if the slugs they took from her match up with what Interpol's already got."

There was another long pause, then Gannon said, "Do you remember the girl I told you about that helped me get Kate's killer?"

"Sure, you told me about her after you got back from France. She was a friend of your SEAL buddy, Boos. You said she was a real trouper. . . . I don't remember her name, why?"

"Her name was Maria Padron and she was murdered on St. Barts four days ago. I'm trying to find the son of a bitch who did it."

This time the silence was on the other end of the line. When Maguire finally spoke all he said was "Jesus H. Christ!"

"Yeah. Get the sudden feeling we're after one and the same person? And his name isn't Carlson."

"You've got his real name?"

"I've got a dead man's name."

"Want to run that by me again?"

"I'll be in D.C. tomorrow," Gannon told him. "If my hunch is right, I'll have facts for you and not supposition."

"What time will you be here?"

"I have a meeting in Georgetown at twelve-thirty with someone I hope will tie this all together. I can be at your office by two."

"I'll be waiting."

-17-

Power in the Pentagon flows from Room 880, on the third floor E Ring between corridors eight and nine, where the main office of the Secretary of Defense is located. One floor below, in a high-security area behind a cipher-locked door with the routing symbol DIA/PW/MIA, is the Defense Intelligence Agency's Special Office for Prisoners of War and Missing in Action.

Run by an army colonel and staffed with thirty-eight civilian and military personnel, most of whom are fluent in various Southeast Asian languages, the office is the central repository for all POW/MIA files—currently numbering 2,393 men still unaccounted for since the end of the Vietnam War.

Retired Army Special Forces master sergeant Nicholas Delvecchio had spent the past sixteen years of his life dealing with the issue of the missing American servicemen. After the fall of Saigon, he had worked with the Joint Casualty Resolution Center in Bangkok, Thailand, until retiring from the army and accepting the position offered by DIA's POW/MIA office. It was more than a job to him, more than simply going through the motions; he cared deeply about the issue, personally knowing two of those still missing in action, and hoped to contribute in some small way to their return, or to finding final resolutions that would put their families' minds at peace.

Delvecchio had felt betrayed when the Carter administration found it politically expedient to reclassify 1,293 of the 2,393 men from Missing in Action status to Killed in Action, Body Not Recoverable. It was an action that relegated the office to negotiating only for their remains with the Vietnamese government or investigating jungle crash sites long ago picked clean by battlefield ghouls and local scavengers, rather than demanding an accounting for them as POWs or MIAs. He believed it all came down to money, the budget-cutting politicians again looking for anyplace to cut costs where the fewest constituents would be affected. The families were easy and tempting targets, receiving the full pay and military benefits of the men still missing in action—housing allotments, PX privileges, medical care, educational benefits, combat pay and flight pay for men who despite their status as MIAs were promoted along with their contemporaries. The pay and benefits often ran as high as seventy thousand tax-free dollars a year, and in some cases fostered abuses of the system—wives who no longer believed, or cared, that their husbands were still alive, had been living with lovers for ten or more years, not officially divorcing, to avoid losing the money and benefits. But Delvecchio considered the government's action a sellout of the hundreds of families who still held hope, no matter how remote, that their loved ones were still alive and might someday be returned to them.

The call he had received at his apartment in Alexandria last evening from Jack Gannon had kept him awake most of the night. Gannon was a longtime friend; they had served together in combat for two years, before Delvecchio was wounded for the fourth time and transferred to a desk job at SOG headquarters in the Cholon section of Saigon. There wasn't much he wouldn't do for Gannon, crediting him with saving his life on his last mission, deep inside North Vietnam, when he had carried him through the jungle for two days, until what was left of their reconnaissance team was finally rescued. But what Gannon had asked of him was in direct violation of office procedures, not to mention a flagrant breach of security regulations. Giving him a printout of the information that was in the computer data bank was one thing; going back into the locked files, taking the actual hard copy documentation, the supporting evidence, and physically removing it from the office, was quite another.

At work that morning, Delvecchio had gone about his daily routine while wrestling with a conflict of emotions. When he finally made his decision, it was because he trusted Gannon implicitly and knew he would not have asked if it weren't vitally important. Just before leaving for lunch, a meal he usually took at a Pentagon cafeteria with some of his coworkers, he told his immediate superior that he needed a few hours of personal time, a request that was granted without question. At eleven forty-five, he drove out of the Pentagon parking lot and headed north on the Jefferson Davis Highway toward the Theodore Roosevelt Memorial Bridge, his briefcase, containing the file, on the seat beside him.

●

Little can be discerned about the makeup and function of a presidential motorcade, beyond the obvious purpose of transportation, as it moves along streets crowded with curious onlookers at speeds averaging forty miles per hour. Unknown to the casual observer, the motorcade is an intricately detailed, highly secure, cohesive unit of expertly trained men concerned with only one thing: the safety of the President of the United States.

The procession of cars, vans, and limousines is led by the pilot car, containing a local police officer and one Secret Service agent. Traveling one-half mile ahead of the motorcade, it serves to check the route in advance, alerting the fixed post uniform police officers that the motorcade is en route, and making certain all intersections along the way are effectively blocked. Next in line is the lead car, which functions as a mobile command post, and again has one local police officer and one Secret Service agent on board. Behind the lead car is the spare limousine, which is occupied by two Secret Service agents (one an agent supervisor); its function is to act as a diversion, obscuring from the public which limousine the President is traveling in, and to take the place of the presidential limousine in the event of a breakdown. Immediately behind the President's limousine is the follow-up vehicle, a van, code-named *Halfback*. Carrying five heavily armed agents, one a gunman in the well, *Halfback*'s role is to protect the rear and each side of the presidential limousine from attack.

Following *Halfback* is the control car, driven by a Secret Service agent and containing members of the President's staff, his military aide with the "football," and a doctor. The control car's assignment is to stay with the presidential limousine in the event of an emergency evacuation of the area. Directly behind the control car is the van carrying the deadly Counter Assault Team (CAT). The five agents inside the van, armed with assault rifles and shotguns, are tasked with working the inner perimeter, responding as a tactical unit to provide immediate and concentrated firepower should anyone attack the motorcade. In the event of such an assault, the President's limousine and *Halfback* instantly evacuate the area, while the CAT team breaks from the motorcade and lays down suppressive fire against the attackers, covering the President's limousine as it makes good its escape.

The remainder of the vehicles are made up of additional staff and press cars, with two notable exceptions. The Intelligence Division car carries two agents whose responsibilities are to receive and act on intelligence updates radioed from W-16, the Secret Service command post in the White House. Any threat-type information W-16 receives from police officers at intersections and along the route of travel, or from agents on the ground at the arrival site, is immediately passed on to the working shift supervisor in the spare limousine and an appropriate response is taken. The last car in a motorcade that usually numbers thirteen to fifteen vehicles—depending on the press cars allotted—is the White House Communications Agency (WHCA) vehicle, code-named *Roadrunner*. Its function is to provide immediate communications capability, directly from the vehicle, between the President and anywhere in the world, through a secure satellite communications system.

In deference to the wishes of the Chief Executive, who had come to be known as the "jumping jack" President for his spur-of-the-moment decisions to travel about the city, the full motorcade and the elaborate precautions taken along the route for "un-scheduled movements" were dispensed with under the reasoning that any travel not announced to the press or public presented little danger to the President's personal safety. The decision elimi-nated the involvement of the D.C. police in such unscheduled movements, and limited the motorcade to what is known as the "Secure Package"—the six vehicles from the lead car to the Counter Assault Team van.

"You don't have to survey all the local streets or secure the entire route by blocking intersections, or put your men on roof-tops if no one knows where the President is going next," the deputy chief of staff had argued with Maguire. "Nobody ever goes to their local Sears store or an out-of-the-way Chinese restaurant on the off chance that the President of the United States is going to be there."

Maguire had reluctantly accepted and made the best of a situa-tion that he could, in the reality of White House politics, do noth-ing to change with continued argument. But two hours ago, upon being informed of the President's desire to go to Fort McNair to jog later that morning, he made the unilateral decision to suspend the relaxed security procedures. After calling the D.C. police Spe-cial Operations Division and requesting a police cruiser as a pilot car, and enough personnel for full intersection control along the entire route, he assigned the working shift supervisor to take the lead car, choosing to ride in the limousine with the President and his Chief of Staff himself. In addition, he sent an advance team and a countersniper team to secure the immediate area of the parade ground at Fort McNair and the track around it where the President liked to run. Dressed in a jogging suit, as was the President, Maguire rode in the front passenger seat alongside the Secret Service agent driver, his automatic pistol concealed in a shoulder holster beneath his jacket, and an Uzi submachine gun secured in a quick-release clamp beneath the dash.

As the motorcade moved along at a faster than usual pace, the President looked up from a position paper his Chief of Staff had just handed him. Glancing out the window as they sped past an intersection, he noticed that the traffic was backed up as far as he could see. The full intersection control by uniform police on motorcycles along the route was not the first change the President had noticed. Upon leaving the White House, he had seen the flags on the fenders of the spare limousine, when ordinarily they were affixed only to his car, a subtle indicator, but one that along with Maguire's presence suggested that the low-profile movement he had become accustomed to while traveling around the city had been quietly upgraded to heightened security measures.

The glass divider in the limousine was down, and looking at the chief of his protective division, he asked, "Any particular reason for the special attention I've been getting lately, Mike?"

"We have a threat case that's got us a little worried, Mr. President," he said, noticing the disapproving gaze he was getting from the Chief of Staff. "It's nothing to be overly concerned about at this point, but we're going to be working you more closely than usual. At times it might seem that we're in your back pocket, sir, but I believe the situation merits additional security precautions."

"Why wasn't I informed of this?" the Chief of Staff asked, giving Maguire a stern look.

"I briefed the deputy chief of staff yesterday afternoon, sir," Maguire said. "He has a complete workup on what we've got so far."

"First I've heard of it," the Chief of Staff said, scribbling a note to himself that Maguire knew would eventually come back to haunt him as a reprimand for breaking the chain of command. But his comments had been in direct response to a question from the President, leaving him on safe, if somewhat shaky, ground, as he had planned. The question of unilaterally beefing up security for the unscheduled movement was another matter altogether, but one he knew he could justify if pressed.

"I'd appreciate it, Mr. President, if for the time being you would wear your body armor every day," he added for good measure, feeling the icy daggers coming from the Chief of Staff, without looking in his direction.

●

Existing on coffee and sandwiches from the cafeteria, Brian Kinsolving had been working on the search to identify Carlson for the better part of three days. He had stayed at his office at CIA's

Counter Narcotics Center until well after midnight, going home to his bachelor apartment only to feed his cat, Bunky, and grab a few hours of sleep before returning to work at five o'clock in the morning. He was getting nowhere with his current approach, and decided to try a different tack and not rely completely on an in-house search.

All intelligence agencies have extensive files to keep track of the agents of allied and opposing services. Their archives contain hundreds of thousands of photographs of known and suspected foreign agents, diplomats, members of trade and cultural delegations, and apolitical paramilitary contract types, including assassins, who work for anyone with the money to pay them. The photographs are exchanged and shared within the intelligence community and are a great help in identifying agents who assume different cover identities and occupations as they move from country to country. There are few, if any, professional intelligence agents who do not eventually end up in the files of at least one or more countries. Kinsolving cabled requests to friendly intelligence agencies in Great Britain, Scandinavia, and Western Europe, asking for any file photographs that matched up with the name Roger Carlson, but so far, the responses received were all negative.

He was running out of ideas when Tony Covington succeeded in convincing CIA's Deputy Director for Operations to allow Kinsolving alone to access the most classified of all the Operations Directorate's files: those stored under the heading of Special Operations.

SO files, with their own computer system and separate databases, required specific code word access allowed only to a select few in the Agency. Kinsolving's access was granted primarily because of the way he was tailoring his search to encompass just the inactive files. He wanted to see only those Special Operations files between the years 1971 and 1975; the mysterious case officer identified only by a coded number, and his agent, Viper, still intrigued him, tugging at his mind since they had first cropped up. Carlson's current profession, his ease of moving around under assumed names, and his familiarity with weapons, suggested by the report from the agent in the Peruvian jungle camp, drew Kinsolving to the conclusion that the man had to have some background in clandestine operations, either paramilitary or military. His tentative identification as an American, and his age further suggested that he could have gained that highly specialized knowledge and training in Vietnam and that the answer might be found in the Vietnam era Special Operations files.

After entering "Carlson" and using a correlation search mode, he looked for intersects with Viper or the code numbered case officer. Finding none, he accessed a subdirectory that had caught his attention; it contained files relating to CIA's involvement with the Phoenix Program, Controlled American Sources (CAS) in Laos, and the Military Assistance Command's Special Operations Group (SOG)—all having conducted covert operations during the Vietnam war. Within two minutes of interrogating the subdirectory, his intuition paid off.

Entering the first four digits of the case officer's code number, he found the screen filled with a lengthy index of operations he had conducted under the auspices of Phoenix, CAS, and SOG. Entering his agent, Viper, brought up another screen, indexing a list of fifteen separate operations in which they were involved together. The last operation listed in the index made the hair on the back of Kinsolving's neck stand up. It had taken place in May of 1975, and was run out of CIA's Bangkok station. Where all the other operations listed still maintained the code number to identify the case officer, this one did not. The entry read: OPERATION MAGIC WAND. CONTROL: P. T. Martindale. PRINCIPAL AGENT: R. E. Carlson (Viper). EXECUTIVE ACTION. It was the last two words that made Kinsolving realize he had finally nailed down his man.

"Got the bastard!" he shouted almost involuntarily. "I got him!"

In response to the outburst, heads popped up above the partitions dividing the office cubicles around the bullpen work area. Kinsolving rapidly typed in other requests that revealed ancillary information, peeling away the layers of mystery surrounding Martindale and his highly specialized agent. But the available information stopped short of revealing R. E. Carlson's true identity, a situation that caused Kinsolving little concern—with the name of his longtime controlling case officer in hand, someone who personally knew Carlson and his true identity, the search was over.

An inquisitive impulse to look for the contents of Viper-related files, or at least a synopsis of their contents, only served to strengthen Kinsolving's conviction that the Carlson he was searching for and the Carlson he found were one and the same person. Typed in bold letters after each of the files in the subdirectory index was the notification: SUPPORTING DATA DELETED DURING ROUTINE PURGING OF FILES. The acknowledgment that the operations had existed was still in the database, along with the principals involved in them, but the details and the purposes they had served were gone, removed for reasons Kinsolving could only guess at, and knew would never be revealed to him, if indeed there was still anyone around who had the answers.

Tony Covington came out of his glassed-in private office at the far end of the bullpen area and went to the young analyst's cubicle. "What have you got?"

Kinsolving consulted his notes and went over his findings with his boss, carefully detailing with pride the steps he had taken to uncover the information.

"Good work," Covington said.

"I thought I'd ask personnel to locate Martindale," Kinsolving said. "Set up a meeting with him."

"First, let's take a look at his file," Covington said, escorting the young analyst back to his office, where he checked the in-house telephone directory and dialed the number for the Personnel Office. Martindale's personal and professional history was hand delivered to Covington thirty minutes later.

The file was in a thick brown folder, with metal clips on the top so that the pages flipped up. Stamped across the front of the file in bold red letters was: INACTIVE.

"Looks like he's no longer with us," Covington said as he scanned the pages that were in reverse chronological order, with the most recent entries first. "And now I know why," he added as he paused to read at length a particular entry.

"He's dead?" Kinsolving said, stiffening at the disheartening thought that had not occurred to him in the excitement of ferreting out his quarry.

"No. He's still alive. Living in Fairfax as of six months ago, according to the most recent update. Forcibly retired in October 1977.''

"Is the reason for dismissal given?"

"Oh, yes," Covington said with a grimace. He had been with the Agency long enough to have been around when Stansfield Turner, then President Carter's newly appointed CIA Director, had convinced the President that the covert operations side of the Agency was bloated and out of control, prompting an ill-advised decision that ultimately resulted in the decimation of the Directorate of Operations. It was an incident that had demoralized Covington, then new to the CIA and assigned to Operations, almost to the point of resigning from CIA himself.

"He left for the same reason about eight hundred other people left in one hell of a hurry," Covington said, "all of them from the Directorate of Operations. It happened in October of 1977 and came to be known as Carter's Halloween Massacre."

Kinsolving remembered hearing about the mass dismissals, but knew nothing of the motivation behind them. "I'm somewhat familiar with the term 'executive action,' " he told Covington, after glancing at his notes. "At least I remember reading about it. A small high-level group who planned and carried out assassinations with official sanction, wasn't it?"

Covington nodded. "Long since shut down," he said. "Though there are still some who insist the Agency should maintain the option."

Again consulting his notes, he said, "Martindale's dismissal explains why Viper and subsequently Carlson disappeared from the files after 1977."

"That's probably when he began his free-lancing career," Covington said. "Guys who've been in black operations that long, and that heavy, don't just hang it up and go home and sell insurance."

"One thing I don't understand," Kinsolving said. "In all of the files I accessed, Martindale's and Carlson's identities were concealed with codes, with the exception of the last entry in the Special Operations files. Why?"

"I can only guess at the answer," Covington said, "but it's an educated guess. The war was over, Martindale wanted to continue to use him, so he sheep-dipped him."

"I'm not familiar with the term."

"It means taking an agent, or a prospective agent, abolishing any evidence of his present and past life, and giving him an entirely different identity, backstopped with all the necessary documentation to hold up under close scrutiny," Covington said. "Whoever Carlson was when he was using the code name Viper, he officially wasn't that person any longer. Having accomplished that, Martindale didn't have to use a code name for him; and he probably created other backstopped cover identities for him as well, if he planned on operating him for a long period of time."

"Who else would know Carlson's real identity?" Kinsolving asked.

"There's a good possibility no one else does, if he was an agent that Martindale recruited and ran himself."

"Someone at the Saigon station must have known about him?"

"Not necessarily. Saigon was the largest station we had at the time. It was like one of those Russian metrushka dolls that tourists buy; a doll within a doll, within a doll. Everything was so highly compartmentalized that no one had the complete picture at any given time. Most case officers had their own in-country agent networks, and if they were getting results, no one asked questions. Most of the time their superiors didn't want to know—which was one way of covering your ass, especially late in the war when anyone with half a brain could see the handwriting on the wall."

"So Martindale could be the only one with the answers?"

"It looks that way."

"Where do we go from here?"

"We don't," Covington said. "We turn it over to Secret Service Intelligence Division."

"Then we're out of it?"

Covington nodded. "Which is precisely where we want to be."

"I don't understand."

"You're aware that the man you've been looking for is an assassin?"

"Of course, that's why we were after him."

"A top-notch assassin, who according to everything you've uncovered, has a great deal of experience, a considerable amount of which, it appears, was gained with the Agency."

Kinsolving still wasn't following his boss's logic. After all of his hard work, he was feeling cheated by not being allowed in on the kill. "We're in a better position to see this through than the Secret Service is."

"And if Carlson somehow manages to elude us all and carry out his contract . . . and kills the President of the United States?"

Kinsolving saw the light. "He was our man at one time, and it was our investigation."

"Right," Covington said. "It's not in our charter anyway, and there are no percentages in putting our heads on the block when it's someone else's area of responsibility. We've done our part, let them take over."

"How much do I give them?"

"The bare essentials. Martindale's name and current address with the information that we have reason to believe he once ran an agent by the name of Carlson, code-named Viper, and the time frame. That's it."

"What if Martindale refuses to talk to them?"

"He's more likely to cooperate with them than with us," Covington said. "According to the psychological profile done at the time of his dismissal, he's a bitter man."

"And if the Secret Service people ask for further information?"

"You tell them there isn't any more," Covington said pointedly. "Because by the end of the day, after I've briefed the Deputy Director for Operations on what you've uncovered, I guarantee you that the files you accessed will no longer exist, so you won't be lying."

-18-

Old brick walls, a timbered ceiling, and hanging plants created a cozy setting in the trendy Georgetown restaurant near the corner of Thirtieth and M streets. A bittersweet memory made Gannon smile as he recalled how his wife had categorized similar places: "long on atmosphere and short on service and good food."

He took a corner table at the back of the room, opposite the door to the kitchen. The ambient noise level was sufficient to obscure a normal conversation, and with his back to the wall, he had an overall view of the other tables.

Nick Delvecchio entered promptly at twelve-thirty, a troubled look on his face until he spotted Gannon in the corner. As he reached the table, Gannon stood and the two men embraced with genuine affection.

"Good to see you, Nick."

"It's good to see you, too. I think."

Gannon got the attention of the waitress and ordered them both a draft ale after she finished reciting the day's luncheon specials. With a nod of approval from Delvecchio, he added a pasta dish that sounded fast and simple.

Delvecchio scanned the nearby tables, filled with young, well-dressed professionals. "How'd you find this place?" he asked. "We stand out like a couple of sequoia trees in Death Valley with all the yuppies in here."

"An Agency guy brought me here once, when they were trying to recruit me."

"Figures; they'd fit right in," Delvecchio said, taking a nervous glance around the restaurant, his briefcase clutched securely in his lap. "We've got history, Jack. That's the only reason I'm doing this."

"Nick, relax," Gannon said calmly. "No one knows I contacted you, and no one will."

"You're not going to go public with anything we discuss?" he said. "Because if you do, it'll come right back to the office; they'll know there's nowhere else it could have come from. And I really like my job."

"I wouldn't do that to you."

Delvecchio nodded an apology. "Sorry. You know what a stickler for regulations I've always been. Hell, I don't even cross against the light."

"One of the reasons you were so damn good at running recon," Gannon said. "You knew your stuff cold and never took unnecessary chances."

"What's so special about this Sincavage?" he asked as he popped the latches on his briefcase and removed a large manila envelope after another apprehensive glance around the room.

"Are you familiar with the contents of the file?"

"Hell, no, I haven't even opened it. You're not going to ask me to leave any of this with you?"

"No." Gannon reached for the envelope and Delvecchio hesitantly handed it across the table. "I just want to see the documentation that supports the finding of Missing in Action."

"He's now carried as Killed in Action, Body Not Recoverable," Delvecchio corrected. "Which means we're no longer looking for him."

Gannon undid the clasp on the envelope and removed a file

folder that opened like a book, with brass paper fasteners holding an inch-thick stack of official reports in place. The document on top was a Report of Casualty, declassified from Secret to Confidential at the end of the war. The one-page form listed Sincavage's name, rank, serial number, and unit, followed by a two-sentence explanation of his last mission: *Missing since 14 July 1971. Last seen on top-secret reconnaissance operation under hostile fire.* The rest of the form contained sections meant to be filled in with biographical data. In Sincavage's case, the information was sketchy to the point of being useless. Under a section titled "Interested Persons" (to be notified), there were no entries.

The next document was the finding of a board of officers convened at Special Operations Group headquarters shortly after Sincavage's disappearance, to hear the evidence and confirm the Missing in Action report. Attached to the document were copies of the debriefings of the men who had participated in the rescue effort to find Sincavage and his reconnaissance team. Jocabetti's statement was there and Gannon noticed that it was essentially the same information he had given him at the VA hospital. Next was a disposition form regarding a series of agent reports verifying that Sincavage and his team had been overrun by the enemy and their bodies could not be found. A copy of a memorandum from a DIA Missing in Action board hearing showed that in light of information received from the Army's Central Identification Laboratory in Hawaii in 1977, Sincavage's MIA status had been reviewed and changed to Killed in Action, Body Not Recoverable.

It was the report from the Central Identification Laboratory in Hawaii (CIL-HI) that caused Gannon to stare in disbelief. "This is the kind of stuff you accept as evidence?" he asked Delvecchio, handing the folder back to him so he could read the report.

Delvecchio scanned the document labeled CIL-HI Case Number 0104-77. The contents, or lack of them, held no surprises for him. He had seen the same thing on numerous occasions. The Central Identification Laboratory, moved from Thailand to Honolulu in 1976, was the army's forensic laboratory where the remains of American servicemen missing in action were sent for identification. The laboratory's record of shoddy work, fabricated lab data, altered reports, and positive identifications based on procedures and conclusions that were scientifically unsupportable was well known to the staff of the POW/MIA office, and on more than one occasion had proved an embarrassment to them.

"This is typical," Delvecchio said, handing the folder back to Gannon. "Last year the families of three MIA's whose remains were positively identified by CIL had them exhumed and examined by independent forensic pathologists. They turned out to be small animal bones."

"It says here that the remains used to identify Jerry Sincavage were eleven bone shards and a small skull fragment," Gannon said. "None larger than two or three inches."

"They've done it with less," Delvecchio said.

"I can't believe anyone accepts this nonsense as conclusive proof."

"There aren't very many who give a damn anymore," Delvecchio said. "The name of the game now is clear the books."

"Who makes the final decision to accept the lab's evidence?"

"CIL sends their findings and their recommendations to the Armed Forces Grave Registration Office here in Washington, where a board decides if a positive identification has been made. They've never repudiated a CIL lab recommendation."

Gannon saw a note typed at the bottom of the report that referred to "further irrefutable evidence enclosed," but no mention of what that evidence was. As he paged through the remaining documents, he felt a small object taped to the inside of the back cover. Turning to the last page, he peeled off the tape that held the object in place, and unwrapped the tissue paper surrounding it.

"So this is their irrefutable evidence," he said, and held up a small pendant suspended from a gold chain. "Talk about gilding the lily."

One and one-half inches in length and three-quarters of an inch high, the small eighteen-karat gold pendant was familiar to both men. It was cast in the shape of the unofficial emblem of the Special Operations Group—a skull, with a dagger through it, and paratrooper wings on either side. It was usually inscribed on the back with the wearer's name and his reconnaissance team, and was worn as a statement of pride in their unit, and in place of dog tags, which were forbidden on "over the fence" top-secret reconnaissance missions.

Gannon turned it over and read the inscription aloud. "J. Sincavage—RT Viper."

"Is there anything in the file about the chain of evidentiary custody?" Delvecchio asked, as taken aback by the inclusion of the pendant as Gannon was.

Gannon flipped back through the file and read over the supplementary information from the Central Identification Laboratory. He found what he was looking for at the bottom of the page.

"The remains and the pendant were turned over to a member of the Joint Casualty Resolution Center in Thailand by a consular affairs officer from the embassy in Bangkok. He claims to have gotten them from a refugee at a camp on the Thai/Cambodian border . . . near Ban Sa-Ngai, while interviewing a Vietnamese man and his wife concerning their immigration status. The wife said she found a shallow grave with the remains of four bodies in it while clearing jungle at a reeducation camp along the Vietnam/ Laotian border, where she and her husband were imprisoned." Gannon slowly shook his head. "Consular affairs officer, my ass. The fine hand of the Agency's all over this."

"It wouldn't be the first time," Delvecchio said.

"There's no way in hell that pendant would have been buried with Sincavage's body. It's worth at least eight hundred dollars; I know, I had one made for myself," Gannon said. "The NVA and the VC were known to smash the teeth out of the skulls of the Americans they killed, just for the small amount of gold in their fillings. And we're supposed to believe they tossed Sincavage's body in a grave with an eight hundred dollar gold pendant and chain around his neck."

"So you think the CIA planted the pendant and the remains with the Joint Casualty Resolution people in Bangkok, then put the fix in at the Central Identification Laboratory?" Delvecchio said.

"Who else has that kind of clout?"

"They must have had a good reason."

"They always do . . . at least one that makes sense to them."

"What got you on to Sincavage in the first place?"

Gannon shook his head. "You don't want to know, Nick."

"You're probably right," Delvecchio said. "That's it, then. You don't need anything else?"

"Nothing. You've been a great help."

"You think Sincavage is still alive and working for the Agency?"

"I sure as hell hope that's not who he's working for," Gannon said. "But I've never known them to go to this kind of trouble unless it was for one of their own."

Again the haunting memory swept across Gannon's mind, causing him to look away and force the unwanted images from his conscious thoughts—images of an evening twenty-two years ago when both he and Sincavage were operating out of the Special Operations Group Command and Control North compound at Da Nang.

Delvecchio noticed the abrupt change in his friend's mood. "This isn't just a professional inquiry, is it, Jack? It's personal."

"Very personal."

●

The distant snap of a small branch underfoot alerted Sincavage to the man's presence. Farther along the jungle trail that led from the camp to the airstrip, he caught a fleeting glimpse of a shadowy human shape in the pale-green light of the thick underbrush. The man continued to follow him on a parallel course to where the plane had been pulled off the end of the grassy runway and into a clearing hacked out of the jungle where the triple canopy trees hid it from view from the air. Sincavage could feel the man's eyes on him as he stowed the rappeling rope and harness and other equipment he had gotten from Anderson aboard the plane, and he again heard the occasional muffled sounds of movement off in the distance as he headed back along the trail.

A few hundred yards from the camp, Sincavage took the offensive. At a spot where the underbrush on both sides of the trail thinned for a short distance, and the man stalking him was forced to go deeper into the jungle to avoid being seen, Sincavage stepped quickly off the trail and circled back to get behind him. With skills and experience far exceeding those of the man who had been following him, he was soon close enough to identify him as someone he had noticed on a number of other occasions, but had dismissed as nothing more than a curious and bored camp worker.

Juan Osorio, unaware that Sincavage was now observing his every move, took his usual precautions before approaching his cache and uncovering the small satellite radio. He was puzzled by the disappearance of the man called Carlson. One moment he was on the trail back to the camp, and the next he was nowhere in sight. But he shrugged it off, assuming that Carlson had picked up his pace and reached the camp ahead of him while he had swung wide to stay in the thick brush.

The man was good at what he did, Osorio thought, and it had become increasingly clear to him what it was that he did, particularly after watching him sighting in the sniper rifle. His skills were impressive, especially the night-illumination shots. At a distance of eight hundred and fifty yards, from atop a hill overlooking the clearing behind the obstacle course, he had put every shot in the kill zone of a human silhouette target lighted only by the reflected glow of a small flashlight he had placed nearby. And in the two days that Osorio had observed him, he had proven highly competent with a wide variety of weapons, and adept at molding the young guerrillas under his charge into the rudiments of a deadly assault force. The urgent request for more information, which he had received from his case officer in Lima, only served to reinforce his belief that the man was indeed someone both deadly and dangerous.

Glancing at his watch to confirm it was time for his scheduled transmission, Osorio brought the radio out of the dense stand of bamboo and knelt in the low underbrush. As he removed the waterproof wrapping and unfolded and oriented the antenna, a sudden dark shadow fell over him, and when he turned to look up, he found himself staring into the cold blue eyes of the man he knew as Carlson.

Without a word, Sincavage shoved him aside and picked up the radio to examine it. Osorio tried to grab it back, reaching for the destruct button to activate the small internal explosive charge designed to fuse and destroy the classified microcircuitry inside the radio. Sincavage slapped him with a vicious backhand blow that sent him sprawling to the ground.

"Let me guess," Sincavage said, his voice calm and carrying a hint of amusement. "DEA? No, too sophisticated. This looks more like something the Agency would have."

Osorio said nothing as he pulled himself to his feet and wiped a trickle of blood from the corner of his mouth with his sleeve.

"The question is," Sincavage said, "what have you managed to tell your Agency friends so far?"

Osorio stepped back and reached for the small automatic pistol beneath his shirt. Sincavage's reaction was swift and practiced, wrenching the pistol from his hand as it cleared the holster and breaking Osorio's wrist in the process.

The explosive cracks of two pistol shots from behind caught him by surprise, and he spun around and dropped to one knee, bringing Osorio's pistol to bear in one lightning quick, fluid motion.

Osorio staggered backward, staring blankly at the two neat round holes seeping blood from his chest cavity as he crumpled to the ground. In the split-second it took Sincavage to locate the source of the shots, Anderson stepped from behind a tree, the nine-millimeter automatic in his hand lowered to his side and no longer posing a threat.

"Sorry if I startled you, mate," the Australian mercenary said as he approached, "but it looked as if you were in need of a bit of help."

Sincavage turned and looked at Osorio's lifeless body lying a few feet away. "I wanted to question him."

"I think he had other things in mind."

"I had it under control," Sincavage said.

"If you say so."

"Why were you following me?" Sincavage asked, watching Anderson closely as he raised the Beretta automatic and snapped it back into his shoulder holster.

"Him," Anderson said, gesturing toward Osorio. "Not you. I saw him sneaking around the perimeter and followed him here."

"How long has he been in camp?"

"Unfortunately, from the beginning," Anderson said. "Which goes a long way toward explaining why an inordinate number of cocaine shipments from here have been confiscated long before they reach the States."

"If I'm right, and he's CIA," Sincavage said, "he's been reporting on your activities as well."

"Well then, we've put an end to that, haven't we?" Anderson said. "And what about your operation? He's surely told his CIA pals about your presence here."

Sincavage nodded absently, his mind calculating the ramifications of his discovery at the camp and how he could best turn it to his advantage. Anderson noticed no undue concern on the face of the man who set his nerves on edge each time they spoke, and indeed there was none. The agent's presence in the camp was an inconvenience to Sincavage, at worst forcing him to accelerate his schedule.

"I'll need a set of aeronautical charts for the routes the smugglers use when they transport shipments from this camp to the States," he told the Australian, "along with your contacts at the refueling stops I'll have to make."

"So, you'll be leavin' us then?"

"What arrangements have you made for the aircraft I'll need to transport my team north?"

"I contacted Calderon; he got what you wanted, a Beechcraft King Air," Anderson said. "It'll be in Cali in two days. You can fly your people out in the Mitsubishi and switch planes there."

Sincavage glanced at the date window on his watch. It was October seventh. "Then we'll be leaving here as planned, on the morning of the tenth."

Sincavage turned and walked back toward the main part of the camp, where his team of six young guerrillas were finishing a lunch of beans and rice. The discovery of the agent had at first made him consider leaving the remote mountain camp early, but if his location and activities were already known, he reasoned, a hasty departure would accomplish nothing. The agent's transmissions were undoubtedly scheduled, and when not received would be a cause for concern, but by the time his control realized something had gone wrong and decided to move on the camp, if indeed they had the capability of mounting a quick reaction raid, he would be gone. He would make no changes, proceeding as planned to arrive in New York City on the morning of October twelfth.

—19—

Maguire was waiting at the northwest gate to the White House grounds when Gannon arrived shortly before two o'clock. Having already logged him in and cleared him for admittance with the Uniform Division guards at the gate, he handed him a laminated pass on a beaded chain, which Gannon slipped around his neck. By the time the two men walked the short distance along West Executive Avenue to the south court of the Old Executive Office Building, deep in conversation, they had exchanged most of the information each had uncovered.

As they entered Maguire's office, Gannon removed the reconnaissance team photograph from his briefcase and pointed out Sincavage. "This was taken in 1971," he told Maguire. "Just before he was listed as missing in action."

Maguire studied the face of the man Gannon had indicated. "It's a Special Operations Group team, isn't it?"

Gannon nodded. "A combined SEALs and SF team for a specific mission."

"Did you know Sincavage in Vietnam?"

"Yes. We served in the same unit for one of my tours," Gannon said, and let it go at that. "According to what you just told me, the man you've been looking for . . . Carlson, was on St. Barts at the time of the drug barons' meeting, he was traveling under false documents, and he turned up in Cartagena, a destination mentioned in the take from the meeting. He's now in Peru at a drug-processing camp that also serves as a training base for Shining Path terrorists; reportedly training a team to assault a motorcade."

"And Interpol's got a Roger Carlson linked to three known assassinations over the past thirteen years," Maguire added.

"What more do you need to go after him?"

"What we've got is a lot of circumstantial evidence, but it's probably strong enough for me to convince the President's National Security Affairs Advisor that Carlson is the drug barons' shooter, and more than enough for me to have him picked up for questioning if he enters the country."

"Delta Force could snatch him out of the camp in Peru," Gannon offered. "We've been gathering intelligence on that place for the past three months. And right now you've got him pinpointed in a remote location with no easy way out. It's the perfect opportunity."

"An extraterritorial operation?" Maguire said. "I don't know if I can get that dog to hunt, but it's sure as hell worth a try."

"Assuming that Carlson and Sincavage are the same person," Gannon said, "and I don't have any doubts that they are, he has friends in high places who went to a great deal of trouble to make it look like he's dead. And we both know who's good at doing that."

"If the answer lies with the Agency," Maguire said, "we may have a hard time getting their cooperation."

"Maybe not as hard as you think," Susan Olsen said from the doorway, having arrived in time to overhear Maguire's last remark. She entered the office and took the chair opposite Gannon, giving him a questioning look.

"Jack Gannon, meet Susan Olsen, with our Intelligence Division," Maguire said.

Gannon nodded a hello, and in reply to Susan's inquiring if he was with the Secret Service, said, "No. Retired military."

"Of course you are," she said with a knowing and flirtatious smile that never failed to pique the interest of any man on whom she chose to use it.

In response to a look from Susan that asked if she could speak freely, Maguire said, "He's okay. What have you got?"

"A Roger Carlson, also code-named Viper, turned up in CIA's files. No details of the whys and wherefores, but they did give up the name of the case officer who controlled him as an agent from nineteen seventy-one through nineteen seventy-seven."

"Sincavage was reported missing in action in nineteen seventy-one," Gannon said, then, as he recalled the inscription on the gold pendant, added, "and the name of the recon team he was running at the time he disappeared was Viper."

"What year did you say his supposed remains were returned and his MIA status changed to KIA, Body Not Recoverable?" Maguire asked.

"Nineteen seventy-seven," Gannon said. "Gets curiouser and curiouser, doesn't it?"

"What's the case officer's name?" Maguire asked Susan.

"Paul Martindale."

"Is he willing to talk to us?"

"I don't know. He's retired and living in Fairfax. They've given us his address, so it looks like CIA's washing their hands of it and dumping it in our laps. I can have our Washington field office send someone over to feel him out."

"No," Maguire said. "I think it might be best if Gannon and I do that."

Susan handed him the CIA memorandum containing Martindale's address and the terse comments they had added, which simply stated that Martindale was no longer with them, having retired in 1977.

Maguire gave her the recon team photo and pointed out Sincavage. "Get FBI to enlarge this guy's face and have their artists age him twenty years, then get your CIA liaison to fax copies down to St. Barts and see if any of the people Carlson came in contact with can ID him."

"Speaking of St. Barts," Susan said, "your hunch was right. Interpol got their act together in a hurry. The slugs from the girl murdered on the sailboat were flown out to Paris within a few hours after I made the request for the ballistics check. A cable came in just as I was leaving the office to come over here; they've tied them to the assassinations attributed to Carlson in Brussels and Hong Kong."

Maguire and Gannon exchanged looks, then Gannon said, "I think it's time to pay Martindale a visit."

"Having a peaceful retirement, Mr. Gannon?" Susan asked, using her best smile as she got up to leave.

"Yes," Gannon said, returning the smile.

"Puttering around the yard, are we? Prize-winning hybrid roses; guppies about to give birth in the fish tank in the den?"

"Something like that."

"How nice," Susan said with a wink, and disappeared down the corridor.

-20-

The small brick ranch-style house sat on a cul-de-sac at the end of a quiet residential street in a Fairfax, Virginia, subdivision of similar middle-class homes. Until last year, when Martindale's wife of forty-two years had died of a heart attack, the one-half acre lot had been a showplace of seasonal blooms in carefully tended flower beds surrounded by a carpet of thick, weedless grass. Now, in contrast to the neatly trimmed lawns and shrubs of the neighboring properties, the lot was sorely neglected.

The man who answered the kitchen door to see Maguire and Gannon standing in the breezeway was tall and barrel-chested. His close-cropped salt-and-pepper hair framed strong, ascetic features dominated by dark-brown opaque eyes that penetrated to the core. His military bearing and lean, taut body made him appear younger than his sixty-eight years, and an overpowering aura of brute strength and self-assurance suggested that he was no stranger to violence and danger.

His eyes locked on Maguire's, then slowly lowered to examine the Secret Service identification presented to him. "What do you want?" The voice wavered slightly with age, but still maintained a gruff edge of authority and impatience with those who would waste his time.

"I'm Mike Maguire, and this is Jack Gannon," Maguire said. "We'd like to talk with you about a national security matter."

"What does it concern?" There was no hint of agreement in the wary, demanding tone.

"A former agent of yours," Gannon said. "Jerry Sincavage."

Martindale's eyes narrowed and his body stiffened. It was as though he had been ambushed, taken by surprise by an all but forgotten name from the past.

Issuing what was more a command than an invitation, he said, "Come in," and held open the aluminum storm door as Maguire and Gannon entered the kitchen area.

Martindale led them down a narrow hallway to a living room cluttered with furniture and artifacts from Southeast Asia. Planters containing oversized bamboo palms in desperate need of pruning framed the picture window looking out onto the street, while ornate oriental sculptures and bric-a-brac vied for attention from shelves and tabletops. Gannon's eyes came to rest on a large stone statue in a corner of the room of a kneeling Buddha that he estimated weighed in excess of two hundred pounds.

"Got that in Laos, up near the Plain of Jars," Martindale said when he noticed Gannon admiring it. "Found it in a temple NVA artillery had blown all to hell. I carried it out myself; lugged it through the damn jungle for three days. Damn near ruptured every organ in my body in the process."

Gannon's eyes moved slowly along walls crammed with photographs that spanned what he estimated to be a career of at least two decades of CIA covert operations. Martindale was distinguishable at various ages in most of them. One in particular caught his attention: he recognized the legendary Special Forces officer, Colonel Bull Simons, standing with Martindale in a group shot that included what Gannon knew to be the first White Star team sent into Laos prior to America's official involvement in the Vietnam War.

"You knew Colonel Simons?" Gannon asked.

"We worked together for a little over a year," Martindale said, curious as to how Gannon knew one of the few men he had ever respected. "How do you know him?"

"I was on the assault team for the Son Tay raid," Gannon said.

The mention of the top-secret mission, led by Simons, to rescue American prisoners of war—a raid that was successfully executed only to find the North Vietnamese prison empty—seemed to soften Martindale's gruff demeanor. Gesturing for his visitors to sit on the sofa, he sank heavily into an overstuffed armchair and reached for a water carafe on the end table, refilling the near-empty glass beside it.

"Who told you about Sincavage?"

"CIA's Counter Narcotics Center, indirectly," Maguire said. "In response to a request from our intelligence division concerning a man by the name of Roger Carlson. He turned up as a former agent of yours."

"What makes you think Sincavage and Carlson are the same man?"

"Strong circumstantial evidence," Maguire said.

Martindale fell silent, his eyes fixed on a distant object across the room. He seemed to drift off, reliving a moment in the past.

"Your friend's Secret Service," he finally said, pointing his glass at Gannon. "You're not. Who are you?" The impatient glare was back.

"Retired military," Gannon said without elaboration.

Martindale continued to stare, slowly nodding his head. "Insult my intelligence once more and you can leave. Now, I'll ask you again: Who are you and what's your interest in this?"

"I'm a retired Special Forces lieutenant colonel, working as a civilian operations and intelligence specialist with the Joint Special Operations Command at Fort Bragg." Purposely leaving out his assignment to Delta Force, he watched to see if his answer satisfied the man whose eyes had never left his as he spoke.

"And why are you interested in Sincavage?"

"I have good reason to believe he killed a friend of mine."

Martindale again nodded slowly as he sipped from the water glass in his hand. "Delta Force, right?"

Gannon held the man's steady gaze without responding.

"That's what I thought." Turning to Maguire he said, "Now, tell me why you're here, and I want to hear all of it. Lie to me; I'll lie to you."

Maguire's initial assessment of Martindale had been correct. The man would not be intimidated by authority into revealing information that was no doubt still highly classified, and he would get nothing from him unless he convinced him that the information he needed was vital to the nation's security. Starting with the drug barons' meeting on St. Barts, he told him all that he and Gannon had learned and surmised in the past five days.

As Maguire spoke, Gannon studied Martindale carefully. There was something about him that wasn't right; something beneath the surface that undermined the solid image of control and self-discipline. His hand trembled slightly as he raised the glass to his mouth, and the way he sipped the contents suggested that what he was drinking was not water. As he reached for the carafe again to refill his glass, he bumped a small jade statue that tumbled to the carpet; his reflexes were too slow to grab it before it fell; the incident disturbed him more than it should.

Despite Martindale's attempts to hide it, what he was suffering from continued to manifest itself. Gannon now realized that the old warrior sitting across from him was a chronic alcoholic in an advanced stage of the disease. He noticed other telltale signs that were impossible to conceal: dilated blood vessels looking like tiny blue spiders on the face and neck, the whites of the eyes streaked with red, and the occasional slurred speech that came and went with a will of its own. Gannon guessed that the carafe on the end table contained either gin or vodka, and that Martindale spent most of his waking hours in an alcoholic haze.

"I need to know everything you can tell me about Jerry Sincavage," Maguire said, having completed briefing Martindale on the information they had gathered, leaving nothing out, and concluding with his belief that Sincavage intended to assassinate the President in six days, during his visit to New York.

"I ran him as an agent for seven years," Martindale said after a long pause and a visible change in attitude that suggested he was willing to cooperate.

"How did you recruit him?"

The distant look returned, this time accompanied with a small smile. "Were either of you familiar with the CAS program during the Vietnam war?"

"It was a CIA operation based in Long Tieng, Laos," Gannon said, recalling the stories of a "secret city" run by CIA in a remote mountain valley. "You inserted reconnaissance teams into northern Laos, North Vietnam, and China. CAS stood for Controlled American Sources, if I remember correctly."

"Close enough," Martindale said. "One of my CAS teams found Sincavage at the side of a trail in Laos; he'd been staggering around the jungle half dead for five days. Shot to hell. I still don't know how he managed to survive."

"Why didn't he return to his unit?" Gannon asked.

"Because when I found out he was the only survivor from his mission, listed as MIA and presumed dead, and he told me the kind of operations he'd been running for the past three years, I decided I could put him to good use," Martindale said. "He was the perfect operative for my purposes at that time, brilliant, resourceful, courageous, a loner who functioned best on his own and really didn't like people . . . and officially dead."

"You forgot to add that he was an amoral sociopath," Gannon said with an enmity that drew a curious look from Maguire.

"That too," Martindale readily agreed, studying Gannon for a moment. "Anyway, once I explained the advantages of staying dead to him, he jumped at my offer."

"Why did you go to the trouble to plant the phony remains and the pendant with the Joint Casualty Resolution Center at the time you retired from the Agency?" Gannon asked.

Martindale's eyes wandered, settling on one of the photographs nearby. There was another long silence before he spoke again.

"Ungrateful sons of bitches," he finally said, slurring the words as he spat them out with a vehemence that curled his lips into a snarl. "Retired? Is that what they told you? Twenty-eight years of dedicated service, five Intelligence Medals, an unblemished career, and I get a Xerox of a dismissal notice that was sent to eight hundred other people, all veteran officers with distinguished careers. The sniveling liberal shits gutted clandestine operations and sent me a goddamn photocopied memorandum as a notice of termination. Nothing about what I'd done to serve my country, not even a thank you and go to hell. The bastards didn't even have the decency to send me an original."

"Is that when you and Sincavage parted company?" Gannon asked.

"I wasn't going to throw him to the wolves," Martindale said. "He was loyal to me, and the best damn operative I ever had, and despite his kinks, he deserved better. I did what I could to make sure they never learned his true identity, in case they ever decided it was in their best interests to kill him to cover their chickenshit asses."

"When did you last see him?" Maguire asked.

"One week after I left the Company," Martindale said. "We said our good-byes over a few beers at the Twin Bridges Marriott, I wished him luck, told him I'd take care of his military records, and never heard from him again."

"What did you mean by taking care of his military service records?" Gannon asked.

"I arranged for them, and all his civilian records, to disappear," Martindale said. "I'm nothing if not thorough, gentlemen. Jerry Sincavage is not only officially dead, he never existed."

Martindale's eyes went out of focus as he drifted back in time to another private memory. "Sincavage was a master of misdirection, you know . . . a goddamn master for a guy that young. Come across a natural like him once in a lifetime. Are you familiar with Ops-34?" he asked Gannon.

Gannon nodded. The Special Operations Group unit had inserted small teams deep inside North Vietnam for a variety of black operations, some run strictly for CIA. "I had some friends who served with me in Ops-35 before they transferred over to it for their second tour."

"Well, Sincavage came up with some of the most ingenious, diabolical concepts imaginable," Martindale said, almost with a fatherly pride. "He was the one who hatched the idea of attaching huge blocks of ice to parachutes and dropping them into the jungle inside North Vietnam at night. When the ice melted, the NVA patrols would find six or eight empty parachutes the next morning and call out an entire regiment to search the area, drawing attention away from where the real team was inserted. They never got wise to that one; we used it until the war ended."

Martindale laughed softly to himself while emptying half of his glass. "And he really outdid himself when I was trying to put together an operation to terminate an NVA general. We'd lost four teams in two weeks trying to get that bastard. Sincavage came up with his own plan, and pulled some unsuspecting NVA defector out of the inner compound at Long Thanh and told him he had been selected for a top-secret mission back into the North. He briefed him on a nonexistent operation, then without him knowing it, stuffed a bunch of forged documents in his rucksack that would incriminate the general we were after, making it look like he was a double agent working for us. He even talked me into planting ten grand in cash on the guy just to make it look good. Then he threw the poor bastard out of a plane over the North with a parachute rigged so the canopy wouldn't blossom. We learned two weeks later that the NVA had found the defector's body, bought the ruse, then court-martialed and shot the NVA general. He was full of ideas like that . . . the beautiful evil bastard."

Gannon had heard rumors of the operations Martindale had just attributed to Sincavage. Everything that had gone on in the secret inner compound at the Long Thanh base located thirty-five miles east of Saigon was classified top secret, and maintained that classification even now, but the stories had gotten around the special operations community since the end of the war.

"What sort of operations did he run for you after the war ended?" Gannon asked.

Martindale hesitated, then said, "He was a mechanic. Are you familiar with the term?"

"Yes," Gannon said, aware that it was a euphemism for a high-level professional assassin.

"And he was a damn good one," Martindale said, taking a long drink that was followed by an involuntary shudder. "He could take you out from fifteen hundred yards or shoot you in the face while he was smiling at you." After a thoughtful pause he added, "Some of us found the best in ourselves when we were doing our worst."

"One thing that doesn't make sense to me," Gannon said.

"Why would Sincavage continue to use the Carlson alias for such a long period of time?"

Martindale shrugged. "It's a common problem a lot of case officers have with deep-cover agents. Sometimes, despite the obvious dangers, they keep using an old alias after being warned that it could compromise them. I always attributed it to being sort of a psychological anchor . . . a tenuous one, but the only one people like Sincavage have to prove to themselves that they really do exist. Some guys, who've been under a long time, or are no longer under contract to the Agency, subscribe to the notion that at least one constant identity is necessary to create a persona they can build a reputation on and present to the people who require their services." Martindale chuckled at a private thought he chose not to share, and then said, "Or they just get cocky, and sooner or later it comes back to haunt them—as you've just proven."

"Is there anything you can tell us about Sincavage that might help us anticipate his moves?" Maguire asked. "Or any contacts from the old days he might use for an operation like this?"

Topping off his glass and slowly sipping the soothing liquid, Martindale remained silent for a long time. Then looking alternately at Gannon and Maguire, he said, "If you know nothing else about Jerry Sincavage, know this: He never played to win or lose, he just played to stay in the game. We all liked being on the edge at one time or another, but he thrived on it; and in the end, he needed it."

In a less than subtle gesture that indicated he had nothing more to say, Martindale got up from his chair, taking his glass with him, and motioned for his guests to use the front door.

"If you're going to try to bring Sincavage down," he said as he walked them to their car, "I wish you luck. And you can believe me when I tell you, you're going to need it."

Gannon turned on Martindale, his eyes hard and unyielding. "The man you're so proud to have had as an agent is nothing more than a sick son of a bitch. And if I catch up with him there won't be enough luck in the world to save his worthless ass."

The remark was more of an emotional outburst than a statement, and Martindale made no comment as Gannon got in the car. The anger evident in Gannon's voice left no doubt in the old intelligence officer's mind that he and Sincavage had crossed paths before and unfinished business remained.

As Maguire backed the car out into the street, he said to Gannon, "I get the feeling that there's something more between you and Sincavage than the murder of Maria Padron?"

Gannon didn't respond immediately, and when he finally spoke, it was in a soft, distant voice that grew with emotion as he again saw the never-to-be-forgotten faces in his mind's eye.

"In sixty-nine, when I was running Recon Team Cobra out of Command and Control North, Sincavage had a team there too. There were about fifty Americans in the unit, and a few hundred indigenous mercenaries the Agency hired to run operations with us. We also had Vietnamese civilians working inside the wire, cooking, doing laundry, cleaning up, things like that."

"Didn't that create security problems?" Maguire asked.

"Yeah, sometimes. SOG headquarters vetted them as best they could, but every once in a while the Viet Cong managed to infiltrate one of their people. But for the most part they were just victims of the war like everyone else in that country. People whose villages were destroyed and had nowhere to go. The pay was better than anything they could make from their own people, and they worked hard."

Gannon paused for a moment and then continued. "There was this young Vietnamese girl, Tiu, she was twenty-six years old, and had a ten-year-old son, Hung. The VC were operating out of her village, and her husband, her whole family were wiped out in an air strike. She ended up at our camp looking for work, a nice kid, couldn't do enough for us, always cheerful and smiling, just glad to have a refuge for her and her son. I really liked her; cared about her. And I got attached to her."

"Romantically?"

"No. Sort of a kid sister. Most of the guys treated her that way. The colonel was pulling some strings to try to get her to the States, and I spent a lot of my stand-down time between missions teaching her English. She was a touch of sanity in that madhouse.

"Anyway, near the end of my last tour, we started losing one or two teams a week on insertion. Shot to hell the second they put a foot on the LZ. It became pretty obvious that the NVA knew we were coming; someone was feeding them information, and it had to be someone inside the compound. The team leaders were getting nervous and the atmosphere was pretty tense. One night when I came out of the mess hall, I heard some screaming from across the compound; it sounded like Tiu. I ran over to see what the hell was going on, and arrived just in time to see Sincavage empty a magazine from his CAR-15 into Tiu and Hung. I tell you, Mike, I almost shot the son of a bitch right there on the spot. I grabbed his weapon from him and started to beat the hell out of him. I don't know how many times I hit him, I just kept at it until three of my buddies pulled me off. The rotten psychotic bastard had decided that Tiu was using Hung to send information to the local VC cadre. He had no evidence, just made himself judge, jury, and executioner and killed them both."

"Was he right?" Maguire asked. "I mean, was she guilty?"

"Hell, no! We found out four days later that one of Sincavage's team, a Cambodian mercenary the CIA had recruited to run recon with us, was meeting in town with known VC. One of Sincavage's own goddamn people was responsible for the leaks."

"Nobody brought him up on charges for killing the girl and her child?"

"I tried," Gannon said. "God knows I tried." The pain he had felt over twenty years ago was still evident in his voice. "And so did the colonel. But it never got any further than SOG headquarters. The word was sent back that the incident was to be forgotten. The pressure had to be coming from the Agency; Sincavage had worked for them when he was with the Phoenix Program and they wanted him operational."

"So they just covered it up?" Maguire said.

Gannon nodded. "That incident was the reason I never went back for another tour; when you could summarily kill someone just because they looked like the enemy, things were getting out of hand—hell, the whole damn country looked like the enemy. Where did you draw the line? I damn near left the service because of it. If being a soldier wasn't the only thing I was good at, I wouldn't have hesitated. Later, when I heard that Sincavage was dead, I felt that at least the scales had been somewhat balanced. And now I find out that he's still alive and responsible for the death of someone else I cared about."

"Well, you might get another chance at him," Maguire said. "After what Martindale just told us, I think we've got enough to get your Delta Force dog to hunt."

"If not, I'll hunt him myself," Gannon said in what was clearly not an idle boast. "And this time I'll play by his rules."

—21—

Contrary to popular belief, decisions can be made and implemented in the White House with amazing speed when the situation requires it. Within one hour after Maguire and Gannon entered the west wing and met with the President's deputy chief of staff, they were taken into the Oval Office. There, in the presence of the Chief of Staff and the National Security Affairs Advisor, they briefed the President, and a decision was reached for a provisional go-ahead for the operation Gannon proposed.

One hour and forty-five minutes later, a top-secret meeting, presided over by the President's National Security Affairs Advisor, convened in the Situation Room in the west wing basement. Gathered around the large oak conference table with Gannon and Maguire were CIA's Deputy Director for Operations, the Chairman of the Joint Chiefs of Staff, the National Security Advisor's deputy for counternarcotics and counterterrorism, the Secret Service's Protective Operations chief, the Assistant Secretary of Defense for Special Operations and Low-intensity Conflict, and the

Delta Force commander, who was already near Washington to attend a meeting in the Pentagon and had been brought to the White House by a driver Maguire had sent.

A large-scale map of the northwestern section of Peru was projected onto the screen at one end of the room as the National Security Advisor took his seat at the head of the table and told Maguire to begin his briefing. Those in attendance listened carefully, some scribbling notes, as Maguire detailed everything he and Gannon had uncovered. When he had finished, the National Security Advisor addressed the group.

"This is to be a highly compartmentalized operation outside the normal chain of command and will be run straight from the National Command Authority. Our jurisdiction in this matter is our right to go anywhere in the world to bring to justice anyone who kills or conspires to kill a United States government official. The President has given approval for a preemptive surgical strike to capture, and I emphasize capture, Sincavage. The only acceptable reason for killing him will be in self-defense, and even then, if the situation allows, the effort should be made to wound and not kill him."

The National Security Advisor paused and nodded toward CIA's Deputy Director for Operations. "The DDO believes, with good reason, that this man has the answers to a lot of questions both CIA and DIA are interested in hearing. And there is a further proviso, that Sincavage and the narcoterrorists at the camp are the only targets of this operation. The secondary purpose of the mission, the one to be used as a cover story if and when the media gets wind of it, will be to destroy the drug-processing camp. You've all been provided with a brief background report on the suspected assassin. Questions and suggestions, gentlemen."

The Chairman of the Joint Chiefs of Staff was the first to speak. "Has any consideration been given to including the Peruvian military in the operation? Perhaps as a combined U.S.-Peruvian drug raid, just to avoid the possible repercussions from a covert operation that violates their national sovereignty?"

"There's the problem of the time involved in conducting combined training rehearsals," the Assistant Secretary of Defense said.

"My understanding of what Maguire gave as the assassin's timetable is that we have a limited window of opportunity."

"I'd advise against inclusion of the Peruvians under any circumstances," CIA's Deputy Director for Operations spoke up. "We have hard intelligence information that the drug barons have penetrated the highest levels of their military establishment. The raid would be compromised before it ever got off the ground."

"I agree with the DDO," the Delta Force commander said. "My men have a rapid deployment capability, and this is precisely the type of mission they train for every day. Without sounding too immodest, we don't need any help from the Peruvians."

"What intelligence do we have on the camp?" the National Security Advisor asked.

"We have an agent on the ground," the Deputy Director for Operations said. "But there may be a problem."

"Define the problem," the National Security Advisor said.

"He has a schedule of communications with our Lima station. As of three hours ago, he's missed his last two transmissions and his alternates."

"Has he been compromised?" the Delta Force commander asked.

"We don't know," the DDO said, "but for the purposes of this meeting, we have to assume that he has."

"Is he your primary source of information on the camp?" It was the Delta Force commander again.

"Along with our satellite surveillance and reconnaissance drone overflights."

"If he's been compromised," the Delta commander said, "we have to consider the probability that Sincavage is aware of his significance and may have already left the camp."

"At this juncture," the DDO said, "I'd have to agree with you."

"Just what do we know about the makeup of the camp?" the National Security Advisor asked.

The DDO referred those present to the folders hastily compiled by Tony Covington at CIA's Counter Narcotics Center and placed before everyone in the room. A series of high-resolution satellite photographs of the immediate area of the camp revealed nothing through the triple canopy, but overlays on the photographs had been used to represent what CIA's technology had managed to ascertain was concealed beneath the dense jungle foliage.

"Our satellites have tracked over the camp at intervals since it was first built," the DDO said. "As you can see from the overlays, the infrared imaging reveals something of the layout."

Holding up a photograph for all to see, he indicated the structures they had identified. "These 'hot spots' are much stronger signatures than those given off by campfires. From the heat signatures we've found in other drug-processing camps, we know they are drying sheds. Some of the smaller heat signatures are dissipated by the tree canopy, but from the reports we got from our agent, we believe they are a cooking area and camp generators. The lesser signatures are believed to be body heat from the people in the camp. It has also been established that there is a commo shack with a secure-voice satellite communications system."

The Chairman of the Joint Chiefs of Staff interrupted. "Didn't your agent give you a detailed layout of the camp?"

"No. We never planned to raid it," the DDO said. "His purpose was to keep us apprised of the guerrilla training program and provide us with information about drug shipments leaving the camp."

Holding up another photograph, the DDO continued. Pointing to an area at the base of the Andean foothills, he indicated the grassy runway located one mile west of the camp, the boulder-strewn clearing close to the main compound, and finally a rough mountain track that was partially visible as it wound its way precipitously into a distant valley.

"We know from our agent that the area is a guerrilla stronghold and that there are no government troops within one hundred and fifty miles. The closest village is twenty-three miles away, with only this one unimproved road leading from it to the camp. There have been reports of Shining Path guerrillas operating in and around the village, but probably no more than a company-size unit."

"How many combatants in the camp at any given time?" the Delta Force commander asked.

"Approximately fifty guerrillas, half of them trainees under the command of an Australian mercenary by the name of Anderson.

The others in the camp, another fifty or so, are unarmed campesinos and a few chemists involved in processing the drugs. One note of interest," the DDO added. "They feel secure enough that they don't post guards around the camp at any time. The guerrillas who are not in training run short-range patrols during the day, but there are no security details after sundown. Their primary purpose appears to be as a reaction force in the event of an attack on the camp."

"How large an assault force do you anticipate needing?" the National Security Advisor asked the Delta Force commander.

"Judging from what I've heard so far, one squadron. That's a total of fifty men."

"And how soon can you be ready to deploy?"

"We'll have to put a four-man reconnaissance/surveillance team in first, to verify that the subject target is still in the camp and to radio back the operational details of the physical layout we'll require for the assault. They'll need twelve hours on the ground to observe the camp."

"And how long will it take to mount the actual assault?" the National Security Advisor asked.

"We can insert the R&S team tomorrow night," the Delta commander said. "The assault will take place the following night, October ninth."

The briefing and discussions continued for another hour, with each man stating his objections to suggestions and proposals with which he disagreed, and contributing to the operation plan in his own area of expertise. Upon the completion of a workable plan and reaching a consensus of support for the Delta Force mission, the National Security Affairs Advisor ended the meeting with the announcement that the President had clearly stated that the chairmen and minority leaders of the Senate and House Select Committees on Intelligence were to be briefed on the mission.

There was no response from the men gathered in the room, but the collective silent groan was palpable. It was not the inclusion of the four politicians that disturbed them, but the knowledge that their staffs would inevitably learn the rudiments of the mission, and they were people with their own agendas and contacts who had on more than one occasion in the past leaked classified intelligence information that had compromised entire operations.

With the meeting adjourned, the Delta Force commander motioned Gannon into a small office off the Situation Room, where he used the secure telephone to call Delta Force headquarters at Fort Bragg to alert his deputy commander to the impending mission.

"I came up here on one of our aircraft," the Delta commander told Gannon after completing the call. "You'll ride back with me. I want you to brief the reconnaissance/surveillance team on the requirements for Sincavage, and the alert-squadron commander and his staff on the follow-on mission."

"I want in on this," Gannon said.

The Delta commander nodded. "For some reason, that doesn't come as a surprise to me, Jack. What did you have in mind?"

"I want to take the R&S team in."

The Delta commander hesitated, then said, "It's going to be a HALO insertion. Are you current?" Even though Gannon was a Master Parachutist and had in excess of two hundred High Altitude Low Opening jumps under his belt, it was a question that needed to be asked in light of the fact that it had been four years since he had been on an assault team for an actual mission.

"I haven't lost any of my skills, if that's what you're worried about. I made three training jumps from thirty thousand feet with C squadron last month."

"Is the motivation for this request personal or professional?" the commander asked, recalling what Gannon had told him prior to the convening of the National Security Council meeting about his previous run-in with Sincavage.

"I can separate the two; I've done it before."

"The mission is to bring Sincavage out alive if at all possible. There's no room for vendettas."

"Have you ever known me to let any personal agendas get in the way of the mission?"

"No, I haven't. Sorry," the Delta commander said, placing a hand on Gannon's shoulder. "The R&S mission is yours."

"Thanks," Gannon said. "I just don't want to stand on the sidelines for this one."

"Done and done," the commander said.

Maguire was waiting outside the Situation Room when Gannon emerged with the Delta commander.

"Susan Olsen just paged me," Maguire said. "CIA's man on St. Barts got a positive ID on the photo we faxed him; the woman at the car rental agency and the manager at the hotel both recognized Sincavage as Carlson."

It was the final piece of evidence that along with the ballistics match proved that Sincavage had been on St. Barts and had killed Maria Padron.

"I'll be in touch," Gannon said, and fell in step with the Delta commander as he left the west wing basement to the car that waited to drive them to Fort Belvoir for the flight back to Fort Bragg.

—22—

Within minutes of the Delta commander's call to his deputy at the Ranch, instructing him to prepare the alert squadron for the reconnaissance/surveillance mission and follow-on raid, telephones began ringing throughout the Fayetteville, North Carolina, area. Those who could not be reached by phone were alerted by pager.

Sergeants First Class Bill Craddock and Ken McMasters had spent a busman's holiday afternoon of sport parachuting, perfecting their free-fall techniques. Now seated around a table on the porch of the Green Beret Parachute Club, drinking Pepsi in lieu of the beer their friends were enjoying, their pagers sounded almost simultaneously. After phoning the Ranch, they both made quick calls to their wives, telling them that they would not be home that evening (pronouncements that were initially greeted with silence, followed by "I love you, honey" and "Take care, Ken. We love you."), then they hurriedly left the club to the knowing looks and thumbs-up gestures of their friends at the table.

Sergeant Major Joe Olivera's pager beeped in an ice-cream

parlor at the Cross Creek Mall where he was eating a banana split with his wife and five-year-old daughter. Upon his return from calling the Ranch, his wife said nothing as he slid into the booth and told her he had to leave; she simply slipped her arm through his and kissed him, and tried not to show the concern she always felt when he was unexpectedly called away.

Neither Joyce Olivera nor the wives of the other two men from C squadron could have imagined that their husbands would, within the hour, be tasked as the reconnaissance/surveillance team for a mission that would require them to free-fall from thirty thousand feet and parachute into the heart of a terrorist camp in the Peruvian jungle. But had they known, it would not have surprised them, nor would it have evoked any pleas to prevent their leaving. Each was painfully aware of the dangers inherent in the profession her husband had chosen, and each had accepted the ever-present threat and learned to suffer her desperate fears in silence.

The men receiving the calls were given an innocuous open code phrase: "Don't forget to bring your lesson plans in tomorrow," that told them there was an immediate alert. Within thirty minutes the troops of C squadron (the alert squadron), and their support personnel were driving through the main gate of the Delta Force compound in an isolated corner of the Fort Bragg complex.

Throughout most of the sprawling headquarters building activities were normal, with no overt indication of an impending operation other than the arrival of the alert squadron, which told those who witnessed it that there was indeed something in the wind. But a charged atmosphere and a sense of mission did pervade the Tactical Operations Center (TOC), contained within the Sensitive Compartmented Intelligence Facility on the lower level. In a smaller room off the TOC, used for highly compartmentalized operations, and to which only a limited number of Delta Force members would be allowed access, the necessary maps, photographs, and charts were being posted in preparation for the operational briefings and mission planning that would be conducted there. Secure radios with satellite links, for communications with the deployed troops, were remoted into the room, and lines were set up that tied the headquarters in to the U.S. government's secure telephone networks.

The men from the alert squadron reported to their squadron bay while the squadron commander and his sergeant major went straight to the Tactical Operations Center. There the deputy commander gave them the warning order: Select three men for a reconnaissance/surveillance team to be led by Jack Gannon, and to be deployed as soon as possible to the cocaine-processing camp in Peru. Their mission was to confirm or deny the presence of the targeted subject, Jerry Sincavage, and collect and report intelligence on the camp and its defenses, and be prepared to provide terminal guidance for a follow-on assault to capture Sincavage and destroy the existing camp.

Back in the squadron bay, the squadron commander passed on the warning order to his troops and chose the three men for the primary R&S mission, and another four-man team as an alternate —whose function it was to fly with the primary team and in the event of casualties during the infiltration, to parachute into an alternate landing zone and handle the casualties and provide replacements, or if necessary, assume the mission, while the primary team handled its own casualties and awaited evacuation when the full squadron assault was launched.

Taking the primary and backup R&S teams and his three troop commanders with him, the squadron commander then returned to the Tactical Operations Center, where the Southcom intelligence analysts waited to begin the area briefing.

Throughout the complex, various staff personnel assisted in the preparation for deployment. Intelligence section (S-2) issued maps and requested additional satellite photographs from the National Photographic Intelligence Center to include in the target folders they were preparing. The intelligence analyst team responsible for the area in which the camp was located searched their files for previous area studies and all updated area-specific information on the camp, including guerrilla activity, locations of lines of communications, potential landing and drop zones, and weather and climatological data.

The air operations officer (S-3 Air) and his staff requested and coordinated the required air support, which included two C-141B Starlifter transport planes, three HH-53H Pave Low III special operations helicopters and two HC-130 aerial tankers for mid-air refueling of the Pave Lows during the flight to the camp. The S-4 arranged for the issue of supplies, transportation to the departure airfield at adjoining Pope Air Force Base, and assisted with the logistics planning for the operation. The medical section issued medical equipment as required and coordinated contingency plans for casualty handling and evacuation. The operations officer (S-3), at the request of the deputy commander, called in *A* squadron's commander and troop commanders, informing them that with *C* squadron being deployed their backup status was now upgraded, making them the alert squadron.

In addition to issuing special equipment and opening the communications network required for the mission, Signal squadron personnel issued CEOIs (communications and electronics operating instructions), which included radio frequencies, brevity codes, and call signs, and code tapes for the speech-security devices.

The well coordinated and highly efficient effort was conducted with cool professionalism, leaving nothing to chance. By twenty-two hundred hours Gannon and the Delta commander arrived back at the Ranch and the R&S teams were fully briefed. Gannon, as the primary team leader, along with the backup team leader, remained in the TOC to compare courses of action for infiltration and to establish an operations schedule. The other members of the R&S teams were sent back to the squadron bay to prepare their equipment.

With most of what every Delta Force trooper needs for any mission already packed and hanging in the team room lockers, very little time is wasted in gathering and selecting gear. Along with their free-fall parachute systems, each man maintains several sets of specialized equipment: one rucksack is prepacked with the gear necessary to operate in a cold-weather environment, another for tropical and subtropical conditions, and yet another contains a variety of individual civilian gear for covert infiltrations where uniforms would compromise their mission. General purpose alert gear, already loaded in the alert vans parked in the squadron bays, is ready for use in the event of an immediate reaction mission, such as an overseas aircraft hijacking.

The squadron's weapons would be selected from their mini-arms room in the bay, where the wide range of weapons issued to all Delta Force troopers—and with which they are highly proficient —were stored. Each man has an M-16E2 rifle, a national match-grade .45-caliber pistol, a 9mm H&K MP-5 submachine gun, and a 5.56mm CAR-15 submachine gun, along with access to a selection of special-purpose weapons, including shotguns, silenced 9mm Beretta semi-automatic pistols, squad automatic weapons (SAW) and M-16s with 40mm M-202 grenade launchers mounted beneath the barrel. It was a formidable and deadly arsenal that fitted most of their needs.

At twenty-three thirty hours, Gannon conducted a separate briefing for the R&S teams on the background of Jerry Sincavage, assigning him the code name "Viper" and issuing each man a blowup of the artist-rendered likeness of their target. The preparations, briefings, and briefbacks went on into the night, with the men of *C* squadron catching a few hours of sleep on the cots in the upper level of the squadron bay, and snacking on sandwiches and coffee brought down from the mess hall.

Gannon's R&S team members, Olivera, McMasters, and Craddock, had trained and worked together for the past three years, having been the first U.S. troops on the ground during the invasion of Panama. Their mission, along with the rest of the twenty-man troop, had been to rescue a highly placed CIA agent from a fortresslike jail, where he was being beaten and tortured. The operation was successful, resulting in forty-seven Panamanian Defense Force casualties versus a sprained ankle Olivera suffered when he had jumped from a fifteen-foot wall into the prison courtyard. The raid to rescue the CIA agent before he was killed by his captors had been their first true combat experience as a team, and they had worked well together, like a lethal, well-oiled machine.

The raid on the jungle camp would be their second taste of combat. Well into the small hours of the night, huddled together in the squadron bay with the backup team, Gannon and his men continued to study the area photographs of the camp and the target folder with the updated intelligence information. Gannon assigned each man specific duties, and as team leader and the most experienced jumper, he planned and coordinated the free-fall infiltration. Olivera, Craddock, and McMasters selected day and night hide sites in the immediate area of the camp, and worked out the details of how the team would conduct the surveillance, assigning coded designations for the known structures within the camp and key terrain features in the surrounding area that were indicated on the overlays of the satellite photographs.

By mid-morning, the C-141Bs from Charleston Air Force Base in South Carolina had arrived. The crew that would fly the R&S teams on the infiltration mission, and the second crew, which would transport the assault squadron to the launch site in Panama, where they would link up with the Pave Low helicopters, were brought to Delta Force headquarters and briefed on their separate missions.

At eleven-hundred hours the primary and backup R&S teams boarded one of the C-141s at Pope Air Force Base for the first leg of their flight, to Howard Air Force Base, Panama, where their mission into Peru would be launched later that night. Olivera, McMasters, and Craddock felt a special sense of pride that they were the ones chosen for Gannon's team. Each thought of the man seated with them as bigger than life, and all knew that he'd been awarded the Medal of Honor and had heard of his exploits in Vietnam with the Special Operations Group. To them he was a true hero—a fact that if spoken aloud would have embarrassed the man they chose to emulate. Deep in his own private thoughts, Gannon, glad to be back in harness again, settled in for the four-and-one-half-hour flight as the huge camouflage-painted bird thundered down the runway and lifted off.

●

Steven Whitney Bradford III was also deep in his private thoughts, and did not notice the attractive young woman who entered the crowded Pizza Hut restaurant in Reston, Virginia. It was not until she took the bench seat opposite him in the corner booth that his mind returned to the present.

"Sorry I'm late," Ann Tyler said. "An aide to the President's National Security Advisor arrived for a hush-hush session with the Senator just as I was about to leave the office."

"Anything important?" Bradford asked. Ann Tyler was a steady customer and, as a staff aide of Senator Ballard, chairman of the Senate Select Committee on Intelligence, was often the source of interesting tidbits concerning the intelligence community, an area which held an endless fascination for Bradford.

"Rumor has it that the President has a problem."

"What kind of problem?" Bradford said, with a little more concern in his voice than he would have liked.

"I'm not sure," Ann said, "but I think it's a threat to his personal safety. Some kind of special mission is being organized to go after an assassin."

Bradford felt a familiar knot forming in his lower stomach. "Where?"

"Peru . . . I believe."

"Do they know who he is, or when and where he's going to do it? Or who else is involved?" The last question was one Bradford wished he had not asked, but its significance was lost on Ann, who had other things on her mind, evidenced by her high-strung behavior.

"I don't know," Ann said, and leaned across the table, touching Bradford lightly on the back of the hand. "Do you have something for me?"

"Do you have something for me?" Bradford said. "Perhaps the fifteen hundred dollars you owe me?"

"Steve, for God's sake, you know I'm good for it. Don't hassle me now."

"I'll expect it by Wednesday at the very latest," Bradford said. "Or find yourself another source."

Their hands met underneath the table, with Ann smiling as she closed her fingers around the three small packets of cocaine.

"You're a dear, Steve," she said, with a look of profound relief that confirmed what Bradford had begun to suspect weeks ago: She was no longer a casual user.

Accompanying her to the parking lot, he sat in his car long after she had driven away. He was staring at the telephone booth outside the service station across the street. Before Ann Tyler had arrived, he had been agonizing over passing on the latest update to the President's New York City schedule: prior to his leaving the city for the trip to Atlanta on the morning of the fourteenth, where he would address the American Broadcasters Association convention, an early-morning run, at 7:00 a.m., at the track around the Central

Park reservoir had been added at the President's request. Despite the fact that it was an off-the-record movement, it was something that the news media would no doubt later report, if indeed they were not tipped off ahead of time and had cameras there to film it, leaving Bradford no choice but to tell his contact in Miami.

But it was the information he had just gotten from Ann Tyler that troubled him now. Calming himself and thinking things through, he decided that it was not something he had to pass on; they had no way of ever finding out that he had any knowledge of it. His outlook brightened considerably at the thought of a successful raid that would remove the threat to the President and consequently the need to supply any more information about his activities, putting an end to the mental torment he had endured since getting caught up in the whole mess. As he drove across the street to the telephone booth, it was the first time in weeks that he felt there might be a way out of his dilemma other than personal disaster.

—23—

A shrill hydraulic whine rose above the steady noise of the jet engines, filling the cavernous interior of the C-141 as the clam-shell doors at the rear of the aircraft opened and the ramp was lowered into position. Outside, a full moon brightened a pitch-black sky, but at thirty thousand feet, the huge aircraft went unseen and unheard from the ground below.

Inside, in the dim red light of the cargo compartment, the four-man primary R&S team breathed evenly through the masks on their helmets, and once again checked to make certain that the line running from the twin bail-out bottles filled with oxygen and at-tached to their harnesses was securely connected. With Gannon acting as jumpmaster, Craddock, McMasters, and Olivera mir-rored his actions as he pulled his clear free-fall goggles down into position, leaving the night-vision goggles resting on top of his helmet, where they would stay until the team had opened their canopies.

With two minutes remaining until they reached the release point for the HALO jump, Gannon pulled out his map and made one final check of the features he had etched in his memory since the previous night. He then knelt on the right side of the open doors and peered out, his eyes scanning the dark, rugged terrain below. Far ahead, to the right of the aircraft and only a few miles from where the jungle-covered foothills rose into towering Andean peaks, he saw the lights of a small mountain village come into view. Crossing quickly to the opposite side of the aircraft, he again looked down and forward. Ten miles south of the village he saw a U-shaped bend in a broad, swift-flowing river, its murky water luminous in the bright moonlight, in clear contrast to the jungle canopy.

Upon hearing the navigator call "one minute," Gannon announced to the aircraft's crew, "Coming off intercom," and disconnected the intercom cord from the plug in his helmet. Signaling the one-minute warning to his teammates, he motioned them to move closer to the edge of the ramp, where they gathered in a tight group beside him. At the "ten seconds" signal from the crew chief, all four men clasped hands—heavily burdened with equipment and subject to buffeting by the aircraft's slipstream, the "four-way off the ramp" with hands joined (a technique developed by the Australian SAS) would help prevent them from being separated during their exit from the plane.

"Radio check," Gannon said into the voice-activated throat microphone attached to his interteam radio, and heard each man give an audible check.

As the red light above the doors went out and the green light flashed on, Gannon said, "On three," and counted off.

On the count of three, he stepped into the dark void, pulling the others off the edge of the ramp with him. The sudden force of the slipstream caused McMasters to flip over and lose his grip, breaking apart the formation as he tumbled out of control. Gannon and the others watched as he recovered to a flat and stable position, then with the instincts of experienced HALO jumpers, they drew their arms and legs in slightly in a coordinated move that increased their rate of descent and brought them vertically even with him.

Catching sight of his teammates, McMasters pulled his arms back and straightened his legs. The adjustment in body position caused him to glide toward them, and bending his knees in preparation for the docking, he grasped the arms of Olivera and McMasters. Once again locked in formation, the four men fell through the night sky, checking their altimeters regularly, and scanning the forbidding terrain below.

"On target," Gannon said over the interteam radio, when he saw that they were halfway between the bend in the river and the lights of the town.

"Break on three," he announced, and began the count as his altimeter reached four thousand feet. On three, the men released their grips and broke formation, diving into a half turn away from each other.

At three thousand feet, they flared their bodies into a modified frog position, slowing their descent as they grasped the ripcords on their right shoulders and pulled. The parachute pack trays opened, releasing the spring-loaded pilot chute that deployed the main canopy. The men all felt the sudden jolt and steady deceleration as their downward momentum fought the resistance of the big parachutes until they swung gently beneath them.

Each team member immediately checked to ensure that the canopies were fully opened, then yanked their brake toggles out of their keepers and looked quickly around to make certain that they were not on a collision course with another jumper. McMasters and Olivera, closing rapidly on each other, steered their highly maneuverable three-hundred-square-foot ram air canopies into a sharp right turn to avoid colliding.

Gannon's voice came over the team radio again. "Give me a count."

"One okay," Craddock said.

"Two okay," McMasters added.

"Three okay," Olivera said.

"Four okay," Gannon said. "Heading two seven zero."

Checking the luminous dials on their compasses, they turned to the heading, putting them on a nearly even vertical plane at intervals of fifteen yards as they slowly descended toward the mountainous jungle terrain. No longer in need of oxygen, they unhooked one side of their masks and pulled their free-fall goggles down under their chins. With their night-vision goggles in position and turned on, an eerie green glow was cast over all they surveyed.

Two miles ahead, Gannon spotted an opening, a light gash in the endless jungle canopy, and immediately recognized it as the grassy airstrip he had seen in the satellite photographs.

"Come left to two four zero," he said as he began the turn. "Drop zone dead ahead, two miles."

Making two rapid diving turns to get below his teammates, he next instructed them, "Stack and follow me."

After Craddock, McMasters, and Olivera had manipulated their brakes and were stacked above him, Gannon turned slowly north, then south, making a wide S turn to bleed off altitude until he was over the drop zone at one thousand feet. As he approached the grassy strip, his eyes moved constantly, checking his proximity to the craggy rock outcroppings of the surrounding hills.

"Turn left, crosswind," he said, and looked back over his right shoulder as he flew past a deep ravine at one end of the runway.

While glancing from left to right, to compensate for the narrow field of vision through the goggles, something had caught his attention; it was a momentary glimpse of a break in the jungle just off to the side, but he was unable to see it now, and dismissed it and returned his undivided attention to the task at hand.

Olivera, Craddock, and McMasters were on the crosswind leg, holding position to remain stacked above him. At five hundred feet they heard him say, "Turn on to final. Prepare release."

All four of the men opened the Velcro closures on their leg straps and made certain the release tabs were within easy reach. As they approached the edge of the drop zone at an altitude of two hundred feet, Gannon gave the final command. "Release and land."

Momentarily letting go of their steering toggles, they yanked the quick-release tabs on their harnesses and felt a tug as the heavy rucksacks dropped fifteen feet below them to hang suspended at the end of the lowering lines. Again grasping their toggles, they glided toward the far end of the drop zone, away from the deep ravine. As each man's rucksack touched down on the grassy strip, they pulled their toggles down steadily to the full brake position, and flared to a stand-up landing as gentle as jumping off a porch step.

Gannon, as team leader, immediately asked for a status report. He got an okay from the other three men, who followed his lead and dropped their parachute harnesses and removed their weapons from where they were secured at their sides for the jump. With practiced precision, the team then gathered their parachutes and rucksacks and quickly withdrew into the underbrush at the side of the airstrip, where they lay silently in a defensive circle, their feet facing inward, listening to the night sounds of the jungle.

The light from the full moon barely penetrated the thick foliage, but it was enough to enhance the image intensification of the night-vision goggles, allowing the team to see a considerable distance into the surrounding thickets. After remaining motionless for ten minutes, until they were sure there was no enemy response to their presence, Gannon gave the command to prepare to move out.

Removing their helmets, they detached their night-vision goggles and snapped them to a rubber strap that held them firmly in place over their eyes. They next disconnected the radios from their helmets and plugged them into their earpieces, then stripped off their one-piece jumpsuits, and put on the boonie hats that matched the camouflage pattern of the lightweight battle-dress uniform they wore underneath.

As Craddock and McMasters gathered and concealed the HALO equipment in the dense underbrush, Gannon took the satellite radio antenna from his rucksack and set it up for his initial entry report.

"Nightstalker," was the single code word he whispered into the radio hand set, indicating that the infiltration was successful, with no injuries or loss of equipment.

Bounced off a communications satellite, the message was received almost instantaneously by the Delta commander and his staff back in the Tactical Operations Center at Delta Force headquarters. It was also heard aboard the C-141. The crew, who had filed a false flight plan to La Paz upon leaving Howard Air Force

Base in Panama, would now report an equally false maintenance problem, cancel the flight plan, and return to Panama with the backup R&S team.

Ten seconds after his initial entry report, Gannon heard the coded response he was waiting for from Delta Force headquarters. Another single word, "Avalanche," acknowledged his report and told him there were no changes in the operations plan. Folding up the antenna and placing it back in his rucksack, he took the point and led the team away from the airstrip in the direction of the camp.

In the pale, filtered moonlight they were phantoms, moving silently through pockets of waist-high ground fog that enveloped the dense triple canopy jungle. The only sounds were the swish of their fatigues and an occasional scrape of a boot on an exposed tree root. They leaned forward against heavy rucksacks and carried their weapons at the ready, sweeping their flanks and the area directly ahead. Their progress was slow, with impenetrable clumps of underbrush necessitating numerous detours from the course Gannon had set.

Nocturnal creatures, startled by their presence, scurried off, causing the team to halt and listen for any human response to the animal noises. Dripping with perspiration despite their slow and careful movement, their hands scratched and bleeding from tangles of thorny wait-a-bit vines, they had traveled less than a hundred yards from the airstrip when Gannon called a halt to observe the trail to the camp where it intersected their line of march.

The camp was not yet in sight, but faint, distant sounds drifted through the jungle to where the team lay silently at the side of the trail, listening. The melancholy sound of someone singing to the accompaniment of a lone guitar, and the steady hum of a generator punctuated by occasional ripples of laughter indicated that the team's infiltration had gone undetected.

"They're at least three quarters of a mile away," Olivera whispered into his throat mike. "We can use a bounding overwatch movement on the trail until we get closer to the camp. Beats the hell out of what we've been doing."

Eager to get the team into their hide sites, and not wanting to waste time and energy unnecessarily, Gannon agreed. As Crad-

dock and McMasters took up covering positions along the trail, he
and Olivera moved quickly ahead, then stopped after a short distance to cover Craddock and McMasters as they moved forward.
The team continued along the trail in this manner until Gannon's
night-vision goggles caught the first glow of campfires long before
they were visible to the naked eye.

With the camp in sight, the team again took cover and grouped
at a huge fallen tree that lay at an angle across the trail, its crown
held up by thick branches and entangled vines, allowing room to
walk beneath it. Fifty feet into the jungle, at the base of the tree,
there was a large hole where its root system had once anchored it
to the earth. Huge buttress roots rose like missile fins from the
fetid jungle floor, and nearby, lightning or decay had brought
others down, opening brief holes to the night sky. Far enough off
the trail, and surrounded by a tangle of ancient tree trunks and
thick underbrush, it was a well concealed and easily identifiable
location that would serve as a rally point. Gannon instructed the
team to cache their rucksacks in the hole beneath the upended root
system, then led them on, unencumbered, to reconnoiter the camp
and select their surveillance hide sites before first light.

•

Nine hundred miles north-northeast of the jungle camp, the C-141
transporting the Delta Force assault squadron and the mission
support personnel from Fort Bragg touched down at Howard Air
Force Base, Panama. Two dark blue Air Force buses with blacked-
out windows awaited their arrival and pulled up to the rear of the
aircraft just as the doors opened and the ramp lowered to the
ground. The squadron quickly disembarked, transferred their
gear, and boarded the vehicles. The drivers knew nothing of the
top-secret mission, nor did the base commander, who was told
only that the arrival of the men was part of a classified Special
Forces training exercise.

Inside an isolated, high-security compound in a remote corner
of the base, the buses stopped in front of an empty hangar where
the men immediately off-loaded their equipment, closed the huge
doors, and shut their activities off from the rest of the base. Outside the hangar, hunkered silent and forbidding on the apron,

were the three Pave Low helicopters that had been flown down from the 20th Special Operations Squadron at Hurlburt Field, Florida. The crews from the Pave Lows, who would fly the assault mission, had joined the Delta Force personnel inside.

The squadron commander waited patiently as members of Signal Squadron set up the communications console at the rear of the hangar. Within minutes they were manning the radios that linked them both to Delta Force headquarters at Fort Bragg and Gannon's team on the ground in Peru.

Three members of the advance team, who had flown down with the first C-141, appeared with boxes of sandwiches and urns of hot coffee for the squadron. The intelligence support cell NCOs went about setting up display boards, posting satellite photos, diagrams, and maps to which they would add the crucial detailed information of the camp layout as it was relayed to them by Gannon and his men.

"Anything come in since we landed?" the squadron commander asked one of the NCOs manning the satellite radio.

"Nothing, boss," the young staff sergeant said. "They should be down for a while longer. The last transmission said they were preparing their hide sites."

"Let me know as soon as they report in."

"Will do."

The squadron commander's primary interest was in the verification that Sincavage was still at the camp. If CIA's agent had been compromised, which now seemed probable, and had led Sincavage to suspect that he was being hunted, a man with his skills could disappear into the dark reaches of the illegal covert world without a trace.

—24—

Gray morning light spread slowly across the horizon as an errant breeze blew down off the Andes, parting and dispersing the ground fog that shrouded the jungle camp in a cool mist. Two old campesinos were the first to stir, rising early to start the cooking fire for the morning meal. As the first thin shafts of sunlight dappled the ground, the din of the jungle rose to its peak—a peak that would diminish to virtual silence in the midday heat. One by one the guerrillas in the large open-sided dormitories swung out of their hammocks and straggled toward the bath house. Most didn't bother to use the highly prized flush toilets inside, and simply relieved themselves at the edge of the jungle.

Gannon hastily scribbled brief notes on the number of men and the locations of their weapons as he watched the camp come to life. Two hours before dawn he had chosen a hide site in a tangled clump of dense underbrush behind the communications shack. From where he lay concealed in a natural depression in the ground, he had an excellent view of the main campsite and was close enough to the communications shack to overhear what went on inside. The collapsible four foot by six foot piece of green iodized chicken wire he had taken from his rucksack and unfolded to place over the top of the depression was expertly woven with pieces of sod and vegetation he had gathered some distance away. It covered him completely, leaving a space of six inches overhead as he lay in a prone position peering out at the camp. As an added precaution, he wore a Ghilley cape over his fatigues—a shroud to which irregular strips of multi-colored burlap, canvas, and camouflage netting in jungle colors were attached. The overall effect was to make him virtually indistinguishable from his surroundings.

Ten yards deeper into the jungle, almost directly behind Gannon and equally well concealed, Sergeant Major Joe Olivera had established his hide site with a twofold purpose: to provide cover for Gannon's close-in position, and with the satellite radio set up beside him, to relay back to headquarters and the squadron in Panama, the reports he received over the interteam radio from the other men.

Although it was against sound principles of operation to have men posted alone, Gannon had no choice but to split Craddock and McMasters up in order to cover both the cocaine-processing part of the camp, and at the far end of the compound, the area where a cluster of huts and an obstacle course were located near the clearing that would serve as the landing zone for the assault squadron.

McMasters had finished excavating his shallow hide site and disposing of the soil farther back in the jungle just before dawn. Hidden twenty feet off the footpath that ran in front of the cluster of small thatched-roof huts, he was still able to observe the vital clearing even though it was fifty yards away and not in his field of vision. Before crawling into his hide site he had set up and concealed a small battery-operated video camera just beyond the obstacle course. Equipped with a low-frequency transmitter, the camera sent its signal back to where McMasters viewed the black and white picture on the three-inch screen of a modified Sony Video Watchman. The wide-angle lens on the camera enabled him to remotely monitor the entire clearing.

Craddock was the first to come up on the interteam radio, reporting on the activity at the drug-processing part of the camp.

"The count is forty-three, so far," he whispered into his voice-activated throat microphone as the men arrived at work after finishing their breakfasts.

"All unarmed worker bees. No perimeter defenses. Strictly an unprotected work area with no sleeping shelters. Judging from what I saw before dawn, the heat lamps in the drying shed are left on, but the area's deserted after work hours."

From his position behind the communications shack, Gannon spotted a short, light-haired man he immediately recognized as the Australian from the photographs the CIA had provided for the briefings. Stomping across the compound, using the gruff tones of authority, the stocky mercenary roused the fifty guerrillas from the mess area. After they retrieved their weapons from where they were stacked in the dormitories, he mustered them into a semblance of a military formation, providing Gannon with a perfect opportunity for an accurate count of every guerrilla under his command.

Gannon continued watching and making mental notes as half the guerrillas formed into five-man patrols and headed out of camp toward the mountain trail that led in the direction of a village in a distant valley. The Australian led the other twenty-five guerrillas down the trail toward the airstrip. Judging from the shouted commands Gannon heard coming from that direction a short time later, he concluded that they were conducting a training session on ambushes and quick-reaction drills.

McMasters, unlike his teammates who had managed to relax and grab a few hours sleep in the squadron bay before leaving Fort Bragg and again before leaving Panama, had gotten little more than a brief catnap in the past forty-eight hours. Tired and groggy, he yawned, then tried to shake the fuzziness from his head as he shifted into a more comfortable position on his side and listened to his teammates reporting their observations to Gannon.

A dull scraping sound brought him fully alert and drew his attention to the hut directly in front of him. As the door opened, two men stepped outside onto the footpath that ran along the edge of the jungle. Moments later two women emerged from another hut, immediately joined by two more men from the hut farthest from his position. All were young Latinos, dressed in camouflage fatigues with bandannas tied around their heads. They were armed with MAC-10 submachine guns, with the exception of one of the women and the taller of the men, who carried portable rocket launchers that McMasters recognized as being German-made Armbrusts. Though unguided, in the hands of someone who knew how to handle them, the powerful anti-armor rockets posed a serious threat to the Pave Low helicopters, a threat that McMasters knew would have to be eliminated as soon as the assault began.

His attention was still on the six young guerrillas when the door of the hut closest to the trail leading to the obstacle course opened. Upon seeing the face of the man who emerged, McMasters smiled and clenched his fist in silent victory. Tall and blond with chiseled features and hard eyes, he matched perfectly the artist's rendering of the man who was the target of their operation. At the moment McMasters was about to whisper into his throat mike and verify Sincavage's presence in the camp, he felt a sudden heavy weight on his ankles.

Slowly turning his head to avoid making any noise, he looked back at his feet and drew a quick, horrified breath that only training and uncommon discipline allowed him to keep from vocalizing into a bloodcurdling scream.

"Ah, shit . . . ahhhh!" His voice was barely a hoarse whisper, but it was carried over the sensitive throat mike to the rest of the team.

"Hide Four, that you?" Gannon said, using the code that designated each of the men. Getting no response he tried again. "Hide Four, this is Hide One. Respond."

"Can't talk now, boss," followed by a low guttural noise was all McMasters managed at the sound of Gannon's voice whispering in his earpiece.

Slithering across McMasters's boots, half in and half out of the shallow trench where he lay concealed beneath a roof of woven sod and brush, was a huge green-and-tan-colored snake—an anaconda, as thick as his upper arm. A forked tongue flicked in and out of a wedge-shaped head the size of a man's hand, sensing its quarry as the lower half of its body thudded into the shallow pit and landed on McMasters's ankles, pinning them to the ground. Eight feet long and weighing well over one hundred fifty pounds, the powerful reptile began coiling around the lower part of McMasters's legs, the crushing pressure sending sharp jolts of pain throughout his body. McMasters froze in position, a reaction that caused the frightening creature to move slowly, rather than encircling rapidly as it would a prey that was trying to escape.

McMasters's eyes were wide with horror. His combat knife was in the sheath strapped around the calf of his right leg, now covered by the snake's body. Any sudden forceful movement or struggle on his part would be heard by Sincavage and the team of guerrillas standing twenty feet away in front of the huts. Remaining motionless in the grip of the awesome killer required willpower and composure that McMasters did not know he possessed until that moment.

The terrified Delta Force trooper's eyes darted back and forth from Sincavage to the snake as he quickly but calmly pulled open the flap of the rucksack that lay at the top of the trench near his head. Reaching inside, he felt the grip of the silenced 9mm Beretta pistol each member of the team had brought with him and flipped off the safety as he pulled it out. Part of the snake's body now completely encircled his lower legs up to his knees. Its head was moving rhythmically back and forth, its tongue flicking, as it inched steadily toward his face. The pain and pressure on his legs was excruciating, and McMasters feared he would involuntarily cry out.

Another frantic glance toward the huts, and he saw that Sincavage and the young guerrillas were preparing to move out. But they were still close enough to hear the bolt clatter of the silenced pistol if it was fired. Seconds seemed an eternity as the pain and pressure increased with each passing moment. Just as McMasters reached the point where he could bear it no longer, Sincavage and his team began to move along the footpath toward the obstacle course. The sound of their voices, the shuffle of boots, and the rattle of the equipment they carried were all that McMasters needed. Holding the tip of the silencer only a fraction of an inch from the snake's head, he squeezed the trigger twice in rapid succession. Both rounds tore through one of the creature's dark, unblinking eyes, causing it to shudder momentarily, then flop limply to the ground.

The pressure on McMasters's lower body was slowly relieved as the thick coils relaxed their death grip.

McMasters immediately glanced in the direction he had last seen Sincavage and his team. They were moving slowly down the path toward the clearing, completely unaware of the life and death struggle that had taken place only twenty feet from where they had stood.

The still frightened trooper lay motionless, gulping in huge breaths and struggling to gain control over his quivering body when Gannon's voice again whispered in his earpiece.

"Hide Four. Report in."

McMasters took one last deep, even breath to steady his voice and said, "This is Hide Four. Got a positive ID on Viper. He just left my area in the direction of the clearing. Six guerrillas were with him. Two with rocket launchers."

"You're sure it's Viper?" Gannon said, the thought of Sincavage being in such close proximity causing the old enmity to stir again.

"Positive."

"Are you okay?" Gannon asked, detecting the uncharacteristic quaver in the young trooper's voice.

There was a pause, then, "I'm okay, boss. But I'll be even better as soon as I unwrap this goddamn snake from my legs."

There was no reply from Gannon, but McMasters heard the low rumble of a stifled laugh through his earpiece, accompanied by similar muffled sounds from Olivera and Craddock.

As the day wore on, Gannon, McMasters, and Craddock continued to observe and note what they saw in a constant stream of whispered reports to Olivera. They concentrated on the number of people in the camp, types and numbers of weapons, security activities, trails, and apparent leaders and their activities. McMasters came up with a crucial piece of intelligence information for the assault squadron. Using the video monitor to observe the clearing that would serve as the landing zone for the assault, he determined from the activities of Sincavage and his team that the area was not mined, as was previously suspected. Another observation, made as he watched the guerrilla team rehearsing a simulated attack on a motorcade, made him single out the young girl with the rocket launcher as his first target when the time came—her accuracy was to be admired, even by someone like McMasters, who was expert with the weapon.

Designating the corner of the airstrip where they had landed as a base starting point—a location clearly visible on the satellite photographs—Olivera began charting the positions of all the camps structures as the team reported them to him. He noted a brief description of each building and each part of the camp, including the apparent purpose it served, and any inhabitants that were observed. An alpha-numerical designation was used as well, a system that would allow the intelligence support cell in the hangar in Panama to layout the entire camp for the assault squadron. When Olivera had his charts complete and his notes organized, he began his transmission by giving the precise location of each team member's hide site—a precaution that in the confusion of battle during the assault, would let the squadron know precisely where the R&S team was.

"Location, Hide One: 225 degrees, 1780 meters from infiltration drop zone. Overlooks probable command post, communications site and living area . . . Break . . . Location Hide Two from Hide One; 175 degrees, 10 meters . . ." he continued on until all the hide sites were plotted, then using similar brevity codes, he described the camp layout.

"Building One Alpha, from Hide One, 318 degrees, 5 meters; commo building. Three meters by three meters. Door on north side. Generator ten meters into jungle off northwest corner . . . Break . . . Building One Bravo, from Hide One, 355 degrees, 30 meters. Living quarters. Five meters by one-five meters, oriented east/west. Open all sides. One lamp on southwest corner . . . Break."

•

Inside the hangar at Howard Air Force Base, Panama, a complete picture of the camp was beginning to take shape. As the R&S team's information continued to come in throughout the day, the squadron's intelligence support cell constantly updated the maps and overlays on the satellite photographs.

The squadron commander studied the large-scale map on

which the information was being plotted. With the verification of Sincavage's presence, and having established that the assault would be coming in almost on top of the hut serving as his quarters, he was committing its exact location to memory and forming a mental picture of the route he would take from the landing zone to reach it. If Sincavage was in his hut at the time of the assault, McMasters was to keep him inside for the fifteen or twenty seconds he estimated it would take him and his three-man snatch team to get there from the clearing. The backup team accompanying him would neutralize the six members of the guerrilla team while he and his men grabbed Sincavage. If he was not in the hut, the plan would be adjusted according to Gannon's information on Sincavage's whereabouts just prior to the arrival of the squadron.

The squadron commander was under no illusions about the difficulty of the task before him. The man they were dealing with was highly trained and experienced. He had not survived multiple combat tours of borderline suicide missions in Vietnam by being careless and unprepared. One of the later reports McMasters had passed along, after observing an outdoor classroom session near the huts, had pointedly reminded the commander of that fact. McMasters had described the instructions Sincavage was giving his guerrilla students in the fine art of disabling a target limousine, and the tactics of a follow-on assault on a motorcade. McMasters's comment had been that "this guy knows his stuff."

At 1320 hours, their final briefings and briefbacks complete, the men of Delta Force C squadron loaded their gear and boarded the waiting helicopters. At 1330 hours the huge Pave Lows squirmed on their landing gear, impatient to be airborne as their powerful turbine engines whined at fever pitch. The first two helicopters to lift off each carried twenty-three Delta Force troopers. The third Pave Low was a flying spare, to be brought into service in the event either of the others developed mechanical problems or crashed. Rising like great prehistoric birds, the three helicopters nosed down, gaining speed and altitude as they turned and headed south across the sparkling blue water of the Gulf of Panama.

—25—

TWENTY-TWO HUNDRED HOURS—
OCTOBER 9TH

Lack of sleep and immobility in the cramped hide site were beginning to take their toll on Olivera. Only the occasional whispered reports from his teammates had kept him from falling sound asleep. As he was about to doze off again, the sudden short beep of an encryption device came over the satellite radio headset he had covering one ear while monitoring the interteam radio in the other. The familiar voice that followed snapped him out of his lethargy and started the adrenaline coursing through his body.

"Thirty minutes out." It was the Delta squadron commander on board the lead helicopter. "Any update on Viper's location?"

"Wait one," Olivera said, and contacted McMasters on the interteam radio.

"Viper's in his hut," McMasters whispered in reply, looking to see if the light still glowed inside. "His lamp's still lit." Fifteen minutes earlier he had watched the six young guerrillas return from the main part of the camp, exhausted after a long day of rigorous training. They had entered their huts, not even bothering to light their lamps, and had not stirred since. "Looks like the others are down for the night. Lamps out."

Olivera relayed Viper's location and the information on the guerrilla team to the squadron commander on board the lead Pave Low.

"Roger that," the squadron commander replied. "Will contact again when twenty minutes out."

Gannon had been keeping track of the personnel in the main part of the camp. The majority of the unarmed campesinos who worked the drug-processing site were in their dormitory, asleep in their hammocks. They were no longer of immediate interest to Gannon, who concentrated on the fifty guerrillas under the Australian mercenary's command. Ten of them sat in small groups around two separate campfires near the kitchen area, four played cards at a dining table by the light of a lantern. He counted another twenty-three lounging about their open-sided dormitory, smoking or sharing bottles of rum and relaxing in their hammocks. The plaintive songs of the lone balladeer the team had heard the previous night entertained another four, and the nine guerrillas he had seen enter the improvised porno theater were still inside, hooting and laughing, and by the sound of their voices, getting drunk while satisfying their prurient needs.

The guerrillas in and around the dormitory were the only ones in close proximity to their weapons. The others had left their AK-47s stacked beside their hammocks, where they had placed them upon returning from their patrols and training exercises. The lack of proper camp security left more than half of the guerrilla force in no position to recover their weapons quickly and organize a proper defense between the time they heard the helicopters and the short time it would take the assault forces to reach them. It was a situation that along with darkness and the element of surprise helped offset the overwhelming odds Gannon and Olivera faced, enabling them to concentrate their fire in a limited area. Based on the observations of the previous night, the camp generators ran until midnight and would provide a further edge—the noise they created would cover the sound of the helicopters until they rose above the hill at the far end of the landing zone and descended into the clearing.

Gannon had lost sight of Anderson, the Australian mercenary they had code-named "Gunslinger," and asked Olivera if he knew his location.

"He was walking in the direction of Hide Three last time I saw him," Olivera replied.

Craddock's voice came over the interteam radio. He was still in his hide site at the drug-processing area even though it had been deserted shortly after sundown. "Gunslinger just passed by, moving toward Hide Four."

"Got him," McMasters whispered as Anderson appeared on the trail bordering the huts. "He's headed toward the clearing. Got an AK-47 with him."

With the time of the assault growing nearer, Olivera had shaken off the creeping drowsiness, and came fully alert and tensed for the action to come when he again heard the voice of the squadron commander come over the headset.

"Twenty minutes out. Any further updates?"

After checking with McMasters, Olivera replied, "No change on Viper. Gunslinger is somewhere in the immediate area of your LZ. Will confirm location and report."

"Roger," the squadron commander said. "Confirm and report on Gunslinger."

With the helicopters only twenty minutes from the camp, Gannon began moving the team out of their hide sites and into position for the assault. He had seen Sincavage three times during the day as he walked through the camp with his trainees, once passing no more than twenty feet from Gannon's hide site. He was disturbed by how strongly the emotions of more than two decades ago took hold of him at the sight of Sincavage, and how vivid his memories were of Tiu and her son and their bullet-riddled bodies, torn and bleeding as Sincavage stood over them, his face showing no more emotion than if he had just shot two squirrels.

He still had that same cold, detached look, and with every fiber of his being, Gannon wanted to change hide sites with McMasters, and personally cover Sincavage's movements until the assault troops arrived, not wanting to take any chance of losing him in the confusion of the squadron's insertion and attack on the camp. And on a more visceral level, he wanted to see the look on Sincavage's face when he dragged him into the jungle and cuffed his hands behind his back and then threw him on board one of the helicopters. But changing positions with McMasters held the danger of discovery and the possibility of bringing a guerrilla force far superior in numbers down on the rest of the team without the squadron there to back them up. His primary responsibility, along with Olivera, was to contain the guerrillas from the time the first sounds of the helicopters alerted them to the impending assault, until the Delta Force troopers reached the main part of the camp. Focusing on the task before him, he forced the thoughts of a confrontation with Sincavage to the back of his mind.

"Hide Four, move close in on Viper's hut," he whispered to McMasters over the interteam radio. "Stay with him at all costs. Hide Three, move to the edge of the LZ and report on Gunslinger's location and activities," he told Craddock.

Leaving his hide site and taking cover at the edge of the jungle beside the communications shack, Gannon directed Olivera to a position on his right flank, a few yards from the porno theater, where he quickly set up and reoriented the antenna for the Satcom radio.

"As soon as we hear the choppers, you take care of the heavy breathers at the movies," he told Olivera. "I'll knock out the radio shack. The moment the squadron hits the ground, we concentrate on the guerrillas' dormitory and take down anyone who acts like a leader."

McMasters voice came over the interteam radio. "Viper's on the move."

Out of his hide site, McMasters had taken cover behind a large tree just inside the edge of the jungle, immediately in front of Sincavage's hut. As Sincavage stepped out onto the path directly in front of him, no more than ten feet away, he was close enough that McMasters could have easily killed him with the silenced Beretta, but with orders to take him alive, he stood silently, watching and waiting. Any botched attempt to grab him at this point posed the threat of alerting the entire camp to the team's presence and endangering the squadron upon arrival.

Sincavage paused to light a cigarette, then turned to walk down the trail toward the clearing where the assault force would soon land. McMasters noticed the Walther PPK semi-automatic pistol tucked inside the waistband at the small of his back, but his attention was drawn to the flashlight and the black duffel bag he carried with him. He had seen the bag earlier that day, when Sincavage had spent an hour target shooting with the break-down sniper rifle he carried inside it.

"He's got the seven-millimeter Magnum with him," McMasters whispered into the throat mike when Sincavage was out of earshot. "And a flashlight."

"Damn!" Gannon said. "He's going night shooting."

"Great timing," McMasters said as he watched Sincavage continue along the trail and out of view.

Craddock's voice came over the radio, so low it was barely audible. "I've got him in sight. He's entered the clearing and walking along the edge, headed for the backstop he used before."

"Where's Gunslinger?" Gannon asked.

Craddock looked back to where Anderson sat ten yards out into the clearing on a large, flat boulder, plainly visible in the moonlight. "He's still here, smoking and stargazing."

"Ten minutes out," Olivera heard the Delta squadron commander say over the Satcom headset. "Is Viper's location still the same?"

"He's moving," Olivera said, and again listened to the team's conversation in his ear piece.

"Hide Four," Gannon said to McMasters. "Move out and stay with Viper. Give him plenty of room, but keep him in sight. Hide Three," he instructed Craddock, "stay with Gunslinger."

"We got Hide Four on Viper," Olivera reported back to the squadron commander on the lead Pave Low. "Will keep you posted. Hide Three reports transponder in place and transmitting."

"Roger. Transponder on," the squadron commander acknowledged.

The minitransponder Craddock had placed at the edge of the

clearing was sending out a signal that the Pave Lows could home in on to lead them directly to the landing zone. The sophisticated navigation equipment on board the helicopters was accurate enough to bring them to within ten yards of the clearing, but the Delta Force troopers were firm believers in redundant systems.

Aboard the troop-carrying Pave Lows, the Delta Force assault squadron rose from the sprawled positions they had assumed while attempting to rest during the long flight from Panama. They lined up, sitting on the floor in the order they would exit the helicopter.

At the jungle camp, Olivera repeated the ten-minute warning to his teammates, causing McMasters to curse softly under his breath as he moved cautiously along the edge of the trail in the direction Viper had gone.

●

Sincavage had noticed Anderson out of the corner of his eye as he entered the clearing, but did nothing to acknowledge his presence. He had disliked the loudmouthed, glad-handing braggart upon meeting him, and was annoyed by his insidious way of finding weak excuses to observe his training sessions. He had twice considered killing him on the off chance that he was reporting his activities to a third party, but unsure of the loyalty of the fifty guerrillas in his charge, had decided against it.

He stopped in front of the shooting backstop at the far end of the clearing and removed a rolled-up human-silhouette target from the duffel bag and tacked it to the plywood facing. A short distance away, he positioned the flashlight until the beam hit the target at an angle that only partially illuminated it. After standing back to observe the effect, he crossed to the tree line where a narrow footpath switchbacked up the side of a hill to a rock ledge that overlooked the shooting backstop at a distance of one hundred yards.

McMasters reached the clearing in time to see Sincavage disappear into the deep shadows at the jungle's edge. With his night-vision goggles in position, he tracked the glow of the small pen-light Sincavage was using to find his way up the steep jungle trail. He also saw Anderson off to his left, and could move no farther into the clearing without stepping into his field of vision. To his right, he stared at the near-impenetrable jungle leading up the hillside in the direction Sincavage was going. Movement over the rough terrain would be extremely difficult and slow, making it impossible for him to keep pace with Sincavage unless he used the same trail.

Frustrated by the sudden turn of events, he stepped back under cover of the jungle and whispered into his throat mike. "Hide Three, this is Hide Four. You've got to take Gunslinger out now. Otherwise I'm going to lose contact with Viper."

"What's the situation?" Gannon broke in.

"We've got what . . . seven minutes?" McMasters said as he glanced at the luminous dial on his watch. "Viper's at an elevated site, away from the noise of the camp. He's gonna hear the choppers any minute and I don't have him in sight."

Gannon made his decision, responding immediately. "Hide Three, eliminate Gunslinger so Hide Four can move in on Viper."

"You want him dead?" Craddock asked.

"Whatever works."

Craddock slipped out of his rucksack and propped it against a tree. Releasing the safety on his silenced pistol, he moved to the edge of the clearing. Anderson was smoking another cigarette, facing away from the man who now began silently stalking him.

McMasters watched impatiently from the side of the trail, alternately glancing from Anderson to the steep terrain at his right. From the glow of Sincavage's penlight, McMasters saw that he had reached the crest of the hill and was now headed toward the rock ledge. In a few moments Anderson would be below him, to his left, and within his field of vision.

A night wind rustled the leaves along the clearing, helping to mask Craddock's cautious approach through the knee-high grass. Rising from a crouch directly behind the unsuspecting mercenary, he swiftly closed to within arm's reach and brought the barrel of the pistol down forcefully across the back of his skull.

Anderson grunted, expelling a sharp breath, then collapsed. Craddock grabbed him beneath the arms and dragged him back into the jungle, where he quickly placed a strip of tape across his mouth and secured his hands behind his back with Velcro wrist cuffs he removed from his rucksack.

The moment McMasters saw Anderson collapse, he had moved from cover and started up the jungle trail in pursuit of Sincavage. With the night-vision goggles illuminating the way, he soon closed the distance.

Sincavage had been lying in a prone position on the rock ledge, adjusting the telescopic sight on the sniper rifle, when the abrupt muted sound from below reached him. He had remained motionless for a long moment, then keeping his eye to the scope, he slowly moved the rifle in the direction he had heard what he at first suspected was merely Anderson clearing his throat. His body tensed when in the bright moonlight, fifty feet below him at the edge of the clearing, he caught a brief glimpse of the mercenary's body from the knees down as it was dragged into the jungle.

Instinct and experience told him that a full-scale attack on the camp was imminent. Moments later, a faint, distant sound served to reinforce that conclusion. It was an unmistakable sound, one that was a permanent part of the memories of those who served in combat in Vietnam, instantly recognizable for the rest of their lives. It faded, lost on the wind that swirled and changed direction as it blew across the rock ledge. And then it was back. One helicopter . . . no, more than one. The low throbbing sound grew louder with each passing second.

Sincavage quickly disassembled the sniper rifle and put it back in the duffel bag. His eyes were scanning now, his senses finely tuned to his surroundings. There was someone on the trail, approaching fast. With the duffel bag slung across his back, he low-crawled off the ledge into the cover of the jungle, where he screwed the silencer onto the barrel of the Walther and rose on one knee to look back in the direction of the trail.

McMasters slowed his approach for fear of being heard as he neared the crest of the hill. He stopped just short of the open area and observed the rock ledge through his night-vision goggles. Viper was nowhere in sight.

"Hide One, this is Hide Four," McMasters whispered into his throat mike. "I've lost him. And I think he's on to us."

"Goddamnit!" Gannon muttered. "Get on him! Fast!"

Olivera immediately relayed the development over the Satcom radio to the squadron commander aboard the lead Pave Low.

"Two minutes out," the squadron commander responded. "Is the LZ secure?"

"That's affirmative," Olivera said after Craddock responded to the question, and added, "Gunslinger is out of the game. Ignore the flashlight on the east end of the clearing."

Gannon's voice, tight and angry, came over the interteam radio. "Hide Three," he said to Craddock, "leave the LZ and cover the guerrillas' huts. Hide Four, continue in pursuit of Viper."

McMasters advanced slowly toward the rock ledge, staying just inside the cover of the jungle. Two of the helicopters were now visible on the horizon through his night-vision goggles, appearing and disappearing as they followed the contour of the land. The third Pave Low, acting as a flying spare, had dropped out of the formation at the ten-minute warning to orbit at a distance. It would stay there for the duration of the mission, ready to respond in the event of a mechanical problem or to conduct search and rescue if the assault helicopters crashed.

"I can see the choppers," McMasters said. "They're about one minute out."

The Pave Lows were not yet close enough to be heard above the ambient noise of the main part of the camp. Gannon estimated that it would be another forty seconds before the huge helicopters, using their terrain-following radar to fly nap-of-the-earth, rose over the hills at the far end of the clearing, their powerful engines shattering the night and sending the camp into a flurry of activity. He and Olivera each laid four hand grenades at their sides and waited for the sound to reach them.

Sincavage spotted McMasters moving slowly toward the ledge. He had a clear shot at him with the silenced Walther, but not knowing if it was one man or a team pursuing him, and certain they would be armed with automatic weapons, he let the opportunity pass. Staying low, he slipped deeper into the jungle, where he circled back to where the trail continued down the opposite side of the hill and exited near his hut.

McMasters was about to return to the clearing, fearing he had lost Sincavage to the jungle, when his night-vision goggles again picked up the glow of the penlight on the back side of the hill. It was moving steadily downward, in the direction of the camp.

"Hide One, this is Hide Four," McMasters said into his throat mike. "I've got Viper in sight."

"Don't lose him again!" Gannon said. "If you have a shot, wound him and take him down."

"Roger that, boss," McMasters replied.

McMasters quickly backtracked to the trail he had used to ascend the hill, and found where it branched off and continued down the other side. With Sincavage aware of his presence, stealth was no longer a consideration, and he moved out at a fast pace, keeping the glowing penlight in sight.

The crescendo of the approaching helicopters increased to a sudden roar as the powerful turbine engines thundered and throbbed, echoing off the surrounding hills and rumbling on through the campsite. Appearing like deadly aberrations in the night, the Pave Lows rose swiftly over the final hill to flare and hover thirty feet above the grassy, boulder-strewn landing zone. Two fifty-foot-long fast ropes were tossed from the rear ramp, and another out the right front door of both helicopters.

With split-second timing, the twenty-three men on board each of the Pave Lows slid down the two-and-one-half-inch-thick soft braided ropes fire-pole fashion, several on each rope at one time, grasping them in their gloved hands and between their knees and feet. Eight seconds later all forty-six Delta Force troops were on the ground and moving off the clearing, their weapons at the ready. Able to communicate with the R&S team over the interteam radio, they heard the four men report their exact locations to the on-rushing troops to avoid being hit by friendly fire.

Confusion and terror reigned throughout the main part of the camp. With the arrival of the helicopters, Gannon and Olivera had each tossed two fragmentation grenades into the radio shack and the porno theater. The guerrillas inside were killed instantly. The thatch and bamboo structures caught fire and burned quickly, sending roiling fireballs into the night.

Two guerrillas sitting at one of the campfires jumped up and began shouting orders to those around the dormitory; the reward for their leadership efforts was to be singled out and killed immediately by two accurate three-shot bursts from Gannon's CAR-15. Olivera lobbed two more grenades at a concentrated group of guerrillas, then covered the area with a barrage of grazing fire from the deadly squad automatic weapon.

The helicopter crews added to the chaos. With the Delta troops on the ground, the two Pave Lows broke to each side of the camp, tossing out firefight simulators. The time-delayed pyrotechnics simulated machine-gun fire, punctuated with random explosions that ripped through the air with the force of grenade blasts. Guerrillas who had run into the jungle to escape the initial attack, now turned and ran back, believing that the camp was surrounded on all sides and that they were caught in a crossfire.

The first Delta assault troops to reach the main part of the camp spread out to encircle the remaining guerrillas, who had now recovered from the initial shock to the point of returning fire from small pockets of resistance under cover of the jungle. The unarmed campesinos ran in all directions, waving their arms to show that they had no weapons, or simply lay flat on the ground, shouting pleas to the unseen attackers not to shoot them.

McMasters reached the bottom of the trail near the huts to see four men from the assault squadron turn and train their weapons on him. Lying strewn across the trail were the bodies of Sincavage's six guerrillas. They had been cut down by Craddock as they bolted from the huts at the sound of the helicopters.

"Hide Four on trail at huts!" he shouted into the throat mike, identifying himself the instant before the Delta troopers were about to fire at his shadowy figure.

The four men immediately lowered their weapons and moved out, heading to where the mountain trail leading to the distant village entered the camp; their assignment was to knock out any vehicles attempting to bring reinforcements. One of the men was armed with a Swedish-made AT-4 antitank rocket launcher.

McMasters saw Craddock lying at the side of the trail, a squadron medic kneeling beside him. "Is it bad?"

"Shoulder wound," the medic answered. "He'll be all right."

The confrontation had cost McMasters precious seconds in his pursuit of Sincavage. He continued across the trail, scanning the jungle with his night-vision goggles. The glow of the penlight was gone. Explosive flashes from the firefight simulators made it impossible to single out Sincavage's telltale light any longer. But McMasters continued to watch, moving his head slowly back and forth, traversing the depths of the jungle, hoping the goggles would catch a brief glimpse of a moving light that would reveal Sincavage's location. But there was nothing. The bright glare of the burning camp structures and the intermittent muzzle flashes from the dwindling battle at the main part of the camp further interfered with his search. He had lost him.

Gannon had lost radio contact with McMasters as he descended the back side of the hill in pursuit of Sincavage. The assault squadron had the main part of the camp under control, and Gannon, taking Olivera with him, left his position, announcing over the interteam radio that they were moving in the direction of the huts. Upon finding them cleared out, he then led Olivera, who had picked up one of the dead guerrillas' rocket launchers, back in the direction of the main part of the camp, halting on the trail when he heard McMasters identify himself to the four Delta troopers.

"Hide Four. What's your position?" he asked over the interteam radio.

"South side of the main camp," McMasters said. "Forty meters into the jungle from the huts."

"Have you got Viper in sight?"

"Negative. I've lost him," McMasters said. "He was moving west; in the direction of the airstrip."

"There may be a plane there," Gannon said. "I noticed something during our infiltration. Didn't have time to check it out."

The Delta trooper assigned to take charge of the Australian mercenary, who had regained consciousness, heard the conversation in his earpiece. Turning to Anderson, he ripped the tape from his mouth and asked, "Is there a plane hidden at the airstrip?"

Anderson hesitated, then shrugged. "Arrogant bastard's nothing to me. There's a twin engine turbo prop pulled off the south end of the strip. Gassed and ready to go."

The trooper relayed the information over the interteam radio.

"Hide Four," Gannon said. "We'll take it from here."

As he neared the main compound, Gannon announced his presence to the troops encircling the area, alerting them that he

and Olivera would be moving at a fast pace across the south side of
the camp onto the trail leading to the airstrip. The volume of fire
from the camp had dwindled to an occasional volley from a diehard
group of seven guerrillas who had taken cover in the kitchen area.
A few threw down their weapons and ran into the jungle as the
Delta Force troops, who were closing in on them, laid down a
withering barrage of covering fire as Gannon and Olivera sprinted
through the camp.

Sincavage reached the airstrip just as the sustained volley of
fire from the camp erupted. He ran to the improvised hangar
hacked out of the jungle at the end of the strip, and climbed into
the cockpit of the MU-2. He breathed a sigh of relief as the turbo
prop engines turned over and roared to life on the first try. Taxiing
out onto the extreme south end of the runway, at the edge of the
deep ravine, he swung the aircraft around, holding it in place with
the brakes as he gradually moved the throttles to full power.

Gannon and Olivera were only a hundred yards from the airstrip when they heard the distinctive high-pitched sound of the
turbo props.

"Lead Pave Low, this is Hide One. Are you monitoring the
interteam frequency?" Gannon said into his throat mike.

"Roger, Hide One. Monitoring," the pilot of the lead helicopter came back.

"Break off and move into position to block the airstrip. Immediately."

"Roger," the pilot replied.

The huge helicopter responded quickly, but too late. Gannon
and Olivera reached the runway to see the streamlined aircraft race
down the grassy strip on its takeoff run. Sincavage held the wheels
on the ground until the last possible moment, then pulled back on
the yoke and rose swiftly into the night, launched off the end of the
runway like a fighter plane catapulted from a carrier deck.

In desperation, Gannon grabbed the rocket launcher from
Olivera, shouldered it and took aim.

"Hey, boss," Olivera said. "They want him alive."

"Judgment call" was all Gannon said, and fired.

The unguided rocket roared from the launcher, closing fast on
the tail section of the plane. But without an internal guidance

system, it was a hopelessly futile effort. The rocket soared upward, passed behind the aircraft's vertical stabilizer, and impacted into the rock face of a hill at the far end of the runway.

The shock waves from the explosion rippled outward and rocked the fast-departing plane. Sincavage saw the brief flash in his peripheral vision and immediately worked the rudder and ailerons. Satisfied that there was no blast damage to the surface controls, he concentrated on his climb out through the jagged peaks on either side.

Gannon stood at the edge of the strip, staring after the plane as it continued to gain speed and altitude. The lead Pave Low had missed the takeoff run by only seconds, and the pilot, following Gannon's orders, did his best to prevent the aircraft's escape. Hovering above the runway, he swung the helicopter broadside so the gunner manning the 7.62 caliber minigun mounted at the left side door had a clear field of fire toward the fleeing plane. But it was again too little, too late. The MU-2 was out of range of the rotating cannon's fusillade, and the Pave Low was too slow by half to pursue it.

•

The MU-2 Solitaire climbed steadily toward a cruising altitude of thirty thousand feet. Sincavage, relaxed and in control once again, checked his instruments and gauges. The tanks had a full load of fuel, having been topped off earlier from the supply kept on hand at the camp, in preparation for his planned departure the following morning. The assault and the loss of his team did not disturb him as much as one would have expected. The guerrillas had been important to his plan, though not vital. But the new circumstances did require a revised strategy—a fallback to an alternative plan, one that was formulating in his mind at that very moment.

With the plane on autopilot, he settled into his seat as his mind flashed back over the night's events. The surprise raid on the camp was not something he had anticipated, given the cocaine cartel's high-level informants inside the Peruvian government. But the fact that there was already a reconnaissance team on the ground prior to the arrival of the assault force led him to suspect that it was not a combined U.S. Drug Enforcement Agency and Peruvian military effort. Delta Force, he guessed. They were the only ones who could have put a mission together that quickly and pulled it off with such timing and precision.

His thoughts focused on a brief encounter that had happened just after the assault forces arrived at the camp. He began analyzing the incident in detail to make certain he had forgotten nothing. After descending the back side of the hill, before continuing on toward the airstrip, he had hidden in the jungle near the huts and watched as the six guerrillas he had trained were shot down as they ran out onto the trail. He had been concealed in a thicket just off the trail, not far from where they fell, when two men had rushed from the main part of the camp and stopped within arm's reach of his position. He could hear their every word. The taller of the two had raised his night-vision goggles and rested them on top of his head, and his face was clearly visible in the bright glow from the burning structures in the main part of the camp. He spoke into a throat microphone to a man with whom he had lost contact.

"Hide Four. Do you have Viper in sight? . . . Respond, Hide Four, do you have Viper in sight?"

It was at that moment, upon hearing his old code name being used, that he realized he was the target of the mission. They were after him, nothing else. And they had come close, very close, to ending his career, if not his life. The realization strangely exhilarated him, a feeling he had known only on rare occasions since Vietnam. The intervening years had been boring and repetitious by comparison. Contract assassinations on unsuspecting victims who posed no challenge . . . a steady diet of that can cause you to lose the edge, make you soft and vulnerable, he thought. And he had been vulnerable tonight.

But the unexpected turn of events had its up side. He was now forced into the position of working alone—and alone was the way he worked best. And the challenge was back. If they had come for him, and only him, then they knew of the assassination plot. Part of that he had anticipated, even carefully fostered and staged. The fact that they had learned his exact location, he attributed to the CIA agent he had discovered on his third day at the camp. But the use of his old code name meant only one thing: they had probably uncovered his true identity as well. At first, the implications of that discovery had been unsettling, but upon thinking it through, he decided it was nothing that could not be countered with careful planning and detailed execution.

And there was something else. A face that kept flashing before his eyes. The face of the man he had seen raise his night-vision goggles as he lay alongside the trail near the huts. He had seen him before. But where? Looked like a hard ass. And then it came to him. Gannon. Jack Gannon, Recon Team Cobra. Command and Control North. Sixty-eight, sixty-nine. Medal of Honor. Small world, huh? The memory of the terrible beating he had taken at Gannon's hands came back. Damn, he could hit. Worst hammering I ever took. Broke my nose and my jaw. Kicked in a couple of ribs too. What the hell had we been fighting about? Some Vietnamese broad . . . and her kid. Yeah, that was it. VC infiltrators. Shot the sneaky bastards. And Gannon tried to bring me up on murder charges. Jesus! Murder charges in 'Nam. Like it really mattered. Wonder if he remembers that?

Turning on an overhead reading light, he angled the flexible goose-necked beam onto his lap and consulted the specially anno- tated aeronautical charts Anderson had given him. The aircraft had a range of eighteen hundred miles with a forty-five-minute fuel reserve, more than enough to reach the first stop en route to the destination he had in mind. With an air speed of three hundred seventy miles per hour, he calculated he would arrive at dawn. Momentarily overriding the autopilot, he banked into a slow turn and rolled out onto a heading that put him on course for a smug- glers' strip outside the resort town of Montego Bay, Jamaica.

-26-

A Department of Defense Gulfstream III jet was waiting at Howard Air Force Base, Panama, to fly Gannon and the Delta Force squadron commander directly to Washington upon their return from Peru. Mike Maguire, as Special Agent in Charge of the Presidential Protective Division, had joined them in a small briefing room on the lower level of the White House west wing, where they recounted the details of the raid on the jungle camp for the Secretary of Defense, the National Security Advisor, and the President's Chief of Staff. Gannon purposely left out his attempt to bring down Sincavage's aircraft with the rocket launcher and his ordering the lead Pave Low to fire on it.

"Approximately thirty-five hundred pounds of cocaine were destroyed," Gannon said as he summed up the operation. "The processing chemicals were also rigged with det cord and C-4 explosive, and blown up, and the drying sheds and other working structures burned to the ground."

"How many noncombatant casualities?" the Secretary of Defense asked, considering the political fallout once word of the Delta Force mission got out.

"Two wounded, none killed," the Delta squadron commander said. "Our medic treated them, and they were both stable and ambulatory when we left the area."

"And the guerrillas?"

"Four escaped into the jungle," Gannon replied. "The rest were killed in action."

"Has the Australian you captured been of any help in establishing where this . . . Sincavage may have gone?" the National Security Advisor asked.

"No, sir," Gannon said. "But I got the tail number from the aircraft he used to make his escape. We passed it on to Customs and Immigration, DEA and the Coast Guard, along with an artist-rendered likeness of the way he looks today."

"You think he's going to enter this country?"

"Yes, sir."

"You can't believe he's still going to try to carry out the assassination attempt in New York City?" the Secretary of Defense said.

Maguire spoke up. "Yes, sir, I do."

"My God, Mike," the Chief of Staff said. "His plan's been exposed, his schedule disrupted, his team killed, all that with only three days until the President's visit and you think he can recoup in time to carry out his original plan?"

"Yes, sir," Maguire said. "From what we've learned about the man, I believe that's exactly what he's going to do."

"Just what have you learned?" From the look on the Secretary of Defense's face, he found the premise as flawed as the Chief of Staff and the National Security Advisor did.

Maguire nodded to Gannon, prompting him to bring up the matters they had discussed prior to the meeting.

"We've learned a lot about his military background, and the things he's done since his meeting with the drug barons eight days ago," Gannon began. "As you all know, he was operated as a contract agent by the CIA for seven years. His former case officer, a man who knows him as well as anyone, had some revealing insights into his abilities and his psychological makeup."

Gannon went on to explain about the innovative covert missions into North Vietnam, repeating what Martindale had told him about Sincavage's skills at deception operations and diverting enemy attentions away from his intended target.

"He isn't the type for obvious frontal assaults. In his case officer's own words, Sincavage is a master of misdirection, and a loner. I don't believe for one second that the team he was training was to be used in his primary attempt on the President's life. There are even indications that he knew his diversionary attempt would be compromised. I believe he was counting on using that to his advantage, to draw attention away from what he was really planning."

"Well then, why would he go to all the trouble to train them?" the Secretary of Defense asked.

"To set them up as sacrificial lambs," Gannon said. "They were to be a misdirection. Once they were stopped everyone would believe the crisis was over, security would be relaxed. No one would ever suspect a second attempt within a two-day period."

"And they would have been stopped," Maguire added. "Assaulting the presidential motorcade is attacking our strength. We train constantly for just that kind of scenario. Their chances of success would have been zero."

"The man obviously intended to use rocket launchers, for God's sake," the National Security Advisor said. "Those damn things will blow any armored limousine to pieces."

"If they hit it," Gannon said. "It's my understanding that the President's limousine travels at an average speed of fifty miles an hour. I'm very familiar with unguided rocket launchers, gentlemen, and I can assure you, hitting a target moving at that speed is next to impossible. Sincavage, with his background, would know that."

"And our motorcade routes are never announced in advance," Maguire said. "Any intelligently planned attack would have to be at arrival and departure points, when the limousine has slowed or stopped. In the case of the New York City trip, that limits it to the airport, the hotel, or the United Nations."

"Three excellent opportunities, I would think," the National Security Advisor said.

"Not when you consider the intensive security measures we

have in place at those locations," Maguire said. "They've been scouted and prepped by our advance teams and local police long before the President ever sets foot in the city. Anyone attempting to fire a rocket launcher at an arrival or departure point would have to have an unobstructed view of the limousine. Which means they would have to be in the front row of spectators or in an elevated position above the crowd. Our counterassault and countersniper advance teams pay particular attention to those areas; consequently they're the most heavily secured. No one would be stupid enough to believe they could get that type of equipment into place unnoticed, let alone have the time to stand in plain view with it on their shoulder until they sighted in and fired."

"Everything we know about the man," Gannon said, "tells us he's not going to roll over and play dead. He's a professional assassin who's always worked alone. His training and working with a team whose only experience was in harassing peasants and gunning down minor, unprotected officials in drive-by shootings from the backs of motorcycles just doesn't hang together. They would have been a distinct liability to him in any number of areas."

"A lone sniper has the best chance of getting away with an attempt on the President's life," Maguire said. "If he can find a site where no countersniper team is covering the area."

"If that's the case, I don't see your problem," the National Security Advisor said. "Forewarned is forearmed. You not only know where and how the attempt is going to be made, you know who's going to do it. That should make things that much simpler."

"With all due respect," Maguire said, "this man is no ordinary threat case. He may just be the best in his profession."

"I'm afraid I can't subscribe to this theory of one man's invincibility," the National Security Advisor said, rising from his chair at the head of the table. "You do what you feel you must to protect the President," he told Maguire, "but as far as I'm concerned, the trip goes off as scheduled."

With the meeting adjourned, the Secretary of Defense and the National Security Advisor left to brief the President in the Oval Office. The Chief of Staff lingered behind, indicating to Maguire that their conversation was not over.

"I've got an addendum to what the National Security Advisor

just said. You have your men protect the President in the same manner they always do, no more and no less. I don't want any convoluted security measures that interfere with his public appearances."

"At least let me use the below-ground garages for the arrivals and departures at the UN and the hotel."

"No, Mike. You did a terrific job; you were instrumental in breaking up an assassination plot in the planning stages. Now it's over. Let it lay. I don't want to see any blatant or obtrusive security measures that give the appearance of a President under siege. No dump trucks blocking intersections along the motorcade route, or any of your heavy-handed tactics that will get the media hyping this nonexistent threat. Do I make myself clear?"

"Put the trip off for another week," Maguire argued. "With the information we have on Sincavage, we'll be able to locate him by then. Get the President to go to Camp David, where we can provide maximum protection. Or if you have to maintain his schedule, change his appearances to indoor locations where we can have a totally controlled situation with a high level of security without it being obvious."

The Chief of Staff's temper flared. "Give it up, Mike. It's not going to happen. You've got nothing to justify what you're asking. Nothing but a hunch."

"What I've got is a potentially disastrous situation on my hands, and you're not giving me any workable options."

"This conversation's over," the Chief of Staff said. "I won't tolerate an armed-camp mentality on the off chance that some nut might make an attempt on the President's life. Just do your job."

"I will, if you let me."

The Chief of Staff paused in the doorway, his face flushed with anger as he leveled a baleful stare at Maguire. "Before you mess with me, Mike, I suggest you check with some people who have."

Maguire knew the futility of any further argument. It had ended the way confrontations with the Chief of Staff always ended, with political objectives holding priority above all else. It was a constant struggle, and occasionally he won small concessions for his security considerations, but he had pushed this as hard as his position allowed. The Chief of Staff was the ultimate decision maker concerning the President's travel, the events he attended, and how they would be staged, and you went up against him only once and survived. Any attempts to circumvent his orders would result in an immediate transfer to a far less desirable position, with nothing having been accomplished and a promising career destroyed in the process.

Gannon had remained silent during the heated exchange. As he left the office with Maguire, he said, "I want to see this through. I'll ask the Delta commander to assign me to work with you until we can locate Sincavage."

"At this point I'd appreciate all the help I can get," Maguire said. "He's going to try it, Jack. I know the son of a bitch is going to try it."

—27—

If someone were looking for a place to disappear off the face of the earth, he would need to look no farther than the Turks and Caicos. An archipelago of eight major islands and thirty-two smaller cays off the southern tip of the Bahamas, the unspoiled and underdeveloped islands are little known to the outside world, with two exceptions—scuba divers, who come to dive among the coral reefs and numerous shipwrecks in cobalt-blue waters where visibility often exceeds two hundred feet, and drug smugglers. Located approximately halfway between Colombia and Florida, the islands have become a major stopover point and transshipment center for cocaine and marijuana smugglers whose cargo is destined for the lucrative markets in the eastern United States.

Only six of the islands are inhabited and have towns, which in most cases are little more than settlements of a few hundred people living in brightly colored houses that line narrow, unpaved roads, where donkey carts are a common sight. South Caicos is the fishing center of the islands, its primary source of income ostensibly being the production of conch and lobster. In reality, that income is far exceeded by what is earned by officials who turn a blind eye to the prodigious amounts of narcotics that flow through the island each year. The heavy presence of smugglers is obvious to anyone who bothers to notice. From the air, dark shapes, recognizable as the tails, wings, and fuselages of sunken aircraft, are clearly visible in the shallow waters close to shore—the results of careless or inexperienced drug-running pilots who had run out of fuel or air speed at the last moment, or misjudged their altitude during a night landing. Jerry Sincavage counted nine separate aircraft wrecks strewn along the coast as he made his approach to the airport.

On the ground, as he taxied off the runway, he saw the telltale signs of smuggling activities everywhere. Single engine planes, light twins, and even heavy transports, far more than could be reasonably explained for a sleepy, backward island, crowded the apron. Some were painted a light-gray color on the bottom of the fuselage and black on the top, making them difficult to see from the ground, or from above when flying over water. With few exceptions, all of the aircraft had mud-spattered landing gear and their propellers and horizontal stabilizers were pitted and dented by gravel and rocks from operating out of unimproved airstrips. One, Sincavage noticed, even had different identification numbers on each side of the fuselage.

What was obvious to the casual observer was also obvious to the local authorities. And Tony Bessario, who sat opposite Sincavage at a table in the airport terminal restaurant, explained how the system worked.

"You pay, you've got no problems," he said. "Everyone connected with this operation is paid off: Customs and Immigration, the local cops and politicians, even the guy in the tower. If you're in a hurry, want a fast turnaround, he'll have you refueled and on your way in twenty minutes. You don't pay, the load you're carrying is gonna get ripped off, and you're probably gonna meet with an unfortunate accident. The players all know the rules; nobody with an ounce of brains bucks the system, and the system looks the other way."

Bessario, born and raised in Miami, was a second-generation

smuggler, having learned all the tricks of the trade from his father, whose final resting place, at the age of fifty-six, was a watery grave at the bottom of a reef off Andros Island. Involved in running drugs since the age of eighteen, Bessario had worked for Raphael Calderon's organization for the past five years. His experience and vast knowledge of the drug interdiction methods of the Coast Guard, Customs, and the DEA, along with a healthy respect for their abilities, had kept him out of jail and out of their files.

The call he had received that morning told him to expect a man named Carlson, and to provide whatever assistance he needed. He had met him at the airport, ready to brief him on the intricacies of avoiding detection, or evading his pursuers if he was discovered while making a illegal flight into the United States.

"You're not going to go unnoticed for very long if you fly up the east coast," Bessario said when Sincavage told him his intentions. "They got tethered radar balloons, airborne radar planes that troll the whole area, and then there's the ground radar. You're going to be a blip on somebody's screen sooner or later. And once they get a lock on you, they'll track your ass the rest of the way and grab you when you put down. My way, you disappear without a trace."

"Your man in Fort Lauderdale is dependable?" Sincavage asked.

"If he wasn't, he wouldn't be working for me. He'll be instructed to stand by for ten hours after you leave here. In the plane you're flying, considering that you'll be wave hopping most of the way, that's about seven hours longer than it'll take you to get there. If you don't make it by then, he'll know you've bought it, or changed plans."

"I'll need a car," Sincavage said.

"You're in luck. There's a Porsche at the other end you can have. It belongs to a guy we had a disagreement with. He won't be needing it anymore."

Sincavage returned his attention to the aeronautical charts spread out on the table, making notes on the intricate procedures Bessario had spent the last two hours explaining to him. He felt refreshed now, having slept for six hours and showered, forgoing a much-needed shave and leaving intact the four-day growth of beard purposely. Before leaving Jamaica he had called Calderon. The Bolivian drug lord had just learned of the raid on the camp in Peru, and was surprised to hear Sincavage's voice. His information on what had happened was spotty, and he had assumed that the hired assassin had been either killed or captured.

From Calderon's point of view, things were getting out of hand and he was beginning to regret ever having put the assassination plot in motion. He had even considered calling Sincavage off, allowing him to keep the twenty million dollars, just to be rid of what he now considered the threat of his own exposure. But the four drug barons secluded at his ranch had been further angered by news of the Americans destroying a jungle laboratory that meant the loss of tens of millions of dollars in production to them. To keep peace within his organization, Calderon was left with no choice but to continue to give his cooperation in carrying out the contract. He began to suspect that the man he had hired was obsessed, and that with or without his help would not be deterred. When he suggested that it might be wise to postpone any attempt on the President's life until a later date, Sincavage replied, "I see things through," and hung up.

After the raid on the camp, and learning that his identity was known, Sincavage immediately realized that travel on commercial airlines was out of the question. He did not know how many of his aliases had been compromised, but he had to assume that they all were, and if the Secret Service suspected he was still intent on killing the President, the train stations, bus terminals, and commercial airports in and around New York would be watched, along with all points of entry into the country.

His original plan, before talking with Bessario, had been to fly north along the east coast of the United States, just outside the radar coverage, then turn inland and land at a small airport in Pennsylvania or New Jersey. From there he had planned to either rent or steal a car and drive to New York. Now Bessario's information called for another change of plans, requiring that he drive from Florida to New York. In light of the information Calderon had passed on about the President's unscheduled run around the Central Park reservoir on the morning of the fourteenth, he had more than enough time to drive the twelve hundred miles and arrive in the city on the morning of October thirteenth. It was a narrow time frame, but would still enable him to scout both the United Nations Plaza and the Waldorf-Astoria Hotel as potential sites while keeping the Central Park reservoir as an alternative, should the others offer an earlier opportunity. He had learned from years of experience that the best time to choose a site for an assassination was not days in advance of his target's arrival, but early on the day of the event, when all of the security forces were getting into position and could be observed and their weak spots determined.

It was just before dusk when he lifted the MU-2 Solitaire off Runway 10 at the South Caicos airport. His sectional charts were clipped to his knee board along with Bessario's instructions as he turned to an easterly heading, climbed to two thousand feet, and passed over the Turks Island Passage that separated the two island groups. In a little under three hours, he would reach the coast of Florida, and begin the cat and mouse game Bessario had told him to expect.

•

The Miami Air Branch of United States Customs is tucked away at the end of a decommissioned runway in a quiet corner of Homestead Air Force Base, beyond the deafening roar of the Phantom jets taking off on their daily training flights. The innocuous-looking cluster of pale yellow buildings includes a hangar, a low-slung prefab structure known as the bull pen, which houses the operations room, and a scattering of mobile homes that serve as offices. The walls inside the operations room are covered with large-scale maps of South American, the Caribbean, and the United States, along with status boards depicting duty rosters, air assets, and information on recent drug busts detailing locations of seizures, amounts seized, number of arrests, and types of aircraft seized. In a small room off the central area is the highly classified computer system that can access data banks containing the names and backgrounds of all known and suspected drug smugglers, their associates, and the identification numbers of their aircraft.

The Customs officers who fly the Citation jets, Blackhawk helicopters, and various other aircraft are the "catch 'em in the act" crews of America's drug interdiction operations, tasked with the "mission impossible" job of tracking, intercepting, and arresting smugglers. Despite their dedication and expertise, with only twenty-four pilots and twelve aircraft at their disposal to stem the flood of narcotics pouring into south Florida on a daily basis, they are little more than a modern analogy to the little Dutch boy with his finger in the dike.

It was shortly after 8:00 P.M. on the evening of October tenth when the operations duty officer answered one of two red telephones on his desk, listened for a minute, then hung up. One of the red phones was a direct line to the Air Force control tower, facilitating immediate clearance for takeoffs, the other, the one the ODO had just hung up, was a direct line to C3-I (Command, Control, Communications, and Intelligence). Located in southwest Miami, near the Metro Zoo, C3-I was the nerve center for the government's drug interdiction program in south Florida, coordinating interagency operations and receiving, among other things, reports from AWACS planes and tethered Aerostat radar balloons on aircraft illegally approaching U.S. borders.

The call from C3-I was an alert that a suspect target had been located. An Air Force AWACS plane from the 963 AWACS Detachment was up working a racetrack pattern between the lower Bahamas and the Turks and Caicos Islands. They had spotted a target traveling without navigation lights and wave hopping at fifty feet off the deck three hundred miles north of South Caicos Island. A quick check revealed that the plane was not on a flight plan.

A radar operator at C3-I in Miami took over the tracking of the suspect aircraft as it flew over Andros Island, then lost it in "the slot"—an area where there was a gap in the radar coverage. Miami C3-I's radar did not, in fact, reach that far south. The tracking information was being relayed to them by data link from Fat Albert, a radar balloon tethered ten thousand feet above Cudjoe Key, Florida, which provided sophisticated look-down coverage for two hundred miles out to sea, detecting suspect targets that flew below the look-up angle of land-based radar.

The C3-I operator, wise to the ways of the smugglers, and aware of the aircraft's last known course and speed, began calculating where it might emerge. His projection proved uncannily accurate, and fifteen minutes later he reacquired the target as it crossed the northern edge of Orange Cay, holding a course for the Florida Keys. The low-level flying and circuitous route of the target aircraft left no doubt in the radar operator's mind that he had found a bad guy.

In the Customs Air Branch operations room at Homestead Air Force Base the operations duty officer pressed the button that sounded a Klaxon throughout the complex. Conversations in the room fell silent and the adrenaline flowed as the announcement came over the public-address system.

"Launch the Citation! This is a scramble! Launch the Citation!"

The on-deck crew ran from the operations room to the hangar, where mechanics stood in front of the sleek, heavily modified business jet waiting for the inertial navigation system to align before disconnecting the auxiliary power unit. With the pilot and the AIO (air interdiction officer) on board, the copilot pulled up the steps and locked the door. Six minutes from the time the Klaxon sounded, the blue and white Citation jet, taxiing at near takeoff speed, turned onto the active runway and moments later roared into the night sky, banking into a right turn over Biscayne Bay. Heading east and staying low until offshore and clear of Miami commercial air traffic, the Citation pilot raised the nose and climbed steadily to fifteen thousand five hundred feet, listening as the radar operator at C3-I gave him the heading toward the suspect aircraft.

"It's an intermittent target," the radar operator told him. "He's in and out of the clutter. Must still be hugging the waves."

"Sure sign of a doper," the pilot said, and turned to the heading given.

The sleek Customs jet was equipped with an exotic array of highly sophisticated electronic detection equipment. Its radar, the same search and fire control radar used in the F-16 fighter, was capable of detecting a target three feet square at a distance of forty miles. Its night-tracking FLIR (Forward-Looking Infrared) detection system turned thermal images into pictures on monitors in both the cockpit and the Air Interdiction Officer's console by way of a repeater. Whatever image was projected on the monitors was simultaneously recorded on the aircraft's videotape system.

As the Citation sped toward the target, at a combined closure rate in excess of six hundred miles per hour, Karen Jacoby sat watching the radar and sensor console at the aft station behind the cockpit. The radar screen's green sighting indicators glimmered and the FLIR screen showed billowing cumulus clouds ahead. Before undergoing training as an air interdiction officer, Jacoby had driven a Customs cigarette boat. Working with a female partner, she had accumulated an impressive arrest record. More than a few seasoned smugglers had gone to jail shaking their heads in disbelief that the two bikini-clad beauties who busted them were Customs officers.

As the Citation crossed over the Florida Keys, the radar was on a four-bar scan, searching from ocean level to nineteen thousand feet out to a distance of eighty miles. Suddenly, a green square appeared in the middle of the screen. Jacoby reacted instantly, sliding the acquisition symbols over the target and squeezing the trigger. The green square changed to a diamond.

"We've got him," she said over the intercom, and gave the heading and distance to the target, now only sixteen miles away.

The radar readout showed zero altitude, indicating that the target was still flying just above the water at two hundred miles per hour. She guessed correctly that the suspect aircraft was a light twin.

Traveling at close to four hundred miles per hour, the Citation quickly closed the distance. When the radar indicated that the target was off his right side, the pilot rolled into a steep diving turn, pulled back the power, and deployed the spoilers. The jet dropped rapidly from fifteen thousand feet and leveled off just above the wave tops. The target aircraft's image, locked into the radar, now showed up on the FLIR screen. Jacoby immediately identified it as a Mitsubishi turbo prop flying ninety feet above the surface of the ocean.

The pilot, experienced and skilled enough to be comfortable with low-level flying, began the intricate and dangerous procedure of identifying a target aircraft at night. With one hand on the yoke and the other on the throttles, his eyes flicking back and forth from the FLIR image to the closure rate on the radar screen, he slowly moved in on the MU-2, pulling to within fifty feet, just below and slightly to one side of its tail. He then drew back further on the power, matching the target's speed to avoid overshooting it, believing that its pilot was unaware of his presence.

Under ordinary circumstances, the pilot of the target aircraft would have no way of knowing the Customs jet was riding his tail. But Sincavage's plane had added advantages. Equipped with forward-looking and rearward-looking radar, and a tail warning receiver, the MU-2 was not the run-of-the-mill doper's plane. Sincavage had been aware of the Citation's presence from the time it leveled off four miles behind him. The tail warning receiver, programmed to scan all Customs and Coast Guard radar bands, had detected the intruder and set off a beeper, alerting Sincavage to turn on his rearward-looking radar. A small screen in the cockpit painted the aircraft behind him and gave him a vector.

The Citation, also flying without navigation lights to avoid being spotted by the target, began inching closer. The bright moonlight reflecting off the ocean was enough for the copilot to read the MU-2's registration number from thirty feet away. Pressing the transmit button on the radio, he contacted C3-I.

"We've got a number on the bogey," the copilot said. "Are you ready to copy?"

"Go," came the reply from C3-I.

"November four two niner Hotel Charlie," the copilot said, and waited while the number was run through the intelligence unit's computer.

"He's not in the system," C3-I said, after a delay of less than a minute. There was another pause, then, "Looks like we've got a special alert on for this guy. Secret Service wants him apprehended and held."

"What are we dealing with?" the pilot asked.

"No details. Just apprehend and hold, using extreme caution."

The pilot was about to request that a Blackhawk helicopter be launched to assist them. After the Citation tracked the target to its destination, the Blackhawk would take over, landing its heavily armed apprehension team to make the arrest. Before the pilot could make the request, C3-I came up on the radio again.

"Be advised, we have no support assets for you."

It was the last thing the pilot wanted to hear. Without the

Blackhawk, they had no way of apprehending the suspect, unless he landed at a major airport with a runway long enough to accommodate the Citation.

"Only one of the Hawks is down for maintenance," he replied to C3-I. "We still got one on standby. Launch him."

"He scrambled on another target just after you took off. Continue tracking your target to his destination. If you can't land with him, radio his location to us and we'll pass it on to the Secret Service and the locals."

The pilot didn't bother to reply. Unless they were extremely lucky, he knew that the chances were good that the target was going to get away.

The invisible hand of Tony Bessario had gone unseen by Customs Air, but its presence was now being felt, as he had promised Sincavage it would be. The tip the operations center had received that had scrambled the Blackhawk to a remote strip in the Everglades had come from one of Bessario's Miami contacts. The Blackhawk was not on a wild goose chase; the apprehension team would soon arrest two first-time smugglers who had reached for the brass ring and flown a Piper Aztec loaded with three hundred kilos of cocaine from South Caicos. They had, however, made a serious mistake in refusing to pay what they considered an exorbitant fee to a South Caicos official that morning. Bessario had been only too glad to accommodate the angry official in his desire to hand out swift and terrible punishment to the offenders.

Sincavage raced north through the Florida Keys, staying down on the deck, less than one hundred feet above the waves as he continued on a course for Miami. At C3-I, the radar operator watched as the Citation followed close behind. They were headed straight for the high-density airspace used by commercial jets landing at and taking off from Miami International Airport. The classified code that the Citation's transponder was sending out told the Miami Air Traffic Control Center that they were flying tactical, in hot pursuit of a smuggler. Any Customs aircraft transmitting that code and using the proper call sign was exempt from FAA regulations, allowing them to fly below prescribed altitudes without navigation lights, violate Terminal Control Areas, and ignore airspeed restrictions in congested areas.

"You're about to mix with the heavy metal," the C3-I radar operator warned as the Citation entered Miami's Terminal Control Area.

"We'll stay below them," the pilot replied, and turned his attention back to the deadly chase.

Sincavage gained altitude as he arrived over Fort Lauderdale, crossing the beach at eight hundred feet. He checked the rearward-looking radar and saw that the Citation had backed off, keeping pace a few hundred feet behind him. After a quick mental review of what the next few minutes of flying would require, he cut back on his power, lowered his landing gear, and lined up for an approach to Fort Lauderdale International Airport.

"He's dropped his gear," Jacoby said from the rear console, where she was hunched over the FLIR screen. Her eyes were fixed on the greenish image of the MU-2 as its airspeed continued to drop. "Looks like our luck's going to hold. He's landing."

Sincavage, tuned to the control tower's frequency, ignored the tower operator's angry demands for the unknown aircraft to identify itself and get clear of the area. He turned onto the downwind leg of the traffic pattern and again checked the position of the Citation on his radar screen. Retracting his gear, he made a sudden rapid descent to four hundred feet and cut across the active runway, to the consternation of the tower operator, who frantically instructed a departing corporate jet to abort its takeoff run.

The unexpected maneuver had caught the Citation pilot and the air interdiction officer completely by surprise.

"Shit!" Jacoby said. "He's off the FLIR, and I've got a radar screen full of targets; there's traffic all over the place."

"He was on to us all the time," the pilot said in disgust. "Bastard must have a blue box."

Sincavage descended to one hundred fifty feet, and began making the abrupt changes of directions that were part of the intricate series of maneuvers Bessario had painstakingly gone over with him.

Aboard the Citation, Jacoby caught a momentary glimpse of the MU-2 on the FLIR screen, then lost it as it made a sharp ninety-degree turn. At distances under one-quarter mile, the Citation's radar coverage was extremely narrow, making it possible for a close-in target to break the radar's lock by making sudden, sharp changes of direction that took it out of the narrow cone of coverage. Reacting quickly, Jacoby unslaved the FLIR from the radar, and tried to reacquire the target.

Sincavage's ninety-degree turn had put him over I-95, tracking north at an altitude of one hundred feet. The silhouette of the darkened aircraft could be occasionally seen against the background of hundreds of automobile headlights along the interstate highway.

Jacoby's heart sank as the target continued making quick changes of direction. The pilot had managed to stay with it through most of the turns, but with the last maneuver it was lost on both radar and the FLIR. When the target broke lock, the radar went to an automatic search mode, but it was a hopeless cause. It was picking up everything in Fort Lauderdale's high-density traffic areas.

The screen glittered with possible targets as Jacoby worked feverishly at the controls, rejecting one and moving on to another when the speed and altitude didn't match those of the MU-2. Her search was further hindered by the strobing effect caused by the fences along the expressway—one of the flaws in the F-16 radar.

The pilot, having lost visual contact with the target, made a series of turns. Both he and the copilot scanned the ground, looking for a moving shadow passing across it that would reveal the presence of the fleeing target. Below them, to the east, were the lights of Fort Lauderdale, to the west, the dark recesses of the Everglades stretched to the horizon. The target was nowhere in sight.

•

Five hundred feet above the outskirts of western Broward County, Sincavage reached into the duffel bag resting on the right seat. He removed the pair of night-vision goggles Bessario had provided and pulled them on. Below him, the dark and forbidding ground brightened considerably. Tuning the radio to the frequency he had been instructed to use, he pressed the mike button and uttered a coded phrase.

"Anvil, this is Hammer," he said, then repeated the phrase.

"Anvil, this is Hammer, do you read?" Two clicks came over the headset Sincavage was wearing. Whoever was listening on the ground had broken squelch twice to tell him that his message had been received.

The VOR indicator on the instrument panel confirmed that Sincavage was where he was supposed to be, and in the distance on his left and right front, he could see the visual reference points that further fixed his position. As he began a slow turn to the right, his eyes searching the ground, a series of lights appeared where moments before there had been nothing but darkness. The small infrared lights, invisible to anyone without night-vision optics, outlined a low-cut pasture. A separate string of the invisible lights, flashing at half-second intervals and arranged in the shape of an arrow, indicated the wind direction. The clandestine airstrip was barely twenty-eight hundred feet in length, but with the MU-2's short takeoff and landing capabilities, it was more than enough.

Sincavage approached on a long final and touched down to a near perfect landing at the point where the infrared runway lights began. The lights flicked off as he rolled out to a stop with more than three hundred feet to spare. He removed the night-vision goggles and watched a long sliver of light appear and grow slowly from the ground up as a large door was raised electronically, revealing the spacious interior of a warehouse that served as a hangar at the far end of the field. A black Porsche coupe, now visible in the hangar light, was parked just outside a small access door off the front of the building, where a man stood motioning with his hand for Sincavage to come ahead. Adding power, he taxied inside and the door closed behind him.

—28—

The Waldorf-Astoria's luxurious presidential suite, overlooking New York City's famed Park Avenue, is located on the thirty-fifth floor of the Waldorf Towers, an exclusive section of the hotel with its own private entrance that lends itself well to the security measures necessary for the protection of visiting dignitaries. For the past six days activity in the quiet, staid building had increased tenfold as a Secret Service advance team prepared for the President's arrival on the afternoon of October thirteenth.

Every room on the thirty-fifth floor, as well as the floors immediately above and below, had been blocked out and reserved for staff members and Secret Service agents—those rooms not needed would remain locked and vacant for the duration of the President's stay. The site agents had taken exhaustive security measures that made any attempt to reach the presidential suite unchallenged a virtual impossibility. One of the elevators in the lobby, dedicated strictly for the use of the President, was modified to stop only on the thirty-fifth floor. Even members of the White House staff, unless accompanying the Chief Executive at his express invitation, had to use another elevator, get off on the floor above or below the President's suite, go through the Secret Service checkpoints and use the stairwell.

By the afternoon of October twelfth, well in advance of the President's arrival, floors thirty-four through thirty-six, having been cleared by Technical Security Division personnel, were sealed off and security posted. Every hotel room, housekeeping supply closet, and nook and cranny had been checked for explosives and trace radiation, and meticulously swept for electronic listening devices. An agent now guarded the door to the presidential suite, while others were posted at each end of the corridor and the elevator landings on all three floors and the lobby.

The visible security on the inner perimeter was daunting enough, but like the tip of an iceberg, it is what remains unseen that is most formidable. Shortly before the President's arrival, the stairwells leading to his floor would be secured by both Secret Service agents and police officers from New York City's Special Operations Division. In a lay-off room, a smaller suite one room up from the President's, a five-man counterassault team, armed with automatic weapons and wearing tactical load-bearing vests and heavy overt body armor, would be poised to respond in an instant to any breach of the inner perimeter and to cover and evacuate the President.

Under normal circumstances, as Special Agent in Charge of the Presidential Protective Division, Mike Maguire would have accompanied the President on *Air Force One* and ridden along with the motorcade. But to Maguire, this trip was far from normal, and after putting his deputy in charge at the White House, he and Gannon had come into the city two days early to supervise and inspect every aspect of the security measures being taken for the President's visit.

Forty-eight hours ago, Maguire had learned of the sighting and disappearance of Sincavage's plane over Fort Lauderdale, and there had been nothing since. At his request, the Intelligence Division had begun a manhunt that blanketed the east coast of the United States. A wanted alert had gone out to all Secret Service field offices, along with instructions to get copies of the artist-rendered likeness of Sincavage into the hands of local and state police and federal agencies from Florida to New York, covering Sincavage's most likely route of travel. Within hours, Secret Service agents had canvassed every car rental agency in the Fort Lauderdale area, but none had seen the man in the picture. The license plates and descriptions of every car stolen or reported missing in Broward County, Florida, for a period of twenty-four hours after the Customs jet had lost track of the MU-2 were reported to the Secret Service's Miami field office. That information was subsequently entered into the computer data bank of the National Crime Information Center, to which all law-enforcement agencies have access, and flagged to indicate Secret Service interest for reasons of national security. Local police were tasked with watching all bus and railroad stations and airports in the New York City area, though Maguire doubted that Sincavage would use any public means of transportation. All that could be done to find him was being done, and Maguire, with Gannon's help, was now concentrating his efforts on preparing for the eventuality of Sincavage reaching the city and attempting to assassinate the President.

The deputy chief of staff, who had arrived in the city a day early to coordinate the fund-raising dinner's agenda with the head of the host committee, was Maguire's only sympathetic ear among the President's staff. The wily politician was fully aware of the various ways that security measures had been upgraded and intensified, but deeming them within the bounds of the Chief of Staff's instructions, did nothing to undermine Maguire's efforts. The increased security was obvious to him because of past experience, but Maguire had been careful to arrange things so they would not be obvious to the press or general public. It was when they met in the corridor outside his suite late on the afternoon of October twelfth that they had their first difference of opinion.

Upon the arrival of *Air Force One* at one-thirty on the afternoon of the thirteenth at LaGuardia Airport's Marine Terminal, the President was scheduled to go directly to the United Nations, where he would address the General Assembly. From there he would proceed to the hotel, where that evening he would attend the fund-raising dinner sponsored by the Republican National Committee. The following morning, after his run in Central Park, the President would return to the airport following a different route than the one used for his arrival. The motorcade routes had been laid out in meticulous detail, with special attention given to avoiding areas where traffic congestion was known to be a problem. Maguire had made one significant change in the procedures usually followed on visits to New York City, and the deputy chief of staff picked up on it immediately, disapproving of what he saw.

"I've looked over the proposed motorcade routes," he told Maguire. "Since they're not being announced in advance, we can forgo the full intersection control. In the past we've stopped at red lights without drawing any undue attention, and that way we avoid adding to the gridlock problem endemic to this city."

"Go along with me on this," Maguire said. "I've worked it out with the police. They can provide motorcycle cops from their Special Operations Division to block off each intersection along the route as the motorcade approaches and passes through, then leapfrog ahead and secure the next one. The traffic tie-ups will be minimal. No intersection will be blocked for more than a few minutes, and we can maintain a rate of speed that ensures the President's safety."

"You've got an armored personnel carrier listed as part of the motorcade," the deputy chief of staff said.

"That was added at the request of the Special Operations Division," Maguire said. "They've used it before; they feel more comfortable if one of their own SWAT teams is present."

"You haven't told them about Sincavage, have you?"

"Not a word," Maguire said. "But they're not stupid. I requested more than twice the number of support personnel from them than I have on other visits. They sense something's up."

"That's not very prudent, Mike. If they suspect you're on alert for a possible assassination attempt, the press is sure as hell going to find out. How did you justify the request for the increase in support?"

"I didn't have to. No one asked," Maguire said. "The New York City police are the last ones to question why people get a little nervous in the Big Apple. One of the detectives I've been working with put it in perspective. He said New York leads the world's cities in the number of people around whom you shouldn't make a sudden move."

The deputy chief of staff chuckled and shook his head. "He won't get any argument from me. I'll back you on this one, Mike, but you're walking a fine line. Your instructions were no heavy-handed tactics, keep that in mind." Casting a suspicious glance at Gannon, who was standing just behind Maguire, he said, "Where does Delta Force fit into this?"

"Sincavage was training a terrorist team at the jungle camp," Gannon said. "I've been assigned as liaison to the Secret Service to determine if a terrorist threat still exists." It was the best reason the Delta commander had been able to come up with to justify Gannon's request to be temporarily assigned to work with Maguire.

"Uh-huh," was all the deputy chief of staff said in reply as he left for a meeting in another part of the hotel.

Gannon had, in fact, worked closely with Maguire, proving invaluable in positioning the countersniper teams. With years of experience working with Delta Force snipers and planning operations, he could tell at a glance the most advantageous surveillance sites for a given area. Maguire had increased the number of teams for the two event sites—the United Nations and the Waldorf-Astoria—from three two-man teams to ten three-man teams for each site. Gannon had selected observation posts that covered every angle of fire, no matter how severe the angle, that a sniper would have at the airport, the entrance to the hotel, the windows in the presidential suite, and the arrival point of the motorcade at the United Nations. Any building over twenty stories high that was being used to cover the President's arrivals and departures was assigned two teams—one posted on the roof and a second in a room halfway down, allowing the second team to cover an area denied the rooftop team due to the severe angle to the street immediately below. At Gannon's suggestion, the size of the area secured was increased as well. Secret Service countersniper teams normally secure an area out to one thousand yards around any event site or arrival and departure point. Gannon had extended that distance to two thousand yards—an extremely difficult shot for even the most accomplished sniper, but still within the realm of possibility.

As the two men waited for the elevator to take them to the lobby, Gannon glanced at a notebook he was carrying. "We still haven't checked out the Central Park reservoir."

"It's an off-the-record movement. Our people and the staff are the only ones who know about it," Maguire said. "I've doubled the size of the detail for the run, and the cops are going to beef up their mounted patrols in the park and put a helicopter up."

"You don't want any countersniper teams covering it?"

"The President will be leaving the city an hour or so later. I'd feel a lot more comfortable with them in position at the airport and the hotel—the sites known to the public."

"Is the President going directly back to the White House from here?"

"No. First to Atlanta, to address the American Broadcasters Association convention that afternoon, then to Houston for a speech at NASA the next day, then back to Washington the same evening to spend four days at Camp David to prepare for the British Prime Minister's visit."

"Has any of that been announced to the press?"

"Not yet."

Gannon again noticed the heightened anxiety Maguire had been exhibiting since their arrival in New York. "We'll get the son of a bitch, Mike. We'll get him."

"I keep thinking about the story that's told to all of our guys on their first day of training with the Presidential Protective Division," Maguire said. "At one-thirty in the afternoon on November 22nd, 1963, John Kennedy was alive and well, riding down Elm Street, I think. A Dallas policeman, about a half mile out in front of the motorcade, saw Lee Harvey Oswald in a window, with a rifle, and assumed he was a Secret Service agent. History changed because of that. Because he didn't say anything. Because he didn't stop the motorcade. You can call it fate, divine intervention, but what it really was was human failure. Monumental human failure. Whenever you organize something as big as an advance for a presidential visit, no matter how thorough or careful you are, somebody isn't going to get the message."

"The best laid plans . . ." Gannon said.

"Yeah. And it's a deadly game, Jack. You can screw up a counterfeiting or forgery case, but screw up protecting the President of the United States and aside from the tragedy of the man dying, you risk destabilizing the entire Western world, and they end up writing thirty-two volumes about precisely how you screwed up. So you either give it one hundred percent or you're kidding yourself. I don't wrap myself in the flag, but I love my country, and my job— hell, it's cost me a good marriage and the love of a damn fine woman. I'm nothing if not dedicated. And I believe that protecting the President of the United States is worthwhile. So I help create this huge organism from nothing, and as the President arrives it's so big and so complicated and you've involved so many people. I mean, it's absolutely amazing that it works at all. It's connected by radio, by telephone, transported by boats, cars, helicopters, airplanes; it's a phenomenon that takes on a life of its own. And it's got to be intricately woven, like a fine tapestry. But no matter how tightly you weave it, at any moment, because of human failure, just one small oversight, in a split second it can unravel right before your eyes with disastrous consequences."

"Delta's operations are pretty much the same," Gannon said. "All you can do is your best, give it everything you've got, and hope it's good enough."

"And even then, sometimes good enough isn't *good enough,*" Maguire said. "Perfect isn't even good enough. I was there when Reagan was shot, you know?"

"I know," Gannon said.

"Six shots fired in one point forty-eight seconds by a guy who was an incompetent pistol shot at best. Less than *two* seconds and four men were wounded. And everyone was doing their job by the numbers. No one had screwed up, and we reacted precisely the way we were trained to react in just that type of situation. Jesus, I never felt so damn worthless in my entire life. I can still see that bright red frothy blood coming out of the President's mouth in the back of the limousine, and remember praying that we'd make it to the hospital in time to save him."

Maguire paused, shaking off the vivid image, then said, "I don't know, maybe I am giving Sincavage too much credit. If I were him,

I'd go to ground until things cooled off. He's got to know we're hunting him."

"Maybe that's why he won't call it off," Gannon said. "No, your gut instincts are right, he's out there somewhere, Mike. And he's on his way here. But we'll get him. One way or another, we'll get him."

●

The fall foliage in the Pocono Mountains of Pennsylvania was at its peak. In the late afternoon sun, brilliant hues of red and gold and amber, accented by dense stands of evergreens, glowed and shimmered across the rolling landscape as far as the eye could see. To the west and north lay the heart of the anthracite coal region, the only place Jerry Sincavage thought of as home, if he thought about any one place in that way. Raised in a series of foster homes in the Wilkes-Barre and Scranton area, he had spent the summers of his teenage years working odd jobs at the resorts scattered throughout the mountains south of the two cities. It was the pleasant memories of the two short summers spent at Lake Harmony that had drawn him back there to prepare himself before going into New York.

He had driven for eleven hours after leaving the Fort Lauderdale area, stopping only for gas and a brief nap in the car at a rest area off I-95 in Virginia before driving the rest of the way straight through to Pennsylvania. The front and rear mounted radar detectors in the Porsche had alerted him at least a half dozen times to speed traps ahead, and state troopers approaching from behind, allowing him to average seventy-five miles per hour for the long, tiresome drive.

He reached Lake Harmony and checked into Split Rock Lodge by nine o'clock on the evening of October eleventh, and slept late the following morning. After a five-mile run and an invigorating swim in the cold, dark waters of the lake, he lingered over breakfast, unwinding and collecting his thoughts. The vacation region was between seasons and the crowds would not return until the December snows came and the ski lifts on the nearby mountains opened. He gave no thought to being recognized; the only people he had known during those early years were other kids, long since forgotten, who had worked the same menial jobs for a chance to spend the summer away from home.

The area was not as he remembered it, but then it had been twenty-six years since he had worked there as a dishwasher in the kitchen of the snack bar that served the beach and swimming pool in front of the lodge. The old, rustic Split Rock Lodge, destroyed by a fire twenty years ago, the desk clerk had told him, had been replaced with a modern building that resembled hundreds of other uninspired, cookie-cutter resort hotels across the country. Where there had once been miles of nature trails and bridle paths winding through deep, natural woods, there were now streets serving developments crowded with tacky weekend cottages that all but destroyed the character and woodsy charm of the place. But the mountains were still there, and the cool, crisp fall air was a welcome relief after the dank humidity of the Peruvian jungle.

After breakfast, he called to verify the number for his contact in New York City, and on the second try reached a man with a pronounced Spanish accent. The man had no new information to pass on and Sincavage told him that he would call the following morning and again late that same night for any updates. After a leisurely walk around the resort grounds, recognizing little of what he remembered from his summers there, he ate lunch on the veranda overlooking the lake while studying street maps of New York, paying particular attention to a large-scale map of Central Park.

It was late afternoon when he drove to Hickory Run State Park, a public campground and picnic area that was closed for the season and deserted. He turned off the main road, unhooked a chain across a gravel drive that wound through a colorful stand of woods, and followed it to where it ended at a large grassy field that served as a campground during the summer. With the Porsche parked well out of sight of anyone driving through the park, he took his duffel bag and walked to a sign listing the campground rules that was nailed to a tree at one end of the field. After tacking a target over the sign, and measuring off the distance until he reached four hundred yards, he then removed the customized sniper rifle from his duffel bag and assembled it. Attaching the scope, he lay in a prone position on grass that smelled of autumn, and went about sighting in the rifle for the last time.

The special cartridges the Australian had given him had proved satisfactory in the target shooting he had done at the jungle camp, but he wanted to test them once more before committing to their use. A few years ago he had tried the first generation of the low-signature, captive-piston ammunition, but the bugs had not been entirely worked out, and it was highly inaccurate at distances exceeding one hundred yards. The improved version, which Anderson had provided, matched the ammunition to a rifle barrel with considerably faster twists than a standard 7mm Magnum, and overcame the early problems of yawing in flight that had seriously affected accuracy and killing power on impact. The unique cartridges were, in effect, a self-contained sound-suppression system that prevented any muzzle blast, flash, smoke, and downrange crack. The sound suppression was exceptional, emitting a noise no louder than a snap of the fingers, thereby eliminating the need for the lengthy external silencer that would normally have been attached to the end of the rifle barrel. The Soviet KGB had developed the specialized ammunition for their "wet affairs" department with only one purpose in mind: termination with extreme prejudice.

Sincavage removed three of the cartridges from the plastic sleeves in which they were packaged and loaded the rifle. He settled into a sturdy platform, sighted in on the target, and worked the bolt action with the speed and smoothness of an accomplished sniper, firing all three rounds in rapid succession. Through his binoculars, he saw that they had impacted in the center of the target in a tight group approximately the circumference of a quarter. Satisfied with the results, he disassembled the rifle, put it back in the duffel bag and stretched out on the grass. He stayed awhile, enjoying the scent of autumn on the cool evening breeze that blew across the clearing as the sun dropped low on the horizon and slowly disappeared behind the mountains.

●

Trooper Stanley Badowski of the Pennsylvania State Police was three hours into an eight-hour shift when he cut through Hickory Run State Park to reach Route 903 on the way to his evening sweep of the Lake Harmony area. It was a slow time of the year in the mountains; the crazy drunks of the ski season wouldn't be around for another two months, and the wild kids of summer were finished tearing up the roads until next year. Only the "blue hairs," as he called them, were out in numbers on the weekends—the geriatric leaf watchers who drove so damn slow and erratic that they created their own brand of traffic hazard. He hadn't written a single speeding ticket in two days and was thoroughly bored with the prospect of driving around for another five hours. That was until the black Porsche with Florida plates swerved out of a side road halfway through the park, spraying a goose tail of gravel behind it.

Sincavage saw the state police cruiser at the same time the rear radar detector blared in his ears. He glanced at the speedometer as the Porsche's powerful three-hundred-and-twenty-horsepower engine accelerated the car through eighty-five miles per hour, too late to back off before the cop's radar got a reading. His mind quickly assessed the situation. It was almost dark, the road was deserted, and there were no houses inside the confines of the park. He glanced in the rearview mirror at the same time the state trooper turned on his light-and-sound show and closed in. With one final appraisal of the surrounding area, Sincavage downshifted and pulled the car off to the side, where another gravel road led to yet another empty campground.

Badowski stopped the cruiser directly behind the Porsche and cut off the roof lights and siren, leaving the engine running and the hazard warning lights flashing brightly in the gathering dusk. Believing he was dealing with nothing more than a simple traffic violator, Badowski opted not to run a make on the Porsche by radioing the license number into the communications operator at headquarters. He simply jotted the number down on his clipboard, scribbling it across the forehead of the face in the photograph on the Secret Service wanted poster that had been issued to him at the start of his shift. Probably some smartass, he thought, eyeing the Porsche, and smiled to himself as he eased his oversized frame and ample stomach out of the car. Well, I'm in just the mood for you, pal, and you're gonna pay through the nose. Trespassing, driving forty miles an hour over the posted speed limit inside the park, and reckless driving . . . that ought to hold you. He hated rich smartass pukes who could afford to spend on a car what it took him three years to earn, and he never failed to single out expensive sports cars, especially foreign ones, for special scrutiny.

Sincavage remained seated at the wheel after putting the driver's side window down and slipping the silenced Walther PPK into the waistband at the front of his trousers beneath his open windbreaker. He glanced in the sideview mirror to see the overweight cop pry himself out from behind the wheel of the cruiser and walk toward him with an arrogant swagger that he swore was part of a required course state troopers everywhere had to pass before graduating and being issued their badges and the ubiquitous mirrored sunglasses.

Badowski approached the driver's side window and bent low to peer inside the low-slung car; the smell of the rich leather interior filled his nostrils, further irritating him on a subconscious level. Radar detectors, he noticed. They were illegal in Pennsylvania and justified another citation.

"You think the laws are for everybody but you?"

"It's hard not to drive this car fast," Sincavage said, trying a friendly approach to mentally disarm the surly cop.

"Hard not to trespass, too, huh? Driver's license and registration," Badowski commanded.

Sincavage saw the trooper's brow furrow and his eyes narrow as he bent even lower and angled his head to get a full-face look at him. There was a brief pause as the image on the wanted poster in the cruiser flashed in Badowski's mind—the scruffy beard did not hide the fact that it was the same man. In that same instant his hand reached for the holster on his right side. He was fast, and his service revolver was quickly drawn and pointed at Sincavage's head.

"Out of the car!" Badowski shouted in his most authoritative voice as he backed a few steps away from the door. "Hands where I can see them!" It was the first time in his seven years as a state trooper that he had pointed his weapon at anything other than a paper target—a fact that would prove significant in the events that followed.

"Hey, easy!" Sincavage said as he popped the door handle and moved his right hand slowly inside his windbreaker and around the grip of the silenced Walther. "You draw your weapon on speeders in this state?" There was a purpose to Sincavage's remarks—to distract the trooper and slow his reaction time by breaking his concentration.

"Out of the car," Badowski shouted. "Now!"

"All right, all right." The door of the Porsche prevented the trooper from seeing Sincavage's hand inside his jacket until he stood to his full height, and at that same moment he brought the Walther up and without hesitation fired two rounds into the startled cop's head.

For Sincavage, the cold-blooded act had been an instinctive, instantaneous reaction, carried out without conscious thought or emotion. Badowski never had a chance, his fate sealed by an occurrence known as lag time—the advantage a person accustomed to bringing a firearm to bear has over an opponent who has never faced a life-threatening situation. The advantage was little more than a second or two, but invariably it was enough to result in the death of the inexperienced shooter.

Badowski toppled like a felled tree. He lay sprawled partway out in the road, a pool of dark-red blood forming and coagulating at the back of his head. Sincavage moved quickly, dragging the cop's body to the cruiser and hefting it into the backseat. After looking both ways on the still-deserted road, he slipped behind the wheel of the cruiser, swung it around the front of the Porsche and turned onto the gravel side road, where he tore out two small posts as he rammed the chain blocking the entrance. At a point where the road curved sharply to the right, he skidded to an abrupt halt, hidden by the forest and completely out of sight of the main road through the park. The clipboard containing the wanted poster had landed facedown when Badowski tossed it onto the front passenger seat, and it went unnoticed as Sincavage shut off the engine and hazard lights and jogged back to where he had left the Porsche.

He got back in the car and sat calmly at the side of the road, considering his options. It was seven-thirty, almost completely dark. New York City was two hours away. It would take him approximately forty-five minutes to reach the New Jersey border at the Delaware Water Gap. There was a chance that the dead cop would not be found by then, or before he reached the city. But he did not consider that a given. There had been something out of sync in the trooper's delay in drawing his weapon, and Sincavage attributed it to wanting to size up the situation before responding with a show of force. The look on the cop's face had seemed to indicate that he had recognized him, but Sincavage thought it more likely that he had radioed in the license number of the Porsche before he pulled him over, and that the car the drug smuggler had given him was, for some reason, entered in the nationwide law enforcement computer system as being stolen. If that was the case, without a timely follow-up response from the trooper who had requested the check, and being unable to raise him on the radio, they would begin looking for him shortly.

He carefully reconsidered his initial reaction, that of leaving immediately for New York, taking the chance that he could make it into the city and ditch the car before the body was discovered. But there were inherent risks in that course of action that did not appeal to his cautious nature—the main concern being driving a car with a high recognition factor that would be easily spotted if the cops were looking for it. Abandoning the Porsche at the lodge and stealing a car from the parking lot was another possibility, but one that had its own time-consuming drawbacks—selecting a car that would not be missed soon after he took it meant finding one that belonged to a night employee at the lodge or a guest who had retired for the evening. Accustomed to operating under pressure and resisting the urge to act impulsively, he was calmly lighting a cigarette when the solution to his problem appeared in the rear-view mirror of the Porsche.

•

Jake Pavlik, a salesman for a bar and restaurant supply company in nearby Stroudsburg, Pennsylvania, often used the shortcut through the park when he was in a hurry to get home at the end of a long day. He had one more stop to make, a small country inn near Lake Harmony. They never placed a big order, but the owner and his wife were nice people and always gave him a free beer or two. A twenty-minute stop at most, and he would be on his way home.

His headlights picked up the Porsche at the side of the road as he rounded a curve a few hundred yards away. There was his dream car. A 928S. Eighty thousand dollars worth of automobile. What he wouldn't give to own one. Maybe someday. But more likely, maybe not. Not locked into a job with limited earning potential, and their first child due in a few months. But then everyone had to have their dreams. He slowed when he saw the tall, lanky man get out of the car and wave his arms. What the hell, he couldn't just leave him stranded in the park at night. Florida plates. Poor guy probably doesn't even know where he is.

"I thought Porsches never broke down," he said as he pulled to a stop next to where the man stood smiling his appreciation.

"You thought right," Sincavage said, jumping into the front passenger seat and placing his duffel bag in the back before the luckless Good Samaritan realized what was happening.

"Drive!" Sincavage said, and jabbed the tip of the silencer into the frightened man's ribs.

Pavlik did as he was told, nearly driving off the side of the road before getting control over the panic that gripped him.

•

One hour and fifteen minutes later, at the wheel of a blue Ford Taurus, Sincavage crossed into New Jersey and got on the turnpike heading north. His mind was focused on what lay ahead, and he gave no more thought to the salesman who had kept up a stream of nervous chatter and pleading until the moment he shot him in the back of the head and rolled him into a culvert on a secondary road near the Pocono Raceway.

—29—

The telephone in the hotel room on the thirty-fourth floor of the Waldorf Towers barely finished the first ring before Maguire sat bolt upright and grabbed the receiver from the nightstand. He shook the sleep from his head and swung his legs over the side of the bed as he listened to the duty agent on the graveyard shift at Intelligence Division headquarters tell him about the report from the Pennsylvania state police.

"The Porsche was registered to a known drug dealer by the name of Carlos Bonilla of Fort Lauderdale, Florida," the duty agent said. "The Broward County Sheriff's Department found his body floating in the inland waterway four days ago; shot twice in the back of the head with a twenty-two, execution style."

"What time was the state trooper's body found?" Maguire asked.

"Nine-fifteen last night. He'd been dead about two hours."

"Where's Lake Harmony?"

"Northeastern part of the state, in the Pocono Mountains."

Only a few hours from New York, Maguire quickly calculated and switched on the lamp to look at his watch. It was three o'clock in the morning. "How was he killed?"

There was a pause while the duty agent consulted his notes. "Shot twice in the forehead. They found two shell casings at the scene, both .380 caliber. No autopsy results yet."

"Did they find anything in the Porsche to give them a lead on the driver?"

"Nothing. Candy wrappers, an empty cigarette pack on the floor in the rear, and a couple of road maps. But they did manage to lift some partial prints."

"They won't do them any good. I want you to check back with the Pennsylvania state police. Talk to the officer in charge of the investigation and find out if there were any cars reported stolen in the immediate area of the shooting last night."

"I already checked. None within a thirty-mile radius," the duty agent said. "But they've got one possibly related incident. Last night around eleven-thirty, a woman in Stroudsburg, that's about thirty-five miles from where the cop was shot, reported her husband missing. She called the state police to see if there had been any accidents. He was due home around eight. He's a salesman; the Pocono mountain area's his territory. They haven't located him yet, but I've got the license number and description of the car he was driving."

Maguire reached for the pen and notepad on the nightstand and copied the information down to pass on to the New York City police.

"You think it's the guy we're looking for?" the duty agent asked.

"Could be. Stay on it, and let me know if the Pennsylvania cops come up with anything else," Maguire said, and hung up after thanking him for the call.

He picked up the phone to call Gannon's room, but decided to let him sleep; there was nothing they could do at three in the morning. Instead he dialed the home number for the New York police captain assigned as his liaison, and passed on the license number and description of the missing salesman's car, asking that it be given immediately to all the city's precincts.

Lying down on the bed, he propped the pillows behind his head and stared at the ceiling, his mind going over and over the myriad details to be seen to before the President's arrival. He felt secure in the knowledge that he was doing everything humanly possible to ensure the President's safety, given the restrictions placed upon him by the Chief of Staff, but the lessons learned from others who had felt that way only to have disaster strike when least expected were never far from his thoughts.

The security measures were extraordinary, far exceeding any he had previously taken, and unless Sincavage was planning a close-in attempt, almost guaranteeing his own death or capture in the process, his chances of success were virtually nonexistent. Everything he had learned about the man suggested that he had highly developed self-preservation instincts, and was not the type to give up his own life to carry out a contract. He was a professional, possibly one of the best in the world. He had to know that his plot had been discovered and that he was being hunted, yet he had not done what any professional would have done and waited to make his attempt at a later date, when security was downgraded and routines returned to normal. Maybe he had, Maguire thought. Maybe it was the stress of the job that was getting to *him,* causing him to fixate on improbable scenarios. Maybe he was burning out; he had seen it happen to others.

Unable to get back to sleep, he pulled a chair up to the window, opened the drapes and stared out at the brilliantly lit Manhattan skyline. The same gut feeling he had had since learning of the escape from the jungle camp again told him that he wasn't tilting at windmills, that the man he was hunting was here, in the city, waiting and planning.

●

At five o'clock in the morning, New York City is an exhausted prizefighter, recuperating after surviving another brutal round with the ceaseless furies of the day. Cars move easily along near-empty avenues, freed from the constant bullying of buses and trucks and the demolition-derby antics of arrogant taxi drivers. The lights from bars and apartment houses that had glowed into the small hours of the night are now extinguished, and in the darkened streets sounds are more intense, more suspect. A truck backfiring during the clamor of the day goes unnoticed; in the predawn hours it echoes through the deserted streets like a cannon shot, raising gooseflesh on the pale skin of the night people—the harmless, confused wanderers who move silently through the shadows, ever mindful of the predators who wait in ambush in alleys littered with beer cans and condoms and empty crack vials and rifled wallets: the debris of conflict and desperation and despair.

Sincavage had stopped to eat at a truck stop in New Jersey, and upon arriving in New York, had driven around the city scouting the locations he planned to visit later that day. It was five-fifteen when he pulled the blue Ford Taurus into the curb on Forty-fourth Street, between Tenth and Eleventh avenues. As he shut off the engine, he was taken by surprise when the passenger-side door flew open and a young girl quickly slid into the front seat uninvited. It was an Indian summer night, and all she wore was lacy lingerie that left nothing to the imagination. Her hand moved easily across his thigh.

"You name it, I do it?" The face was young, with a trace of small-town innocence lost, but the voice was tough and street-scarred.

Sincavage released his grip on the pistol inside his waistband and stared into the eyes of a kid he knew could not be more than seventeen years old.

"Come on, handsome, I'll make you moan and groan and cry out words you didn't even know you knew."

Sincavage cracked a small smile and got out of the car, tossing the keys in the hooker's lap. "Take it, it's yours."

"Hey, I ain't no car thief. I'm a whore."

"Count your blessings, kid," Sincavage said, taking his duffel bag from the backseat. "You could be dead."

He looked back to see the teenage hooker rummaging through the glove compartment before she ran toward a pay phone at the corner, her ridiculously high heels tapping out a staccato rhythm on the quiet street. She would call her pimp, who would call his friends, and the car would soon be stripped of everything the scavengers could sell, including the license plates, leaving an unrecognizable hulk to join the hundreds of other abandoned cars throughout the city.

Walking back toward Tenth Avenue, Sincavage came abreast of a darkened alleyway and caught a sudden movement out of the corner of his eye. Two shadows became feral night stalkers, intent on the duffel bag slung over his shoulder. Their switchblades clicked open in unison as they moved out onto the sidewalk, poised and ready to strike until they saw their victim stand firm, his eyes challenging as his right hand slipped inside his open windbreaker. With a quick jerk of his head, the taller of the two called off the attack and they silently retreated into the alley to wait for easier prey.

Sincavage was sized up three more times without incident before he reached Fifty-ninth Street, at the southern boundary of Central Park. As he followed the park's eastern border, walking north along Fifth Avenue, his thoughts went back to the last time he had visited the city, thirteen years ago, his final assignment for the CIA. A KGB officer, working undercover of the Soviet Mission to the United Nations, had been targeted for elimination. Sincavage never knew why, he had simply carried out the contract. It was near here, he recalled, as he passed one of the walkways entering the park adjacent to East Sixty-sixth Street. It had been a cold February night, just before midnight, and it had been snowing. He could almost feel again the large wet flakes as they gently caressed his face, and hear the silence of the empty avenues and see the white mantle that covered the ground and clung to the barren trees. He had followed the unsuspecting Russian from a restaurant on the Upper East Side to where he made a detour through the park on his way back to the Soviet Mission. He had shot him near a statue, pausing, transfixed, to watch the snow falling all around him, mixing with the bright red blood from two neat head wounds.

Sincavage snapped out of his macabre reverie as he left the sidewalk and entered the park at East Sixty-ninth Street. The city grew even quieter as he followed a meandering tree-lined path and was swallowed up by the peaceful sylvan setting of woods and meadows and watery expanses that sparkled with mirror images of the elegant apartment buildings towering over the perimeter of the park. The occasional whoosh of cars on the broad avenues faded to a whisper, punctuated by the muted clank of manhole covers rattling under their weight.

The city seemed to vanish altogether as he reached the wooded thickets and rolling grassy mounds of an area known as the Ramble. He paused beneath a darkened lamppost to let his eyes adjust to his surroundings and heard the distant sound of a hacking cough somewhere off to his left. He remained motionless, listening and watching. Near the edge of a clump of bushes, a bundle of rags stirred and sighed and then was still again. He counted four more wretched silhouettes of the homeless, lying huddled in fitful sleep about the area. He heard the hacking cough again, and moved toward it, stopping at a park bench deep in the shadows of an overhanging tree. He stared down at a figure curled into a fetal position on the bench, a filthy blanket pulled over his head.

One end of a thin strand of rope was tied to the man's wrist, the other end knotted around the handle of a shopping cart that overflowed with a collection of refuse scavenged from the city's trash receptacles. He reached down and pulled the blanket away from the man's face.

Harry Duncan awoke with a start. "Don't hit me! Please don't hit me!" he cried, covering his face with his hands and curling into an even tighter ball.

"Relax, I'm not going to hit you," Sincavage said. "I've got a proposition for you."

"Ah, Jesus," Duncan said. "I ain't into that kind of stuff. Come on, mac, just leave me alone. I ain't botherin' nobody."

"A business proposition," Sincavage said, as the stench of cheap wine and body odor reached him. He took a wad of twenty-dollar bills from his pocket and peeled one off. "Here's a twenty. Let's talk."

Duncan rose slowly to a sitting position and stared suspiciously at Sincavage and the twenty, which he quickly stuffed into the pocket of his trousers. "Talk about what?"

"How much for your coat?"

Duncan looked at the tattered and filthy full-length overcoat he wore over two other jackets. "You wanna buy my coat?"

"Sixty dollars," Sincavage said. "Another twenty for that stupid-looking hat." It was a short-brimmed longshoreman's hat that looked as though small animals had been chewing on it.

Duncan thought for a moment. "A hundred bucks for the both of them," he said, forcing a smile that revealed stained and broken teeth.

Sincavage held back a laugh. "All right, a hundred. Hand them over." The only reason he hadn't simply killed the pathetic creature seated before him was due to a rare compassion he had developed at an early age for society's castoffs. There had been legions of them in the coal regions of Pennsylvania when the mines had closed and they had nowhere to go but the local bars and the parks. One of his foster fathers, a man who had treated him well, had ended up that way, crying to him in an alcoholic stupor one night that he could no longer afford to take care of him.

Duncan removed the overcoat and watched as Sincavage slipped it on. "Nice fit," he said, and handed him the cap. "Wear it cocked to one side, gives you the Rocky look. People think twice before they mess with you."

Sincavage placed the grimy cap at a jaunty angle and laughed softly to himself as he looked at the contents of the shopping cart.

Never one to let an opportunity pass him by, and with visions of a month's supply of wine dancing through his foggy mind, Duncan reached into the cart and pulled out a thick woolen sweater that was stained and torn. "This would look nice with the coat, ya know."

"Another hundred for the cart and everything in it," Sincavage said.

"Oh, I don't know," Duncan said. "There's some pretty nice stuff in there. And the cart's in good shape, a little rust—"

"Don't press your luck." The voice had turned hard and menacing.

Harry Duncan had survived the past three years on the streets of New York partly because of his ability to read people and their intent. What he saw in the eyes of the stranger told him he was about to lose it all. "Another hundred's good. No problem."

Sincavage paid the balance of the money and untied the rope from the handle of the cart. He buried his duffel bag under a layer of newspapers and shabby clothing and moved slowly back along the path, pushing the cart before him.

"You need anything else, I could probably get it for you," Duncan called after him, but got no reply as his mysterious benefactor disappeared over a wooded rise.

To be homeless in New York City is to be invisible. And when Jerry Sincavage emerged from the park onto Fifth Avenue at Seventy-ninth Street, he became invisible to the millions of people who crowded the great city's streets every day. He could linger in an alley or a doorway or on any street corner without drawing attention. His behavior, no matter how bizarre, would be ignored, the eyes of passersby averted in a conscious effort to avoid him and deny his existence.

From beneath his cap, he pulled clumps of hair down over his forehead and around his ears. He moved slowly along the sandstone wall bordering the park, settling into a shuffling gait, his eyes cast downward, affecting a beaten, dejected posture that along with his stubbly beard and shopping cart and newly acquired clothes made him indistinguishable from the countless others condemned to live a nonexistence. He paused to get his bearings, then headed north as the first faint traces of dawn light appeared on the horizon.

—30—

The crowd assembling behind the police barricades at the United Nations had begun gathering at noon, swelling considerably as the time of the President's arrival drew near. At two o'clock, with the motorcade only twenty minutes away, the security forces had been in place for over an hour, putting into practice what the Secret Service site advance agents assigned to the U.N. Plaza had been planning for the past week. Following the instructions of Maguire and Gannon, and with the help of the New York City police officers working with them, they had saturated the area with strategically placed personnel without making the heightened security obvious to the press or public.

Every building fronting on the U.N. Plaza had been surveyed, along with other "threat buildings" out to two thousand yards that had windows or rooftops with unobstructed views of the President's arrival and departure point at the oval driveway in front of the Secretariat building. The countersniper advance teams had gone through each of them with the building supervisors, checking the rooftops for anyplace a sniper could hide, then floor by floor, determining which windows opened and which did not, and which way they opened and if there were any vacant rooms or offices.

Constantly practicing their deadly trade of locating, identifying, and neutralizing snipers, the Secret Service countersniper teams were some of the best marksmen in the world. Their custom-built 7mm Magnum JARs (which they, tongue-in-cheek, referred to as Just Another Rifle) are air gauged and chronographed after every hundred rounds to check for signs of barrel deterioration, and computerized ballistic trajectories are used to make adjustments for differences in altitude, barometric pressure, and temperature, insuring first-round accuracy anywhere in the world. Once establishing that a person is an imminent threat to the President of the United States, they are more than capable of surgically removing that threat in an instant.

Each of the ten three-man countersniper teams assigned to observe the threat buildings at the United Nations site had drawn its own map, plotting the distances with range finders and depicting the buildings within its area of responsibility. One hour before the President's scheduled arrival, using binoculars and tripod-mounted spotting scopes from their elevated vantage points, the teams began the continuous scanning process, looking for windows that were not supposed to be open, suspicious persons or objects that appeared in those that were closed, or any objects on the rooftops that were not there during the initial survey. One man on each team was the primary marksman, another the primary observer, the third, using binoculars, did quick scans of each building, followed by a slow detailed check of every window on every floor. All three men were equally trained and traded off positions to avoid the eye fatigue that developed after extended periods of looking through high-powered optics. Far below them, parked in unmarked cars in the immediate area of the designated threat buildings, was a response team for each countersniper team, consisting of a Secret Service agent and a plainclothes New York cop, ready to respond to any situation spotted from the rooftop positions.

Circling fifteen hundred feet above the highly organized scene, aboard *Huntsman,* the Secret Service observation helicopter, Gan-

non and Maguire had been tracking the progress of the presidential motorcade, watching for signs of suspicious vehicles or unexpected traffic congestion along the route.

As the motorcade approached the immediate area of the
United Nations Plaza, Maguire's thoughts shifted to the scene that
would shortly unfold at street level. The agents working the inner,
middle, and outer perimeters of the President's arrival and departure points were trained in their own unique area of protective
operations: Attack on the Principal. Once the President left the
limousine, two agents would lead the formation surrounding him
as he moved along the barricaded crowd. Two more would walk
immediately in front of him while two were shoulder to shoulder
directly behind him. Farther back, two additional agents would
secure the rear of the box formation, immediately followed by the
"gunman"—an agent armed with an Uzi submachine gun concealed in a black nylon breakaway shoulder bag; the shoulder strap
for the bag actually being the sling for the Uzi.

All were expert crowd watchers, prepared to react to any attack
on the President, whether from a single assassin or an all-out
terrorist assault. Much of their expertise was intuitive, but it was an
acquired intuitiveness. Constantly scanning the crowds, they were
trained to study faces and hands and body posture, each agent
responsible for evaluating a possible hostile situation within his arc
of observation—the mirrored sunglasses, rather than an affecta-
tion, served to hide the eyes, allowing an agent to study an individual without giving away the focus of his attention.

Maguire had worked the formation around the President
countless times, and was well aware of the enormous pressure of
the constant detailed vigilance required of the agents given the
critical assignment. Is there a frown that stands out among the
smiling, expectant faces? Are there nervous head movements or
darting eyes not fixed on the approaching President, where they
should be? A topcoat worn when it wasn't needed, or a folded
umbrella on a sunny day? Is anyone moving through the otherwise
static crowd, possibly searching for the best line of fire. Is there
anyone with an arm bandaged and in a sling, or carrying a briefcase
or blueprint container—all places to conceal a weapon or an explosive device. Any sudden arm movements? And hands—the trained

eyes of the agents working the box formation around the President move continuously over the front lines of the well-wishers. Anyone with his hands in his pockets draws immediate attention. Without a word, without so much as eye contact, the unseen hand is squeezed inside the pocket by an agent to make certain it is empty, then abruptly pulled out, where it is plainly visible, the agent moving on before the startled onlooker realizes what has happened.

Maguire always took special precautions when there were publicly stated threats by Middle Eastern groups or terrorists. His agents were provided with photographs of known members of those groups well in advance and instructed to pay particular attention to corresponding ethnic types visible in the crowd. His standing order was that no potential threat situation ever be taken lightly, regardless of how improbable or innocuous it appears at first glance. Photographers were always closely scrutinized; a good camera angle is also a good angle of fire, and a camera bag provides excellent concealment for a handgun. And there was no chauvinism or age discrimination. Women as well as children were given equal attention.

The reaction of the agents to any potential threat was graduated. If a suspect person was out of reach of an agent in the immediate vicinity of the President, the agent, speaking into his sleeve microphone, vectored a member of the Intelligence Team working the middle perimeter toward the suspect, while the agents in the box formation subtly positioned themselves between the President and the possible threat. When confronted with a "within arm's reach" situation by an armed assailant, where the agent had neither the time nor the room to draw his own weapon, his constant, repetitive training came into play. With only the body armor worn beneath his shirt for protection, he aggressively went after the assailant, placing his body between the weapon and the President—a completely unnatural reaction in the face of gunfire, when diving for cover was the strongest instinct. An agent's own weapon was never drawn until it was clear that an attack was in progress; Maguire had learned from hard experience that a panicked crowd was a threat in itself. But once the suspect produced a weapon, he was no longer a potential threat; he was a target to be downed immediately. Every effort was made not to endanger the lives of innocent bystanders, but the top priority was eliminating the threat and covering and evacuating the President.

The security fence and guard posts enclosing the entrance to the area around the United Nations Secretariat building made Maguire's job somewhat easier than it would have been at a less restricted site, allowing him to exercise rigid control over the number of people in immediate proximity to the President. He had ordered a separate area, inside the security gate, cordoned off for the press and camera crews and welcoming dignitaries and selected members of their staffs. United Nations delegates and employees were routed around the area, and those allowed inside were thoroughly vetted no matter how well known, and issued lapel pins recognizable at a glance to set them apart. With the President due shortly, the huge crowd behind the barricades had peaked, but the scene was orderly and controlled to Maguire's satisfaction.

"Turning off Second Avenue onto East Forty-second Street," the helicopter pilot said over his radio, relaying the location of the motorcade to the personnel on the ground. "E.T.A. three minutes."

Maguire and Gannon, seated in the rear of the helicopter and wearing headsets, were both monitoring the Secret Service frequency when an urgent voice came over the radio identifying himself as "Hercules," the code name for the countersniper teams. He was calling his Response Team on the street below his observation post on top of the General Assembly building.

"Hercules Four to Response Team Four," the voice said. "Man in a window with an unidentified object. Could be a rifle. Fourteenth floor of the U.N. Plaza apartments. Building _B,_ he added, designating which of the twin apartment towers it was. "Third window in from the east side."

"Response Team Four, on our way," the Secret Service agent replied without delay, and along with the police officer working with him, jumped from the car and ran the short distance from the sidewalk into the building.

The pilot of the helicopter, needing no instructions on what to do, immediately broke away from his aerial surveillance of the motorcade. Banking into a steep turn, he swung out over the East

River and headed toward the apartment building. He descended to an altitude that put him level with the open window on the four-teenth floor, intent on distracting the suspected shooter and block-ing his view of the motorcade arrival point.

"It can't be Sincavage," Gannon said, quickly counting off the floors and locating the window. "He wouldn't show himself before he had a shot."

Maguire's eyes were hard on the same window as he spoke into the boom mike attached to the headset. "Slow down the motor-cade," he ordered. "Be prepared to go around the block."

The pilot swooped expertly into position opposite the open window, hovering dangerously close to the building. A startled figure backed away, dropping whatever he was holding in his hands.

The Response Team rushed from the elevator and burst into the apartment. "All clear," the Secret Service agent reported as he appeared in the window moments later. "It was a kid with a long telephoto lens on a video camera."

Maguire radioed the motorcade to proceed and the helicopter climbed away, flying a circular pattern out over the East River as the President's limousine turned the corner onto First Avenue.

Gannon and Maguire exchanged looks. There was no sign of relief in either expression. The man they wanted was yet to be accounted for.

•

Forty-eight blocks north of the United Nations Plaza, Jerry Sincav-age sat on a park bench near the steps leading up to the track around the Central Park reservoir. He had spent the early morning hours scouting the area facing the stretch of the one and one-half mile oval track that passed in front of the marble columns and balustrade of the Engineers' Gate entrance to the reservoir at Fifth Avenue and Ninetieth Street. After studying the street maps, he had correctly determined that the area was the most likely place for the President to begin his run. Its location in relation to the Wal-dorf-Astoria Hotel made it the most convenient and logical choice.

Across the street, one block down from where he sat and di-rectly behind the Guggenheim Museum at the corner of Eighty-ninth Street, a construction site rose twelve stories, overlooking the reservoir and part of the track. He had spotted its potential within minutes of his arrival that morning, and had to smile at his stroke of good fortune. The building was in the early stages of construction, consisting of little more than steel beams and plank flooring. The open-cage construction elevator was locked after work hours, but a series of ladders inside the skeletal structure gave access to each level.

In the predawn light, he had climbed to the eleventh floor and found a place of concealment that left little to be desired. Stacks of construction materials were scattered about the flooring, covered by tarps to protect them from the elements. Anyone lying beneath one of the tarps, surrounded by the stacks of materials, could not be seen from above or below. From the completely concealed position, he had an unobstructed diagonal view of the parking area in front of the steps leading up to the reservoir, as well as a sixty-yard stretch of the jogging track that was clear of any overhanging branches from the trees lining the edge. The distance from the construction site to the track was less than two hundred yards. An easy shot for someone of his abilities.

A successful escape from the site after the assassination would be a matter of timing. The rappeling rope he had in his duffel bag was long enough to allow him to rapidly descend into the alleyway behind the museum, dropping the last eight feet to the ground. He had secured the rope in place, and made three practice descents, reaching the alleyway in just over twelve seconds each time. The conical-shaped structure on top of the Guggenheim Museum ob-scured the first five stories of the construction site from anyone on ground level on the park side of Fifth Avenue, limiting his actual exposure time from the moment he left his place of concealment to under six seconds. Without the sound of a shot to aid them in determining his location, it would take at least thirty seconds to figure out the trajectory of the bullet and begin flooding the area with security personnel.

The alleyway below the construction site ran behind the mu-seum and exited onto Eighty-eighth Street, where in the confusion following the assassination, he would, with a little luck and careful planning, be able to make it across the street and disappear into the park. After retrieving the rope and putting it back in his duffel bag, he had climbed down from the building and spent the better part of an hour walking and retracing possible escape routes from the alleyway into the park. The fact that vehicle and pedestrian traffic on Eighty-eighth Street and along Fifth Avenue in front of the park had increased dramatically by six-thirty in the morning was not lost on him; it would prove useful in providing a screen to aid in his escape.

At seven o'clock, he had stationed himself on the park bench across the street to observe the early morning activities in the immediate area, noting that the construction crew did not begin work until eight-thirty, ninety minutes later than the President's scheduled run. At nine-fifteen, three Secret Service cars and two blue and whites from the New York City police department pulled into the parking area near the entrance to the reservoir. Sincavage again could not believe his luck. Two of the agents stood no more than ten feet away, on the landing at the top of the marble steps, discussing where the presidential limousine and the rest of the scaled-down motorcade would park and where the President and the security detail assigned to jog along with him would enter and exit the track. All of the locations were in the line of fire from the place of concealment he had chosen at the construction site.

Another agent approached and pointed out the location he had selected to position the counterassault team vehicle that contained the five agents armed with assault rifles and shotguns. Sincavage, overhearing most of their discussion, realized that the vehicle would be parked beneath trees, and would not have a clear view of the construction site, making it highly unlikely that they would catch even a split-second glimpse of him before he disappeared behind the rear wall of the museum.

None of the agents had cast more than a cursory glance in the direction of the unshaved, disheveled man sitting on the park bench, ostensibly sorting through a collection of refuse in a shopping cart. By ten-thirty, after walking around the reservoir and selecting static observation posts at strategic points, they had left. The absence of any countersniper teams surveying the buildings and rooftops in the area was the last piece of information Sincavage needed to feel entirely comfortable with the site he had chosen.

He left the park shortly after the Secret Service agents and police, and pushing his cart before him, walked the thirty-nine blocks to the corner of Fiftieth Street and Lexington Avenue, where he slowly circled the block around the Waldorf-Astoria Hotel. He was impressed by what he saw. Every building that presented even the most improbable line of fire was covered by countersniper teams, and the overall security at street level around the entrance to the Towers was such that any attempt made on the President as he entered or exited the building would be suicidal. Sincavage immediately dismissed the hotel as a possibility, as he did the airport and United Nations arrival and departure sites without bothering to visit them, suspecting that the security measures would be just as thorough and pervasive.

Even if his intentions had not been known to the Secret Service, and normal security procedures were in effect, none of the sites would have held the promise of the off-the-record run at the reservoir. Back at the construction site, he began scouting a variety of escape routes through the park to the opposite side, where he planned to exit onto Central Park West. He decided he would spend the night in his place of concealment on the eleventh floor, allowing for a premature arrival by the President without risking his opportunity of getting into position. In the early afternoon, he sat in the woods near the edge of the section of track that was within his line of sight from the building. A constant stream of joggers were out running, and he counted off the number of seconds it took them to cover the distance, determining that even if the President jogged at a fast pace, he would have at least a fifteen-second window for his shot before his target was obscured from view by overhanging branches.

The construction site could not have suited him any better had it been put there specifically for his purpose. He would have five separate opportunities: when the President arrived and got out of the limousine, as he walked up the steps to the track, as he began to jog, when he finished his run and came back down the steps, and as he returned to the limousine. It was more than he could have hoped for.

By three o'clock in the afternoon, he was growing tired. After eating two oversized soft pretzels bought from a vendor across the street, he stretched out on the bench and, using his duffel bag as a pillow, slept for the first time in thirty hours.

•

The sound of horses' hooves echoed off the pavement as the two New York City mounted policemen left the bridle path below the Central Park reservoir and passed in front of the Engineers' Gate, continuing on in the direction of where the path began again and ran south through the park.

"You notice the duffel bag under that wino's head back there," the cop on the lead horse said as they passed in front of the bench where Sincavage lay stretched out on his stomach.

"Yeah," the sergeant said. "I saw it. Looked like ballistic nylon. In good condition."

"Pretty expensive bag for a bum." With a gentle check of the reins, the cop stopped his horse and turned in the saddle to look back. "Ten to one he ripped it off. Let's check him out."

"Give it a rest, Santoli. The poor bastard's not worth the paperwork."

"You got an attitude problem, Sarge."

"What I've got is another half hour until the end of tour. And that loser comes under the heading of a bullshit collar."

Santoli shrugged, and with a subtle tap from the heels of his boots, nudged his horse onto the bridle path and on through the park.

Sincavage slowly moved his arm from beneath his body, releasing his grip on the Walther tucked into his waistband. He opened one eye to watch the two cops from the mounted police unit disappear around a bend in the wooded path, then he slipped back into the restful half-sleep he had managed before the sound of the approaching horses had awakened him.

—31—

Steven Whitney Bradford III had spent most of the day in the banquet room on the third floor of the Waldorf-Astoria Hotel, overseeing the preparations for the ten-thousand-dollar-a-plate dinner that the President would address at eight o'clock that night. The exclusive guest list of one hundred and ten of the Republican party's heaviest contributors read like a who's who of the upper echelon of American business and industry.

Bradford and his boss, Tom Gibson, the head of the President's Staff Advance Office, had choreographed the evening's activities from start to finish. Using the master guest list, arranged in order of their importance by the deputy chief of staff, they selected which guests would sit at which tables, decided when "Ruffles and Flourishes" would be played, who would introduce the President, what time his speech would begin, and supervised the arrangement of the dais, carefully positioning the podium and the head table and the camera and lighting angles to ensure that the

President would be seen and photographed in the most flattering light.

Security measures, the most extensive Bradford had ever seen for an indoor event, were coordinated with the Secret Service agent in charge of the banquet room site. They had spent the better part of the afternoon with him, deciding where the walk-through magnetometers would be positioned to screen the guests as they arrived, and arguing over their plan to have the President enter at the opposite end from the dais and walk down the center of the room, greeting and shaking hands with the guests. The Secret Service compromise was to agree to the President entering from the opposite end of the room, but insisting that he stay to one side, along the wall, where they could position an agent in front of him and behind him, allowing them to concentrate on the people on only one side. They had also insisted that the walk through the crowded banquet room not be repeated when his speech was over, dictating that the President would leave by way of a door in the no-man's-land behind the dais.

Bradford had visited the hotel kitchen with the inspector from the Food and Drug Administration, and listened to the Secret Service agent in charge of security for the chefs and waiters give his final instructions to the head of the kitchen staff. All of the waiters working the banquet were issued identification tags, and the four highly screened long-term employees who were chosen to work the dais and the President's table were issued special tags that set them apart from the others. The food carts and trays were to be checked for hidden weapons and explosives before being taken inside, and the head of the kitchen staff, who personally knew all of the selected employees, was to be on hand for the entire evening to verify that each person entering the banquet room was indeed the one to whom the identification tag had been issued.

Shortly after four o'clock in the afternoon, the President arrived at the hotel from the United Nations and went directly to his suite on the thirty-fifth floor of the Towers. By five o'clock, the meticulous planning for the banquet was completed, and Bradford headed back to his room to shower and dress for the evening. He was standing in the corridor about to board an arriving elevator when Tom Gibson stepped off and pulled him to one side for a private conversation.

"This is very hush-hush," he told Bradford in his best conspiratorial whisper. "Not a word to anyone. The deputy chief of staff has asked me to make some special arrangements for the President."

Bradford nodded his understanding that what he was about to hear was not to be repeated. A twinge of anxiety brought back a facial tic that he had developed over the past week and thought he had finally brought under control with the timely use of Valium. He did not want to hear any more privileged information that he would feel pressured to pass on, and began to feel physically ill at the thought of it.

"Are you feeling all right?" Gibson asked, noticing his subordinate's discomfort.

"It's nothing a hot shower and a few hours to put my feet up won't cure," Bradford said.

"Good. Because I have a job for you," Gibson said. "Today is the President's anniversary. He wants to surprise the First Lady with a visit to a place they used to go when they were first married. Apparently they haven't been there in years."

"Here in the city?"

Gibson nodded. "The Café Carlyle. It's supposed to be a rather posh place. I thought you might be familiar with it."

"It's at Seventy-sixth and Madison, in the Carlyle Hotel," Bradford said. "A small, intimate piano bar. The usual entertainment is a singer doing Broadway show tunes and standards; Rodgers and Hart, Cole Porter. It's popular with the Upper East Side crowd."

"The deputy chief of staff made it clear that this is to be a quiet evening. A romantic interlude, so to speak. I want you to handle it, discreetly."

"What about the Secret Service?"

"The deputy chief of staff is giving them their instructions. You and one of their agents will go there an hour or so before the President and the First Lady leave the hotel, to reserve a table and make the necessary arrangements."

"What time will they be arriving?"

"The President wants to leave here shortly after the banquet, around nine-thirty. Make certain you get him the best possible table," Gibson said, and gave Bradford a fraternal clap on the shoulder as he continued down the corridor and entered the banquet room.

•

The deputy chief of staff stood in the sitting room of his suite, glaring at Maguire. His patience with the Special Agent in Charge of the Presidential Protective Division was growing thin.

"Why wasn't I told about this before now?" Maguire said.

"Because the President only informed us an hour ago."

"I'll need more time to secure the immediate area and get everyone in place."

The deputy chief of staff's temper flared. "For Christ's sake, Mike, this is to be a low profile off-the-record movement. The manager at the café won't even know about it until an hour or so before the President arrives. There will be no advance notice to anyone, and your people can seal the place off once he's inside. The risk factor from a security standpoint is nonexistent."

"I want some people up there well in advance to—"

"This is New York City," the deputy chief of staff snapped, cutting him off in mid-sentence. "If a horde of Secret Service agents show up hours before the President's due to arrive, it won't take thirty seconds before someone realizes what's going on and tips off the media; the place will be staked out by camera crews and reporters all night."

"I'll see to it that they don't get anywhere near him."

"No. You'll let your working shift supervisor take care of it. I've already given him explicit instructions on how this is to be handled."

Maguire's anger over having his authority usurped was clearly visible in his expression.

The deputy chief of staff, out of respect for the professionalism and dedication of the man standing before him, took a softer tone. "You can only cry wolf so many times, Mike. If you turn an evening that has special meaning to the President into a three-ring circus against his express wishes, you'll lose every friend you have around here. And if the Chief of Staff has anything to say about it, and he will, you'll end up being transferred to the ass end of nowhere to finish out your career."

"Considering the circumstances, that's a risk I'm willing to take," Maguire said.

"Well, it's not your decision to make. So back off. You've done a bang-up job with the security for this trip, and after the banquet, the President has no more publicly announced appearances. You'll have plenty of time to hunt down your man, if he's still out there."

"He's out there," Maguire said, but knew there was no point in further argument. He had heard nothing more about the Pennsylvania State Police investigation, and the salesman's missing car had not been found in the city. The airport arrival, the appearance at the United Nations, and the arrival at the hotel had all gone off without incident, and he had nothing but a hunch, a gut-level feeling, on which to hang an argument for expanding the already intensified security measures.

The deputy chief of staff had been right in his assessment of the President's late-night visit to the Café Carlyle; it was not a high-risk situation. But as Maguire left the suite on the thirty-fourth floor of the Towers and joined Gannon in the lobby, he could not help feeling that it was not over yet, and that Sincavage would still attempt to carry out the assassination.

•

Steven Whitney Bradford III sat in the telephone booth in the lobby of the hotel for a long time, anguishing over the call he was about to make. This time the information on the President's movements was limited to an even smaller number of White House staff members and Secret Service agents, exposing him to possible discovery if the assassination plot was carried out. But realizing that he had long ago sealed his fate with the shadowy member of the drug cartel from Miami, he saw no choice but to play out the hand he had been dealt. The President's visit to the Café Carlyle would be public knowledge in the morning, and he preferred not to think about the consequences if he failed to pass the information along. It took him nearly five full minutes to stop his hands from shaking when he dialed the number.

"Payment in full before I give you the information," he told the man with the Spanish accent on the other end of the line. "Five kilos for each piece of information, as promised. Fifteen kilos in all, with what I have to tell you tonight."

Bradford listened as the man gave him the address for the meeting. It was to be in Brooklyn, the drug dealer's home turf, an area where he felt comfortable and in control.

"Brooklyn's fine." Bradford was unfamiliar with the section of the borough where the exchange was to take place, but was not about to argue as long as he was being paid in full and could bring to an end what had been the most desperate time of his life. "I'll be there at nine," he said, and hung up.

He placed another call, to a college friend who was now a Wall Street broker with a small but lucrative cocaine business of his own. Nervous about handling what for him was a large amount of cocaine to have in his possession at one time, he had met with his friend over lunch on the day he had arrived in the city and arranged to sell the anticipated ten kilos at a below-market price that would net him three hundred thousand dollars. His broker friend was pleased to learn of the additional five kilos of high-grade cocaine, and agreed to payment of the original sum, plus an additional one hundred and fifty thousand dollars, with bearer bonds and negotiable securities that Bradford could pick up that night at his Sutton Place South apartment.

Bradford looked at his watch as he left the telephone booth and crossed the lobby to exit the hotel onto Park Avenue. It was seventhirty. He had arranged to meet the Secret Service advance agent at the Café Carlyle at eight o'clock. His business with the café manager would take no more than fifteen minutes, leaving him ample time to get to Brooklyn for the meeting. Climbing into a taxi in front of the hotel, he swallowed a Valium and slumped in the seat, promising himself that if he could get through this night, he would get out of the drug business completely and never again allow himself to be put in a position where others had control over his life.

—32—

Mike Hagen, four years out of the academy, was the quintessential Irish cop. Behind the baby-faced good looks, mischievous blue eyes, and crooked grin, a fiery temper simmered just beneath the surface. His physical strength was out of all proportion to his size. He was just over five feet nine inches tall, weighed one hundred and sixty pounds, and was a banger who could hurt you with either hand. A left hook, an overhand right, even a solid jab had sent opponents reeling, stunned and on their way to defeat. His record as an amateur middleweight, fighting for the Patrolmen's Benevolent Association boxing team, was twenty-three wins and one loss. All his victories were early-round knockouts; his one defeat had been at the hands of a Hispanic sergeant on the Chicago PBA team who, aware of his reputation as a power puncher, had gouged him in the eye in the first round, and taking advantage of his impaired vision, had worked him over while running from him for the rest of the fight. The victory Hagen relished most had been during an international match. He had flattened a member of the team from

Northern Ireland, a young Protestant lad, in forty-seven seconds of the first round. Hagen's mother, a devout Catholic, only one generation removed from the "old sod," had assured him that that deed alone would assure his direct ascendance to heaven.

Hagen was working anticrime out of Brooklyn's 70th Precinct, an assignment that suited his personality, allowing for more independence and individual initiative. It also meant that he was out of the "bag," as the uniform was referred to by those on the job, and wore plainclothes and patrolled in an unmarked car. His friend and partner, Tommy Delesandro, a year older and a few inches taller than Hagen, was a solid, thickly muscled two hundred and twenty pounder who didn't bother much with throwing punches. If a suspect or a perp he was tossing or arresting turned out to be a cop fighter, Delesandro merely wrestled him to the ground and sat on him while he cuffed him. Saves wear and tear on the knuckles, he had told Hagen, who never went looking for it, but when presented with an unexpected and free sparring partner, regardless of size, always welcomed the opportunity to hone his skills.

Tough and authoritative without being abusive, Hagen and Delesandro were good cops. Second-generation cops who loved the job and accepted the responsibilities and aggravation that went with it. This week they were working nights—six to twos—the six in the evening until two in the morning tour. It was the tour they preferred. More happened during those hours. The night creatures, out in force, lurked in the shadows, dealing crack, mugging helpless victims, planning neighborhood robberies, or shooting each other in drug-dealing territorial disputes.

Tonight had been no different; in fact, a little busier than most. They had already collared three teenage blacks attempting to break through the roof of a clothing store, chased a mugger only to lose him in a maze of passageways in a block of apartment buildings, and had called in a blue and white to haul away a mildly demented public masturbator and flasher whom Delesandro had appropriately called a dumb jerkoff. Forgoing their usual routine of returning to the station house for their meal break and working out in the weight room above the garage, they shared a pizza while parked at the curb along Caton Avenue, adjacent to the huge playground and recreation area known as the Parade Grounds.

The four- and five-story brick apartment buildings that lined the side streets leading off the avenue had once been thriving neighborhoods of middle-class Jewish and Italian families in pursuit of the American dream. They were now rundown tenements on some of the most crime-ridden streets in the city, known as "Crack Heaven" in the vernacular of the cops in the 70th Precinct. The Italians and the Jews had long since moved on to safer and more prosperous neighborhoods, leaving the area to the blacks and newly arrived Colombians and Haitians—working class and welfare families, too poor to escape the vicious crack dealers that now controlled their streets. Hagen and Delesandro had gotten used to responding to the countless nightly "man with a gun" calls from Central. Calls that, more often than not, turned out to be nothing more than the frightened and desperate efforts of the decent hard-working people who lived in the neighborhoods to get the cops to chase the crack dealers from the steps and lobbies of their apartment buildings.

A brief rain shower ended as the two cops sat eating their pizza in the unmarked car on the darkened, deserted avenue. Hagen looked out the window and shook his head in disgust.

"Look at this skelly place," he said. "It rains anywhere else in the world, things look clean and new. Here, it looks like some giant dog slobbered all over it."

"You got a way with words, Mike, ya know," Delesandro said, folding a slice of pizza in half. "Like all the cross-kissing, whiskey-drinking, poetry-reading, bottle-throwing Irish."

"Don't start with me, you spaghetti-bending Gindaloon bastard," Hagen said, in the spirit of the good-natured banter the two men engaged in to ease the boredom and pressures of the job.

Hagen's eyes were moving constantly over the area around the car as he ate. They were cop's eyes that took nothing for granted, and they locked on to a lone figure approaching from Ocean Avenue, walking along the outside of the fence that enclosed the Parade Grounds.

"Will you look at this?" Hagen said in disbelief.

"Looka wha," Delesandro said through a mouthful of pizza.

"This idiot over here. Where the hell does he think he is, the Upper East Side?"

Delesandro cocked his head in the direction his partner indicated and saw a well-dressed white man pass by on the opposite side of the street, unaware of their presence among the other cars parked at the curb. The sight of white people in the neighborhood, other than cops, was rare enough, but one walking alone and dressed the way this one was sent an open invitation to every mugger in the precinct.

"He's either lost, or he's got a death wish," Delesandro said. "We'd better clue him in."

Hagen's eyes followed the man as he paused and looked around, then continued on, checking the street signs at each intersection before he stopped midway through the block where Argyle Road ran south off Caton Avenue. His behavior told Hagen that the man was there for a reason, looking for someone or something.

"I don't think he's lost. Let's play this out. See what he's up to."

"Dumb bastard should have a big *V* for victim painted on his back," Delesandro said.

A sudden flash of headlights in the side-view mirror caught Hagen's attention. "Get down!" he said to Delesandro.

The two men slouched deep in the front seat, peering over the dashboard as a black Mercedes with tinted windows hissed by on the wet pavement. The big, expensive sedan stopped next to where the man they were watching stood anxiously glancing about, repeatedly checking the pocket of his raincoat, the way an armed man does who is not accustomed to carrying a weapon.

"What have we here," Hagen said as he saw the driver get out and walk to the rear of the Mercedes.

The two cops raised themselves slightly higher in the seat for a better view, and watched as the driver of the Mercedes opened the trunk and removed a tan leather carry-on bag, which he handed to the man on the sidewalk after a brief conversation. Before Hagen and Delesandro could react, the man climbed back into the Mercedes and drove off. The man with the carry-on bag turned and began to walk back in the direction of Ocean Avenue, his nervous behavior indicating that he had not counted on being left to fend for himself.

"Let's check this out," Hagen said.

The man with the leather bag stopped walking and put his hand inside the pocket of his raincoat when he saw the two men get out of the car and approach from the other side of the street. He turned and broke into a run in the opposite direction when Hagen called out, identifying himself as a police officer. The two cops gave chase, with Hagen quickly overtaking the fleeing man, and with a hard shove bounced him off the chain-link fence enclosing the Parade Grounds. Ducking to avoid the carry-on bag as it was swung at his head, Hagen countered with a solid blow to the kidney that sent the man to his knees.

"You have no probable cause," Steven Whitney Bradford III gasped as he slowly pulled himself to his feet.

"Hey, Tommy," Hagen said to his partner, who had grabbed the leather bag and was in the process of opening it. "We got a legal genius here, says we have no probable cause. What do you think?"

Delesandro let out a long, low whistle at the sight of the contents of the bag. "I don't know, but I'd say fifteen keys of what looks an awful lot like coke might be probable cause."

"I didn't know what was in there," Bradford cried out.

Hagen quickly and expertly patted him down, removing a chrome-plated .25-caliber automatic pistol from the pocket of his raincoat.

"I have a permit for that," Bradford lied.

"That's the least of your problems, pal. You have the right to remain silent," Hagen began as he spun him around to face the fence and handcuffed him.

"This is all a mistake," Bradford said, close to tears, his legs wobbling beneath him as Hagen escorted him back to the unmarked police car and shoved him into the rear seat.

—33—

At the same moment Steven Whitney Bradford III was being locked in the detention cage on the first floor of the 70th Precinct station house at 154 Lawrence Avenue in Brooklyn, Jerry Sincavage was hanging up the public telephone on the northeast corner of Eighty-eighth Street and Madison Avenue in Manhattan.

His final call to his New York contact, before climbing to the eleventh floor of the construction site where he planned to spend the night, had yielded unexpected results. The Café Carlyle, according to his contact, was only twelve blocks south of his present location. The President's quiet visit had potential. If a chance for a shot presented itself, there would be the added advantage of darkness, and the park was only one block away. And again, as with the run at the reservoir, the President would not be wearing his lightweight body armor, not for a quiet evening with his wife where no crowds would be present. But even if he could not find a suitable place of concealment in sight of where his target entered and exited the building, he would have the opportunity to get a preview of the security measures the Secret Service put into effect for a scaled-down, off-the-record movement, enabling him to make any necessary adjustments in his plans for the following morning.

It was nine forty-five when Sincavage crossed to the west side of the avenue and headed south, his eyes cast downward as he again affected a shuffling gait and stayed close to the curb as though searching the gutter for the esoteric treasures valued only by people of the street. A blue and white patrol car from the 19th Precinct streamed by, responding to an assist call to aid with a medical emergency. The two uniformed police officers in the car took no notice of the homeless wretch with the shopping cart moving slowly along Madison Avenue.

•

The Secret Service shift supervisor in charge of security for the President's visit to the Café Carlyle had followed the deputy chief of staff's explicit instructions. The motorcade, usually numbering thirteen to fifteen vehicles, consisted only of the lead car, serving as a mobile command post, and carrying two Intelligence Division agents; the President's limousine, in which the supervisor rode up front with the driver; and *Halfback,* the follow-up van that contained seven heavily armed agents. Leaving a narrow lane open for the crosstown traffic, the supervisor had ordered the vehicles double parked on Seventy-seventh Street between Madison and Park avenues, just around the corner from the entrance to the café. The agents staying with the motorcade were instructed to remain inside the vehicles rather than announcing their presence by standing around on the sidewalk.

Inside the café, the shift supervisor and the agent who had driven the limousine sat unobtrusively at a table against the far wall; they had a clear view of the entrance and the President and the First Lady, who sat at a corner table near the piano. Three of the agents from *Halfback* were also posted inside the building. One was in the serving kitchen off the main room of the café, and two, with Uzi submachine guns concealed in shoulder bags, were outside the room in the small lobby accessing the street, securing both ends of the corridor that led through the public rooms and on into the main lobby of the Carlyle Hotel.

There were two shows each evening at the café, one starting at nine-thirty and the second at eleven-thirty. By choosing the earlier show, the President had avoided the late-night crowd, and the room was barely half full, partly due to the manager, who in compliance with the shift supervisor's request had turned away anyone who arrived after the President and the First Lady, explaining that the tables for the early show were all reserved. The sophisticated ambiance of the stylish room was reminiscent of a bygone era, whispering of New York in its heyday, a black-and-white vignette of tuxedos and smart conversation. The appearance of the President and the First Lady had created an initial stir among the people already in the room, but the jaded New York crowd, accustomed to having celebrities in their midst, soon settled down to occasional glances and nods of acknowledgment in the direction of the famous couple, who sat holding hands and smiling in quiet conversation.

The shift supervisor, through his sleeve microphone and the innocuous earpiece connected to the miniature radio clipped to his belt, was able to monitor and respond to all the agents under his command. With everything under control, he relaxed somewhat, settling back in the padded bench seat against the wall to enjoy the music.

●

Gannon and Maguire were having dinner in a small restaurant on Lexington Avenue, across from the rear entrance to the Waldorf-Astoria, when Maguire's pager went off. Using the telephone at the checkout counter, he dialed the number for the White House Command Center signal board in the hotel, and was patched through to the caller who was waiting on the line for him. After listening to the distraught voice of a man he hardly knew, he returned to the table with a puzzled look on his face.

"What is it?" Gannon asked.

"Someone from the President's Staff Advance Office has been arrested. Steve Bradford."

"Anything serious?"

"He wouldn't say," Maguire said. "What I can't figure out is why he called me. I know him to say hello, but I've never said more than a dozen words to him. Says it's urgent and he won't talk to anyone but me."

Maguire's expression suddenly changed. He recalled something he had read in CIA's evaluation of the intelligence information gained from the conversation recorded during Sincavage's meeting with the drug barons on St. Barts. The audio technicians had deduced from the bits and pieces of dialogue recovered from the spotty take that the drug barons had an inside informant who was in a position to pass along information on changes in the President's schedules before they were released to the press and public. Maguire had attributed it to the not unusual occurrence of someone in the Staff Advance Office simply trying to impress friends with their insider knowledge. The phone call he had just received from Bradford gave him the chilling feeling that the hasty dismissal of CIA's suspicions was coming back to haunt him.

"Remember what I said about monumental human failure?" he said to Gannon. "Well, I think it's just happened again; and this time it's my fault."

"What are you talking about?"

"I'll tell you on the way. Let's go," he said, and tossed enough money on the table to more than cover his bill as he and Gannon rushed from the restaurant.

Taking one of the Secret Service cars parked in the garage beneath the hotel, Maguire sped through the streets of lower Manhattan. His initial impulse was to radio the Secret Service detail with the President and alert them to a possible problem. But if his hunch was wrong—and it was only a hunch—he would make a fool of himself and cause problems for the shift supervisor as well if he ruined the President's anniversary evening.

Raised in the city, and having attended Brooklyn College, he was familiar with the borough, and running every red light along the way, he reached the 70th Precinct station house twenty minutes after leaving the hotel garage.

—34—

The entrance lobby of the 70th Precinct station house was filled with the usual nightly assortment of cops and handcuffed criminals. Maguire and Gannon angled their way through to the tall desk and got the attention of the sergeant who had just finished a heated exchange with a lawyer complaining about the treatment of his client.

"I'm here to see Steve Bradford," Maguire said, showing his Secret Service identification. "He was arrested earlier this evening."

The sergeant looked closely at Maguire, comparing the photograph on the identification card with the man presenting it. "Bradford," he said, and consulted the blotter for the arresting officers. "Hagen and Delesandro," he called out above the clamor of the room to no one in particular.

"Anticrime," a cop standing near the vending machines against the wall shouted back.

"Downstairs," the sergeant told Maguire, "make a left past roll call, down the hall, door on your right."

Maguire and Gannon took the steps to the basement and followed the directions to the small room shared by the anticrime squad and SNEU (Street Narcotics Enforcement Unit). The door was cracked open, and inside two young cops in sweatshirts and jeans sat hunched over battered desks, pecking away at typewriters. A television perched on top of a filing cabinet was tuned to a Mets game, and as Gannon stepped into the cramped and cluttered office, he noticed a small cage containing a family of kangaroo mice on top of another cabinet.

"Hagen and Delesandro?" Maguire asked.

"That takes care of us," Hagen said, continuing to type. "Now, how about you?"

"Mike Maguire, Secret Service," Maguire said, again producing his identification. "This is Jack Gannon. We're here to see a man you arrested earlier this evening. Steven Whitney Bradford."

"The Third," Hagen said with a grin. "Don't forget the Third part. Hey, Tommy, looks like the yuppie wasn't bullshitting."

Delesandro pulled a completed arrest report from the typewriter and looked up. "That clown we busted really works for the President?"

"Staff Advance Office," Maguire said. "I'd like to talk with him. We're in a hurry."

"Sure," Hagen said. "He's upstairs in the cage."

Delesandro recounted the details of Bradford's arrest for Gannon and Maguire as they followed the two cops back upstairs to an area off the main lobby.

"Tommy got the license number from the Mercedes," Hagen said. "We ran a make on it. Registered to a Carlos Guizado. Mid-level drug dealer. Colombian. Couple of our guys working narcotics have been trying to nail his ass for the past year."

Maguire's eyes met Gannon's. Both men immediately realized the significance of what Hagen had just told them. "Has Bradford made a statement?" Maguire asked.

"Nada," Delesandro said. "Said he wanted to talk to you first. You want to fill us in on what's going on?"

"Not yet," Maguire said.

Hagen led them down a corridor and into a large room that served as a lineup area. The detention cage was off to one side.

Bradford sat on the bench, his elbows on his knees, staring at the floor. He got to his feet at the sight of Maguire. "I need to talk to you immediately," he said, positioning himself at the door to the cage.

"Me too," a wild-eyed man standing behind Bradford said, and promptly pulled open his raincoat to flash the naked body underneath.

"Knock it off, you goddamn pervert," Delesandro said, opening the cage and holding the flasher back as Bradford stepped outside.

"We need a place to talk privately," Maguire said.

Hagen led them to an interrogation room at the end of the corridor. "We'll be out here in the hall if you need us."

Bradford entered the sparsely furnished room and slumped into a chair at one end of a small table. Gannon closed the door behind them and stood off to the side as Maguire sat across from the badly shaken young man whose face was a mask of fear and anxiety.

"I want some guarantees," Bradford said. His eyes flicked toward Gannon, his voice trembling as he spoke.

Maguire fixed Bradford with a hard, angry stare. "I'll guarantee that you'll be an old man before you get out of prison unless I get some straight answers right now. Have you been passing on information about the President's unscheduled movements?"

Bradford squirmed in his chair. His eyes welled with tears as he avoided Maguire's gaze.

"Answer me, goddamnit!"

Bradford stared at the floor in silence, then summoning up what false courage he had left, said, "I want a guarantee of immunity from prosecution; I don't want to go to prison. If I don't get it; I've got nothing to say until I talk to a lawyer. And by then it's going to be too late to do you any good."

Gannon startled even Maguire as he stormed across the room and grabbed Bradford by the neck with one hand, pulled him out of the chair, and pinned him against the wall. Bradford's feet were off the floor as Gannon increased pressure on his throat and spoke in a low, menacing voice.

"Those two cops out in the hall can't lay a hand on you, neither can the Secret Service," he told Bradford, whose eyes were wide with fear. "But I'm not bound by their rules, and so help me God, I'll beat you to within an inch of your worthless life if you don't answer the questions."

"Let me go," Bradford gasped. "Please let me go."

"Jack," Maguire said. "Let him go."

Gannon calmed himself from the pent-up rage that had caused him to act. There had been a rush of memories of Maria Padron and Tiu and her son, and the indifferent look on Sincavage's face as he stood over the two bodies, and he had lost control. He released his grip on the desperate man's throat, and Bradford's feet again touched the floor.

"They would have killed me," Bradford said, crying now, his body trembling as he sat down.

"Did you tell anyone about the Café Carlyle?" Maguire said. He leaned across the table, his face close to Bradford's.

"Please, I need some help. I can't go to prison." He was watching Gannon out of the corner of his eye, and flinched when the man who had terrified him simply shifted his weight.

"Answer the question!"

Bradford slowly nodded his head. It was all that Maguire needed. He jumped from the chair and threw open the door. "He's all yours, there'll be federal charges later," he told the two startled cops standing in the corridor as he and Gannon raced from the station house to the Secret Service car outside at the curb.

•

Sincavage found the unlocked wrought-iron gate between the two brownstones on East Seventy-eighth Street shortly after locating the motorcade around the corner from the entrance to the Café Carlyle. Beyond the gate, a narrow passageway led to the rear of a four-story brick structure that was sandwiched between two taller buildings and fronted on Madison Avenue. A metal ladder attached to the wall provided access to a lower-level roof, and using the rappeling rope with the rubber-tipped grappling hook attached to one end, Sincavage slung his duffel bag over his shoulder and easily scaled the thirty feet to the upper level. He stayed low, behind the ornamental cornices along the front edge, and crossed over to where the next building rose six stories higher than the one he was on. The wall rising to his right hid him from view in the direction of the café, and where the roof met the wall of the adjoining building, there was a corner nook that provided excellent cover for an urban sniper site.

His view of the entrance to the café was at an acceptable angle, and unobstructed, except for a small area where three large shrubs in containers sat at the edge of the sidewalk. The distance the President would have to walk to where the motorcade was parked provided more than enough time for an unhurried shot under near-perfect conditions.

Sincavage removed the sniper rifle from his duffel bag and carefully assembled it. He estimated his height above the street at no more than fifty feet. With a distance of approximately one hundred yards to the target area, the ballistic drop of the projectile would be negligible, and there was no noticeable crosswind. He used the adjusting knobs on the scope to set both windage and elevation at zero, then removed the lens covers from both ends and set the scope on its lowest magnification of three-point-five power.

Lying in a prone position, he raised the weapon to his shoulder, making certain the barrel of the rifle did not extend beyond the edge of the roof. He placed his eye to the telescopic sight and focused on the sidewalk in front of the café. The area was well lit, and there were no lights shining directly toward him that would blind him when viewed through the scope. He next twisted the adjustable two-inch objective lens at the front of the scope until he was satisfied that he had the optimum amount of light in the sight picture for a clear shot at his target.

Rolling onto his side and opening the bolt of the rifle, he inserted one of the low-signature rounds into the chamber, then closed and locked the bolt. He looped his left wrist through and around the heavy leather sling, and pulled the butt of the weapon up with his right hand, placing it just to the inside of his shoulder muscle. Again lying flat on his stomach, he shifted slightly until the rifle pointed naturally, with no strain on his body, in a direct line with the entrance to the café. He placed his cheekbone on the stock next to where the thumb of his right hand gripped it, and positioned his eye comfortably just behind the scope. The cross hairs precisely intersected the spot at which he intended to shoot. He removed his eye from the scope and began breathing slowly and evenly, keeping his body and mind relaxed as he waited for his target to appear.

—35—

Gannon did little more than pause at the red lights he encountered during the high-speed race back to Manhattan. Seated beside him, Maguire used the secure-voice radio in the Secret Service car to contact the White House Command Center signal board at the Waldorf-Astoria, who patched him through to the shift supervisor at the Café Carlyle. As Maguire spoke, his conversation was being monitored by all the agents with the presidential motorcade, bringing them to a heightened state of alert.

"Keep Timberwolf and Tranquility inside until further notice," Maguire said, using the code names for the President and the First Lady. "We've got a hot one working."

The shift supervisor at the corner table inside the café raised his index finger to seat the earpiece of his radio more firmly in his ear. He strained to hear Maguire's voice over the sound of the piano player, who was midway through a Cole Porter tune. Raising his left arm, he spoke softly into his sleeve microphone, drawing no attention from the people at the surrounding tables, who were engrossed in the performance.

"I'll seal off the Madison Avenue entrance to the building and bring two more agents from *Halfback* into the lobby," he told Maguire.

"No," Maguire said. "If Sincavage is watching the building he'll pick up on the increased activity. I don't want him spooked. Maintain your present positions. I've got *Huntsman* in the air, he'll be flying a pattern over the East River until I tell him to move in. The counterassault team and a countersniper team are on the way from the hotel site and should be arriving at your location from the Park Avenue side shortly. Everyone is to stay off Madison Avenue until I arrive."

Gannon swerved to avoid a taxi as he came down off the ramp from the traffic circle around the Pan Am building and sped through a red light at the intersection of Park Avenue and East Forty-sixth Street. Eight minutes later, he slowed to turn onto East Seventy-seventh Street and stopped where a Secret Service car was positioned to seal off the entrance to the one-way street at the Park Avenue end. The agent immediately passed him through, and Gannon parked alongside the counterassault team van midway up the block. The CAT team and the countersniper team had arrived only minutes earlier and were waiting inside their vehicles as instructed. The leaders of the two highly specialized teams stepped out onto the sidewalk when they saw Maguire and Gannon get out of their car and approach.

"I want you on top of the Carlyle Hotel," Maguire told the leader of the three-man countersniper team. "Use Park Avenue to go around the block, and take your men in through the Seventy-sixth Street entrance. Get hotel security to take you to the roof."

"What are we looking for?" the team leader asked.

"Probably a lone sniper," Maguire said. "If I'm right, he's on the roof of a building within two or three hundred yards of the entrance to the café."

The countersniper team leader signaled to his men, who jumped from the car and followed him at a dead run in the direction of Park Avenue.

Maguire turned to the counterassault team leader. "Take three of your men and use the same entrance to the hotel. Back up the agents already posted inside the building and seal off the corridor leading from the main lobby to the café."

The CAT team leader left without a word, and with three of his men, also armed with assault rifles, disappeared in the direction the countersniper team had gone.

The shift leader provided Gannon and Maguire with miniature radios, which they clipped on their belts, running the wires for the earpieces and sleeve microphones inside their jackets.

Maguire got a Sig-Sauer 9mm automatic pistol from the counterassault team vehicle and handed it to Gannon. "As soon as they locate him," Maguire said, "I'll have the building sealed off and we'll move in."

●

The lobby of the quiet, sophisticated hotel was empty except for a bellman and the elevator operators. The assistant manager, who had earlier been discreetly informed of the President and the First Lady being in the Café Carlyle, responded immediately to the countersniper team leader's request. A hotel security guard appeared at the front desk within two minutes of their arrival. Another was sent to reassure the doorman at the Seventy-sixth Street entrance that the hotel was not under attack by the three armed men who had raced past him without a word, only to be followed moments later by another four men carrying assault rifles.

The security guard with the team, a former Force Recon Marine who had worked with snipers in Vietnam, was a competent professional and understood the needs of the men he was escorting. "What area do you want to look down on?"

"Buildings on Madison Avenue with a line of fire to the café entrance."

"You don't want the roof," the security guard told the countersniper team leader as they rode the elevator. "It's forty stories up and too cramped. There's only a narrow walkway around the water tower."

"What do you suggest?"

"More than half of this hotel is private apartments. There's an empty one on the twenty-first floor. It's got a big terrace that overlooks Madison Avenue and wraps around the side too. It's up high enough to look down on everything for three blocks and it puts you closer to the surrounding rooftops."

The team leader gave his approval, and they rushed from the elevator and followed the security guard into the spacious duplex apartment. His appraisal had been correct, the terrace overlooked everything in both directions on the west side of Madison Avenue for three blocks. In the near distance, only a block away, Central Park was framed by sparkling skyscrapers, and below them, the darkened rooftops of the expensive stores and luxury apartments that lined the broad avenue were within easy view.

With practiced proficiency, the three-man team quickly set up their equipment. The team leader, acting as the primary marksman, removed his sniper rifle from its carrying case while his teammates opened an equipment bag and took out two night-vision spotting scopes and what the security guard thought were two standard spotlights.

The lights the two men acting as observers held in their hands were in fact two-hundred-thousand-candlepower searchlights fitted with infrared filters over the lenses. Capable of illuminating a broad area out to eight hundred yards, the powerful light was visible only when viewed through night-vision optics. Anyone caught in the beam without night-vision optics was totally unaware that they were under surveillance.

The two observers put the tripod-mounted scopes into position at the edge of the terrace and turned on the searchlights after securing them to the adapters at the sides of the tripods, where they would track in the same direction the scopes moved. They began scanning the rooftops below, pausing at each object defined in the green-tinted light of the lens.

The observer covering the rooftops north of the terrace stopped his slow pan and swung back to a point he had just passed. He turned the knurled ring on the eyepiece of the scope and zeroed in on the roof of a four-story building in the middle of the second block up from the entrance to the café. Tucked into the corner, where the roof met the wall of an adjoining building, the image of a man, lying in a prone position with a rifle to his shoulder, came clearly into focus.

"Got him!" the countersniper said excitedly into the portable radio he held in his hand. "Lone sniper. West side of the avenue." He quickly swung the scope downward to read the numbers on the arch over the entrance to the building. "Ten-oh-two Madison. Approximately ninety yards north of your location."

"Everyone hold their positions," Maguire ordered.

Motioning to Gannon to follow, the two men ran to the end of the street, where they could peer around the corner at the building, exposing their heads only for the few seconds it took to fix the location in their minds.

"There aren't any alleyways between the buildings on Madison," Maguire said. "He must have gained access to the rear from a side street."

"We can go around the block on Park Avenue and use Seventy-ninth Street to get to the other side," Gannon said. "His attention is directed toward the café; we can make it across without coming into his line of sight."

Maguire nodded in agreement, then spoke into his sleeve microphone. "Hercules," he said, using the code name for the countersniper team in the Carlyle Hotel. "We're going to make an approach to the rear of the building. If the subject moves I want to know immediately."

"Roger," the team leader replied.

Maguire turned to the four remaining CAT agents standing next to the counterassault team vehicle. "If Hercules sees the target move, on my command I want you to secure the immediate area of the sidewalk outside the entrance to the café."

The voice of the shift supervisor inside the café came over the radio. "Shall I inform Timberwolf of the situation?"

"Only if he's ready to leave and we still haven't secured the area," Maguire said.

•

David Armitage lived most of his life vicariously, a fact that accounted for the telescope he kept at the window of his twenty-first-floor apartment at the corner of Fifth Avenue and Seventy-sixth Street. His points of observation during the daylight hours were the benches and pathways across the street in Central Park. At night, he moved to the opposite side of his living room and watched the windows of the upper stories of the Carlyle Hotel and nearby apartment buildings. More often than not, his voyeuristic tendencies were satisfied. Tonight, a quick check of the Carlyle's windows facing the park had paid off. A couple in a suite on the twentieth floor, not bothering to close the draperies, and leaving a nightstand lamp on, lay naked on a king-size bed, giving each other full-body massages.

Armitage had watched with mounting excitement, and ultimately satisfaction, as the erotic massages turned into a short-lived but passionate bout of lovemaking. Looking for more of the same, he aimed one floor higher, on a level even with his own window. He was moving his telescope slowly along the side of the building when something caught his eye. Two men were on the terrace of a corner apartment setting up their own telescopes. When a third man appeared with a rifle in his hands, Armitage called the police, telling them what he had seen without giving his name.

•

With some of the city's most wealthy and influential citizens living on Manhattan's Upper East Side, police response time in the exclusive neighborhood is quick and forceful. Four patrol cars from the 19th Precinct, their sirens wailing and roof lights flashing, converged on the Carlyle Hotel within minutes of the anonymous phone call. Two of the cars screeched to a halt in front of the entrance to the café; the other two swung off Madison onto Seventy-sixth Street, covering the main entrance to the hotel.

Sincavage watched as two more blue and whites arrived from the direction of Central Park, joining those already angled into the curb in front of the café. The uniformed officers were out of their cars, two stood partway out in the street, craning their necks and pointing toward the roof of the Carlyle. On the side street where the motorcade was parked, Sincavage saw a man with an M-16 rifle appear at the corner and glance in the direction of the cops, then run back out of sight.

•

"What the hell is going on?" Maguire said into his sleeve microphone. He had heard the sirens just as he and Gannon had reached the intersection of Madison Avenue and Seventy-ninth Street and were about to cross to the opposite side.

"Cops," the countersniper team leader replied from the terrace high above the street. "I count six blue and whites."

"What are they doing?"

"I've got a feeling they're looking for us," the team leader said.

Inside the café, the shift supervisor was monitoring the exchanges. "Is Timberwolf in any danger?" he whispered into his microphone.

"Negative," came a response from one of the agents just outside the inner door to the café. Another "Negative" was heard from an agent in the main lobby of the hotel.

"We'd better move," Gannon said to Maguire. "Sincavage has got to realize he's been compromised."

"Goddamnit!" Maguire muttered in disgust, and peered around the corner toward the roof of the building where Sincavage had been seen.

●

Sincavage followed the instincts that told him the commotion in the street below was directly related to his presence, and placed him in imminent danger. He removed the binoculars from his duffel bag and slowly scanned the roof and upper floors of the hotel. As he moved back and forth along each level, he stopped to study the silhouettes on the terrace of a corner apartment on the twenty-first floor. The heads and shoulders of three men were visible. Two had spotter scopes. The third had a sniper rifle, pointed directly at him.

Rolling onto his side against the adjoining wall, out of view of the man sighting in on him, Sincavage quickly disassembled his rifle and stuffed it into the duffel bag, along with the binoculars. He got to his feet, and staying in crouch, began to back away from the edge of the roof.

"The subject is moving," Maguire heard the countersniper team leader report. "I have a shot."

"Do not shoot!" Maguire immediately replied. Aside from wanting to take Sincavage alive, they had no justifiable provocation to fire on the man until he placed someone's life in immediate danger. "Everyone hold their positions."

Despite his desire to move the CAT team agents still with the motorcade into position to cover the front of the building where Sincavage was spotted, and to send three more from *Halfback* across to Fifth Avenue to approach from the opposite direction and cover the most likely escape route, his primary responsibility was the President's safety. With that foremost in his mind, he ordered the CAT team agents to station themselves outside the entrance to the café and to apprise the police on the scene of the situation. Talking to *Huntsman,* who was listening on the same frequency while circling six hundred feet above the East River, seven blocks away, he ordered the helicopter to move in.

Sincavage slung the duffel bag over his shoulder as he reached the edge of the roof above the passageway behind the building. He grabbed hold of the rappeling rope as he lowered himself over the side, and quickly and expertly dropped to the lower-level roof, squeezing the rope only once with an iron grip that slowed the speed of his descent.

Maguire reached the west side of Madison Avenue, with Gannon ten yards behind after pausing for traffic. He rounded the corner onto Seventy-eighth Street to see a man run from a passageway forty feet away on the other side of the street. He reached for his weapon just as Sincavage saw him and turned in his direction, a silenced pistol in his hand. A powerful blow struck the right side of Maguire's head and slammed him against the wall of a building, where he crumpled to the sidewalk, stunned and close to losing consciousness.

Gannon reached his side seconds later. He dropped to one knee and took aim at the fleeing man, who was now running at full speed and nearing the end of the block. A woman pedestrian turned the corner and entered his line of fire. He released pressure on the trigger, holding off the shot for fear of hitting her. He watched as Sincavage lowered his shoulder and knocked the woman to the ground without breaking stride as he ran on toward Fifth Avenue. The woman was again in Gannon's line of fire as she struggled to her feet.

"Go after him!" Maguire was lucid and his eyes were focused as he pulled himself to a sitting position and slumped against the side of the building. Blood streamed down the right side of his head, making the superficial scalp wound appear worse than it was. "I'll be okay, the bullet just creased my head."

Tires howled and brakes screeched as a car traveling at a fast rate of speed veered to avoiding hitting Sincavage when he reached the center of the avenue. There was a loud thud, and Gannon saw the car strike Sincavage a glancing blow, rolling him over the right front fender, only to have him spring to his feet and continue on.

Gannon bolted from the sidewalk like a sprinter from starting blocks. He reached the end of the street just as Sincavage vaulted the four-foot wall around Central Park and disappeared from sight.

Gannon raised the sleeve of his jacket to his mouth as he ran across Fifth Avenue. *"Huntsman,"* he called to the Secret Service helicopter. "Sincavage entered the park at Seventy-eighth Street. I'm only a few seconds behind him. See if you can spot him."

Huntsman was hovering near the roof of the building Sincavage had just left. Gaining altitude to clear the taller buildings along Fifth Avenue, he was over the park in seconds, the powerful search-lights mounted beneath the cockpit sweeping the pathways and open grassy areas below.

Gannon cleared the wall in stride and thrashed through a tangle of dense shrubs to emerge onto a path leading deeper into the park. His eyes moved rapidly over the area ahead as he ran. The light from a crescent moon cast a pale glow over the pathways and open areas, and the lamplights were of some help, but Gannon saw no sign of Sincavage. He stopped and listened for the sound of someone running, but heard nothing.

"Huntsman," Gannon said into the microphone as he looked up and located the helicopter. "I've lost him. You're due south of me, approximately four hundred yards. Move in and cover the area immediately in front of me."

Gannon saw the searchlights from the helicopter swing in his direction and draw closer as he began to jog along the path. As his eyes flicked back and forth across his flanks, he caught a quick glimpse of something ahead of him, running through a small children's playground off to his left. He stopped and watched as the shadowy figure of a man cut deeper into the park. *Huntsman's* searchlights swept over him long enough for Gannon to see that he was tall, and was wearing a long overcoat and a narrow-brimmed slouch hat and had something slung across his back.

Gannon gave chase. The man ran only a short distance before stopping to turn and fire twice. In the heat of the moment, as he dove off the pathway into the grass and rolled to his knees behind a park bench, it did not occur to Gannon that the shots had not been silenced.

"Give it up, Sincavage!" he shouted, knowing that the warning would do no good. Ignoring another wild shot that ricocheted off a nearby lamppost, he took careful aim and fired three rounds in rapid succession. Through the sights of his pistol, he saw the man drop to the ground and roll down an embankment and out of view.

Still sitting slumped against the building, and on the verge of blacking out, Maguire had heard the volley of distant shots. "Jack! You all right?"

"He's down!" Gannon said over the radio, and moved cautiously, his weapon at the ready, toward the spot where he had seen the man fall.

He found him sprawled facedown at the base of a tree, a black carry-all bag lying on the grass near where he had tumbled down the embankment. Gannon felt the blood-soaked area in the center of the man's chest as he rolled him over. His face was in deep shadow, and it was not until a few moments later, when *Huntsman* swooped down, his lights flashing across the motionless body, that Gannon stared at the unfamiliar features of a boy barely out of his teens and realized that the person he had shot was not Sincavage.

Billy Delgato died for the wrong reason that night. He had just robbed a young couple sitting on a bench overlooking the park's Conservatory Water. Threatening to shoot the girl, he had relieved them of their wallets, watches, and pocket money, which he had tossed into the carry-all along with the proceeds from an earlier robbery. He was running from the scene when he heard the man he believed to be a cop running after him. The man was fast, and was gaining on him. When his drug-ravaged body could run no farther, he had stopped and stood his ground, and died.

•

The muffled sounds of the shots had gone unnoticed, or purposely unacknowledged, when they reached Central Park West, as did the poorly dressed, disheveled man with a black nylon duffel bag slung over his shoulder. The man had slowed his pace when he reached the other side of the broad avenue, then paused to look back in the direction of the park before disappearing among the shadows of the narrow brownstones on West Sixty-eighth Street.

Epilogue

Six miles west of the small, rural town of Thurmont, Maryland, Gannon spotted the NO TRESPASSING sign at the entrance to a narrow dirt road that cut into the woods. Maguire slowed to turn off the main road through Catoctin Mountain Park, and followed the overgrown track to where it ended at a turn-around deep in a colorful autumn forest of chestnut, oak, and hickory trees. He pulled in behind two state police cruisers, and he and Gannon got out and took a path that led a few hundred yards into the dense woods and ended near a section of the double chain-link fence topped with razor wire that enclosed the 143 acres of the Camp David presidential retreat.

It had been four days since Sincavage had escaped and disappeared without a trace. The city-wide manhunt had yielded nothing, as Gannon and Maguire had expected it would. With the assassin still at large, and the media's sensationalistic coverage of the uncovered plot on the President's life, the run at the reservoir had been canceled. With the heightened security measures

Maguire had insisted upon—and this time got without argument—
the President had gone on to Atlanta and Houston, returning to
Washington two days later, where he immediately left for the seclu-
sion of Camp David to prepare for his upcoming meeting with the
British Prime Minister.

Steven Whitney Bradford III was out on bail, and had little in
the way of pertinent information, only able to give them the names
of the two drug dealers with whom he had been in contact. The
drug dealers had denied everything, and through the efforts of
their high-priced lawyers, were also released on bail, only to disappear two days later. The body of the missing salesman in Pennsylvania had been found, and the ballistics reports from the slugs
recovered from his head, and from the head of the slain trooper,
had been matched by Interpol with the previous killings attributed
to Sincavage. But that was where the trail of information ended.

At the insistence of his grateful superiors, Maguire had taken a
week's convalescence leave to recuperate from the mild concus-
sion caused by the bullet that had creased his skull. He had returned to Washington and his Georgetown apartment, where Gannon had arrived the previous night to spend the weekend. Out of
ideas and approaches to the problem of finding Sincavage, the two
old friends had settled in front of the large-screen television in
Maguire's den for an afternoon of college football. The call from
the Secret Service Intelligence Division came at one-thirty in the
afternoon.

Seventy-five miles northwest of Washington, near the perimeter of the Camp David compound, there had been a mysterious
crash of an unknown type of light aircraft the night before. The
Maryland State Police lieutenant in charge of the investigation had
called in the Secret Service because of the proximity of the incident
to Camp David, and his suspicions that it was connected with the
nationwide hunt for the man who had attempted to kill the President.

Maguire had driven the distance to the site in under an hour,
and when he and Gannon emerged onto the scene from the
wooded path, the county coroner was just completing a cursory
examination of a badly charred body that lay strapped across the

seat of the twisted tubular aluminum frame of what looked like a small go-cart with a shielded propeller mounted at the rear.

"Not much you can tell from what's left of him," the coroner said, rising to his feet and addressing Maguire. "The gas tank on this thing apparently exploded and set him on fire. Lucky for him it looks like his neck was broken on impact and killed him before he could burn to death."

Gannon walked slowly around the wreckage, then looked up to see a three-hundred-square-foot Ram Air parachute tangled in the upper branches of a tree directly over the crash site.

One of the state troopers at the scene noticed the focus of Gannon's attention. "There's a local parachute and hang-gliding club at the county airport," he said. "We got a report this morning that someone broke into their clubhouse last night and stole a parachute and this contraption." He pointed to the wreckage on the ground. "I think they called it a power hang-glider."

"It's a Power Chute," Gannon said, recognizing it for what it was. Before it had become popular with civilian sport parachutists, Delta Force had tested the innovative piece of equipment two years ago during its mid-stages of development by a British manufacturer, who had already sold its merits to the Special Air Service. Delta had been equally impressed with its practical application for clandestinely getting men into and out of isolated areas.

The lightweight tri-wheeled cart was equipped with a rear-mounted thirty-eight-horsepower engine that turned the propeller with enough force to push the cart along at a rate of speed that fully inflated the parachute canopy attached to the top of the frame. Needing less than twenty yards to get airborne, the Power Chute was capable of launching a three-hundred-and-fifty-pound payload off virtually any type of terrain, could attain an altitude of ten thousand feet, and cruise at forty miles per hour for a distance of over sixty miles. With a glide ratio of two-to-one with the power off, from ten thousand feet the operator could, using the steering toggles for the parachute, travel another four miles while descending silently to the ground.

"You said there was a separate parachute stolen from the same place," Gannon said to the trooper. "Where is it?" Gannon looked to see if remnants of it were strapped to the charred body in the wreckage. They were not.

"Don't know," the trooper said. "Everything we found is over there." He indicated a small grassy spot where the lieutenant and Maguire were examining the neatly arranged articles that had been found at the site.

Gannon crossed to where the lieutenant was holding up a disassembled 7mm Magnum sniper rifle and telling Maguire that it had been thrown clear of the wreckage and was found twenty feet away inside a black ballistic nylon duffel bag with the other items spread out before him.

"Look at this ammunition," the lieutenant said as he removed one of the low-signature cartridges from its individual plastic sleeve. "I've never seen anything like it."

"May I?" Gannon said, and took the cartridge to examine it, recognizing it immediately, but handing it back without comment.

"There are some maps of this area and Baltimore, and street maps of New York City," the lieutenant went on, holding up the maps. "A few articles of clothing, and a silenced Walther PPK pistol. I'll tell you what I think: I think this is the guy you've been looking for. It all adds up."

Gannon caught Maguire's eye and motioned him off to the side for a private conversation. "What do you think?"

"The body's charred beyond recognition, but according to the coroner the man was probably the same size and weight as Sincavage. And the sniper rifle is the same type your people reported seeing him with in Peru."

"And I guarantee you the silenced pistol will prove to be a perfect ballistics match," Gannon added.

"Why do I get the feeling you have some doubts about all this?"

"We're supposed to assume that Sincavage stole the Power Chute with the intention of infiltrating Camp David by cutting the engine a few miles out, gliding the rest of the way under canopy, and touching down inside the compound. How practical is that?"

"There are places he could have landed at night without being seen," Maguire said. "Near the stables or the skeet range, or the tennis courts."

"What would have been his chances of getting anywhere near the President?"

"He wouldn't have had a prayer," Maguire said. "Camp David is the one place we feel totally confident of our ability to protect the President when he's away from the White House. There's a company of Marine guards patrolling the outer and middle perimeters, and then our own agents securing the inner perimeter. He might have been able to land unseen, but the motion detectors and other electronic surveillance equipment throughout the compound would have picked him up as soon as he started moving around."

Gannon fixed his gaze on the wreckage and the charred remains. "I flew the Power Chute when Delta was evaluating it. It only has one seat, but you can bring out a wounded man with you by securing him across your lap. Or you can carry the body of a dead man by strapping him to the seat and the frame and sitting on him."

"What's your point?"

"That body over there is lying sideways across the seat, held in by just the seat belt. The straps from the shoulder harness aren't attached to the snap links on the belt as they should be."

"The snap links could have been knocked loose in the crash, and the body twisted sideways from the force of the impact."

"Or that body was already dead when Sincavage strapped it across the seat. A time-delayed incendiary device, like the one used on the sailboat in St. Barts, could have been attached to the gas tank and set to ignite after the crash. He might have even soaked the body in gasoline before taking off, to make sure it burned beyond recognition."

"You're forgetting something," Maguire said. "Sincavage had to be at the controls to fly the thing to the point where it would crash where it did. You're not suggesting he rode it into the trees?"

"One of the state troopers told me that a parachute was stolen from the same place as the Power Chute," Gannon said. "He could have guided it down to twelve hundred feet above the ground, then bailed out."

"That sounds a little risky, just to take the heat off."

"I don't think that's what this is all about," Gannon said. "Regardless of what we might suspect, there's enough here to make a strong case for that body being Sincavage. The media's going to buy it, and the drug barons who hired Sincavage will hear about it. They'll believe he's dead, and Sincavage can disappear with his twenty million."

"I don't know, Jack. He was good, but sooner or later everyone makes mistakes. I think he just made his last one. And besides, I can't see a guy like Sincavage voluntarily packing it in."

"He's too smart not to," Gannon said. "He's finished as a professional assassin. He no longer has the anonymity he's counted on for the past nineteen years. We know who he is, and every law-enforcement agency in the world has a photograph of him by now. Do you remember what Martindale, the case officer who controlled him for seven years said about him?"

"Yeah. He was a master of misdirection."

"Well, I think the master just finished off his career with one final stroke of genius."

"If you're right, and he's still alive and going into permanent retirement," Maguire said, "it's going to be damn near impossible to find him. Twenty million can buy an awful lot of privacy, plastic surgery, and official cooperation."

"Oh, I'll find him," Gannon said. "Sooner or later he'll make a mistake, and then I'll find him."

●

The tall blond man who had been spending his nights at the shelter for the homeless in Baltimore's inner city had not shown up for the evening meal for the past two days. There were few who noticed his absence, and those who did only knew his first name, and that he was an alcoholic. No one would report him missing, and consequently no one would search for him, and no one would ever know that a stranger, similar in appearance, had approached him in a darkened alley, offered him a cigarette, then snapped his neck and stuffed him into the trunk of a stolen car.

●

The boarding gate for the evening flight from Washington's National Airport to San Juan, Puerto Rico, was crowded and noisy. The attractive flight attendant at the entrance to the aircraft smiled politely as the passengers filed in and presented their boarding passes. She paused briefly, intrigued by the intense blue eyes of the tall dark-haired man with the neatly trimmed mustache who returned her smile and took a seat in the first-class section. There was something about him that appealed greatly to her. An aura of rugged individualism was how she described it to the other flight attendant who was working the first-class section. Later in the flight she would flirt with him, and accept his invitation for dinner that night in San Juan. She had noticed the scar on the back of his right hand as he reached for his drink, and took it as confirmation that her initial assessment was correct; this was not a man who had lived a protected, uneventful life.